Kelley Armstrong is the author of *Bitten*, *Stolen* and *Dime Store Magic*. Her fourth book in the series *Industrial Magic* is published in September 2004. She lives in Ontario with her husband and two children.

STOLEN

KELLEY ARMSTRONG

www.orbitbooks.co.uk

An *Orbit* Book

First published in Great Britain
by Time Warner Paperbacks in 2003

First published by Orbit in 2004

Copyright © Kelley Armstrong, 2003

A CIP catalogue record for this book is available from
the British Library.

ISBN 1 84149 354 6

Typeset in Goudy Old Style
by Palimpsest Book Production Limited,
Polmont, Stirlingshire
Printed and bound in Great Britain
by Clays Ltd, St Ives plc

Orbit
An imprint of
Time Warner Book Group UK
Brettenham House
Lancaster Place
London WC2E 7EN

To my mother, for buying my first writing journal and expecting me to fill it.

ACKNOWLEDGMENTS

With thanks . . .

To my agent, Helen Heller, my miracle worker.
To Sarah Manges at Viking US, for always going the extra mile for me.
To Anne Collins at Random House Canada, for all her wonderful advice.
To Antonia Hodgson at Time Warner Books UK for her early and ongoing support.
To Bev Irwin for her professional advice on the medical segments.

Finally, to my family, for almost always letting me retreat undisturbed to my writing dungeon and for forgiving the snarling that erupts when they trespass.

CONTENTS

PROLOGUE

He hated the forest. Hated its eternal pockets of damp and darkness. Hated its endless tangle of trees and bushes. Hated its smell of decay – dead vegetation, dead animals, everything dying, even the living creatures incessantly pursuing their next meal, one failure away from the slow descent into death. Soon his body would be one more stink fouling the air, maybe buried, maybe left for the carrion feeders, his death postponing theirs for another day. He would die. He knew that, not with the single-minded intent of the suicidal or the hopeless despair of the doomed, but with the simple acceptance of a man who knows he is only hours from passing out of this world into the next. Here in this stinking, dark, damp hell of a place, he would die.

He didn't seek death. If he could, he'd avoid it. But he couldn't. He'd tried, planning his breakout for days, conserving his energy, forcing himself to eat, to sleep. Then he'd escaped, surprising himself really. He'd never truly believed it would work. Of course, it hadn't actually worked, just appeared to, like a mirage shimmering in the desert, only the oasis hadn't turned to sand and sun, but damp and dark. He'd escaped the compound to find himself in the forest. Still hopeful, he'd run. And run. And gone nowhere. They were coming now. Hunting him.

He could hear the hound baying, fast on his trail. There must be ways to trick it, but he had no idea how. Born and raised in the city, he knew how to avoid detection there, how to become invisible in plain sight, to effect an appearance so mediocre that people could stare right at him and see no one. He knew how to greet neighbors in his apartment building, eyes lowered, a brief nod, no words, so if anyone asked about the occupants of 412, no one really knew who lived there: Was that the elderly couple? The young family? The blind girl? Never rude or friendly enough to attract attention, disappearing in a sea of people too intent on their own lives to notice his. There he was a master of invisibility. But here, in the forest? He hadn't set foot in one since he was ten, when his parents finally despaired of ever making an outdoorsman out of him and let him stay with his grandmother while his siblings went hiking and camping. He was lost here. Completely lost. The hound would find him and the hunters would kill him.

'You won't help me, will you?' he said, speaking the words in his mind.

For a long moment, Qiona didn't reply. He could sense her, the spirit who guided him, in the back corner of his mind, the farthest she ever went from him since she'd first made herself known when he was a child too young to speak.

'Do you want me to?' she asked finally.

'You won't. Even if I want it. This is what you want. For me to join you. You won't stop that.'

The hound started to sing, joy infusing its voice with melody as it closed in on its target. Someone shouted.

Qiona sighed, the sound fluttering like a breeze through his mind. 'What do you want me to do?'

'Which way is out?' he asked.

More silence. More shouts.

'That way,' she said.

He knew which way she meant, though he couldn't see her. An ayami had presence and substance but no form, an idea impossible to explain to anyone who wasn't a shaman and as easy for a shaman to understand as the concept of water or sky.

Turning left, he ran. Branches whipped his face and bare chest and arms, raising welts like the marks of a flagellant. And equally self-inflicted, he thought. Part of him wanted to stop. Give up. Accept. But he couldn't. He wasn't ready to surrender his life yet. Simple human pleasures still held too much allure: English muffins with butter and strawberry jam at the Talbot Café, the second-story balcony, farthest table on the left, the sun on his forearms, tattered mystery novel in one hand, coffee mug in the other, people yelling, laughing on the busy street below. Silly things, Qiona would sniff. She was jealous, of course, as she was of anything she couldn't share, anything that kept him bound to his body. He did want to join her, but not yet. Not just yet. So he ran.

'Stop running,' Qiona said.

He ignored her.

'Slow down,' she said. 'Pace yourself.'

He ignored her.

She withdrew, her anger a flash fire in his brain, bright and hot, then smoldering, waiting to flare again. He'd stopped hearing the hound, but only because his blood pounded too loudly. His lungs blazed. Each breath scorched through him, like swallowing fire. He ignored it. That was easy. He ignored most of his body's commands, from hunger to sex to pain. His body was only a vehicle, a medium for transmitting things like strawberry jam, laughter, and sunlight to his soul. Now after a life-time of ignoring his body, he asked it to save him and it didn't know how. From behind him came the bay of the hound. Was it louder now? Closer?

'Climb a tree,' Qiona said.

'It's not the dogs I'm afraid of. It's the men.'

'Slow down then. Turn. Confuse them. You're making a straight trail. Slow down.'

He couldn't. The end of the forest was near. It had to be. His only chance was to get there before the dogs did. Ignoring the pain, he summoned every remaining vestige of strength and shot forward.

'Slow down!' Qiona shouted. 'Watch—'

His left foot hit a small rise, but he adjusted, throwing his right foot out for balance. Yet his right foot came down on empty air. As he pitched forward, he saw the streambed below, at the bottom of a small gully eroded by decades of water flow. He flipped over the edge of it, convulsed in midair, trying to think of how to land without injury, but again he didn't know how. As he hit the gravel below, he heard the hound. Heard its song of triumph so loud his eardrums threatened to split. Twisting to get up, he saw three canine heads come over the gully edge, one hound, two massive guard dogs. The hound lifted its head and bayed. The other two paused only a second, then leapt.

'Get out!' Qiona screamed. 'Get out now!'

No! He wasn't ready to leave. He resisted the urge to throw his soul free of his body, clenching himself into a ball as if that would keep it in. He saw the undersides of the dogs as they flew off the cliff. One landed atop him, knocking out his last bit of breath. Teeth dug into his forearm. He felt a tremendous wrenching. Then he soared upward. Qiona was dragging him from his body, away from the pain of dying.

'Don't look back,' she said.

Of course, he did. He had to know. As he looked down, he saw the dogs. The hound was still at the top of the gully, howling and waiting for the men. The two other dogs didn't wait. They tore his body apart in a shower of blood and flesh.

'No,' he moaned. 'No.'

Qiona comforted him with whispers and kisses, pleaded with him to look away. She'd tried to save him from the pain, but she couldn't. He felt it as he looked down at the dogs destroying his body, felt not the pain of their teeth, but the agony of unbelievable loss and grief. It was over. All over.

'If I hadn't tripped,' he said. 'If I'd run faster . . .'

Qiona turned him then, so he could look out across the forest. The expanse of trees went on and on, ending in a road so far away the cars looked like bugs crawling across the earth. He glanced back at his body, a mangled mess of blood and bone. The men stepped from the forest. He ignored them. They didn't matter anymore. Nothing did. He turned to Qiona and let her take him away.

'Dead,' Tucker said to Matasumi as he walked into the cell-block guard station. He scraped the mud of the forest off his boots. 'Dogs got him before we did.'

'I told you I wanted him alive.'

'And I told you we need more hounds. Rottweilers are for guarding, not hunting. A hound will wait for the hunter. A rottie kills. Doesn't know how to do anything else.' Tucker removed his boots and laid them on the mat, perfectly aligned with the wall, laces tucked in. Then he took an identical but clean pair and pulled them on. 'Can't see how it matters much. Guy was half-dead anyway. Weak. Useless.'

'He was a shaman,' Matasumi said. 'Shamans don't need to be Olympic athletes. All their power is in their mind.'

Tucker snorted. 'And it did him a whole lotta good against those dogs, let me tell you. They didn't leave a piece of him bigger than my fist.'

As Matasumi turned, someone swung open the door and clipped him in the chin.

'Whoops,' Winsloe said with a grin. 'Sorry, old man. Damn things need windows.'

Bauer brushed past him. 'Where's the shaman?'

'He didn't . . . survive,' Matasumi said.

'Dogs,' Tucker added.

Bauer shook her head and kept walking. A guard grabbed the interior door, holding it open as she walked through. Winsloe and the guard trailed after her. Matasumi brought up the rear. Tucker stayed at the guard station, presumably to discipline whoever had let the shaman escape, though the others didn't bother to ask. Such details were beneath them. That's why they'd hired Tucker.

The next door was thick steel with an elongated handle. Bauer paused in front of a small camera. A beam scanned her retina. One of the two lights above the door flashed green. The other stayed red until she grasped the door handle and the sensor checked her handprint. When the second light turned green, she opened the door and strode through. The guard followed. As Winsloe stepped forward, Matasumi reached for his arm, but missed. Alarms shrieked. Lights flashed. The sound of a half-dozen steel-toed boots clomped in synchronized quick-step down a distant corridor. Matasumi snatched the two-way radio from the table.

'Please call them back,' Matasumi said. 'It was only Mr. Winsloe. Again.'

'Yes, sir,' Tucker's voice crackled through the radio. 'Would you remind Mr. Winsloe that each retinal and hand scan combination will authorize the passage of only one staff member and a second party.'

They both knew Winsloe didn't need to be reminded of any such thing, since he'd designed the system. Matasumi stabbed the radio's disconnect button. Winsloe only grinned.

'Sorry, old man,' Winsloe said. 'Just testing the sensors.'

He stepped back to the retina scanner. After the computer recognized him, the first light turned green. He grabbed the door handle, the second light flashed green, and the door opened. Matasumi could have followed without the scans, as the guard had, but he let the door close and followed the proper procedure. The admittance of a second party was intended to allow the passage of captives from one section of the compound to another, at a rate of only one captive per staff member. It was not supposed to allow two staff to pass together. Matasumi would remind Tucker to speak to his guards about this. They were all authorized to pass through these doors and should be doing so correctly, not taking shortcuts.

Past the security door, the interior hall looked like a hotel corridor, each side flanked by rooms furnished with a double bed, a small table, two chairs, and a door leading to a bathroom. Not luxury accommodations by any means, but simple and clean, like the upper end of the spectrum for the budget-conscious traveler, though the occupants of these rooms wouldn't be doing much traveling. These doors only opened from the outside.

The wall between the rooms and the corridor was a specially designed glass more durable than steel bars – and much nicer to look at. From the hallway, an observer could study the occupants like lab rats, which was the idea. The door to each room was also glass so the watcher's view wasn't obstructed. Even the facing wall of each bathroom was clear Plexiglas. The transparent bathroom walls were a recent renovation, not because the observers had decided they wanted to study their subjects' elimination practices, but because they'd found that when all four walls of the bathrooms were opaque, some of the subjects spent entire days in there to escape the constant scrutiny.

The exterior glass wall was actually one-way glass. They'd

debated that, one-way versus two-way. Bauer had allowed Matasumi to make the final decision, and he'd sent his research assistants scurrying after every psychology treatise on the effects of continual observation. After weighing the evidence, he'd decided one-way glass would be less intrusive. By hiding the observers from sight, they were less likely to agitate the subjects. He'd been wrong. At least with two-way glass the subjects knew when they were being watched. With one-way, they knew they were being watched – none were naive enough to mistake the full-wall mirror for decoration – but they didn't know when, so they were on perpetual alert, which had a regrettably damning effect on their mental and physical health.

The group passed the four occupied cells. One subject had his chair turned toward the rear wall and sat motionless, ignoring the magazines, the books, the television, the radio, everything that had been provided for his diversion. He sat with his back to the one-way glass and did nothing. That one had been at the compound nearly a month. Another occupant had arrived only this morning. She also sat in her chair, but facing the one-way glass, glaring at it. Defiant . . . for now. It wouldn't last.

Tess, the one research assistant Matasumi had brought to the project, stood by the defiant occupant's cell, ticking notations on her clipboard. She looked up and nodded as they passed.

'Anything?' Bauer asked.

Tess glanced at Matasumi, shunting her reply to him. 'Not yet.'

'Because she can't or won't?' Bauer asked.

Another glance at Matasumi. 'It appears . . . I would say . . .'

'Well?'

Tess inhaled. 'Her attitude suggests that if she could do more, she would.'

'Can't, then,' Winsloe said. 'We need a Coven witch. Why we bothered with this one—'

Bauer interrupted, 'We bothered because she's supposed to be extremely powerful.'

'According to Katzen,' Winsloe said. 'If you believe him. I don't. Sorcerer or not, the guy's full of shit. He's supposed to be helping us catch these freaks. Instead, all he does is tell us where to look, then sits back while our guys take all the risks. For what? This?' He jabbed a finger at the captive. 'Our second useless witch. If we keep listening to Katzen, we're going to miss out on some real finds.'

'Such as vampires and werewolves?' Bauer's lips curved in a small smile. 'You're still miffed because Katzen says they don't exist.'

'Vampires and werewolves,' Matasumi muttered. 'We are in the middle of unlocking unimaginable mental power, true magic. We have potential access to sorcerers, necromancers, shamans, witches, every conceivable vessel of magic . . . and he wants creatures that suck blood and howl at the moon. We are conducting serious scientific research here, not chasing bogeymen.'

Winsloe stepped in front of Matasumi, towering six inches over him. 'No, old man, you're conducting serious scientific research here. Sondra is looking for her holy grail. And me, I'm in it for fun. But I'm also bankrolling this little project, so if I say I want to hunt a werewolf, you'd better find me one to hunt.'

'If you want to hunt a werewolf, then I'd suggest you put one in those video games of yours, because we can't provide what doesn't exist.'

'Oh, we'll find something for Ty to hunt,' Bauer said. 'If we can't find one of his monsters, we'll have Katzen summon something suitably demonic.'

'A demon?' Winsloe said. 'Now that'd be cool.'

'I'm sure it would,' Bauer murmured and pushed open the door into the shaman's former cell.

DEMONIC

'Please tell me you don't believe in that stuff,' said a voice beside my shoulder.

I looked at my seat-mate. Mid-forties, business suit, laptop, pale strip around his ring finger where he'd removed his wedding band. Nice touch. Very inconspicuous.

'You shouldn't read crap like that,' he said, flashing a mouthful of coffee stains. 'It'll rot your brain.'

I nodded, smiled politely, and hoped he'd go away, at least as far away as he could on an airplane flying at an altitude of several thousand feet. Then I went back to reading the pages I'd printed from the believe.com web site.

'Does that really say werewolves?' my seat-mate said. 'Like fangs and fur? Michael Landon? *I was a Teenage Werewolf?*'

'Michael . . . ?'

'Uh, an old movie. Before my time. Video, you know.'

Another polite nod. Another not-so-polite attempt to return to my work.

'Is that for real?' my seat-mate asked. 'Someone's selling information on werewolves? Werewolves? What kind of people would buy crap like that?'

'I would.'

He stopped, finger poised above my papers, struggling to convince himself that someone could believe in werewolves and not be a complete nutcase, at least not if that someone was young, female, and stuck in the adjoining seat for another hour. I decided to help.

'For sure,' I said, affecting my best breathless blond accent. 'I mean, like, werewolves are in. Vampires are so five minutes ago. Gothic, ugh. Me and my friends, we tried it once, but when I dyed my hair black, it went green.'

'That's, uh—'

'Green! Can you believe it? And the clothes they wanted us to wear? Totally gross. So then, like, Chase, he said, what about werewolves? He heard about this group in Miami, so we talked to them and they said vampires were out. Werewolves were the new thing. Chase and I, we went to see them, and they had these costumes, fur and teeth and stuff, and we put them on and popped these pills and presto, we were werewolves.'

'Uh, really?' he said, eyes darting about for an escape route. 'Well, I'm sure—'

'We could run and jump around and howl, and we went out hunting, and one of the guys caught this rabbit, and, like, I know it sounds gross, but we were so hungry and the smell of the blood—'

'Could you excuse me,' the man interrupted. 'I need to use the washroom.'

'Sure. You look a little green. Probably airsickness. My friend Tabby has that real bad. I hope you're feeling better, 'cause I was going to ask if you wanted to come with me tonight. There's this werewolf group in Pittsburgh. They're having a Grand Howl tonight. I'm meeting Chase there. He's kinda my boyfriend, but he switch-hits, you know, and he's really cute. I think you'd like him.'

The man mumbled something and sprinted into the corridor faster than one would think possible for a guy who looked like he hadn't exceeded strolling speed since high school.

'Wait 'til I tell you about the Grand Howl,' I called after him. 'They're so cool.'

Ten minutes later, he still hadn't returned. Damn shame. That airsickness can be a real son of a bitch.

I returned to my reading. believe.com was a web site that sold information on the paranormal, a supernatural eBay. Scary that such things existed. Even scarier that they could turn a profit. believe.com had an entire category devoted to auctioning off pieces of spaceship wrecks that, at last count, had 320 items for sale. Werewolves didn't even warrant their own classification. They were lumped into 'Zombies, Werewolves, and Other Miscellaneous Demonic Phenomena.' Miscellaneous demonic phenomena? The demonic part kind of stung. I was not demonic. Well, maybe driving some hapless guy from his airplane seat wasn't exactly nice, but it certainly wasn't demonic. A miscellaneous demonic phenomenon would have shoved him out the escape hatch. I'd barely even been tempted to do that.

Yes, I was a werewolf, had been since I was twenty, nearly twelve years ago. Unlike me, most werewolves are born werewolves, though they can't change forms until they reach adulthood. The gene is passed from father to son – daughters need not apply. The only way for a woman to become a werewolf is to be bitten by a werewolf and survive. That's rare, not the biting part, but the surviving part. I'd lived mainly because I was taken in by the Pack – which is exactly what it sounds like: a social structure based on the wolf pack, with an Alpha, protected territory, and clearly defined rules, rule one being that we didn't kill humans unless absolutely necessary. If we got the munchies, we pulled into the nearest fast-food drive-thru like everybody else. Non-Pack werewolves, whom we called mutts, ate humans because they couldn't bother fighting the urge to hunt and kill, and humans were the most plentiful target. Pack wolves hunted deer and rabbits. Yes, I'd killed and eaten Bambi and Thumper. Sometimes I wondered if people wouldn't consider that even more shocking, in a world where a dog thrown from a car garners more media attention than murdered children. But I digress.

As part of the Pack, I lived with the Alpha – Jeremy Danvers – and Clayton Danvers, his adopted son/bodyguard/ second in command, who was also my partner/lover/bane of my existence . . . But that gets complicated. Back to the point. Like everyone else in the Pack, I had responsibilities. One of my jobs was to monitor the Internet for signs that some mutt was calling attention to himself. One place I looked was believe.com, though I rarely found anything deserving more than a dismissive read-over. Last February I'd followed up something in Georgia, not so much because the listing sounded major alarms, but because New York State had been in the middle of a week-long snowstorm and anyplace south of the Carolinas sounded like heaven.

The posting I was reading now was different. It had the alarms clanging so hard that I'd read it Tuesday, left a message for the seller immediately, and set up a meeting with her in Pittsburgh for Friday, waiting three days only because I didn't want to seem too eager.

The posting read: 'Werewolves. Valuable information for sale. True believers only. Two homeless killed in Phoenix 1993–94. Initially believed to be dog kills. Throats ripped. Bodies partially eaten. One oversized canine print found near second body. All other prints wiped away (very tidy dogs?). Zoologist identified print as extremely large wolf. Police investigated local zoos and concluded zoologist mistaken. Third victim was prostitute. Told roommate she had an all-night invitation. Found dead three days later. Pattern matched earlier kills. Roommate led police to hotel used by victim. Found evidence of cleaned-up blood in room. Police reluctant to switch focus to human killer. Decided third victim was copycat (copydog?) killing. Case remains open. All details public record. Check *Arizona Republic* to verify. Vendor has more. Media welcome.'

Fascinating story. And completely true. Jeremy was responsible for checking newspaper accounts of maulings and other potential werewolf activity. In the *Arizona Republic* he'd found the article describing the second kill. The first hadn't made it into the papers – one dead homeless person wasn't news. I'd gone to investigate, arriving too late to help the third victim, but in time to ensure there wasn't a fourth. The guilty mutt was buried under six feet of desert sand. The Pack didn't look kindly on man-killers.

We hadn't been worried about the police investigation. In my experience, homicide detectives are a bright bunch, smart enough to know there's no such thing as werewolves. If they found mauling with canine evidence, they saw a dog kill. If they found mauling with human evidence, they saw a psychopath kill. If they found mauling with both human and canine evidence, they saw a psychopath with a dog or a murder site disturbed by a dog. They never, ever, saw a partially eaten body, footprints, and dog fur and said, 'My God, we've got a werewolf!' Even wackos who believed in werewolves didn't see such murders as werewolf kills. They were too busy looking for crazed, half-human beasts who bay at the full moon, snatch babies from cradles, and leave prints that mysteriously change from paws to feet. So when I read something like this, I had to worry about what other information the vendor was selling.

The 'media welcome' part worried me too. Almost all believe.com listings ended with 'media need not inquire.' Though vendors pretended the warning was meant to discourage tabloid journalists who'd mangle their stories, they were really worried that a legit reporter would show up and humiliate them. When I went to investigate such claims, I used the guise of being a member of a paranormal society. This time, since the vendor had no problem with media, I was pretending to be a journalist, which wasn't much of a stretch, since that was my profession, though my typical beat was freelancing articles on Canadian politics, which never included any mention of demonic phenomena, though it might explain the rise of the neo-conservatives.

Once in Pittsburgh, I caught a cab, registered at my hotel, dropped off my stuff, and headed to the meeting. I was supposed to meet the vendor – Ms. Winterbourne – outside a place called Tea for Two. It was exactly what it sounded like, a cutesy shop selling afternoon tea and light lunches. The exterior was whitewashed brick with pale pink and powder blue trim. Rows of antique teapots lined the window sills. Inside were tiny bistro tables with white linen cloths and wrought-iron chairs. Then, after all this work to make the place as nauseatingly sweet as possible, someone had stuck a piece of hand-markered cardboard in the front window informing passersby that the shop also sold coffee, espresso, latte, and 'other coffee-based beverages.'

Ms. Winterbourne had promised to meet me in front of the shop at three-thirty. I arrived at three-thirty-five, peeked inside, and didn't find anyone waiting, so I went out again. Loitering in front of a tearoom wasn't like hanging around a coffee shop. After a few minutes, people inside began staring. A server came out and asked if she could 'help me.' I assured her I was waiting for someone, in case she mistook me for a vagrant soliciting leftover scones.

At four o'clock, a young woman approached. When I turned, she smiled. She wasn't very tall, more than a half-foot shorter than my five-ten. Probably in her early twenties. Long curly brown hair, regular features, and green eyes – the type of young woman most often described as 'cute,' that catchall description meaning she wasn't a beauty but there was nothing to drive her into the realm of ugliness. She wore sunglasses, a brimmed hat, and a sundress that flattered the kind of figure men love and women hate, the full curves so maligned in a world of Jenny Craig and Slim-Fast.

'Elena?' she asked, her voice a deep contralto. 'Elena . . . Andrews?'

'Uh – yes,' I said. 'Ms. Winterbourne?'

She smiled. 'One of them. I'm Paige. My aunt will be along shortly. You're early.'

'No,' I said, returning her smile full-wattage. 'You're late.'

She blinked, thrown off by my bluntness. 'Weren't we supposed to meet at four-thirty?'

'Three-thirty.'

'I was sure—'

I pulled the printout of our e-mail correspondence from my pocket.

'Oh,' she said, after a quick glance. 'Three-thirty. I'm so sorry. I must have jotted it down wrong. I'm glad I stopped by early then. I'd better call my aunt and tell her.'

As she took a cell phone from her purse, I stepped away to give her privacy, though with my heightened auditory senses I could have heard the murmured conversation a hundred feet off. Through the phone, I heard an older woman sigh. She promised to join us as soon as possible and asked – warned? – her niece not to start without her.

'Well,' Paige said, clicking off the phone. 'My apologies again, Ms. Andrews. May I call you Elena?'

'Please. Should we wait inside?'

'Actually, it's a bad place for something like this. Aunt

Ruth and I had coffee here this morning. Food's great, but it's much too quiet. You can hear conversations from across the room. I guess we should have realized that, but we're not very experienced at this sort of thing.'

'No?'

She laughed, a throaty chuckle. 'I suppose you hear a lot of that. People not wanting to admit they're into this kind of stuff. We're into it. I won't deny that. But this is our first . . . what would you call it? Sale? Anyway, since the tearoom turned out to be a bad choice, we had some platters made up and took them to our hotel. We'll hold the meeting there.'

'Hotel?' I'd thought she lived in Pittsburgh. Vendors usually arranged meetings in their hometown.

'It's a few blocks over. An easy walk. Guaranteed privacy.'

Big warning bells here. Any woman, even one as femininity-challenged as me, knew better than to traipse into the hotel room of a stranger. It was like a horror movie where the heroine goes alone into the abandoned house after all her friends die horrible deaths and the audience sits there yelling, 'Don't go, you stupid bitch!' Well, I was the one shouting, 'Go on, but grab the Uzi!' Walking headfirst into danger was one thing; walking in unarmed was another. Lucky for me, I was armed with Supergirl strength. And if that didn't do the trick, my Clark Kent act came with fangs and claws. One glance at this woman, barely five-two, nearly a decade my junior, told me I didn't have anything to worry about. Of course, I had to fake concern. It was expected.

'Umm, well . . .' I said, glancing over my shoulder. 'I'd prefer a public place. No offense . . .'

'None taken,' she said. 'But all my stuff is back at the hotel. How about we stop by there, and if you still don't feel comfortable, we can grab my things, meet up with my aunt, and go somewhere else. Good?'

'I guess so,' I said, and followed her down the street.

TEA

The hotel was one of those old places with a ballroom-sized front lobby, glass chandeliers, and elevator operators dressed like organ grinders. Paige's room was on the fourth floor, second one left of the elevator. She unlocked the door and held it open for me. I hesitated.

'I could stick something under the door to prop it open,' she said.

Her face was all open innocence, but I didn't miss the mocking lilt in her voice, maybe because I was much taller and in better physical condition. Even without werewolf strength, I could take her in a fight. Still, that wasn't to say there wasn't some ape with a semiautomatic lurking behind the door. All the muscles in the world won't stop a bullet to the head.

I glanced around and stepped inside. She took a pad of paper from the table and held it up, gesturing toward the closing door.

'That won't be necessary,' I said.

'The phone's right here.' She lifted the receiver so I could hear the dial tone. 'Would you like me to move it closer? I'm pretty sure Pittsburgh has nine-one-one services.'

Okay. Now she was making fun of me. Stupid little twit. Probably one of those airheads who parked in deserted underground lots at night and bragged of their courage. The impulsiveness of youth, I thought, with the maturity of someone almost two years into her thirties.

When I didn't reply, Paige said something about making tea and vanished into the adjoining room of the suite. I was in the living-room part, which contained a small table, two chairs, a sofa, a recliner, and a television. A partly open door led into the bedroom. Through it, I could see suitcases lined against the side wall and several dresses hung on a rack. By the front door there were three pairs of shoes, all women's. No sign of a male occupant. So far the Winterbournes seemed to be above-board. Not that I really expected some guy with a semiautomatic to leap from behind the door. I was suspicious by nature. Being a werewolf does that to you.

As I sat at the table, I eyed the platters from the tearoom. Sandwiches, cookies, and pastries. I could have devoured all three platefuls as a snack. Another werewolf thing. Like most animals, we spent a large part of our lives engaged in the three Fs of basic survival: feeding, fighting, and . . . reproduction. The food part was necessity. We burned calories like fire burns kindling – without a constant supply, our energy fizzled out. I had to be careful when I ate in front of humans. It wasn't fair. The guys could down three Big Macs and no one batted an eye. I got strange looks if I finished two.

'So this information you're selling,' I said as Paige returned. 'It's as good as the Phoenix case, right?'

'Better,' she said, setting the tea tray on the table. 'It's proof that werewolves exist.'

'You believe in werewolves?'

'Don't you?'

'I believe in anything that'll sell magazines.'

'So you don't believe in werewolves?' Her lips curved in an annoying half-smile.

'No offense, but it's not my thing. I write the stuff. I sell it to magazines. People like you buy it. Ninety percent of the readers don't believe it themselves. It's harmless fantasy.'

'Best to keep it that way, isn't it? Harmless fantasy. If you start believing in werewolves, then you have to admit the possibility of other things, witches and sorcerers and shamans. Not to mention vampires and ghosts. Then there's demons, and that's a whole can of worms you don't want to open.'

Okay. Now she was definitely making fun of me. Did someone stick a big 'mock me' sign on my back? Maybe I was taking this more personally than it was intended. Look at it from her point of view. As a believer, she probably looked on nonbelievers the same way nonbelievers looked at her, as a pathetic ignoramus. Here I was, ready to buy information to perpetrate a myth I didn't even believe in, selling my integrity for next month's rent. A journalistic whore. Didn't I deserve a little mockery?

'Where's the information?' I asked, as politely as I could manage.

She reached over to the side table, where a folder lay. For a moment, she leafed through it, lips pursed. Then she took a sheet and laid it between us. It was a photograph showing the head and shoulders of a middle-aged man, Asian, a pinched nose and dour mouth softened by doe-like eyes.

'Do you recognize him?'

'I don't think so,' I said. 'But it's a pretty ordinary face.'

'How about this one? Not quite so ordinary.'

The next photo showed a man in his early thirties. He wore his dark-red hair in a long ponytail, a fashion statement that didn't suit anyone over the age of twenty-five. Like most guys who continued the hairstyle past its prime, he seemed to be compensating for a hairline that had already receded farther than the Bay of Fundy at low tide. His face was paunchy, once semi-handsome features vanishing as fast as his hair.

'Now him I recognize,' I said.

'You do?'

'Of course. Come on. I'd have to live in Tibet not to recognize him. Hell, even journalists in Tibet read *Time* and *Newsweek*. He's been covered by them, what, five times in the last year? Ty Winsloe. Billionaire and computer geek extraordinaire.'

'So you've never met him personally?'

'Me? I wish. No matter how many interviews he's given, a Ty Winsloe exclusive would still be a career breakthrough for a no-name reporter like me.'

She frowned, as if I'd answered the wrong question. Instead of saying anything, though, she fanned both pictures in front of me and waited.

'Okay, I give,' I said. 'What does this have to do with werewolf proof? Please, please, please don't tell me these guys are werewolves. Is that your game? Put one decent story on the web, lure some dumb journalist down here, then weave a whopper about werewolf billionaires?'

'Ty Winsloe is not a werewolf, Elena. If he was, you'd know it.'

'How . . . ?' I shook my head. 'Maybe there's some confusion here. Like I said in my e-mail, this is my first werewolf story. If there are experts in the field, that's a scary thought, but I'm not one of them.'

'You're not here to write a story, Elena. You're a journalist, but not this kind.'

'Ah,' I said. 'So, tell me, why am I here?'

'To protect your Pack.'

I blinked. Words jammed in my throat. As the silence dragged past three seconds, I struggled to fill it. 'My – my what?'

'Your Pack. The others. Other werewolves.'

'Ah, so I'm a' – I forced a patronizing smile – 'a werewolf.'

My heart thudded so loudly I could hear it. This had never happened to me before. I'd run into suspicions, but only general questions about my behavior – like 'What are you doing in the forest after dark?' – but never anything that tied me to being a werewolf. In the normal world, normal people didn't go around accusing people of being werewolves. One person, someone I was close to, actually saw me change forms and convinced himself he'd been hallucinating.

'Elena Antonov Michaels,' Paige said, 'Antonov being your mother's maiden name. Born September 22, 1969.

Both parents killed in an auto accident in 1974. Raised in numerous foster homes in southern Ontario. Attended the University of Toronto. Dropped out in her third year. Returned several years later to complete a bachelor's degree in journalism. Reason for the hiatus? A bite. From a lover. Clayton Danvers. No middle name. Born January 15, 1962—'

I didn't hear the rest. Blood pounded in my ears. The floor swayed beneath me. I gripped the table edge to steady myself and struggled to my feet. Paige's lips moved. I didn't hear what she said. I didn't care.

Something snapped me back into my chair. Pressure wound around my legs as if someone was tying them down. I jerked up but couldn't stand. Looking down, I saw nothing restraining me.

Paige stood. I bucked against the chair. My legs wouldn't budge. Panic seeped into my chest. I pushed it back. This was a trick. A simple trick.

'Whatever you're doing,' I said. 'I'd suggest you stop it. I'm going to count to three.'

'Don't threaten—'

'One.'

'—me, Elena. I can do—'

'Two.'

'—a lot more than bind—'

'Three.'

'—you to that chair.'

I crashed both fists up into the bottom of the table and sent it jetting into the air. As the pressure on my legs vanished, I vaulted across the now-empty space between us

27

and slammed Paige against the wall. She started saying something. I grabbed her by the neck, stopping the words in her throat.

'Well, it would seem I arrived just in time,' a voice said behind us.

I looked over my shoulder to see a woman walk into the room. She was at least seventy, short and plump, with white hair, a flowered dress, and a matching pearl necklace and earring set, the perfect image of a TV grandmother circa 1950.

'I'm Ruth, Paige's great-aunt,' she said, as serenely as if I was enjoying tea with her niece instead of throttling her. 'Trying to handle matters on your own again, Paige? Now look what you've done. Those bruises will take weeks to fade and we didn't bring any turtlenecks.'

I loosened my grip around Paige's neck and struggled for a suitable reply. None came. What could I say? Demand an explanation? Too dangerous, implying I had something to hide. Better to act as if Paige's accusation was crazy and I was getting the hell out of here. Once away from the situation, I could figure out my next move. I shot Paige the wary look people use when dealing with someone of limited sanity and sidestepped toward the door.

'Please don't.' Ruth laid a hand on my arm, firm but not restraining. 'We must speak with you, Elena. Perhaps I can handle this better.'

At that, Paige reddened and looked away. I eased my arm out of Ruth's grip and took another step toward the door.

'Please don't, Elena. I can restrain you, but I'd rather not resort to that.'

I lunged at the door and grabbed the handle with both hands. Ruth said something. My hands froze. I jerked them back from the door handle, but they wouldn't come loose. I tried to turn the handle. My fingers wouldn't respond.

'This is the way the spell should work,' Ruth said, her voice and face radiating the calm of a seasoned teacher handling a recalcitrant child. 'It won't break until I give the command.'

She said a few words. My hands flew free, throwing me off-balance. As I stumbled back, Ruth put out a hand to steady me. I recovered and stepped away fast.

'Please stay,' she said. 'Binding spells have their place, but they're not terribly civilized.'

'Binding spells?' I said, flexing my still-numb hands.

'Witchcraft,' Ruth said. 'But I'm sure you figured that out. Whether you want to believe it may be quite another matter. Let's start over, shall we? I'm Ruth Winterbourne. That impetuous young woman behind you is my niece Paige. We need to speak to you.'

HOCUS-POCUS

I wanted to run. Throw open the door, run, and not stop until Ruth and Paige Winterbourne were gone, not just out of my sight, but out of my head as well. I wanted to run until my legs ached and my lungs burned and I could think of nothing but stopping, unable to spare a moment's energy dealing with what had happened. Not the most mature response. I know that. But it was what I was good at. Running. I'd been doing it all my life. Even when I didn't run, when I dug in my heels and confronted my fears, there was always a part of me running as fast as it could.

I knew what I should do. Stay and work this out, refute Paige's claims and discover how much these women knew. If Paige had simply said she knew I was a werewolf, as disturbing as that would have been, I could have handled it. But when she recited my bio, though it was all accessible through public records, the violation was somehow more personal. Then bringing up my history with Clay as matter-of-factly as she'd recited my birth date, well, every fiber screamed for me to run, get out of there, get some distance, deal with it later. Only Ruth's demonstration of power kept me from running. It also gave me a moment to stop and think.

Did I want to return to Jeremy and say that two strangers had accused me of being a werewolf and I'd bolted? Oh, he wouldn't be angry. He'd understand. That was the worst of it. I didn't want him to understand why I'd screwed up. I wanted him to be proud of me. Yes, I know, I was much too old to be seeking approval from a surrogate father-figure, but that's the way it was. After Clay bit me, Jeremy had taken care of me, putting his life on hold to put mine back together. Each time I undertook one of these investigations, I was showing Jeremy that he hadn't made a mistake, that I'd prove my value to the Pack by repaying his efforts tenfold. Now, faced for the first time with imminent exposure, was I going to return to New York and say, 'Sorry, Jer, but I couldn't deal'? Not in this lifetime. If I ran, I'd keep running. Everything I'd worked so hard for in the last year – letting myself accept my life at Stonehaven, with the Pack, with Clay – would all be thrown away and I'd go back to being as miserable and screwed-up as I'd been eighteen months ago.

So I stayed. Ruth and I came to an agreement. I'd hear her out, admitting nothing. If I wanted, I could treat her story like the ramblings of a senile old woman and pretend to stick around just to be polite.

We sat at the table, Paige on the far side, chair pulled back. She hadn't said a word since her aunt arrived.

'Do you believe in witches?' Ruth asked as she poured me a cup of tea.

'Wicca?' I said carefully.

'No. Witches. Hereditary witches. Like hereditary were-wolves.'

She put up a hand as I started to protest.

'I'm not asking for an admission, remember? You're humoring an old lady. Well, if you don't – or didn't – believe in witches, then I have to assume you don't believe in anything more fantastical. All right, then. Let's start from scratch. Pretend there are witches and . . . other things. Pretend, too, that these beings – races we call them – know about one another and gather periodically to disseminate information and deal with potential exposure. Now, at one point, werewolves were part of this collaboration—'

I opened my mouth, but Ruth again raised her hand.

'All right,' Ruth said. 'You don't need a history lesson. We didn't come here for that. As Paige may have said, we came to warn you. Did she get to that part?'

'I showed her the photos,' Paige said. 'We didn't get to the explanation.'

'Allow me then. These men – humans – have been giving us some trouble. Quite a bit of trouble. Confrontations, accusations, kidnappings. It would seem they know more than they should.'

'Those two?' I said, pointing at the folder. 'Ty Winsloe? Kidnapping witches? You're losing me. This doesn't make sense.'

'What does anymore?' Ruth said with a tiny smile. 'Once upon a time all we had to worry about was bonfires and Grand Inquisitors. Now we have evil computer magnates. I won't go into detail, partly because I suspect you won't stick around long enough to listen and partly because I'm hoping a little curiosity might bring your pack to our meeting.'

'I really—'

'They know about the werewolves and they're looking for them, just as they're looking for the rest of us.'

I leaned back in my chair and looked from Ruth to Paige. Ruth watched me, green eyes bright and sharp. Paige pretended to be watching me, but those same green eyes on her were hooded and distant, looking at me but not seeing me.

'You know how this sounds, don't you?' I said. 'Pretend I *am* a werewolf. You two lure me here with some bullshit story and tell me you're witches. Not only are you witches but you're part of some supernatural United Nations. As delegates of this UN, you've decided to contact me with this story about demonic computer geeks—'

'They're not demonic,' Ruth said. 'As I said, they're human.'

'You guys really take this stuff seriously, don't you?'

'It is serious,' Paige said, cool stare freezing. 'Maybe we made a mistake choosing you—'

'And about that. Why choose me? Or did you put that story on the Internet and assume only a werewolf would reply? Let's say this conspiracy exists and there are guys out there looking for werewolves. What's to stop them from responding to your ad?'

'We did get a lot of inquiries,' Ruth said. 'But we were waiting for yours.'

'Mine?'

'A few years ago, our council had a run-in with a werewolf. Not one of your Pack. An outsider. We've kept tabs on him, in case we ever needed to contact the werewolves. When this trouble began, we found him and . . . persuaded him to share some information with us. He knew about your Pack, who led it, who was in it, where they lived. Moreover, he knew all about you and your background. Being the only female werewolf, it seems you've achieved quite legendary status among your race.'

She smiled. I returned a blank stare.

Ruth continued, 'He knew you followed up on realistic werewolf sightings, watching for misbehavior. Quite interesting. We do the same, monitoring witches who've left the Coven. So we decided to try getting in touch with you that way before attempting direct contact.'

'Why me?'

'You're part of the Pack. As well, being the only female, you seemed a . . . better choice of contact. Perhaps easier to talk to than your male counterparts.'

In other words, more gullible? Less likely to counter threat with violence? If they wanted the latter, they should have gone straight to the top. Jeremy was the most levelheaded among us. He was also the most open-minded. He'd have been the best choice for this meeting. Wouldn't it have made more sense to take their concerns directly to the Alpha anyway? Unless, for some reason, they didn't want to do that.

'You still realize how this sounds,' I said. 'Forget how and why you chose me. You bring me here, issuing B-movie lines like "We know who you are." Sorry, but I'm looking for the hidden camera. Let's say I believe all this hocus-pocus. Why, if this UN doesn't include werewolves, would you suddenly want to contact them now? If you are witches, you must have run into bad guys before.'

'We risk exposure as often as you do,' Ruth said. 'But it's

always been one race at a time. This is different. This involves all of us, which is why we must band together.'

'One for all and all for one,' I muttered.

'This isn't a joke,' Paige said.

'You still don't believe us, do you?' Ruth asked. 'Even about the witch part, despite our little demonstration.'

'We could do a bigger one,' Paige said. 'Say, zip your mouth shut. Permanently.'

'Paige,' Ruth warned. 'Forgive my niece's youthful exuberance. If you'd like, though, I could certainly give you a better demonstration. Nothing as uncivilized as a binding spell, of course.'

'No thanks,' I said.

'Why?' Paige asked. 'Because you don't believe? Or because you don't want to?'

'I did what I said I'd do. I stayed. I listened. Now I'm leaving.'

As I stood, Ruth touched my arm. 'At least tell your leader what we've said. We're meeting in two days. Delegates from the major races will be there to discuss the problem. We'd like your pack to join us. Here's my card.'

She handed me a business card. I half-expected to see 'Ruth Winterbourne, Spells and Potions.' Instead, it was a card for 'Winterbourne Designs, Custom Apparel for Women.' The address listed was in Massachusetts, though disappointingly not Salem.

'Yes,' Ruth said with a smile. 'It's a real business card for a real business. Not much money in hexes these days.'

'I don't—'

'Put it in your pocket and we'll pretend you're going to

throw it away once I'm out of sight. If you call, use my cell phone number. We're heading straight from here to the meeting in Vermont. It wouldn't be a long drive from New York if you decide to come out. I hope you do.'

I mumbled something noncommittal, pocketed the card, and left.

Afterward, I spent more time thinking about witches than billionaire conspiracy theories. The thought of other 'supernatural' beings intrigued me, though I found it hard to believe. Okay, skepticism from someone who routinely morphed into a wolf may sound hypocritical, but I couldn't help it. I'd been a werewolf for nearly six months before I believed they existed. I'd changed forms, I'd seen Jeremy change forms, yet still managed to convince myself that it wasn't real. Serious denial. Maybe it was easier to believe werewolves were a one-time aberration of nature, the way some people – myself included – think the universe contains only one populated planet. The thought of zombies and vampires wandering the earth was just too weird. But Ruth hadn't mentioned zombies or vampires. She'd only said witches and . . . other things. I could believe in witches. The idea that some people could harness the earth's powers was much easier to accept than the idea that, say, some people could transform into wolves.

When I walked into my hotel room, the phone was ringing. I stood in the doorway, contemplated a quick about-face, then resigned myself to answering it. Besides, it might not be who I expected.

'What the hell are you doing in Pittsburgh?!' the caller roared before I even got the receiver to my ear. I looked for a volume button on the phone, couldn't find one, and considered 'accidentally' hitting the plunger.

'Nice to hear from you, too, Clayton. My flight was fine, thanks. How's Detroit?'

'Hotter than Hades,' he muttered, his Southern drawl resurrected as his voice dropped to non-eardrum-shattering decibels. 'Smells worse, too. Why didn't you call and tell me you were going to Pittsburgh?'

'Because you would have insisted on meeting me here. I don't need—'

'Too late. I'm already packing.'

'I don't need your help, and I don't need your protection.'

'And my company, darling? I suppose you don't need that either.'

'Give it a rest. You only left yesterday, and I'll be joining you on Monday.'

'Then I can save you two flights. I'll drive down tonight, and when you're done there, I can bring you back to Detroit—'

'No.'

'I'm just trying to be—'

'Controlling, possessive, overprotective.'

'I miss you.'

'Nice try. The answer's still no. I can handle this.'

'So what exactly are you handling?'

'I'll tell you tomorrow,' I said. 'After I speak to Jeremy.'

'Anything good?'

'Maybe.'

'Fun?' he asked.

'Definite mayhem possibilities.'

'Come on. Tell me.'

'Later.'

'Tease,' he growled.

'You want to hear teasing?' I asked.

'Sure, if you want me in Pittsburgh in an hour.'

'It's a six-hour drive.'

'Wanna bet?'

We went on like this for a while, forty-five minutes actually. Before we ended the conversation Clay had agreed – most grudgingly – not to follow me to Pittsburgh. I had to admit that since we'd been back together, he really had been working at being less controlling, possessive, and over-protective. Not that he was giving up and letting me lead a semi-independent life. We kept separate bedrooms, but that was as far as it went. He still expected me to be with him twenty-four hours a day. Even the separate bedroom thing was a joke. Having my own room only meant I had a place to store my stuff. Wherever I slept, Clay slept.

As part of my own relationship-saving efforts, I'd had to admit that this togetherness thing was part of Clay's nature. Bitten as a child, he'd forgotten ever having been human, and nothing in his later experiences convinced him he was missing out on anything. He was more wolf than human. About the togetherness thing, Clay would argue that you'd never see a wolf telling its mate that it had to 'get away for a while' or needed 'some personal space.' They formed lifelong bonds that seemed to work out just fine despite the grievous lack of relationship therapy.

Clay and I had been together nearly twelve years. Well, 'together' was a mild exaggeration. We'd started out twelve years ago, then there was the biting thing. After ten years of bouncing back and forth, I'd broken down and admitted to myself that I loved him and couldn't live without him – all that Harlequin romance stuff. Still, our relationship was hardly the sort of thing Harlequin would endorse. Clay and I went together like fire and gasoline – intense heat, incredible fireworks, and, occasionally, devastating destruction. I'd come to realize that was how we were. It wasn't a calm, stable relationship, it never would be, and, frankly, neither of us wanted that. Blissful domesticity was for other people. Give us fireworks and explosions, of both the positive and negative variety, and we were as blissful as we got.

I couldn't sleep that night.

I lay in bed, staring at the ceiling, fighting off an unease that kept me from closing my eyes.

First, there was the question of the witches. Were they witches or not? Either way, I didn't trust their motivation. Too much of what they'd said didn't make sense. I should have called Jeremy as soon as I'd left their hotel. He wasn't going to be happy when he found out I'd waited a full day to tell him. At least two people knew I was a werewolf and I hadn't told either Clay or Jeremy. Where the hell was my head at? Should I call Jeremy now? It was 2:45 A.M. My flight left at 8:00. This could wait. Could it? Should it?

I went for a run to clear my head. Jogging, I mean. While Changing into a wolf and running around Pittsburgh might be fun, it was definitely not the kind of excitement I needed. I pulled on shorts and a T-shirt, left my hotel room, and followed a maze of alleys to a deserted industrial area. Big cities weren't the place for late-night jogs. Anyone seeing a young woman running around Pittsburgh at 3:00 A.M. was going to be looking for the guy chasing her.

I'd jogged about a quarter-mile when I realized someone was following me. No big surprise. Like I said, young women jogging at night attract attention, usually the wrong kind. Sure, if some guy jumped me, I could slam him into the nearest brick wall and there'd be one less potential rapist for the world to worry about. But that meant a body to clean up in a strange city. Not only that, but I couldn't do it. I can talk the talk, but I ain't that tough. Even if some mugger pulled a gun on me and I had to kill him, I'd regret it. I'd wonder if I'd overreacted, if maybe this was the guy's first offense and a good scare would have set him straight, if maybe he had a wife and kids at home and only wanted a few bucks for food. Better to avoid getting into a situation where such action might be necessary. Wild wolves survived by avoiding confrontation with humans. Smart werewolves did the same.

When I heard soft running footfalls nearby, I first made sure it wasn't a coincidence. I turned down the next three streets and circled full around to where I'd been. The footsteps followed. Next I got downwind and checked the scent, in case it was another werewolf. As the only female werewolf in a country with a couple dozen males, I was considered a trophy. The fact that my lover was the most feared and hated werewolf around only added to my value. If mutts didn't want to fuck me, they wanted to fuck Clay over – and the chance to do both at once was more than some could resist. Though I didn't know of any mutts in the Pittsburgh area, they were a nomadic lot and my dossiers were always out of date.

My pursuer wasn't a mutt. Werewolves had a distinct underlying scent and this guy didn't. It was a guy – a man, I mean. Other than that, his smell didn't give me much to go on. No aftershave. A touch of body odor, as if his deodorant had reached its time limit. Otherwise clean. Very clean. I didn't expect that with a rapist or mugger. Yes, I know not every creep is a scruffy, unshaven vagrant. Most aren't. But they aren't usually hygiene fanatics either. Curiosity aroused, I decided to get a look at my stalker.

Still eager to avoid confrontation, I did both at once, getting a closer look while sneaking away. To find him, I stopped in the middle of the empty street, bent over, and retied my shoes. Then I muttered under my breath, yanked them undone, and redid them. By the third tie-up, stalker-guy got antsy, probably cursing me for stopping in the road instead of some nice shadowy corner. He leaned out of his hiding spot, giving himself away with a blur of motion in the otherwise still street. He was hiding in a building alcove to my left.

Straightening, I launched into a set of hamstring stretches. Midway through my second set, I took off. Running full out, I raced into the alley alongside the building where my stalker hid. By the time he came after me, I was behind the adjacent building. I stopped in a rear doorway and searched the ground. A few yards to my left, I saw what

I wanted. Something dark and missile-like. A half-dozen beer bottles scattered around the door. Grabbing the nearest one, I pitched it down the back alley. It crashed somewhere behind the next building. Fortunately, my stalker wasn't deaf. When he got to the end of the side alley, he turned toward the crash and headed in that direction, moving away from me.

Keeping in the shadows, I watched the man as he walked away. Six-two, maybe six-three. Average weight. Dressed in dark pants and jacket. Some kind of hat. Baseball cap? He slowed, paused, getting his bearings. Then he hunkered down and crept forward, head moving from side to side, like a sniper creeping through the jungle. Something dangled from his hand. A gun. A big gun. Right, Elena. You're being stalked through Pittsburgh by an armed Vietnam vet. That's what I got for watching *Platoon* with Clay last week. The guy was probably carrying a bottle of Wild Turkey.

Sticking close to the wall, I slunk toward my stalker. Light from a naked bulb flashed off what he held in his hand. Definitely a gun. I narrowed my eyes to get a better look at his outfit. He wore black fatigues. Okay, enough with the *Platoon* flashbacks. Fatigues didn't come in black, at least I didn't think they did. The guy wore black baggy pants, an equally baggy jacket, a dark ball-cap, and dark, thick-soled boots.

He stopped. I flattened myself against the wall and waited. Tugging off his ball-cap with one hand, he scratched his head with the other. In the silence of the night, his fingernails rasped through his short hair. Very short hair.

Like military buzz-cut short. Keeping his cap off, he took something from his pocket, flicked his wrist, and lifted it to his ear.

'She come out that way?' he murmured into the two-way radio. I assumed it was a radio because I didn't see him punch in a phone number. 'Yeah . . . no. She musta made me. Spooked and ran. Caught me off guard . . . yeah . . . no, no. I woulda noticed that. Kinda hard to miss a wolf out here.'

Wolf? Did he say wolf?

This really wasn't my day.

HOUDINI

'No,' my stalker said into his radio. 'What? . . . Yeah. Probably. You gonna check with Tucker? . . . Nah, I'll walk. Tell Pierce to park it around back . . . Yeah? Well, it's not far . . . See ya in a couple.'

He stuffed the radio into his pocket. Then he lifted his gun and did something to make it smaller, folded back the barrel or unscrewed it or something. Hey, I'm Canadian. I don't know street guns. Somehow he made the weapon half the size, lifted his jacket, and stuck it in a holster.

I followed stalker-guy back to the street. There he met up with a second man, also dressed in the whole cat-burglar/gothic-fatigue getup. Both removed their ball-caps and shoved them in a collapsible knapsack. Then they unzipped their jackets, making themselves look as normal as possible without revealing the guns. They headed east. I followed.

By the third turn, I knew where they were going. We were still a half-mile away, but I knew. As I expected, they walked three blocks, made a left, made a right, walked three more blocks, and ended up in front of the hotel where I'd met the Winterbournes that afternoon. So my concern about gun-toting men hiding in the Winterbournes' hotel room hadn't been so paranoid after all. Only instead of having their cohorts/minions jump me there, they'd waited to go after me under cover of night.

I expected the men to walk straight in the front lobby. When they didn't I was surprised, then realized two guys dressed in black walking into the lobby of an expensive hotel at 4:00 A.M. would raise a few eyebrows . . . and a few alarms. Invited or not, they were taking the back route. They skirted around to a side door. My stalker leaned against the wall, blocking my view, while his friend fiddled with the lock. Two minutes passed. Then the door opened and they slipped inside. I counted to twenty, then went after them.

The two men took the stairs. They climbed to the fourth floor, opened the exit door, and peered out. After a few moments of discussion, my stalker's companion slipped into the hall, leaving stalker-guy in the stairwell.

Now I had a dilemma. From my vantage point below the stalker, I couldn't see anything – not him and certainly not his companion, even though the door was propped open. I did have an option. When I'd come in with Paige, I'd noticed a second set of stairs on the far side of the lobby. I could exit on the third floor, find the alternate stairs, go up to the fifth, and circle back to the staircase. From the steps above, I'd be able to see. Plus, the stalker would be more likely to expect danger from below, someone coming up from ground level. On the other hand, the plan also meant I'd be out of hearing and smelling range for at least a few minutes. Was it better to stay where I could use those two senses?

The longer I waited, the more risky it would be to leave. I crept down the stairs to the third floor.

Circling around wasn't a problem. The exits were marked at each end of the hall. I came back to the first stairwell, took off my shoes, slipped through the fifth-floor door, and eased down the stairs until I was a half-dozen steps from the fourth-floor landing where stalker-guy waited. Sliding my shoes back on, I crouched to peer through the railing. Perfect. Now I had sound, smell, and sight. My stalker's partner was at room 406. The Winterbournes'. He was crouched before the door, fiddling with lock-pick tools. So they weren't invited guests. Maybe the Winterbournes had been telling the truth about being in danger. At least, telling the truth about *themselves* being in danger. And me? Well, I wouldn't have been in Pittsburgh if it weren't for them, right? Somehow I doubted these militia-wannabes would have been stalking me tonight if I'd stayed home. Whether or not the Winterbournes were complicit in this, I could still blame them for it. Lucky thing, because I definitely wanted to blame them for something.

Stalker-guy rolled from his heels to his toes, muttering under his breath. Down the hall, his companion wiped his sweaty face on his shoulder. He stood, stretched, and crouched again. Several times he tried the door handle, then turned to his partner and shook his head. Finally my stalker waved him back. I quickstepped up three stairs, out of sight. They came into the stairwell and closed the door.

'No go,' lock-pick guy said. 'I don't get it. I'm sure I popped the lock, but it won't open.'

'Dead bolt?'

Lock-pick guy shook his head. 'I checked out the place this morning. Old-fashioned key locks.'

'Call Tucker. I saw a pay phone out front. Ground line. I'll wait here.'

Lock-pick guy trotted down the stairs. As the first-floor door swung shut behind him, I heard another door opened, this one on the fourth floor. Stalker-guy cracked open the exit to look down the hall. Then he made a noise deep in his throat, a stifled chuckle. I sneaked down a few steps, crouched again, and looked through the door crack.

Paige Winterbourne stood in the hall, arms folded across her chest, dressed in a green silk chemise and matching wrap. Frowning, she surveyed the corridor. Then she stopped and stared at the exit where we hid. Though the door was open only a couple of inches, she must have seen light or shadow peeking through. As she watched, stalker-guy hesitated, holding the door handle, ready to close it. If she'd gone back into her room to call security, he would have bolted. But she didn't. She narrowed her eyes and started toward us. Yet another horror movie cliché. When the ditzy ingénue hears a bump in the night, does she retreat to safety and phone for help? Of course not. She has to see what's behind that partly open door. All Paige needed now was to lose the negligée, so she could run naked and screaming down the hall when she flung open the door and found the killer lurking behind it.

Stalker-guy broke from the script. Instead of waiting for Paige to throw open the door, he took out his gun and snapped it back together. Then he eased the door open another half-inch and lifted the gun to the door crack. Last year, I'd seen an innocent woman gunned down because of me. Whether Paige was innocent or not was a matter of some debate, but I doubted she deserved to be murdered in a hotel hallway. I leaped over the railing and landed on the man's back. He fell forward. I grabbed his head and twisted his neck. The simplest, quietest, and cleanest kill.

As he dropped face-first to the floor, I looked up to see Paige holding the door open and staring.

'Stand guard,' I said. 'Is your room unlocked?'

'My—? Umm, yes.'

I hoisted the dead man onto my shoulder and pushed past her into the hall. 'I said to stand guard. He wasn't alone.'

'Where are you ⇒ oh, wait. My room? You can't put him—' She stopped. 'Take him to the suite next to ours. The near side. It's empty.'

'All the better.'

'I can unlock the door with a spell,' she said.

She hurried down the hallway alongside me, murmuring words in a foreign language. While she was talking, I covered my hand with my shirt, reached over, and snapped the vacant room's door knob.

'Run back and get the gun,' I said. 'Then wake your aunt and get in here.'

Paige hesitated, like a knee-jerk reaction against taking orders. She seemed to think better of arguing and paused only a second before jogging to the stairwell. I dragged the dead man into the bathroom, closed the door, and checked his pockets for ID. Nothing. Seeing the two-way radio in his pocket reminded me that there was a second gunman, and Paige and her aunt were taking their sweet time evacuating their room.

I opened the bathroom door as they walked into the vacant room. Paige was still wearing her chemise and wrapper. Ruth's long housecoat covered her nightwear. Both carried a change of clothing and their purses.

'Good idea,' I said. 'Is all your ID in there?'

'No sense leaving them any clues if they break in,' Paige said. 'If we have to, we can leave the rest of the stuff behind.'

'Paige told me what happened,' Ruth said. 'We're very grateful. Also very impressed. You have excellent reflexes.'

'Self-defense classes,' I said.

'Still not admitting to the werewolf thing?' Paige asked.

I walked to the bathroom and held open the door. 'Either of you ever see this guy before? Don't touch anything. The cops will dust for prints.'

'Cops?' Paige repeated.

'Yes, cops. Who do you think will handle the murder investigation? Hotel security?'

'Murder? You mean he's dead?'

'No. He's resting comfortably,' I said. 'People always sleep best with their heads at a ninety-degree angle. He looks comfortable, doesn't he?'

'There's no need for sarcasm,' Paige said tightly. 'Maybe you're used to hauling corpses around, but I'm not.'

'Sheltered life. You're supposed to be a witch and you've never had to kill anyone?'

Paige's voice tightened another notch. 'We use alternate methods of defense.'

'Like what? Cast a spell to make your attackers think

happy thoughts? Turn their guns into flowers? Peace and love for all?'

'I'd have used a binding spell,' Paige said. 'Kept the guy alive so we could question him. Wow. There's a novel idea. If you hadn't killed him, maybe we could have talked to him.'

'Oh, that's right. Paige's ultra-efficient binding spell. Tell you what. Next time I see a guy pointing a gun at you, I'll let you do things your way. You start your invocation and see if you can finish before he guns you down. Deal?'

Paige lifted the gun, opened it, removed a tranquilizer dart, and held it up. 'No one wanted to kill me.'

'Are you sure about that?' a male voice asked.

Paige and I jumped. Even Ruth looked up, startled. In the corner of the bedroom stood a man dressed in the same black fatigues as the dead man on the floor. He was average height and weight, with average brown hair cut short but not military short. Only one distinguishing feature – a paper-thin scar running from temple to nose – assured me I'd never seen this man before. I glanced toward the hall door. It was still closed and locked. Paige's change of clothing lay undisturbed in front of it. So how'd this guy get in?

'I'm glad to hear you wouldn't have killed poor Mark,' the man said, sitting on the edge of the bed, stretching his legs and crossing his ankles. 'Very sporting of you. I guess what they say about witches is true. So selfless, so concerned for others, so unbelievably naive.'

I stepped toward him.

'Don't!' Paige hissed.

'This is the werewolf?' The man turned dirt-brown eyes on me in a smirking once-over. 'Better than I expected. So, are you coming along, wolf-girl? Or do things have to get' – his smirk broadened to a grin – 'physical.'

I glanced at Paige and Ruth.

'Oh, they're coming too,' the man said. 'But I'm not worried about them. Only witches, you know. They'll do what they're told.'

Paige made a noise in her throat, but Ruth laid a restraining hand on her arm.

'So you're kidnapping us?' I asked.

The man yawned. 'Looks that way, doesn't it?'

'What's in it for you?' Paige asked.

'See?' The man looked at me. 'That's witches for you. Make me feel guilty. Appeal to my kinder, gentler side. Which might work, if I had one.'

'So you're working for Ty Winsloe?' I said.

'Oh, come on, ladies. As much as I'd love to chat about my motivations and the Yankees' chance at the World Series—'

I lunged at him, sailing the five feet between us. My hands went out, ready to catch him in the chest and topple him backward. But they didn't. Instead I hit empty air and tumbled onto the bed, twisting fast to right myself before the counterattack. It didn't come. I whirled around to see the man standing by the bedroom door, the same bored expression on his face.

'Is that the best you can do?' He sighed. 'Major disappointment.'

I advanced on him, slowly, eyes locked on his. When I was close enough to hear his heartbeat, I stopped. He grinned again and his eyes sparked with boyish anticipation, like a kid impatient for the game to begin. His throat pulsed, words moving up to his mouth. Before he could say anything, I swung my right foot out, hooked his legs, and yanked. He pitched backward. Then he vanished, one second dropping like a brick, the next – not there. Just not there.

'Clever,' he said from somewhere behind me.

I spun to see him standing in the bathroom by the dead body.

'You're getting the hang of it,' he said, a grin illuminating his eyes. 'I'd love to give you another chance, but my compatriots are coming. Can't let them find me playing with the enemy. They wouldn't understand. Humans.'

He bent to the tranquilizer gun Paige had dropped. Ruth's lips moved. The man stopped in mid-reach, fingers close enough to flex and touch the metal. But his hand didn't move.

'Go!' Ruth said, snatching her purse from the floor. 'It won't last.'

Paige sprinted across the room, grabbed my arm, and dragged me toward the door. I jerked away and turned back to the man. He was immobilized. It didn't matter if it wouldn't last. I didn't need long. I stepped toward him. Paige grabbed my arm.

'No time!' she said. 'He could break it any second.'

'Go on,' I said.

'No,' Ruth said.

Together they propelled me out the door. I resisted, but it was clear they weren't going anywhere without me, and I wasn't about to risk anyone's life, including my own. So I ran for the stairwell. They followed.

We'd gone down almost two flights of steps when I heard the tramp of footsteps coming up from the bottom. I wheeled around and shoved Paige back up. As we ran for the third-floor exit, someone shouted from below. The clomp of footsteps turned to a fast beat as they hightailed it up the stairs after us.

I pushed past Ruth and Paige and led them down the hall to the opposite stairwell. Our pursuers were just coming onto the third floor as we bolted through the other door. Down the stairs. Out the first-floor emergency exit. Alarms blared.

Paige turned to the north. I grabbed her arm and wrenched her back.

'That's the street,' I hissed, pushing her in front of me as we ran south.

'They won't gun us down in front of people,' she called back at me.

'Wanna bet? How many people do you think are out there at four-thirty in the morning?'

'Just run,' Ruth said. 'Please.'

The alarms seemed to slow the men down. Maybe someone stopped them. I didn't know and didn't care. All that mattered was that we made it to the south end of the alley, turned west, and were halfway down that one before I heard our pursuers come out of the hotel, barking orders. The west alley ended. Our choices were south to a dead end or north to the street. With Ruth and Paige in their nightgowns, I wasn't sure running to the possible safety of the street was such a good idea. But 'dead end' had a really ominous ring to it. So I turned north and kept running.

Actually, 'running' was an overstatement. Call it a fast jog. While Paige managed to stay beside me, forcing her elderly aunt to run at my normal pace would have been as much a death warrant as leaving her behind.

Partway to the street, we hit a narrow alley that went off to the west and I veered down it. The men were now rounding the north corner, their heavy breathing like the baying of hounds at our heels. I was glad Ruth and Paige couldn't hear it. Ahead, a garbage dumpster blocked the west route. I could see a turn to the south and assumed there was a north fork as well. There wasn't. Worse yet, the south fork ended in an eight-foot wall.

'Over the dumpster,' I whispered. 'I'll jump on and pull you up.'

Ruth shook her head. 'Down there,' she wheezed, pointing south.

'But there's no—'

'Hide,' she said.

I squinted down the dark alley. There was no cover there but shadows. I turned to Ruth to say as much, then saw her face. It was crimson, her chest heaving, such rasping breath making her wince. She couldn't go any farther.

Nodding, I shepherded them down the south alley and motioned for us to stand against the west wall, where the shadows were deepest. I put Ruth, in her pale yellow night-gown, on the far side, sheltered by Paige and me. It wouldn't help. They'd see us. One glance down this alley and we were caught. All I could do now was prepare to confront them.

We were barely settled into the shadows when three men

skidded to a halt in front of the dumpster. One was lock-pick guy, the other was Houdini from the hotel room, and the third was yet another military-style clone.

'Don't move,' Paige whispered, touching my arm.

I didn't think it would help, but if it made them feel better, I'd stay still until we were discovered. The men looked at the dumpster, then glanced down the south alley, too quick to see us. Lock-pick guy walked from one end of the dumpster to the other.

'Blocked,' he said. 'No way but over.'

'Eight feet?' the new guy said. 'With an old lady? No way.'

Houdini leaned against the north brick wall, took a cigarette from his pocket, and struck a match. The flame lit his face for a second, then sputtered into darkness. He took a drag while the two military guys argued over the likelihood of our having scaled the dumpster. Hello! We were twenty feet away, in almost plain sight. But no one ever said the military recruited for brains. Besides, the more I saw of these guys, the more I doubted they were acting under the auspices of any wing of the U.S. military. So what were they? Retired military maybe? More likely discharged. Or those militia groups who pop up with alarming frequency on American newscasts. It didn't matter. Bright, they were not.

As I turned back to Houdini, he looked right back at me. He knew exactly where we were. Why didn't he tell his comrades? Because he wanted us to sweat. Extending the game of cat and mouse. He lifted the cigarette and inhaled. The red ember glowed in the night, then fell, end over end, blinking in the darkness before hitting the ground in a shower of sparks. As he stepped toward the south alley, I tensed and held my breath. His eyes scanned the alley, on us then not on us. Cute. Pretend you can't see us. Lull us into a false sense of security. Sadistic bastard. I held my breath and prepared for the attack.

LEGION

Houdini walked less than a foot from me, looked at the opposite wall, then swiveled his gaze my way. Here it comes. He was taking his sweet time, pretending not to see me. Then, he'd suddenly meet my eyes and bingo, lap up the fear he expected to see there. I gritted my teeth as his head turned toward mine. But his gaze kept moving, right over my face, eyes not even flickering to mine. He grunted. A muscle beneath his scar spasmed. He turned to the wall at the end of the alley and looked up. Then he vanished. A crackle of paper erupted from the other side of the wall. A curse. Then he was back, striding toward the military goons.

'Undisturbed trash on the other side of the wall,' he said. 'They didn't go that way. Either over the dumpster or you guys took a wrong turn. I'll check the other side of the dumpster, but I'm betting on the latter. Humans.'

His companions started to grouse, but Houdini had already vanished. A minute later he returned.

'Puddles,' he said. 'With no wet tracks leading out of them. You fucked up.'

Lock-pick guy glared. 'If you're such a great tracker, why didn't you take the lead?'

'Not my job,' Houdini said, walking east down the alley. 'I'm special ops.'

'That's right,' lock-pick guy called after him. 'You have super powers. So you should have been able to beam yourself down to the hotel exit before they escaped. Oh, sorry. I forgot. You're not that powerful, are you?'

Houdini didn't turn, just extended his middle finger in the air and kept walking. Lock-pick guy glanced at the dumpster again, then peered down the south alley. Unless he was night-blind, he should have seen us. But he didn't. He snapped something at the third man and they took off after Houdini.

When they were out of earshot, Ruth leaned toward me and whispered, 'Cover spell. I would have mentioned it, but there wasn't time.'

I listened to the retreating footsteps, waited until they were gone, then turned to her. 'It worked, but I don't suppose you have something a bit more disabling in that bag of tricks, in case they come back.'

Ruth chuckled. 'Sorry. Our spells are designed for defense, not offense.'

'We have some aggressive spells,' Paige said. 'But they take time to prepare.'

Ruth's mouth tightened. 'We don't use them. That's not our way.'

I remembered what Houdini said about witches. Personally, I'd rather stop my attackers permanently, but witches seemed to have a different philosophy.

Thinking of Houdini, I had to ask, 'What was that guy?'

'Half-demon with teleport abilities,' Paige said. 'Limited range, probably no more than five to ten feet. Offspring of a minor demon, hence the diluted power. My guess is that's the best Winsloe and his bunch have. That's why they want better specimens.'

'Specimens?' I said.

'We'll explain at the meeting,' Ruth said. 'Right now we need to get someplace safe.'

'I can get us over the dumpster,' I said. 'Messy, but safer than heading back to the hotel.'

Ruth nodded and we hurried up the alley. Going over the dumpster wasn't the most pleasant route, but it was easy enough. A six-foot jump was nothing for a werewolf. Neither was hauling up two average-sized women. The stench was the worst of it, enough to make me lose my appetite, which was a feat in itself. We made it down the other side without hearing a sound from the other alley. Our pursuers were long gone.

Once over the dumpster, I followed my nose to an all-night doughnut shop. We managed to sneak through the parking lot and scoot into the washroom without attracting attention. I bought coffee and doughnuts and took them into the washroom where Paige and Ruth were cleaning up. While they ate, I snuck through the door labeled 'employees only' and raided the staff lockers for clothes. I wasn't sure what would fit, but anything had to be better than night-gowns, so I grabbed what I found and took it into the bathroom. We agreed it was time to split up.

'Take care,' Ruth said as I prepared to leave. 'Watch your

back and go straight to the airport. We'll see you at the meeting.'

I hesitated, not wanting to leave the impression that by joining them that night, I was ready to join their meeting, but Ruth had already turned away and started talking to Paige. So I murmured my goodbyes and left.

I returned to my hotel and told the desk clerk I'd gone for an early jog and left my card-key upstairs. He escorted me up to my room, opened it, and waited while I pretended to be looking for the card-key, actually checking for hidden guests. Once he left, I grabbed my stuff, got out, caught a cab to the airport, and called Jeremy.

By the time I called Jeremy, my brain had shifted into overdrive. While I'd been running and worrying about escaping, I hadn't had time to think much about what I was seeing. Now I had too much time, and my mind took full advantage of it. Witches and binding spells. Teleporting demons and armed militia men. Tranquilizer guns and kidnapping plans. Whatever happened to the good old days when all I had to worry about was crazed mutts? Werewolves I could handle. But this? What the hell was this?

I blurted the whole story to Jeremy in a semi-coherent rush of words, thankful I'd found a private phone booth and didn't need to worry about watching what I said. Jeremy waited until I was done, paused to make sure there wasn't more, then said, 'That doesn't sound good.'

I had to laugh. As I did, I felt the tension ease from my neck and shoulders, and relaxed for the first time that night.

60

Typical Jeremy. Master of understatement. I could have told him a nuclear warhead had escaped from Russia and was heading for New York and he'd have said the same thing in the same calm, unruffled tone.

'And no,' I said, 'I haven't been drinking or ingesting illegal narcotics.'

He chuckled. 'I believe you. Where are you now?'

'At the airport.'

'Good. Don't fly to Syracuse. Buy a ticket for Buffalo and watch out for curious onlookers. I'll meet you at the airport.'

By the time my plane touched down, I'd relaxed enough to feel pretty foolish about calling Jeremy in a near-panic and making him drive nearly three hours to Buffalo. There must be a logical, nonsupernatural explanation for what I'd seen that night. I didn't know what it might be, but I was sure it existed.

As the crowd of disembarking passengers carried me into the lobby, I looked over their heads for Jeremy and spotted him immediately. At six-two, Jeremy might not be the tallest guy in the room, but he usually stood a few inches above his neighbors, high enough for me to catch a glimpse of black eyes topped by arching black brows and black bangs always a few weeks overdue for a cut. When he'd last condescended to let me cut his hair, I'd noticed the first strands of white. Not surprising considering Jeremy was fifty-two. We aged slowly – Jeremy looked in his mid-thirties – and he was probably past due for some gray, but I'd still teased him unmercifully. With Jeremy, any flaw was worth picking on. He didn't have nearly enough of them.

When he finally saw me, his lips curved in the barest of smiles, then he nodded and waited for me to come to him. Typical.

'Okay,' I said as I drew up beside him. 'Tell me I overreacted.'

He took my bag. 'Certainly not. Far better than ignoring it and, say, not calling me as soon as you found out about these women.'

'Sorry.'

He waved off the apology. 'We're on top of it now. We're heading straight to Vermont. I've packed our bags. It doesn't seem wise to return to Stonehaven until we know more about this threat.'

'So we're going to the meeting?'

'We don't have much choice. These wit – women seem to have all the answers.'

'So we're getting information from them, not joining them?'

Jeremy chuckled. 'You sound relieved. Don't worry, Elena. The Pack doesn't need any outside help.'

'I tried calling Clay from the airport, but he was out. I left a message saying we needed to talk to him. Should I try him now?'

'He got your message and called home. I explained what happened. I think it's best if he doesn't join us for this meeting. Somehow I doubt he'd be on his best behavior.'

'I can see it now. Charging into the meeting, demanding answers, and threatening to throw someone out the nearest window if those answers don't come fast enough. And that *would* be his best behavior.'

'Exactly. Not quite the entrance I had in mind. So I downplayed the danger and told him you and I could handle it. I'll keep him updated, and if things prove difficult, he can join us.'

'What about Nick and Antonio? They're in Europe for another two weeks.'

'Three,' he said. 'I phoned and told Tonio to be on the alert. If we need them, we'll call. Otherwise, even if this threat is real, Europe may be the best place for them. Out of danger.'

'So it's just the two of us.'

Another chuckle. 'I'm sure we'll survive.'

We spent the night at a cottage Jeremy had rented in Vermont. Despite the busy season, he'd managed to find a place where the original guests had canceled their reservation at the last minute. Not only was it in a secluded, wooded region, but it surpassed 'suitable' and approached perfect, a lakeside chalet far from vacationer traffic. I'd have been lucky to get us reservations at a third-rate highway motel. Trust Jeremy to find Eden with less than a day's notice.

The meeting was being held in Sparta, Vermont. On the drive, Jeremy had called Ruth's cell number and told her we'd arrive Monday, though the meeting started Sunday. Actually, we planned to show up Sunday, but he figured the lie might help us. If we were walking into a trap, by arriving early, we'd catch them off-guard.

As each passing hour pushed Pittsburgh further into my memory, my skepticism returned. What had I really seen?

Nothing a good troupe of magicians or illusionists couldn't pull off. Cover spells and teleporting demons? Right. In the light of day, such things seemed ridiculous. Phantasms of night and nerves. Much more likely we were indeed walking into a trap, a clever but very human trap. At the very least, we were about to meet some seriously deluded people.

The next morning, as we drove down the highway off the mountain, I could see Sparta ahead, nestled in the valley, lone white church on the mountainside, spire wreathed with cloud or late-day fog. Wood-sided houses, all colors of the rainbow, peeked up from the August greenery. Holsteins and red barns dotted the few fields carved out of the wilderness. Pink cottages ringed a lake to the south. It was picture-perfect . . . from a distance. The closer you drove, the more you noticed the signs of decay. The brightly colored houses screamed for paint or vinyl siding. The barn foundations were crumbling into piles of stone that barely supported the woodwork above. Rusty fences and rotted posts let cows escape into neighboring fields. The lakeside cottages didn't look big enough to hold a double bed, let alone a bathroom. On the edge of town we passed a sign welcoming us to Sparta, population 600. The cemetery across the road held more people than the village itself. A dying town, bolstered by one remaining source of tourism, a massive campground outside the village limits, jam-packed with trailers and motor homes and not a tent in sight.

The town center swarmed with tourists, some from the trailer park, others presumably from nearby cottages. Not that downtown Sparta was any kind of shopping mecca.

There was an Exxon gas station, the *House of Wang* Chinese restaurant, *Lynn's Cut and Curl*, the *Yankee Trader* general store – with signs boasting of video games and hand-scooped ice cream – and the ever-present coffee shop, called simply *Joe's*. From what I could see, there were only three streets in Sparta, the highway plus cross streets on either end, Baker to the west and New Moon to the east. The two side streets were lined with houses differentiated only by their colors, everything from baby blue to deep violet to lime-green. Despite the abundance of open land beyond the town, lawns were barely big enough to warrant a power mower. Flowers came in two varieties: marigold and begonia. Country-craft wreaths hung from front doors, and signs hung from porches proclaiming 'The Millers: John, Beth, Sandy, Lori, and Duke. Welcome All!'

'Odd that they'd pick such a small town for their meeting,' I said.

'Maybe,' Jeremy said, 'but how many of those people walking around do you think actually live here?'

I saw his point. Both sides of the highway were jammed with SUVs and minivans. Families strolled the street, licking ice-cream cones and sipping canned diet soda. Strangers probably outnumbered townies ten to one. A few more wouldn't be noticed.

'Ooops, we passed it,' I said. 'Sign for the Legion Hall back there. Sorry.'

Jeremy pulled into a parking lot, waited for a brigade of baby strollers to pass, then turned the Explorer around and headed back. The Legion Hall was at the end of Baker, a good half-mile beyond the last house on the street. Jeremy slowed to look at the hall, then continued down another hundred feet and pulled into a dead-end lane. We found a path leading toward the Legion Hall through a patch of woods. We debated taking it, but decided against it. While it might have given us a chance to sneak up and look around, there was also the risk that someone from the meeting would pick that moment to pop outdoors and catch us lurking among the trees. Not exactly a dignified entrance.

Taking the road, we still approached with care. When we got to the hall, I surveyed the parking lot and counted four vehicles: two mid-sized rental cars, a Jeep with California plates, and an Accord with Massachusetts plates.

'I see the witches drove,' I said, gesturing at the Accord. 'So much for teleport spells and magic broomsticks. And look at this place. It's a Legion Hall. We're going to a meeting of supernatural races in a Legion Hall. On a beautiful summer day, with not even a thunderclap in the background. Couldn't they have found a rotting Victorian mansion somewhere?'

'The mausoleum at the cemetery was booked. If you look up in the far left corner under the eaves, I believe I see a cobweb.'

'That's a streamer. A pink streamer. From a wedding reception.'

'Well, I'm sure you'll find some cobwebs inside.'

'Sure, right next to the Ladies' Auxiliary snack table.'

Jeremy bent to read the schedule posted behind a cracked glass case.

'So what are we booked under?' I asked. 'The New Age Alternate Lifestyle conference?'

'No, the Corporate Technology Workshop.'

'Great. Witches without broomsticks, teleport spells, or imaginations. What's next? If there are vampires in there, they probably drink artificial blood plasma substitute. Sterilized, of course.'

'If there are vampires, they'd be in their crypts right now. It's daylight.'

'So, in that case, I can logically conclude that vampires don't exist, right? If they did, they'd be at the meeting. And if they were coming to the meeting, it'd be held at night. Ergo a daytime meeting means no vampires. Bonus.'

'Not a big vampire fan?'

'It's not that. Think about it. Witches, sorcerers, magicians, whatever . . . they're minor-league bad. If such things existed, they wouldn't be more than gifted humans. Werewolves are major league. No magic sleight of hand can top our big trick. Add superhuman strength, preternatural senses, and a really nasty attitude—'

'Speak for yourself.'

'Present company excepted. Point being, witches have nothing on us. But vampires. Vampires could be more powerful. They certainly get better press. I might walk into that meeting and find out I'm not the baddest thing in the room.'

'Maybe not, but you'll still be the baddest thing *alive* in the room.'

I grinned. 'The undead angle. Hadn't thought of that.'

'Proper categorization is the key. Now let's get inside.'

Jeremy pulled on the door. It didn't budge.

'Locked,' he said.

He paused a moment, as if considering whether to knock, but I knew he wouldn't. The Alpha of the werewolves did not wait to be admitted to any so-called meeting of the supernatural. Jeremy yanked on the door, but it didn't break, didn't even quaver.

'Guess the powers are bound to fail once you hit a certain age,' I said. 'Allow me.'

Jeremy stepped aside with a mocking half-bow. I grabbed the door handle and heaved with enough force that the door should have flown from its hinges. It didn't move.

'Oh,' I said.

'Oh, indeed. Perhaps you could huff and puff and blow the door down.'

An image from Pittsburgh came to me. Lock-pick guy complaining about the Winterbournes' hotel-room door.

'A spell,' I said. 'They've cast a spell on it. Guess we have to knock.'

'Be my guest.'

That was embarrassing. Werewolves knocking at the door. What was the world coming to? Still, we had no choice. I knocked and a few moments later, Paige answered.

Her eyes widened as she opened the door. 'You're early.'

'Is that a problem?' Jeremy asked, his voice pure silk.

Paige glanced up at him, hesitated, then shook her head. 'No, of course not. Come in and meet everyone.'

INTRODUCTIONS

As Paige led us down the hall, we could see the main room ahead. There were four people on folding chairs around a folding wooden table, the type of furniture found in church basements everywhere. Looking at the four, I was relieved – or perhaps slightly disappointed – to note a complete absence of cloven hooves and unsightly body appendages. The four looked as if they could have really been at a conference, albeit a casual midsummer conference in cottage country.

Ruth sat beside an empty chair. Like Paige, she wore a sundress. Across from them was a woman in her mid-forties, slender with short auburn hair. Beside her sat a young man with broad shoulders, a boyish face, and light brown hair tipped blond. On his left was a man on the far side of middle age, heavyset and graying. He looked aboriginal, probably Inuit, his smooth face a mask of meditative calm. So this was a gathering of the most powerful supernatural beings in North America? Oh, please. Central casting could have found a more likely bunch by plundering the Sunday night television lineup.

Across the room was the Ladies' Auxiliary snack table.

Well, not exactly, but close enough. The only thing missing was the blue-haired matron doling out goodies and guarding her cash box. There was a table with a coffee urn, a margarine tub of white powder that was more likely to be creamer than cocaine, a pyramid of Styrofoam cups – one filled with sugar cubes – and a plate of powdered doughnuts. On the rear wall, a handwritten sign reminded snackers that coffee and doughnuts were a quarter each, followed by a line in red clarifying that this meant fifty cents for both a doughnut and coffee, not a quarter for the two combined. I really hoped the Legion folks were responsible for the goodies and the sign. Otherwise . . . well, I didn't want to consider the alternative. Let's just say if anyone passed around a plate for membership dues, I was out of there.

Beside the table was a flip-board and, on the top page of the flipboard, the meeting agenda. I kid you not. They had an agenda, not just a rough list of topics, but a full schedule starting with greetings and refreshments at 10:00, background at 10:30, roundtable at 11:45, followed by lunch from 12:15 to 1:15. I glanced over my shoulder to see Jeremy reading the schedule, lips twitching.

'At least they're organized,' he murmured, too low for Paige to hear.

Everyone turned as we walked in. Ruth stood, features rearranging themselves in a welcoming smile as she hid her surprise.

'Hello,' she said. 'I thought you weren't coming until Monday.'

'Our plans for the weekend fell through.'

'Oh? Oh, well, yes. Come in then. Everyone, this is Jeremy . . . Jeremy Danvers, the . . . leader . . . I hope that's right, leader? . . . of the—'

'Jeremy is fine,' he finished. 'This is Elena.'

The young man with the blond-tipped hair grinned. 'The infamous werewolves? Funny, you don't look like werewolves. No connecting eyebrows, no hairy palms. Damn. Another myth shot to hell. And I thought all werewolves were male. That's definitely not a guy.'

'Women's lib,' I said. 'We're everywhere now.'

The young man's grin broadened. 'Is nothing sacred?'

'Elena is the only female werewolf,' Paige said as she walked to the empty chair. 'Werewolves are made two ways, by inheriting the genes or by being bitten. Most werewolves are hereditary, since few people bitten by a werewolf survive. Because the genes pass only through the male line, female werewolves are extremely rare.'

The young man rolled his eyes. 'Next on the Discovery Channel, an in-depth examination of werewolves and feminism by Paige Winterbourne.'

'Go to hell, Adam.'

'Don't rush me.'

'Ignore them, please,' Ruth said. 'Adam and Paige have known each other since they were children. Sometimes I suspect they haven't come very far in the intervening years. Now, introductions. This one beside me is Paige and that young man is Adam, in case that wasn't perfectly obvious. Our younger generation. The poor man stuck between the two is Kenneth.'

The middle-aged man blinked, as if startled back to earth.

He looked at us and gave a confused smile.

'On Adam's other side is Cassandra.'

The auburn-haired woman's smile didn't reach her eyes, which studied us with interest but little emotion.

'That's not what you really want to know, is it?' Adam said. 'At least, that's not the good part, not *who* we are, but *what* we are, right? Though it's probably better to explain the two separately or it ends up sounding like an AA meeting for the damned. "Hi, my name is Adam and I'm a half-demon."'

'A half . . . ?' I said.

'Exactly what it sounds like. Mom's human. Dad's the living embodiment of absolute evil. Luckily, I got my looks from mom's side. My father's not exactly GQ material. Don't ask me what my mother was thinking. Obviously one too many tequila shots that night.'

'Demons take human form to rape or seduce human women,' Paige said. 'Half-demons are always human in appearance. They inherit other qualities from their fathers. Each has different powers, depending on the type of demon that sired them.'

'The X-Men of the Underworld,' Adam said. 'Now that Paige has so neatly summed up my biology, here are the goods on the rest. Paige and Ruth, witches, but you knew that. Cass, vampire. Ken, shaman. You know what a shaman is?'

'Yes,' Jeremy said.

'So that's it. The major supernatural races, all in one place, like Satan's Ark.'

'Adam, please,' Ruth said. She turned to us. 'Adam likes

to joke, but I can assure you, we are not evil, not Satanists, nothing of the sort.'

'Just regular folks,' Adam said. 'With a few quirks.'

I glanced at Adam. So this was a half-demon. Uh-huh. I'd never heard of half-demons before Pittsburgh, but I was sure if such things existed, they shouldn't look like this guy. Any portrayal of demons I'd ever seen was quite clear on several points: They had cloven hooves, scales, horns, and tails. Logically, then, a half-demon should at least have bad skin. He should not be a baby-faced, all-American boy who looked like he should be greeting guests at Disney World. Maybe that was the idea. Maybe half-demons were supposed to look charming and innocuous. It would be far easier to tempt mortals to evil without scales and horns ruining that all-important first impression. Perhaps beneath that wide-eyed exterior lurked a soul of pure evil.

'Chairs,' Adam said, scrambling to his feet. 'You guys need chairs. Hold on. I'll be back in a flash.'

Maybe it was a deeply hidden wellspring of evil. Very deeply hidden.

Then there was Cassandra. A vampire? Who was she kidding? She looked as much like an undead bloodsucker as I looked like a half-wolf monster. Okay, bad analogy. The point was that Cassandra could not be a vampire. It wasn't just her appearance. Granted, she looked less like a crypt-dwelling fiend than a Wall Street exec, the kind of woman whose tailored dresses, perfect manicure, and nearly flawless makeup were a trap waiting to spring on anyone who mistook the outer package as a sign of inner softness. But the problem went deeper than that. Much deeper. First, there were no fangs, not even oversized canines. Second, she sat in a room with sunlight streaming through the windows. Third, there was no way in hell – pardon the pun – you could tell me that any woman could style her hair and apply her makeup that well if she couldn't see her reflection. Even with a three-way mirror, I can't get my hair back in a clip without tendrils escaping every which way.

Jeremy must have been thinking the same thing because he started by saying, 'Before we begin, we need to clear up one thing. I don't mean to sound suspicious—'

'Don't apologize,' Cassandra said. 'You should be suspicious.'

Jeremy nodded. 'Although Adam so neatly categorized everyone, you can see where we might be in need of more . . . concrete evidence.'

I said, 'To put it bluntly, how do we know you are what you say you are? You say you're a vampire, but . . .'

'Everyone knows vampires don't exist,' Cassandra said.

'It is a bit hard to swallow,' I said. 'Vampires, witches, shamans, demons.'

'Are you listening to yourself?' Paige said. 'You don't believe in the supernatural? You're a werewolf!'

'Alleged werewolf.'

Paige rolled her eyes. 'Here we go again. You still don't believe we're witches, do you? Even after we cast multiple spells to save your life—'

'Save my life?' I sputtered. 'You were the one padding down a hotel hallway in your nightgown, so eager to see the bad guy lurking behind door number one.'

Adam laughed. Paige shot him a glare.

'Okay,' I said, 'let's pretend I believe in vampires and witches. How do I know that's what you guys are? Do you know how many wackos out there think they're vampires? Trust me, you don't want to know. It'll keep you up at night.'

'I've seen them,' Cassandra said. 'Black lipstick, black nail polish, absolutely zero fashion sense. Wherever did they get the idea vampires are color-blind?' She lifted her pen and offered it to me. 'You could stab me with this. Just not in the heart, please.'

'Too messy,' I said.

She settled back in her chair, eyes on me as if no one else was in the room. I could feel the curiosity in her gaze now as it moved across my face, studying me. Her lips curved in a smile, still cool, but now tinged with friendly interest.

'I could bite you,' she said.

'I'd only bite you back.'

The smile touched her hazel eyes. 'Interesting thought. What do you think would happen? A vampire/werewolf hybrid? Or would it have no effect? Intriguing idea, but impractical at the moment. We could compare fangs.'

'Definitely a guy thing.'

She laughed. 'Quite right.'

'Maybe you can explain something then,' I said. 'If you *are* a vampire . . .' I looked at the sunlight streaming through the window.

'Why am I not exploding in a cloud of dust? I've often wondered that myself. As Adam would say, "Damn, another myth shot to hell." I'm quite glad that one isn't true. An eternity without Caribbean beach vacations would be more than I could handle. It was much more disheartening when

I discovered I couldn't fly. But as for a demonstration, perhaps this will do.'

Cassandra laid her left hand on the table, lifted the pen, and jammed it down into her outstretched palm, driving it a half-inch into her hand. Ruth shuddered and looked away. Cassandra examined the damage with cool detachment, as if she'd stabbed the tabletop instead.

'A poor job of it,' she said. 'Unlike werewolves, we don't have super strength. That's the best I can manage, but it should prove my point.'

She tugged the pen out, then lifted her palm for me to examine. The puncture was as clean as a nail hole through a waxen dummy. As I watched, the edges of the wound moved together, the flesh reconstituting itself. Within a minute, her skin was smooth and unblemished.

'No pain, no blood, no fuss,' she said. 'Good enough?'

'Yes,' Jeremy said. 'Thank you.'

'My turn?' Paige said. 'What can I do to convince you, Elena? Conjure up a demon?'

'Paige!' Ruth's eyes widened in alarm. She quickly turned to us. 'Let me assure you, we do not conjure demons. Besides a few simple self-protection spells, witches practice only benevolent magic.'

'An it harm none, do what thou wilt,' Cassandra murmured.

Ruth whispered something to Paige, who nodded, shrugged, rolled her eyes, clearly adopting the ever-popular defense of the young: 'Geez, I was only kidding.' Had she been kidding? Not about conjuring a demon, but about being able to do it? Ruth said they practiced only so-called white magic. Was that all they *could* do? Or all they *would* do? Was a certain apprentice spell-caster not too happy with her predefined role as the direct descendant of the Good Witch of the North? Hmmm.

'That's enough for the demonstrations,' Jeremy said. 'Right now, I'd like to learn more about these men who stalked Elena.'

'I heard about that,' Adam said, grinning at me. 'The first casualty of war. Way to go. I'm jealous.'

'You would be,' Paige said.

Ruth glanced at the two with a look 90 percent exasperated affection and 10 percent gentle warning. They shut up as quickly as if they'd received a tongue-lashing. Ruth paused, as if making sure they were going to be quiet, then began her story.

AGENDA

Five weeks ago, a shaman had been kidnapped and had contacted Kenneth via astral projection – whatever that was. By the time he contacted Kenneth, he was in rough shape. A shaman was never physically strong to begin with, so it didn't take much rough treatment to injure one – or so Ruth explained. Because of his weak condition, his report was patchy and at times incoherent. From what Kenneth could make out, the shaman had been kidnapped by two men and taken to a compound a full day's drive from his home in Virginia. There, two other men had questioned him about his powers and abilities. In the early days of his captivity, the shaman had enough strength to astral-project through the compound at night, searching for clues about who had captured him and why. He'd learned the names of the two men who'd questioned him, Lawrence Matasumi and Tyrone Winsloe. Winsloe's name meant nothing to the shaman or Kenneth. Apparently knowledge of current events didn't rank high in shaman priorities.

While this shaman had been astral-projecting, he'd found that he wasn't the only supernatural being in the compound. His captors also had a teleporting half-demon – likely

Houdini – on their staff. He also heard that a sorcerer was assisting them, though he never saw the man. As for the other captives, when he first astral-projected, he found a witch, two half-demons, and a Vodoun priest. Then the witch disappeared and he learned that another, stronger witch had been targeted to take her place.

That was all the shaman knew. He'd promised to contact Kenneth again the next day but never did. When Kenneth conveyed the information to Ruth, Paige recognized Winsloe's name and used the Internet to track down Lawrence Matasumi, a renowned parapsychology researcher.

'Have you had any luck finding these men?' Jeremy asked when Ruth finished.

'Find them?' Adam said. 'Hell, no. We figured we'd hide out and pray they don't find us.'

'Actually, we've been debating that very matter,' Ruth said, ignoring or missing Adam's sarcasm.

'Have we?' Adam said. 'I thought it was decided. Reactive, not proactive. That's our way. Well, it's the way of the witches, and since they lead these meetings—'

'Why, Adam,' Paige said, 'are you expressing an interest in a greater leadership role? More responsibilities?'

He only grinned. 'Perish the thought. I was only saying that, as our esteemed leaders, the witches generally make such strategic decisions, and they've decided we're ducking for cover.'

'We need to discuss the matter further,' Cassandra said. 'This is a new situation for us. We've never had to worry about finding those who threaten us. If someone thinks they have proof of vampires, they aren't interested in exploring the intricacies of our lives. They're calculating how much money they'll get in the book deal. Finding them isn't a problem. They're waving big red flags saying, "Find me, please" – find me and make me rich.'

'But with these guys it's different,' I said. 'So, different threat, different response, right? They're hiding, so you need to find them.'

'And do what?' Paige asked. 'Ask them to stop harassing us?'

Jeremy looked at Ruth. 'If we find the threat, we eliminate it. That's our way.'

'Sign me up,' Adam said.

'We are going to take action,' Ruth said. 'You know that, Adam, although our idea of action may not match yours. This is a serious threat, and I'm not comfortable even gathering here to discuss it. No matter how careful we were in setting up this meeting, we have seven supernatural beings in one place, each of whom these men would love to collect.'

'Is that what they're doing?' Jeremy asked. 'Collecting?'

'We aren't clear on their motives,' Ruth said. 'That wasn't something Roger – the kidnapped shaman – was able to determine. From what he observed, we gather that they're studying us, trying to get to the root of our powers.'

'So they can find a way to use them for themselves,' Paige said.

Ruth frowned. 'We aren't sure of that. I don't like jumping to conclusions, but yes, that would seem to be a viable motivation. The presence of Lawrence Matasumi on their team would suggest strong scientific interests.'

'And the presence of Ty Winsloe means someone's

expecting to cash in big time,' Paige said. 'Winsloe's no philanthropist. The guy wouldn't cross the road to save an old lady unless she'd leave him her estate for his inconvenience.'

A small frown from Ruth. 'Perhaps. The point is, though, that they seem to want to harness our powers. For personal gain or in the name of science, it doesn't matter.'

'They can't get my powers,' Adam said. 'Strictly hereditary.'

'You sure about that?' Paige said. 'Maybe if they take you apart, organ by organ, they can find exactly what in your physiological structure gives you these powers. Of course, whether they found it or not wouldn't matter much to you, since you'd be in a bunch of little autopsy bags.'

'Nice visuals, Paige,' Adam said.

'The point is,' Ruth said, 'we don't know what they can get from us. Some things, like minor spells, can be learned. As for becoming a werewolf or vampire, that's a frighteningly simple matter. What if these men began selling the ability to become a werewolf?'

'Hope they wouldn't charge much,' I muttered.

'I'm sure plenty of people would see the advantages to superhuman strength,' Ruth said.

'Not to mention prolonged youth,' Paige added. 'You'd have morons lining up ten deep for that one. The latest alternative to plastic surgery: Become a werewolf.'

'The point is,' Ruth said, again, 'that by having the ability to do these things, to freely – or not so freely – distribute these powers, these men could upset the balance of nature. People would die. Humankind would be at risk, threatened by the worst kind of excesses, immortal dictators, spell-casting tyrants, serial killers who could take the form of wolves—'

'Been there, done that,' I murmured low enough for only Jeremy to hear. A smile sparked in his eyes, but he kept his face impassive.

'We have to think beyond ourselves,' Ruth said.

'Do we?' Cassandra asked. 'I know that's how you feel, Ruth, but I'm not terribly concerned with protecting humankind from self-destruction. I care what this threat means to *me*. If you tell me these men want to kidnap me, that's a good enough reason for me to take this seriously. The question is, what are we going to do about it?'

That certainly was the question. And we spent the next seven hours discussing it, sending Adam and Paige out to get lunch at one and barely stopping the debate long enough to eat.

So what was Ruth's plan? Well, step one was for each delegate to notify his or her fellow monsters. Sounds simple and logical, right? Of course, Jeremy would notify the rest of the Pack. He'd never dream of doing otherwise. Now that he realized the extent of the danger, he'd tell Clay to join us right away. That done, he'd only need to make one other phone call. Two deaths in last year's skirmish with the mutts had reduced us to a pack of five. Besides Clay, Jeremy, and myself there were only Antonio Sorrentino and his son, Nick. There were always a half-dozen or so mutts trying to get admitted to the Pack, and with our diminished numbers, Jeremy was considering two or three, but he was in no rush to make a decision, so for now we were five. Two easy phone calls. But that wasn't what the witches wanted. They wanted us to notify the mutts. Say what? As Jeremy explained, mutts were nomadic. Territory was for the Pack. Only one mutt had territory, and that was a special arrangement. Then Ruth wanted us to notify this particular mutt and let him contact the others. Okay. Sure. I could see it now. I'd call Karl Marsten, ask him to pass on the word to his 'fellow mutts' and he'd laugh himself into a stomach rupture. He'd still be laughing when he hung up on me.

Ruth didn't understand how things worked. Like us, the witches had a small central group, which they called the Coven. More witches lived outside the Coven than in it, like the Pack and the mutts. Outside witches were considered an inferior class, like the mutts. But, unlike us, witches didn't *admit* the others were inferior. Oh, no. According to Ruth, outside witches were poor misguided souls in need of protection and conversion. She reminded me of an early Christian missionary talking about Native Americans, and I noticed Paige squirming as her aunt spoke. Unlike missionaries, though, Ruth didn't want these outside witches to join their 'church' – their Coven. Oh, no. They only wanted them to live good and proper lives on their own. The Coven was special.

If we thought the logistics of notifying werewolves was tough, informing vampires and half-demons was almost impossible. Cassandra knew where to find all of the couple dozen living (should I say existing?) vampires, but she had zero interest in apprising all but a handful and made it clear that she wasn't wasting her time on such a ridiculous task. Let the others look after themselves. As for half-demons, there were apparently over a hundred in North America alone, about 50 percent of whom, if notified, would be lining up to apply for jobs with the enemy.

Now, of course Ruth didn't want us to contact each and every member of our race, but they expected us to at least notify a few and ask them to pass the word along. That was more than anyone, except Kenneth, was willing to do. Jeremy, Cassandra, and Adam all agreed it was a waste of time. After a few hours arguing the point, they abandoned it and moved to step two.

Everyone agreed on step two: Learn more about the enemy. How to go about this was another matter, but everyone agreed on the principal idea. We had to know more. And step three? Don't even ask about step three. The group was divided between witches and shamans wanting to find a way to discourage or discredit our antagonists, and werewolves and half-demons wanting to eliminate them. Cassandra didn't care much one way or the other, so long as these people went away and left her alone.

At seven we were still talking. Everyone was getting tired and a wee bit cranky. When Ruth suggested we order in dinner, the answer was a resounding 'No!' We needed a break. We'd drive to nearby Kingston for dinner, then come back to the meeting. As Ruth said earlier, our gathering was dangerous in itself. We all wanted to decide on a course of action that day and get the hell out of Sparta.

As the meeting disbanded for dinner, everyone except Paige walked to the parking lot en masse. Maybe she had to fix up her notes. Or maybe she was the cleanup crew.

When we got outside, Kenneth and Cassandra headed to separate rental cars. Jeremy and I were walking to the Explorer when Ruth called him over. Jeremy motioned me toward the SUV and strode back to Ruth.

'Scary bunch, huh?' said a voice to my left.

I turned to see Adam jog up beside me.

He grinned. 'So, what was the scariest part? The flip-board agenda? The powdered doughnuts?'

'Please tell me the witches aren't charging a quarter for coffee and doughnuts.'

'No, no, no. Didn't you see the sign. It's *fifty* cents for a coffee and a doughnut. A quarter each. Seriously, though, that's Legion stuff. But the flip-board and the schedule were definitely Ruth's doing. A guy who used to be a delegate told me that, years ago, the witches had a mission statement and a code of conduct for these meetings. I think he was kidding, but I've never been sure.'

'So they're always so . . . earnest?'

Adam laughed. 'Earnest. That's a good word to describe witches. Well, maybe not Paige, but certainly Ruth and the rest of them. Deadly serious. This is important stuff, damn it.' He rolled his eyes. 'Everyone's gotta have a hobby, and with the witches, it's organizing these meetings. Hey, is it true you gave Paige those bruises around her neck?'

'It was a misunderstanding.'

He grinned. 'I'll bet. I'll also bet she deserved it. Paige can be a major pain, but she can also be a lot of fun. You have to be careful which side of her you land on.' He glanced back at Jeremy and Ruth. 'So, you think your leader can talk these guys into taking action?'

'If he can't, we'll do it ourselves. We aren't accustomed to taking orders from others.'

'My kinda people. That's what we need in these meetings. A strong, nonpassive leader.'

'A male leader?'

Adam lifted both hands to ward me off. 'I didn't say that. It's not a gender thing. It's a race thing. Witches and shamans aren't like us. And vamps? Well, they're not like anyone, which is exactly how they like it. Cass can kick ass if she wants. Not super-strong or anything, like she said, but that regenerative stuff is real handy in a fight. Guy shoots you, you just keep walking and grab the gun. Very cool.'

'So they're immortal?'

'Nah. Not exactly anyway. They can regenerate, they live for hundreds of years, and they're damned tough to kill. Close enough to immortal for me.'

Before I could ask anything more, Paige joined us.

'I'm going with you,' she said to Adam. 'Kenneth offered to drive Ruth. I'd go along, but at the speed he drives, I'd faint from hunger before we reached the restaurant.' She glanced at me. 'Want to come with us?'

I was about to decline when Jeremy waved me over, saving me the trouble of coming up with a polite excuse. I said I'd see them at the restaurant and jogged over to Jeremy.

BURNED

We'd elected to eat at an Italian restaurant. Bad choice. Though it was nearly eight, the place was crowded. This part of Vermont didn't offer much in the way of fine dining, so it seemed as if everyone within a fifty-mile radius who didn't like hamburgers was here. There was no hope of getting a table for seven, so we agreed to split up. When the server found us a table for six and a table for two, Cassandra offered to take the small table. At first I thought she wanted to eat alone, which wouldn't have surprised me, but instead she invited me to join her. I wasn't the only one shocked by that. Paige stared at me as if trying to figure out what could possibly possess Cassandra to pick me as her dining companion. I think she'd have been less surprised if Cassandra invited me to *be* dinner instead. Even Kenneth blinked, which seemed a sure sign that a dinner invitation from Cassandra was not a common event. I'll admit, I was flattered. Cassandra didn't seem the type who'd need, much less want, company.

Cassandra and I sat apart from the others, out on the patio. I wondered whether she'd eat dinner. She ordered chicken parmigiana and white wine. While she drank the wine, she only had a few bites of the chicken, then shifted the food around on her plate to make it look as if she'd eaten more. Maybe she was eating later. I really didn't want to think about that. Culinary squeamishness may seem absurd coming from someone who chows down on raw rabbit, but there was a difference between what appealed to me as a wolf and what appealed to me as a human. As good as freshly killed deer tasted after a hunt, I didn't like to think about it while eating seafood linguini.

'You're curious,' Cassandra said after our meals arrived. 'But you don't ask questions. Odd for a journalist.'

How much had Ruth and Paige told everyone else about me?

'Depends on the type of journalist,' I said. 'I do politics and social issues. Strictly public-life stuff. Very little dirt-digging of a personal nature.'

'So you avoid personal questions. Probably because you don't want anyone asking them back. If you're curious, you can ask. I don't mind.'

'Okay,' I said . . . and asked nothing.

After a few minutes of silence, I decided I really should ask something. Not just anything, but the big question. After all, it was staring me in the face, from Cassandra's barely touched plate.

I gestured at her dinner. 'So, I guess you're not big on chicken.'

'Solids in general. I can eat a few bites, but more gives me a nasty case of indigestion.'

She waited, face expressionless, but a smile shimmering in her eyes.

'There's no sense asking, is there?' I said, sipping my wine. 'Asking if vampires – you know – would be like asking if werewolves change into wolves. It's the hallmark of the species.'

'Actually, in my case, you'd be mistaken. I know, I know, you read so many stories. But they're just not true. I most emphatically do not sleep in a coffin.' She paused, then arched her eyebrows. 'Oh, isn't that what you meant?'

'I meant, obviously you drink—' I gestured at my wine glass.

'Burgundy? I prefer white. Yes, I can drink wine. Thank heaven for small mercies. It's only solids that give me trouble. Let me help you out, Elena. I believe the word you're looking for is "blood."'

'That's it. Slipped my mind.'

She laughed, a throaty laugh that startled the server coming out the patio door. We ordered refills on our wine, then waited until he'd left.

'So what is it these days?' I said. 'Home deliveries from the blood bank?'

'Afraid not.'

'A special deal with the butcher?'

'The FDA would likely disapprove. Sadly, we're stuck getting our meals the old-fashioned way.'

'Ah.'

'Ah, indeed,' she said with another laugh. 'Yes, I drink it straight from the source. Some rules, though. No children. No one under thirty. Makes it more sporting.'

'Did I mention I'm twenty-eight?'

'That's not what I heard.' She grinned. 'No need to worry.

Common courtesy dictates that we never drain the lifeblood of anyone to whom we've been formally introduced.'

She cut a few bits of chicken and moved them around on her plate. 'To be honest, I've tried animal blood and blood banks. They don't work. Living that way is like subsisting on bread and water. We exist, but barely. Some still do it. I'm too selfish. If I'm alive, I want to be completely alive. The only apology I can make is that I try to choose those who welcome death, the old, the sick, the suicidal. I'm deluding myself, of course. I can tell that a man wants to die, but I have no way of knowing if he's about to climb a twenty-story building or temporarily depressed over a broken affair. Life would be so much simpler if we lost our souls when we were reborn, if we forfeited the ability to feel, to know right from wrong. But I suppose that's why they call it a curse. We still know.'

'But you don't have a choice.'

'Oh, there's always a choice. Self-annihilation. Some do it. Most consider it, but the will to survive is ultimately too strong. If it means the choice between their death and mine, altruism be damned. The motto of the truly strong. Or the incredibly selfish.'

We were quiet a moment, then she said, 'I take it werewolves aren't cannibals, then?'

'You mean eating humans, not other werewolves, which strictly speaking, would be cannibalism.'

'You don't consider yourselves human?'

'To varying degrees. Myself, I still think half-human, half-wolf. Cla— Others don't. They consider werewolves a separate species. I'm not avoiding the question. Pack wolves are forbidden to eat humans. We wouldn't anyway. It doesn't make sense. Eating humans wouldn't serve any other purpose than to sate a hunger that can as easily be satisfied with a deer.'

'It's that easy then?'

'I wish. Unfortunately, there's not just the hunger. There's the hunting instinct, and I'll admit, humans satisfy that far better than any animal.'

Cassandra's eyes glittered. 'The Most Dangerous Game.'

The thought struck me then, how odd it was to be discussing this with another woman. I shook it off and continued, 'Trouble is, it's hard to hunt without killing. It's possible, but dangerous, risking the chance you won't be able to stop yourself before the kill. Non-Pack werewolves hunt, kill, and eat people. The temptation is too great, and most aren't interested in controlling their impulses.'

The server came out then to get our dessert order. I was about to pass, as I usually did when dining with other women, then realized it didn't matter. Cassandra wouldn't care if I ate three pieces of cake. So I ordered tiramisu and a coffee. Cassandra seconded the coffee. As the server turned to leave, Cassandra reached and grabbed his wrist.

'Decaf actually,' she said.

As she spoke, she kept her hand on his wrist, thumb outstretched across his pulse. The server was young and Latin-handsome, big dark eyes and smooth olive skin. Did he notice she held his arm too long? Not a chance. As she called him back and changed her order, she kept her eyes on his like he was the most fascinating thing in the room. And he stared back like a mouse entranced by a cobra. If she'd asked him to step into the back alley with her, he'd have tripped over his feet to obey. When she finally released his arm, he blinked, then something like disappointment crossed his face. He promised to hurry with the coffees and returned to the dining room.

'Sometimes I almost can't resist,' Cassandra said after he'd gone. 'Even when I'm not hungry. The intoxication of power. A nasty but unbreakable addiction, don't you think?'

'It's . . . tempting.'

Cassandra laughed. 'You don't have to pretend with me, Elena. Power is a glorious thing, especially for women. I spent forty-six years as a human woman in seventeenth-century Europe. I'd have killed for a chance at power.' Her lips curved in a wicked grin. 'But I guess I did, didn't I? The choices one makes.' She leaned back and studied me, then smiled again. 'I think you and I will get along quite well. A rare treat for me, meeting a huntress who isn't another self-absorbed vampire.'

Our coffees and my dessert arrived then. I asked Cassandra what it was like to live as long as she had, and she regaled me with stories for the rest of the meal.

After dinner, Adam repeated Paige's offer to join them on the way back to the Legion Hall. Again, I was about to decline, but this time Jeremy overheard and insisted I go along, probably hoping the two youngest delegates would talk more freely without their elders around. In an aside, he promised to follow us in the Explorer.

Unlike Jeremy, Adam hadn't found parking in the small lot behind the restaurant, so the three of us left the others and headed up a side street. Ahead, on the other side of the road, I saw the old Jeep from the Legion Hall parking lot, the one with the California plates.

'Yours?' I asked Adam.

'Unfortunately.'

'That's some drive.'

'A long drive. In a Jeep, a very, very long drive. I think I shook loose two fillings this time. Getting above the speed limit is nearly impossible. And passing? Forget it. It'd be easier driving *over* slow traffic. Next time, I'm saving my pennies so I can fly out.'

'You say that every time,' Paige said. 'Robert would buy you a plane ticket any day, but you always refuse. You love driving that piece of crap.'

'The blush is wearing off the romance. One more – Shit!'

I looked up to see a massive Yukon backing into the spot in front of Adam's Jeep. The gap was barely big enough to fit a compact. The behemoth SUV kept reversing until it was mere inches from the Jeep's front bumper. Another car was parked less than a foot from the Jeep's rear end.

'Hey!' Adam called as he jogged toward the Yukon. 'Hold on!'

A forty-something woman in the passenger seat turned and fixed Adam with an expressionless stare.

'I'm stuck in behind you,' he said, flashing a wide grin. 'Could you just pull forward a second? I'll get her out of there and you'll have lots of room.'

The passenger window was down, but the woman didn't answer. She looked over at the driver's seat. No words were exchanged. The driver's door opened and a man in a golf shirt got out. His wife did the same.

'Hey!' Adam called. 'Did you hear me? You boxed me in. If you can pull forward, I'll be out of there in a flash.'

The man clicked his remote. The alarm chirped. His wife fell in step beside him and they headed for the restaurant.

'Assholes,' Paige muttered. 'Own a fifty-thousand-dollar gas-guzzler and you own the whole damned road.'

'I'll talk to them,' I said. 'Maybe he'll listen to a woman.'

'Don't.' She grabbed my arm. 'We'll catch up with the others and come back for the Jeep later.'

'I'm only going to talk to them.'

She glanced at Adam, who was starting after the couple. 'It's not you I'm worried about.'

The man turned now, lip curling as he threw some insult at Adam.

'What did you say?' Adam yelled back.

'Oh, shit,' Paige murmured.

The man turned his back on Adam.

'What did you say?' Adam shouted.

As Adam advanced on the man, I made a split-second decision to interfere. We were trying to lie low and couldn't afford to call attention to ourselves with a brawl that might involve the police. Adam should have known this, but I guess even most easy-going young men can be subject to surges of testosterone.

As I turned to go after Adam, Paige grabbed my arm.

'Hold on,' she said. 'You don't—'

I shook her off and started running, ignoring her trailing footsteps and warning shouts. As I drew closer to Adam, I smelled fire. Not smoke or burning wood or sulfur, but the subtler odor of fire itself. Ignoring it, I grabbed Adam's wrist and whirled him around.

'Forget it,' I said as he turned. 'Jeremy can drive us—'

Adam faced me now, and I knew where the smell of fire came from. His eyes glowed crimson. The whites were luminescent red, sparking absolute, bottomless rage.

'Get your hands off me,' he rumbled.

There was no trace of Adam's voice in the words, no sign of him in his face. Heat emanated from his body in waves. It was like standing too close to a bonfire. Sweat sprang from my pores. I turned my face from the heat, still holding his wrist. He grabbed me, each hand gripping a forearm. Something sizzled. I heard that first, had a second to wonder what it was, then blinding pain seared through my arms. He let go and I stumbled backward. Red welts leaped up on either forearm.

Paige grabbed me from behind, steadying me. I shoved her away and turned back to Adam. He was striding toward a vacant alley.

'He's okay,' Paige said. 'He'll get it under control now.'

The Explorer rounded the corner. I waved my arms for Jeremy to stop and yanked open the passenger door before the SUV hit a full stop. As I jumped in, Jeremy's gaze went to my burned arms and his mouth tightened, but he said nothing. He waited until I was inside, then hit the accelerator.

DISSECTION

I explained what happened as we drove. Once outside town, Jeremy pulled into a gas station, parked in front of the phone booth, and got out. A few minutes later he returned and took us back onto the highway.

'Ruth?' I asked.

'I told her we're not returning to the meeting tonight. She heard what happened. Very apologetic. She asked if we'd come if they meet again tomorrow. I said I didn't know, so she wants me to call back tonight and see what they decided.'

'Will you?'

'Probably. My first priority is protecting the Pack. To do that, we may need to join these people temporarily, while they investigate this threat. They have resources we can't match. At dinner we discussed this astral projection the shamans do, and it sounds like an invaluable tool for learning more about these men you encountered in Pittsburgh. Beyond that, though, I have no intention of sticking around to help them. We fight our own battles.'

In the silence that followed, I reflected on our day, on the overwhelming things we'd discovered. Overwhelming for me, at least. Jeremy seemed not only unfazed but unsurprised by it all. I could chalk this up to his usual equanimity, but his response to everything seemed too calm, even for him.

'You knew,' I said. 'You knew there were other . . . things out there. Besides us.'

'I'd heard rumors. When I was a child. Long nights, after a Meet, occasionally talk would turn to the possibility of other creatures, vampires, spell-casters, and the like. Someone remembered an uncle who once encountered a being with strange powers, that sort of thing. Much the way humans might discuss aliens or ghosts. Some believed. Most didn't.'

'You did?'

'It seems improbable that we'd be the only legendary creature with its basis in reality.' He drove in silence a moment, then continued. 'Once, not long before his death, my grandfather told me that his grandfather claimed to have sat on a council of what Ruth would call "supernatural beings." My grandfather suspected the story may have simply been the confused imaginings of an old man, but he thought he should pass it on to me. If it was true, if other creatures existed, then someone in the Pack should be aware of the possibility.'

'Shouldn't everyone in the Pack have been aware of the possibility?' I said. 'No offense, Jer, but I really would have appreciated a warning.'

'To be honest, the thought never crossed my mind. I never tried to discover whether my grandfather's story was true or not. The point seemed moot. I have no interest in other beings, and we're safer if they have no interest in us. Yes, I suppose one of you could accidentally come across one, but considering how few of us exist, and how few of them exist, the chances of not only meeting but recognizing one another seemed infinitesimal. Certainly it's never happened before, not in my lifetime or my grandfather's. Now it appears these witches have been aware of us for a very long time. I never considered that possibility.'

'Are you admitting you made a mistake?'

His lips twitched in the barest smile. 'I'm admitting to an oversight. It would only be a mistake if I considered the possibility and chose to ignore it.'

'But if werewolves did sit on this council at one time, why isn't it in the Legacy?' I said, referring to the Pack's history book.

'I don't know. If, as Ruth says, werewolves broke from the council, they may have chosen to remove that portion of their history from the Legacy.'

'Maybe for good reason,' I said, brushing my fingertips over my burned arms.

Jeremy glanced at me and nodded. 'Maybe so.'

At the cabin, Jeremy washed and dressed my burns, then asked if I was ready for bed or wanted to stay up longer.

'Were you staying up?' I asked.

'If you were.'

'If you were, I will, but if you're tired . . . ?'

'Are you tir—' Jeremy stopped. A small half-smile flitted across his lips and I knew what he was thinking. We could go on like this all night, neither of us willing to voice an opinion that might inconvenience the other. With Clay or Nick or Antonio, I made my wants and opinions known without hesitation. Survival of the loudest. With Jeremy, his unerring civility resurrected my upbringing, and a simple choice could evolve into an endless 'After you,' 'No, I insist, after you' farce. If Clay were there, he'd make up our minds for us before the second round of the dance. Without him, we were on our own.

'I'm going to stay up awhile,' I said.

'I'll keep you company.'

'You don't have to.'

'I know. We'll sit on the deck. Go out, and I'll fix us a snack.'

I went outside. Minutes later, Jeremy followed with two glasses of milk and a bag of cookies.

'Nothing stronger around to dull the pain,' he said, handing me the milk. 'You'll have to settle for simple comfort.'

Jeremy sat beside me. We gazed out over the water for a few minutes, the crunch of cookies echoing in the silence. Smoke from a campfire floated across the lake.

'We should build a fire,' I said.

'No matches.'

'Damn. Where's Adam when you need him?'

Jeremy gave a half-smile. 'We'll have a bonfire for you back at Stonehaven. Plenty of matches there. Marshmallows too. If only I can remember how to carve a roasting stick.'

'You know how?'

He chuckled. 'Hard to believe, isn't it? Yes, I did some camping as a child. Dominic used to rent a cottage every summer, got Tonio and his brothers out of the city, back to nature. They'd take me along.'

As Jeremy lapsed into silence, I struggled to think of a way to keep him talking. Jeremy didn't talk about his childhood. Not ever. I'd had hints from others that it wasn't the most idyllic youth, but Jeremy kept mum on the subject. Now that he'd cracked opened that window, I wasn't about to let it close again so easily.

'Where did you go?' I asked.

'Not far. Vermont, New Hampshire.'

'Was it fun?'

Another half-smile. 'Very. I didn't care about the back to nature part. Stonehaven has all that. But it let Tonio and me play at being real kids, to play *with* other kids. Of course, we met other children at school. But we always went to private school. As Alpha, Dominic enforced that for Pack sons. If their fathers couldn't afford to send them, he paid for it. Strict environmental control. Home for weekends and holidays, minimal interaction with humans. On vacation, though, we could cut loose, so long as we used false names and all that.'

'You had to use fake names? How old were you?'

'Young. Tonio was older, of course. But I was the one who made up our stories. It was fun, actually, inventing a new identity every summer. One year we were minor nobility visiting from England. Our accents were atrocious. Another year we were Mafia brats. Tonio loved that one. Gave him a chance to practice his Italian and make the local bullies quake.'

'I can imagine.'

'Great fun, until the kids started offering us their ice-cream money. Tonio drew the line there. Integrity above all, even if it meant turning down extra food. We were debating whether to admit the whole mob thing was a hoax when Malcolm showed up to take me back to Stonehaven. Early as always.'

Malcolm had been Jeremy's father, though I never heard Jeremy call him by anything but his first name.

'He missed you?' I asked.

Jeremy laughed. Not his usual chuckle but a whoop of laughter that startled me so much I nearly dropped my cookie.

'No,' he said, composing himself. 'Malcolm most assuredly did not miss me. He did that every summer, stop by to see how I was doing. If I was having fun, which I always was, he decided it was time for me to come home.'

I didn't know what to say to that, so I said nothing.

Jeremy continued, 'After a few years, I started out-maneuvering him. As soon as Malcolm arrived, I'd have a massive attack of homesickness. Desperately miserable. Dying to leave. Then, of course, he'd make me stay the rest of the summer. The Sorrentinos played along. They knew what it was like for me at home.' He gave a wry half-smile. 'You, Clayton, and me. Three housemates, all with rotten childhoods. What are the chances?'

'Clay had a good childhood.'

'Barring the small matter of being turned into a werewolf at the age of five and spending the next few years hiding in the bayou, eating rats and drunks.'

'I meant after that. After you rescued him. He's always

said he had a good childhood at Stonehaven.'

'When he wasn't being expelled from school for dissecting the class guinea pig?'

'It was already dead.'

Jeremy chuckled. 'I can still hear him saying that. Over thirty years later and I can hear it perfectly. Clay's first Pack meeting. I'm trying to pretend everything's fine, not let anyone know about the expulsion. Then Daniel roars in and announces it to the whole Pack. "Clayton got kicked out of school for cutting up a guinea pig." Clay tears into the room, marches over to Daniel, glares up at him – they were the same age, but Clay was at least a head shorter – and shouts, "It was already dead!"'

'Which explained everything.'

'Absolutely.' Jeremy smiled and shook his head. 'Between the dissected class pet and the toy animal fiasco, I had to question whether I was cut out for surrogate parenthood.'

'Toy animals?'

'Clay hasn't told you that one?' Jeremy drained his glass, picked up mine, and stood.

I grabbed his pant leg. 'Tell me.'

'When I come back.'

I groaned and waited. And waited. Took him much too long to pour that milk. Playing the whole thing for full effect.

'Toy animals,' I said when he finally returned.

'Right. Clay had problems with the other children at school. I assume you know that.'

I nodded. 'He didn't fit in and didn't try. Small for his age. Antisocial. The accent only made it worse. I wondered about that when I met him. He said he'd lived in New York State for twenty years, but he sounded like he'd just stepped off the train from Louisiana. He said when he was a kid, other children mocked his accent. So he kept it. Clay's perverse logic.'

'Anything to set him apart. So, after the guinea pig disaster, I home-schooled him until the following September, then sent him to a different school and asked the principal to notify me of any behavioral problems. I swear I spent three afternoons a week in parent-teacher conferences. Mostly it was little things, but one day the teacher said Clay was having trouble at recess. The other kids were complaining that he was following them around, watching them, that sort of thing.'

'Stalking them,' I said. 'Scouting for weaknesses.'

'Exactly. Now, I wasn't worried he'd do anything. I was very strict on that point. No devouring classmates.' Jeremy rolled his eyes. 'Other parents warn their kids not to talk to strangers. I had to warn mine not to eat them. Anyway, this teacher says Clay isn't showing an interest in normal recess pursuits, like playing with toys. Toys. I knew I was missing something. Clay was the most un-childlike child I'd ever met, so I tended to forget he should be doing childish things. After the conference, I drove straight to the toy store and bought bags of toys. He ignored them all . . . all except this set of plastic animals – cows, horses, sheep, deer, camels, and so on. He'd take them into his room and stay there for hours. I congratulated myself on my great insight, assuming he liked the animals because he felt some kinship to them. Then I found the book.'

Jeremy paused.

'What book?' I asked, because I knew I was supposed to.

'*Gibson's Guide to Animal Anatomy*. He'd stolen it from the school library and dog-eared a bunch of pages. So I took a closer look at the plastic toys. They were all marked with strategically placed red Xs.'

'Identifying the vital organs,' I said. 'For hunting.'

'Exactly.'

'So what'd you do?'

'Gave him a long lecture about stealing and made him return the book immediately.'

I threw my head back and laughed. Jeremy rested his hand around my waist, a rare gesture of closeness that I enjoyed for as long as possible.

'How about a run?' he asked after a few minutes. 'We could both use one to work off some stress after today.'

I was getting tired, but I never would have said so. Werewolves preferred to run with others – the pack instinct. As with so many other things, Jeremy was different. He preferred solitude once he'd Changed. He'd sometimes join us in a Pack hunt but rarely went for a regular run with a partner. So, when he offered, I could have been ready to drop from exhaustion and I wouldn't have refused.

We walked into the woods, taking the path until we were deep enough to find places for our Change. We'd gone about twenty feet when Jeremy turned to stare over my shoulder.

'What?' I asked.

'Headlights slowing at the top of the drive,' he murmured.

The driveway sloped steeply from the road to the cottage, putting the car on a hilltop, so all we could see was the glow of twin lights. As we waited, the lights vanished and the rumble of the engine died. A car door opened and shut. Footsteps walked to the edge of the hill. A stone pinged from beneath a shoe, clattering down the incline. A pause. Someone listening for a response to the noise. Then the whisper of long grass against pant legs. A glimmer of darkness above us, movement without form. Then moving south, downwind. Intentionally downwind. A tree creaked to our right. I jumped. Only the wind.

Jeremy was watching, listening, smelling, only a tightness in his jawline betraying his tension. I looked at him, but he didn't look back. Too busy watching. And waiting. The scuffle of dead twigs underfoot. Silence again. A loon cried across the lake. Again I jumped. Then a rock tumbled down the hillside to my right. As I turned, I caught a blur of motion to my left. Misdirection. Shit. Too late. The blur was on me, knocking my legs out from under me. Hands grabbed me as I went down, flipping me over onto my back and pinning my arms at my sides. I hit the ground with my attacker atop me.

GUESTS

'**M**iss me?' Clay asked, grinning down at me.

I kicked up, somersaulting him over my head and into a stack of firewood. The wood toppled over him, knocking his breath out.

'Guess not,' he wheezed, somehow still grinning.

'Can I kill him?' I asked Jeremy. 'Please.'

'Maim, but don't kill. We may still need him.' Jeremy offered Clay a hand and yanked him to his feet with a bit more force than necessary. 'I'm glad to see you got my message, but I didn't think you'd be here this fast. Did you have any trouble getting out of your course?'

No, Clay wasn't a student at the University of Michigan. He was a professor. Well, not actually a professor. I mean, not permanently. He was a research-based anthropologist who occasionally did short lecture series, not because he liked to – Clay didn't *like* doing anything that involved contact with humans – but because the odd foray into the world of interpersonal academics was an evil necessary for keeping up his network of contacts and thus maintaining his career. Most people who'd met Clay, on hearing his occupation, said something along the lines of 'I thought you needed a Ph.D. to do that.' Clearly the vision of Clay and a doctorate degree did not go together. Yes, he had one – I can vouch for that, having seen the diploma at the bottom of his sock drawer. Anyone who met Clay, though, could be forgiven for the mistake. He didn't talk like someone with an advanced degree. And he sure didn't look like a Ph.D candidate. Clay was one of those detestable people blessed with both genius-level intelligence and drop-dead-gorgeous looks. Blue eyes, dark blond curls, and a rugged face straight out of a magazine. Match that with a powerful body and you have a package that wouldn't go unnoticed in the middle of a Chippendales convention. He hated it. Clay would have been overjoyed to wake up one morning and find himself transformed into the kind of guy who got lingering gazes only when his fly was down. I, on the other hand, shallow creature that I am, would not be so pleased.

Clay told Jeremy that his lecture series had been part of an interim course, so he'd had no problem talking to the regular prof and rescheduling his portion for the end of the session. As he explained this, I practiced my grade-three math skills.

'You left Clay a message on my cell phone, which he took with him to Detroit, right?' I asked.

Jeremy nodded.

'And when did you leave that message?'

'Before dinner. After you left to sit with Cassandra I used the pay phone in the lobby.'

'Uh-huh. About four hours ago, then. So assuming Clay

took the shortest route from Detroit, through Ontario, into Quebec and down, that's well over six hundred miles. A Porsche traveling at, say, ninety miles an hour, with no stops or slowdowns, would take at least seven hours to make the trip. Anyone see a problem with this math?'

'I wasn't actually in Detroit when Jer called,' Clay said.

'Uh-huh.'

'I was a bit . . . closer.'

'How close?'

'Ummm, say . . . Vermont.'

'You sneaky son of a bitch! You've been here the whole time, haven't you? What did you do, follow us around?'

'I was protecting you.'

I resisted the urge to stomp my feet on the ground. Not the most mature way to launch an argument, but sometimes frustration blew maturity out of the water. Clay did that to me. I settled for one ground-shaking stomp.

'I don't need protection,' I said. 'How many scrapes have I been in? Too many to count, and no one's killed me yet, have they?'

'Oh, there's good logic. Shall I wait until someone does, darling? Then I'm allowed to protect you? Guard your grave maybe?'

'I ordered you to stay in Detroit, Clayton,' Jeremy said.

'You said I didn't *need* to come along,' Clay said. 'You didn't say *couldn't*.'

'You knew what I meant,' Jeremy said. 'We'll discuss this later. Come back to the cottage now and we'll fill you in on anything you don't already know.'

We headed back toward the cabin. When we were nearly

out of the woods, Jeremy stopped and raised a hand, silencing us.

'Did you rent a pickup?' he whispered to Clay.

'Nah, some little shit-box. Figured the Boxster might be a bit conspicuous in these parts. Why?' He followed Jeremy's gaze. 'That's not mine.'

I looked up the hill to see a pickup truck parked at the end of the drive.

'What time is it?' Clay asked.

'Too late for making out,' I said. 'Too early for hunting or fishing.'

'I'd say we have company,' Jeremy said. 'I'll stand watch. You two circle the cottage and greet our guests.'

Clay and I crept from the forest. The south side of the cabin was dark and quiet. As I listened, I caught the crunch of dead leaves from the north side. I waved for Clay to take the lake side while I slipped across the drive.

On the north side of the cottage I found my quarry, a single man standing lookout. I crept through the trees until I was beside the man. He was probably fifty, but with the physique and bearing of a man half that age. His stance was ramrod straight, eyes trained on the driveway, unblinking. A professional. Retired military, possibly, given the half-inch buzz cut and clothes so stiff I suspected he starched his underwear. He held his gun at his right side, lowered but tense, ready to flip up and fire like a pump-action toy. Where did Winsloe do his recruiting? *Soldier of Fortune*? With the way these guys were popping up, it looked like he'd bought himself a whole damned army.

Clay stepped from the forest, coming out behind the

gunman. He caught my eye through the trees. I nodded and crouched. As he eased forward, some drunken lout across the lake yelled. The lookout spun around, but Clay was already in mid-flight. I leaped and knocked the gun from the man's hand as Clay grabbed him around the neck. A dull snap. Then silence.

Clay lowered the dead man to the ground. I opened the gun chamber. The bullets inside shone too brightly for lead. I flashed them to Clay as he dragged the body into the woods.

'Silver bullets,' I whispered. 'Not standard equipment for a B&E.'

Clay nodded.

'Front or back?' I asked.

'You pick.'

I headed for the front door. It was cracked open. As I slunk along the wall, there was a muted pop from behind the cabin as Clay broke the rear lock. When I was close enough to see through the front-door crack, I paused. No light, sound, or movement came from within. With my toe, I prodded the door open farther. Still nothing. I crouched and crept through, staying low enough that I wouldn't catch anyone's attention – or catch a bullet fired blindly at chest level.

The front and back doors were opposite one another, linked by a common hall, so as soon as I sneaked inside, I saw Clay. He lifted his brows. Hear anything? I shook my head. As we stepped into the main room, he pointed overhead and mouthed 'light.' I looked toward the staircase. Upstairs a light flickered, like a moving flashlight. Clay gestured from me to him, then pointed up again. We were both going. He led.

Three-quarters of the way up the stairs, one creaked. That was inevitable, wasn't it? I think carpenters do that on purpose, make at least one creaky step so no one can ever steal up or down undetected. We froze and listened. Silence. Clay stepped on the next tread, stooped, and leaned forward, peeking into the upper hall. He shook his head. Nothing. After a moment's pause, he climbed the last three steps. He went left into the back bedroom, where the light was coming from. I stood at the top of the stairs, back to the far wall, guarding the front bedroom, the steps, and Clay all at once.

'Shit,' he whispered.

I turned. Jeremy had been using the back bedroom. He or one of the intruders had left on the nightstand light. In front of it, a pedestal fan rotated at the slowest speed, blades intermittently blocking the bulb, giving the impression of flickering light. As I shook my head, footsteps sounded on the main level. The hatch to the basement slapped shut.

'That's it,' a man's voice said. 'They're not here.'

'Then we'll wait,' another said. 'Get Brant and we'll leave.'

Footfalls on the front porch. 'Brant's gone.'

'Probably taking a piss. Fucking wonderful lookout. Go start the truck, then. He'll figure it out.'

Clay whispered. 'I'll head them off at the back. You take the front. Get them into the woods. Away from their truck – and Jeremy.'

I hurried toward the stairs, expecting Clay to follow me.

I should have known better. Why take the stairs when there was a more dramatic departure at hand? Still, it wasn't pure theatrics. Clay's exit did distract the two men from hearing me run out of the house. I was leaping off the front porch when the second-story bathroom window smashed. A shower of glass rained down on the two men. As they looked up, Clay dropped to the ground in front of them.

'Going somewhere?' he said.

Before either man could react, Clay kicked the pistol from the hand of the man on the left. The man on the right spun, saw me, lifted his gun, and fired. I dodged sideways, but something pricked my calf. A tranquilizer dart. Clay had realized which man had the more dangerous weapon and disarmed him, leaving the tranquilizer gun for round two.

The first man ducked Clay's next kick and thundered into the forest. Clay followed. The other man stood watching me, tranquilizer gun poised. I plucked the dart from my leg and charged. His eyes widened as if he'd expected me to keel over on the spot. Obviously anyone who thought they needed silver bullets to kill a werewolf also didn't know they'd need an elephant-sized wallop of sedative to drop us. As he aimed again, I dove for his legs, caught them and jerked backward, pulling him down with me. The gun sailed to the side. His hand flew up, not toward me, but left, reaching out across the ground. Shit. The other gun. The real gun.

I rolled sideways and knocked the gun out of his reach. He got to his knees, raised his fist, then paused. Guys did this. It was like some ingrained school-yard rule. Boys don't hit girls. Not ever. They usually only hesitated a moment before realizing there were exceptions to every rule. Still, it gave me time to duck, which I did. I brought my fist up into his gut. He doubled over, still kneeling. I grabbed his hair and slammed his face into the ground. He recovered fast, though. Too fast for me to snap his neck. His gaze went straight for the gun. As he lunged forward, I snatched it out of his reach, swung my arm back, and plowed the barrel into his heart. His eyes went wide, and he looked down at the gun protruding from his chest, touched the trickle of blood oozing from the wound, frowned in confusion, swayed once on his feet, then toppled backward.

Clay stepped from the forest, looked down at the man, and tilted his head.

'Hey, darling,' he said. 'That's cheating. Werewolves don't use guns.'

'I know. I'm so ashamed.'

He laughed. 'How you feeling after that dart?'

'Not even a yawn.'

'Good, 'cause we have one left. Guy headed into the bog. Figured I'd come back and see if you needed help before we give chase. He won't get far.'

'Change, then,' Jeremy said, walking up behind us. 'It's safer. Are your arms all right, Elena?'

I peeled off the bandages, wincing as they came free. We healed fast, but the process still took longer than a few hours.

'I'll be okay,' I said.

'Good. Go on, then. I'll look after these two.'

Clay and I left to find places to Change.

*   *   *

After twelve years, I had Changing down to a science, a simple set of steps that I followed to keep myself from focusing on the upcoming pain. Step one: Find a clearing in the woods, preferably well away from everyone else, since no woman, vain or not, wanted to be seen in the middle of a Change. Step two: Remove clothing and fold neatly – this was the plan, though somehow my stuff always ended up hanging inside out from tree branches. Step three: Get into position, on all fours, head between my shoulders, joints loose, muscles relaxed. Step four: Concentrate. Step five: Try not to scream.

When I'd finished my Change, I rested, then stood and stretched. I loved stretching as a wolf, exploring the changes in my structure, the new way my muscles interacted. I started from the paws, pressing my nails into the soil and pushing against the ground with all four legs. Then I arched my back, hearing a vertebrae or two pop, luxuriating in the total absence of any back or neck stiffness, the little aches and pains of bipedalism that humans learn to accept. I moved the end of my spine, curling my tail over my back, then let it drop and swung it from side to side, tail hairs swishing against my hind legs. Finally, the head. I rotated my ears and searched for at least one new sound, maybe a woodpecker a mile away or a beetle burrowing in the earth beside me. I played the same game with my nose, sniffing and finding something new, cow manure from a field five miles off or roses blooming in a cottage garden. I couldn't do the same with my eyes. If anything, my sight was worse as a wolf, but I blinked and looked around, orienting my night vision. I didn't see in black and white, like most animals, but in a muted palette of colors. Finally, I pulled back my lips in a mock snarl and shook my head. There. Stretches complete. Time for the workout.

AMUSEMENTS

S ince Clay left him, the man had covered a lot of ground. He'd run at least two miles – all in the same quarter-mile radius, circling and zigzagging endlessly. Some people have no sense of direction. Tragic, really.

Clay had driven him into a boggy area where no cottagers had reason to venture and thus no cottagers had carved paths. As we drew close, we could hear the man out there, the squelching of his boots constructing an aural map of his movements. East a dozen feet, veering a few inches south with each step, then turning abruptly southwest, moving twenty feet angling north, another turn, a few more steps – and he was pretty much back where he'd started. Clay's sigh tremored through his flanks. No challenge. No fun.

At this point, we should have finished the guy off – gone down into the bog, one in front, one in rear, jumped him, tore out his throat, and called it a day. That would have been the responsible thing to do, dispatch the threat without risk or fuss. After all, this was a job, damn it, it wasn't supposed to be fun. Still, there was one problem. Mud. Mud oozed between my toes, and the cold water inched up my forelegs. I lifted one front paw. It came up a thick, black club, mud coating every hair. As I put my paw down, it shot forward on the slick ground. I couldn't work like this. It wasn't safe. There was only one option. We had to get the guy out of the bog. Which meant we had to chase him. And, damn, I felt bad about that.

We split up, circling in opposite directions around the man fumbling in the mud. I took the south and found the ground was still marshy. When we met up at the far side, Clay swung his head north, telling me the ground there was dry. I paused then and audibly located the man again. Southwest, maybe fifty feet away. Clay rubbed against my side and growled softly. He circled me, brushing along my flank, tail tickling across my muzzle, then walking around the other side. I shifted closer, ducked my muzzle under his throat and pressed it there. Anticipation quavered through his body, a palpable vibration against my cheek. He nuzzled my ear and nibbled the edge of it. I nudged him, then stepped back. 'Ready?' I asked with a glance. His mouth fell open in a grin, and he was gone.

I slogged through the mud after Clay. We went south-southwest. About twenty feet south of our target, we stopped. Then we headed north. Ahead, the man was still squelching through the bog, punctuating every few steps with a muttered oath. Having decided he'd lost Clay miles back, he was intent on getting out of what must have seemed the largest bog in North America. As we drew closer, we slowed, trying to quiet the sound of our approach. Not that it really mattered. This guy was so engrossed in escaping the endless bog that we probably could have bounded up wearing castanets and he wouldn't have heard us. We came within a dozen feet of him and stopped. Although the breeze was at our back, we were now close enough to smell him even upwind. Clay brushed against my side to get my attention. When I looked over, he lifted his muzzle to the sky, miming a howl. I snorted and shook my head. Warning our prey had its attractions, but I wanted to try something different.

I inched through the scrubby brush. When the man's scent hit gagging intensity, I paused and checked his direction. Moving due north, his back to me. Perfect. I ducked my head, eased my belly to the mud and crept along until I could see the man pushing through a sumac. He could just as easily have gone around the scraggly tree, but he was fumbling in near darkness, having either dropped his flashlight or left it with his dead partner. Other than the sumac, the area surrounding him was clear. I backed up – much tougher to coordinate as a wolf than a human. Clay slid forward to meet me. When he was alongside, I dropped my forequarters to the ground and waggled my rear in the air. He grunted and tilted his head to one side, a clear 'What the hell are you doing?' I snorted, stood, and repeated the performance, this time bouncing back and forth. It took a second, but he finally got it. He brushed against me one last time, burrowing his muzzle into my neck. Then he turned and loped northwest.

I went north again, creeping only a few feet farther before seeing the man. He was plowing through ankle-deep water, curses coming at two for every step. I swiveled my ears right and caught the sound of Clay's paws clumping through the mud. When he was parallel to me, he stopped, blue eyes glinting in the darkness. I didn't need to communicate my location to him. My pale fur glowed under all but the darkest skies. Turning toward the man, I double-checked his location. He'd gone maybe two steps in the intervening moment. I added those extra two feet to my position. Then I crouched, forequarters down, rear in the air, wiggling as I shifted position and tested my back legs. Up, down, side, side, down again, tense, hold . . . perfect. I moved my concentration to my front legs, coiling the muscles. One last check on the target. No change in position. Good. Now launch.

I sailed through the air. The undergrowth crackled on takeoff. The man heard it, turned, lifted his hands to ward me off, not noticing that my trajectory wouldn't bring me within a yard of him. I landed to his right. I dropped my head between my shoulders and growled. His eyes flashed from surprise to comprehension. That was what I wanted, why I hadn't let Clay warn him. I wanted to see his expression when he realized exactly what he was facing, for once not being mistaken for a wolf or wild dog. I wanted to see the understanding, the horror, and, finally, the bladder-releasing panic. He gaped for one long moment, jaw open, no part of him moving, not even breathing. Then the panic hit. He whirled around and almost tripped over Clay. He shrieked then, a rabbity squeal of terror. Clay drew back his lips, fangs flashing in the moonlight. He growled, and the man bolted for the clearest opening, north toward the dry ground.

It wasn't much of a chase in the bog, more like two mud wrestlers pursuing a third, all three sliding more than they were running. Once we hit dry ground, the man broke into a headlong run. We sprinted after him. It was an unfair race. Running full out, a wolf is faster than most professional athletes. This guy was in excellent shape, but no professional, and he had the additional disadvantage of near exhaustion, mounting panic, and lousy night vision. We could have taken him with one burst of speed. Instead we slowed to a lope. We had to give the guy a chance, right? Of course, fairness was our only motivation. We weren't really trying to prolong the chase.

We loped after him for a good mile across an open field. The stink of his panic rushed back at us, filling my nose and saturating my brain. The ground flew under my feet, my muscles contracting and expanding in a syncopation so absolute that the feeling was nearly as heady as the scent of his fear. His labored breaths rasped like sandpaper against the silence of the night. I blocked that out, listening instead to the steady huff of Clay's panting as he ran beside me. Once or twice Clay veered close enough to brush against me. The intoxication of the chase was complete. Then, with one new scent on the breeze, reality took over. Diesel fumes. There was a road ahead. Alarm zinged through me, then was washed away in a wave of common sense. It was approximately three A.M. on a Monday morning in the middle of cottage country. The chances of hitting traffic congestion ahead were zero. The chances of encountering even one car were nearly as low. All we had to do was get this guy across the road and keep going.

Though I could still smell diesel, it wasn't intermingled with the scent of asphalt. A dirt road. Better still. We crested a small rise and saw the road ahead, an empty ribbon of brown weaving through the hills. The man clambered up the ditch on the near side. As we leaped off the hillock, a flash of light illuminated the road for one second, then vanished. I paused. For a moment, all was dark. Then the light flashed again. Two round lights in the distance, bobbing over the hills. The man saw it too. He found a last burst of speed and ran toward the oncoming vehicle, arms waving. Clay shot out from behind me. As the car dipped into the last valley, Clay vaulted across the road, sprang at the man, and knocked him flying into the ditch. A pickup came over the last hill, motorboat rumbling behind it. It cruised up alongside us and kept going.

I raced across the road. Clay and the man were at the bottom of the ditch, tumbling together, Clay snapping, trying to get a good hold as the man squirmed to escape. Both were covered in mud, making Clay's job tougher and the man's easier. The man contorted sideways and reached for the bottom of his pant leg. In a flash, I realized what he was after. I yelped a warning to Clay. The man's hand clamped on something under his cuff. As he yanked it out, Clay dove for his hand. A flash of light. A crack of thunder. A shower of blood. Clay's blood.

I flew down the ditch, knocked the gun from the man's hand, and turned on him. His eyes widened. I leaped at him, grabbed his throat, and tore. Blood jetted. The man convulsed. I flung him from side to side until his throat tore away and his body sailed into the bushes. Something prodded my flank and I spun to see Clay there. Blood streamed from the back of his fore-haunch. I pushed him down on his side, licked the wound clean, and examined it. The bullet had passed through the skin and muscle connecting his front leg to his chest. It stank of gun-powder and burned flesh, and as soon as I cleaned the wound, it filled with blood again. I cleaned, then gauged the flow of blood. No longer streaming, it had slowed to a steady drip. Ugly, but not life-threatening. As I pulled back for another look, Clay licked the side of my muzzle and burrowed his nose against my cheek. A low rumble, like a growling purr, vibrated through him. I bent to check his wound again, but he blocked my view and nudged me backward into the woods. Mission accomplished. No mortal injuries. Time to Change back.

After I Changed, I returned to where the corpse still lay on the ground. Clay leaped out behind me, swatting my rear, and grabbing me around the waist before I could retaliate. As he bent to kiss me, I dodged his lips to check his wound. The gunshot was now through the back of his upper arm, several inches from his torso – one spot on us as wolves didn't always correspond with the same spot as humans. Blood oozed from the hole. I bent for a closer look, but he snatched my chin, lifted it, and kissed me.

'You need to get that checked,' I mumbled through the kiss.

He hooked my left foot and I fell backward against his good arm.

'You really need to—'

He lowered me to the ground. I dug in my heels and locked my knees.

'Jeremy should look—'

He stifled the rest by kissing harder. I wrenched free of his arm and danced backward. He grinned and started to advance.

'Arm's fine, then?' I said.

'Don't care if it isn't.'

'Good. Then you won't mind working for it.'

I spun and bolted. I didn't get far. This side of the road was forest, and thick woods weren't kind to humans, particularly naked running humans. I circled a clump of trees. Clay followed me around once, then changed direction and tried to grab me from the other side. I laughed and raced back and across the clearing. As I darted around again, he dove at my feet and snagged one. I stumbled, but regained my balance as he hit the ground, hand still around my ankle. Squirming out from his grasp, I broke free and scrambled away. A hoarse laugh resounded through the trees, followed by scuffling as he got to his feet. I shot behind the stand of trees and waited to see which direction he'd pick. I heard him run toward me. Then silence. I waited. More silence.

Crouching below eye level, I inched clockwise around the trees. Nothing. I spun around, expected him at my rear. He wasn't there. I paused, then crept counterclockwise until I was back on the clearing side of the trees. No sign of him. I listened, sniffed, looked . . . nothing. As I stepped backward into the clearing, I caught a blur of motion to my left, from behind a massive oak. I wheeled away, but too slow. Clay grabbed me around the waist and sent us both to the ground with a hard thump.

His mouth went back to mine, tongue slipping between

my teeth. I tossed him on his back. As I struggled to get up, he flipped me over again, hands pinning mine to the ground. I struggled, more for the feel of it, his body moving on mine, the weight of him, the rough scratch of his chest and leg hairs against my skin, the contractions of his muscles as they worked to keep me down. The blood from his wound smeared across us, mixing with the man's dried blood on me. There was blood on his lips and in his mouth. Closing my eyes, I tasted the sharp tang and explored deeper with my tongue.

The ground below us was slick with damp leaves coated in layers of fresh mud and blood. We slipped and slid across it, grappling and laughing and kissing and groping, then Clay grabbed my hips and plunged into me. I gasped, and he threw his head back, laughing. We wrestled some more, rolling and thrusting together, not bothering to find a rhythm. The ground chafed and twigs poked in the damnedest places, but we kept going, kissing until we were out of breath, then laughing and tussling some more. I closed my eyes and drank in everything, the tripping of my heart, the smell of damp leaves and blood, the sound of Clay's glorious laugh.

When I opened my eyes, he was grinning down at me. He never closed his eyes when we made love, never looked away, always watching my face and letting me see everything in his eyes. I saw the first shudder of climax, the widening of his eyes, the slow moving of his lips saying my name. Gasping, I felt my body tense in waves of perfect sensation as I joined him.

* * *

'Miss me?' he said a few minutes later, still lying on me, slowly slipping from inside me.

I tilted my head back to look up at him and grinned. 'In ways.'

'Ouch. Cruel. Very cruel.'

'At least I appreciate you for one thing.'

'Only one thing?'

His hand moved to my breast, teasing the nipple between his fingers, then bringing his lips down for backup. I closed my eyes and groaned.

'Or maybe several things,' I murmured. 'That's one of them. Want to compile a list?'

He chuckled, the vibration tingling through my breast.

'No list, please,' said a deep voice somewhere to our right. 'I'll be waiting here all night. I already had to wait through round one.'

I turned my head to see Jeremy walk through the trees. 'Sorry,' I said.

'Don't be. But I'd like to get this cleaned up before dawn.'

Clay groaned and lifted himself onto his elbows, still lying on me.

'Yes,' Jeremy continued. 'Terribly inconsiderate of me, expecting you to dispose of the corpses you created before you finished your reunion romp. I apologize most sincerely. Now get off your ass, Clayton, and get to work.'

Clay sighed, gave me one last kiss and got to his feet. I stood and walked over to the body of the dead man. Yes, I was still naked, and, yes, Jeremy was standing right there and, no, I didn't try to cover myself or anything so ridiculously prudish. Jeremy had seen me naked, had sketched me naked, had tripped over me lazing around naked. We were werewolves, remember? That meant that after we Changed, we were always naked and, most often, nowhere near our clothing. We got used to being naked and, after a while, clothed/unclothed, it was all pretty much the same.

'I don't suppose you brought our clothes?' I said. 'Shouldn't matter, so long as we don't meet any early morning anglers on the way back.'

'Actually, I did bring them, but considering the amount of mud and blood on both of you, I think we'd better stick to nudity for a while longer. You'll be clean soon enough.'

I didn't ask what he meant by that. I dropped to my knees beside the dead man and searched for a wallet or ID. Jeremy walked back to the ditch and returned with a spade, which he tossed to Clay.

'Bury him here?' Clay asked.

'No. Dig a hole by his neck, turn him over, and drain the blood. We'll take him back to the cottage for disposal. It's about a half-mile back. I was hoping for a closer kill.'

'No choice in the matter,' I said. 'We found him in a bog, chased him here to dry ground, then he pulled a gun. Shot Clay in the arm.'

Jeremy frowned, walked over to Clay and examined the wound.

'Clean shot,' he said. 'Does it hurt?'

Clay lifted his arm above shoulder level. 'Only if I do this.'

'Then don't do that.'

'Couldn't resist, could you?' I said.

Clay grinned. Jeremy's lips curved in the barest smile, then he clapped Clay on the back.

'Get to it, then. Drain the body so we can move him.'

'There's no ID,' I said.

Jeremy nodded. As Clay lifted the shovel to dig, Jeremy and I jumped in at the same time, both realizing it wasn't something he should do with a bad arm. After a brief argument – I argued, Jeremy held the shovel and refused to release it – I let Jeremy dig the hole, then I tipped the body over it. Once the blood had drained, we filled in the hole with the surrounding blood-soaked leaves, then covered it with soil and took the corpse back to the cottage.

It was still deep night when we returned to the cabin. Jeremy and I carried two corpses to a treed strip of bank along the lake. Clay stayed back with the third, saying he had to 'do something' with it. Neither Jeremy nor I asked for details. With Clay, it was better not to know.

I stood on the embankment, still naked. We'd tied thick rope around the neck and legs of each corpse and weighted them with concrete blocks from a cottage demolition up the road.

'Wow,' I said to Jeremy as I lowered myself to the ground and dipped my legs into the icy water. 'I get to make someone "swim with the fishes." This is cool. My first Mafia-style disposal. You realize what this means. If I get caught, I'm going to have to turn State's witness against all you guys. Then I'll sell my story for a million bucks. But I'll never get to enjoy it, 'cause I'll live out the rest of my miserable existence in a shanty in the Appalachians, eating muskrat stew, jumping every time I hear a noise, waiting for the day when one of you hunts me down like the traitorous bitch I am.'

I paused. 'Hold on. Maybe this isn't so cool after all. Can't we just bury him?'

'Get in the water, Elena.'

I sighed. 'Being a gangster ain't what it used to be. Al Capone, where have you gone?'

Jeremy pushed me off the bank. I hit the water with a splash.

'And try to be quiet,' he said.

'I didn't—'

He threw the man down to me, dunking me underwater with the weight. When I resurfaced, Jeremy was gone. I swam into the middle of the lake, dragging the weighted corpse behind me. Then I dove to check the depth. It was at least fifty feet. This guy wouldn't surface any time soon. To be sure, I snagged him in a tangle of some underwater plants. Then I returned for the second body.

Clay still wasn't back when I got to the shore. Jeremy passed me corpse number two, and I swam back out to repeat the procedure, dropping this one a hundred feet farther west, in hopes that if one surfaced, the other wouldn't also be found. Sometimes it scared me that I even thought of such considerations. I had too much experience with these things. Way too much.

As I resurfaced after dumping the body, arms grabbed me around the waist and jettisoned me out of the lake. Coming down I hit the water with a tidal-wave splash. I grabbed Clay by the neck and dragged him under, holding him there for a second – maybe longer – before releasing him.

'Did Jeremy tell you the part about being quiet?' I hissed as he came up for air.

He grinned. 'I am being quiet. You're the one splashing around.'

I lunged for him. He grabbed me, pulled me against him and kissed me. His lips were ice cold, his breath steaming hot. I kissed him deeper, wrapping my arms and legs around him, then ducking him under the water again.

'I *did* miss you,' I said as he surfaced.

He tilted his head and knocked his open palm against one ear. 'Sorry, darling. Water in the ears, I think. I coulda sworn you admitted that you missed me.'

I pulled a face, then turned and started to swim, heading for shore. Clay caught my leg and hauled me back.

'I missed you, too,' he said, pulling me upright against him. He traced his fingers up my inner thigh. 'We should be getting in. Think we can trick Jeremy if we come to shore farther down?'

'For a few minutes.'

'Long enough?'

'Long enough for now.'

He grinned. 'Good. Wanna race?'

'What's the prize?'

'Winner's choice.'

I lunged forward. He grabbed my ankle again, yanked me back, then took off ahead.

By the time we got to the cabin, Jeremy already had the Explorer packed. We wouldn't stay at the cottage any longer, for obvious reasons. Before leaving, Jeremy disinfected Clay's wound and my burned arms, then dressed both. Then we left to find a place for the night. While we'd been disposing of the bodies, Jeremy had called Ruth and, without mentioning our guests, discovered the group was convening again in the morning. Someone had told these men where to find us. Only five other people knew we were in Vermont. All five of them would be at the meeting tomorrow. So would we.

CONFRONTATION

The meeting was due to start at eight. We got up at seven but were still late. An hour wasn't enough time for three people in our tiny motel room to shower, shave (no, being a werewolf doesn't give me extraneous hair; the guys shaved, not me), dress, leave, grab takeout, eat, and drive to Sparta. To save time, Clay and I even shared a shower, which for some reason didn't manage to save any time at all. Go figure.

Before we'd dumped the bodies, Jeremy had emptied their pockets. Even if we weren't curious about their identity, it was standard operating procedure to destroy the ID before dumping a body. Like I said, we had way too much experience with this stuff. As with the guy I'd checked, one of the other two didn't have any wallet, ID, or cash on him. The third guy had two twenties and a driver's license in his rear pocket. Emergency cash and a license in case he was pulled over. Bare minimum. These guys had known what they were doing. Jeremy had checked the driver's license and proclaimed it a fake. An impressive fake, but a fake. Jeremy would know. He manufactured all our phony ID, something else we had far too much experience with.

We arrived at the Legion Hall at nine-thirty. All four cars were in the lot. Again the witches had used a spell to lock the door but this time we didn't knock. Clay tore the door off its hinges and we walked inside. As I entered the room, Ruth stopped talking. Everyone looked up.

'Where have you been?' Ruth asked.

I grinned, baring my teeth. 'Hunting.'

'Wanna see what we caught?' Clay asked from behind me.

He strode to the table and tossed a garbage bag on it. Cassandra was the only one who looked at him, wondering who he was. Everybody else stared at the bag. No one moved to take it. Then Cassandra reached forward, lifted one side of the bag, and looked in. After a second, she let the plastic fall from her hand and sat back in her chair. Her eyes moved from Clay to me and back to Clay, face blank, no shock, no disgust, nothing. Paige peeled back the plastic and recoiled fast.

The third man's head lay on its side, eyes wide and dull. Paige jumped to her feet and tried to yank the plastic back over it. The head rolled with the sudden movement. She bit off a scream.

'Interesting form of introduction,' Cassandra said, looking at Clay. 'May I ask who you might be?'

'Clayton Danvers,' Paige muttered between her teeth. 'The werewolf Pack's guard dog.'

'The question isn't who's Clay,' I said, 'but who's that guy in the bag? Anyone up for volunteering information?'

'We found this man at our cottage last night,' Jeremy said. 'He was with two others who, I can assure you, are equally dead. They came armed with silver bullets.'

'Silver—' Adam began. 'Shit, isn't that supposed to—' He stopped and looked around at the others. 'You think we sent these guys?'

'Look at him,' Paige said, turning to me. 'Clean-shaven, military brush cut. Just like the guys in Pittsburgh. Obviously—'

'Obviously nothing,' Clay said. 'Either the whole Pittsburgh thing was a setup or you dressed these guys to look like Elena's stalker so, if it backfired, we'd draw the *obvious* conclusion. If these men were part of this kidnapping scheme, why would they come after Jeremy and Elena when you guys were all holed up here in a late-night meeting. You'd be the *obvious* choice.'

'Maybe they wanted a werewolf,' Paige said. 'Besides, we always cast protective spells around our meetings. They wouldn't have been able to get to us.'

'So you expected trouble?' I said. 'Thanks for warning us. But that doesn't explain how they got here. First they show up in Pittsburgh, then here. How?'

'They must have followed—' Paige stopped, then murmured '—someone.'

'They followed you,' Cassandra said, turning on Ruth. 'You led them right to us.'

'Perhaps you weren't behind last night's attack,' Jeremy said, 'but you hardly can be absolved of blame. Ensuring you weren't followed from Pittsburgh is an elementary safety precaution. If that's how this group operates, then I have no interest in aligning my Pack with you, even temporarily. As you can see' – he gestured at the bag – 'we can take care of ourselves. We will continue to do so without your help. Anyone who comes after us or interferes with us again will be treated the same as those three men last night. Anyone. For any reason.'

We left. No one came after us.

I drove the Explorer back to the hotel. It was packed and ready to go. All we had to do was pick up Clay's rental car.

'Where to next?' I asked as we stood in the hotel parking lot.

'Montreal,' Clay said. 'We need to return the car.'

I turned to the econo-box rental, noticing the Quebec license plates. 'Why the hell did you leave your car in Montreal?'

'You think I was gonna cruise Vermont looking for a rental agency when I was driving right past a big city?'

'How about I drive straight home and you guys meet me there?'

'You're coming to Montreal, Elena,' Jeremy said

Jeremy headed to the econo-box and folded himself into the tiny passenger seat. Yes, he would have been more comfortable in his Explorer, but that would mean listening to Clay curse the loathed SUV for a few hundred miles. Given the choice between leg cramps and a migraine, Jeremy would choose the former. Riding in the SUV with me and leaving Clay alone in the rental wasn't an option. Until the danger passed, Clay would stick close to Jeremy, protecting his Alpha as instinct dictated.

Once Jeremy was in the car, Clay walked over, wrapped his hands around my waist, and pulled me against him.

'I'll make it up to you,' he murmured against my ear. 'Tonight. We'll go for a run.'

'In the city?'

He grinned. 'You arguing?'

'Jeremy will.'

'We'll take him along. I'll talk him into it on the drive. Speaking of which, you wanna liven the ride up a bit?'

'Race?'

'You read my mind, darling.'

'A four-banger verses a V6?'

'It's the driver, not the car.'

'You're on. First one to Montreal gets to pick where we run tonight.'

'One catch,' Clay said. 'We have to play safe and stay in sight. If I can't see you in my rearview mirror, I'm slowing down.'

'Rearview mirror? Baby, you ain't seeing me through nothing but the windshield.'

He grinned. 'We'll see about that.'

Racing through the back roads of Vermont was great fun. Once we got to Highway 87, things would get decidedly dull, but on the two-lane back roads we had to contend with mountains, valleys, towns, blind curves, lane-hogging campers, and poky sightseers. Plenty of close calls. Plenty of excitement. The bad guys didn't need to kill us. If they waited long enough, we'd do it ourselves.

After about a half-hour, I was stuck behind Clay. My

fault. We'd been leapfrogging for miles. I'd been in the lead, then I'd come up behind a fifth-wheeler with a camper on the back and made the mistake of leaving a safe cushion between it and me, which Clay, of course, had zipped into. Now we were stuck on a winding road behind this dullard who insisted on doing the speed limit. Finally, I noticed a straightaway long enough to pass. But Clay didn't pull out. After a moment's thought, I realized why. He couldn't see past the fifth-wheeler. I could. The advantage of driving an SUV – improved vision. Hah! So on the next suitable straightaway, as Clay fishtailed trying unsuccessfully to see around the fifth-wheeler, I pulled out and passed. Once around the truck, I zipped past a car and a tractor trailer. Then I floored it. Clay's subcompact vanished amid an unending stream of tourist traffic. He'd be pissed that I'd broken his 'stay in sight' rule, but it served him right, thinking he could outrace me no matter what he drove. Clay's self-confidence could always use shake-up. He'd catch me soon enough.

I burned up ten miles with no sign of Clay in the rearview mirror, then slowed. No sense pushing my luck or I'd have Jeremy on my back too. Jeremy let us play our games, but if I went too far, he'd tear a strip out of me. Besides, I was getting near the highway, and I wanted to be sure Clay was behind me by then. So I eased down to the speed limit, turned the corner onto the gravel road leading to the highway, cranked up the radio, and relaxed.

A mile or two later, as I was cruising along enjoying the scenery, something appeared in front of me. Something big. Right in front of me. So close I didn't have time to see if it was a moose or a deer or a person. Nor did I have time to think. I reacted. I jerked the steering wheel and hit the brakes. Too hard on both counts. I saw the flash of a face on the roadway. Then the Explorer spun left, and for a second, I thought it might flip over. It didn't. Instead it slammed into the far ditch. The airbag exploded, knocking me in the face like a punching bag. Before I could recover, the driver's door clicked open.

'Are you okay?' a woman's voice asked. She pulled the airbag from my face and frowned. 'Are you okay? That man ran right in front of you. I couldn't believe it.'

I gave my head a shake, groggy, punch-drunk. 'A man? Did I hit him?'

'No. Would have served him right if you had.' The woman shook her head. 'I guess I shouldn't say that. Let's get you out of there.'

As she helped me out, I got a better look at her. Mid- to late forties. Dark blond hair cut in a chin-length pageboy. Linen dress. Simple goldchain necklace. Face drawn in concern.

'Come sit in the back of my car,' she said. 'I've called an ambulance.'

I hesitated, swaying on my feet. 'My friends are coming.'

'Good.' She guided me to her car, a sleek black Mercedes, opened the back door, and helped me inside. 'We'll wait here for them. How do you feel?'

'Like someone KO'd me in round one.'

She laughed. 'Can't say I know what that feels like, but I can imagine. You're pale, but your color's coming back. Pulse feels fine.'

137

I felt her fingers against my wrist. Then I felt something else there. A prick. A rush of icy cold. As I yanked my hand back, the driver's door opened. A man got in. He turned to grin back at me.

'Just couldn't wait for another sparring match, huh?'

His face flashed in my memory, but my brain was fogging fast and I couldn't place him. Then, as my muscles went slack, I remembered.

The half-demon from Pittsburgh. Houdini.

My head hit the seat. Everything went black.

PRISON

For hours, I fought to regain consciousness, rousing enough to know something was wrong but unable to pull myself awake, like a swimmer who sees the water's surface above but can't reach it. Each time I jetted toward awareness, the tranquilizer's undercurrent dragged me back. Once I felt the rumbling of a van. Then I heard voices. The third time all was still and silent.

On the fourth round, I managed to open my eyes and kept them open, certain if I closed them I'd be lost. For at least an hour, I lay there, winning against the urge to sleep, but without the strength to do more than stare at a beige wall. Was it beige? Or taupe? Maybe sand. Definitely latex. Eggshell latex. Scary that I knew so much about paint. Scarier still that I was lying there, paralyzed from the eyelids down and trying to figure out what shade my captors had painted my prison. My encyclopedic knowledge of paint was Jeremy's fault. He redecorated obsessively. I mean obsessively. He had his reasons, which were no one's business but his own. If wallpapering the dining room every two years quelled whatever ghosts haunted him, I bit my tongue and pasted. As for why I was thinking about paint at such a ridiculously inopportune moment, well, there wasn't much else I could think about, was there? I could fret and worry and drive myself into a panic wondering where I was and what my captors planned to do with me, but that wouldn't change anything. I couldn't lift my head. I couldn't open my mouth. I couldn't do anything but gaze at this stupid wall, and if brooding over the paint color kept my nerves calm, so be it.

Taupe. Yes, I was pretty sure it was taupe. My upper lip tingled, like dental anesthesia wearing off. I wrinkled my nose. Slight movement. A smell. Fresh paint. Wonderful. Back to the decorating again. I inhaled deeper. Only paint, the scent so strong it drowned out anything else. No, wait. Something else mingled with the paint. Something familiar. Something . . . Blood. Mine? I sniffed again. Not mine, which wasn't terribly reassuring. As I rolled my eyes up, I could see dark splotches under a hastily applied layer of paint. Blood-sprayed walls. Never a good sign.

I screwed up my face. All muscles functional. Great. Now if someone attacked me, I could bite him, provide he was helpful enough to put some vital body part in my mouth. The tingling moved down my neck. I looked up. White ceiling. Distant noise. Voices. No, one voice. Someone talking? I listened closer and heard the hyper-babble of a DJ. After a Guinness-breaking feat of long-windedness, he stopped. A guitar twanged from the far-off radio. County music. Damn. They'd resorted to torture already.

Hand and arm movement. Hallelujah. Digging my elbows into the bed, I propped up my torso and looked around. Four walls. Three taupe. The fourth mirrored. One-way glass. Lovely. By my feet, a bathroom. I could tell it was a bathroom and not a closet because I could see the toilet, not through the door, but through the front wall, which was clear glass. Grade-school bathroom peeping had left someone with a very disturbing fetish.

More smells. A woman. The room was permeated with her smell. The bed on which I lay had been fitted with fresh, lemon-scented sheets, but the other woman's smell had soaked through to the mattress below. A note of familiarity. Someone I knew? The woman who'd drugged me? No, Someone else. Teasingly familiar . . . The association clicked. I recognized her scent because it bore overtones from the smell of the blood on the walls. Not a good way to make an acquaintance, and judging by the quantity of dark splotches under the paint, a face-to-face meeting wouldn't be forthcoming. Not in this life at least.

Hold on. I had hips. Well not really – my baggy-seated jeans always proved otherwise. I mean my anatomical, curve-free hips had movement and feeling. Then legs. Yes! I swung my legs over the edge of the bed and pitched forward onto the floor. Okay, the legs weren't quite back yet. Nice carpet though. Industrial-weave loom. A pleasing blend of gray and brown, great for hiding those pesky blood splatters.

After a few minutes, I was able to struggle to my feet. I looked around. Now what? Assuming these were the same people who'd captured that shaman, there should be other prisoners in adjoining cells. Maybe I could communicate with them.

'Hello?' I said. Then louder. 'Hello?'

No response. Doubtless the walls were too thick for jail-house whispering. Even the air coming through the foot-square ceiling vent smelled filtered and processed. Still, if I could hear a radio playing . . . I looked around for a speaker. There was an intercom by the door, but the music didn't sound tinny, so I doubted they were piping it in. As I listened, I caught the sound of someone shouting, voice raw, screaming barely intelligible curses. I gauged the distance of the noise. Very muted, probably more than fifty feet away. So it was good soundproofing, but it wasn't werewolf-proof.

As the shouter took a much-needed vocal break, I heard scratching. Rats? Mice? No, I'd smell them. Besides, my cell was nothing if not clean, as sterilized as a McDonald's kitchen on health inspection day. I rotated my head to pick up the sound. It came from the corridor. Scratch, scratch, pause, scratch, scratch, scratch, swoosh. The swoosh of paper. Someone lifting a page, shuffling it, then scratch, scratch – pen on paper. Someone writing outside my cell. I stood, turned away from the hallway, walked three steps, then whirled to face the door. The noise stopped. I bared my teeth, snarled, then inclined my open mouth closer to the mirrored wall and picked at a piece of imaginary food caught between my teeth. Frenzied scribbling ensued. Okay, now I knew *what* the note-taker was watching. And I didn't recall signing any consent forms.

I strode to the door and pounded on the glass. Though it didn't budge under the onslaught, my fists boomed with each strike. I didn't shout. If they couldn't hear my pounding, they certainly wouldn't hear my yelling. A long minute passed. Then the intercom above my head buzzed.

'Yes?' a woman's voice. Young. Studiously neutral.

'I want to speak to someone in charge,' I said.

'I'm afraid that won't be possible,' she said, pen scribbling.

I pounded harder.

'Please don't do that.' Calm, approaching boredom. Pen still scratching.

I drew back my fist and slammed it into the glass. The blow shuddered through the glass and my arm. The pen stopped.

'I understand you're upset, but that won't help. Violence never solves anything.'

Says who?

I turned away, as if backing down, then whammed a roundhouse kick against the side wall. One chunk of plaster flew free, revealing a strip of solid metal. I hooked my fingertips behind the metal and gave an experimental tug. No give. But I wasn't really trying. Now if I ripped away enough of this plaster, I could get my fingers behind the metal and give a real good pull . . .

Heavy footsteps clomped outside my cell. Ah, progress.

The intercom clicked.

'Please step away from the wall,' a male voice intoned.

He sounded like one of those car alarms from the '90s, where if you made the ghastly error of walking within six inches of some yuppie's Beemer, a mechanical voice warned you to move away, like you might brush against it and leave fingerprints. The last time we'd encountered one of those, Clay had leaped onto the hood of the car, leaving much more than fingerprints. The car owner had been within hearing distance. You've never seen a pudgy forty-something move so fast. Then he'd seen Clay and decided the damage really wasn't so bad after all. Following Clay's example, I did not step away from the wall. I smashed my fist into the plaster between the metal brackets, leaving a nice hole into the adjoining cell.

The door flew open. A man's face flashed into the room, then withdrew. The door slammed shut. A radio squawked.

'Base one, this is alpha. Request immediate backup to cell block one, unit eight.'

'You messing with my girl?' a lazy Midwest drawl asked, voice hissing with static. Houdini. 'You sound a wee mite panicked there, soldier-boy. Want me to come down and hold your hand?'

'Reese? What the hell are you doing in the— Never mind.'

Click. End of static.

'Cocky bastard.'

'No kidding,' I said.

Silence. Then 'Shit,' and a snap as the intercom died.

'Get me someone in charge,' I said. 'Now.'

A muttered exchange, indecipherable through the glass. Then boots stalking away. I decided not to worry the hole in the wall further. Not yet at least. Instead I hunkered down and peered through it. I might have been gazing into a mirror, a reverse image of my own cell. Only this one was empty. Or so it appeared. I thought of calling through the opening, but hadn't heard the note-taker leave, and there was no sense talking to a potential cell-mate while I had an audience. So I waited.

Twenty minutes passed. Then the intercom clicked on.

'My name is Doctor Lawrence Matasumi,' a man said in perfectly unaccented American, the region-free tones usually heard only from national new-show anchors. 'I would like to speak to you now, Ms. Michaels.' – As if it was his idea. – 'Please step into the bathroom, lower the seat, straddle the toilet facing the tank, place your hands outstretched behind you, and do not turn your head until instructed.'

Somehow he made such ludicrous instructions sound perfectly rational. I thought of a comeback, but squelched it. This didn't sound like a man who'd appreciate bathroom humor.

While I was sitting on the john, the exterior door whooshed open, like breaking a vacuum seal. Footsteps entered. One set of loafers, one set of low heels, and two – no, three – pairs of boots.

'Please do not turn your head,' Matasumi said, though I hadn't moved. 'Keep you hands outstretched. A guard will enter the bathroom and secure your hands behind your back. Please do not resist.'

He was so polite about it, how could I disobey? Especially considering the twin snaps of gun safety catches that accompanied his instructions. Someone walked into the bathroom and grasped my hands, his touch firm and impersonal – just business, ma'am. He pulled my arms together and clapped cold metal bands around my wrists.

'The guard will now lead you into the main room. You may take a seat on the chair provided. When you are seated comfortably, the guard will secure your feet and arms to the chair.'

Okay, this was getting tedious.

'You sure you don't want him to secure my feet first?' I asked. 'Throw me over his shoulder and carry me to the chair?'

'Please rise from the toilet and proceed into the main room.'

'Can I look now?' I asked. 'Maybe you should blindfold me.'

'Please proceed to the main room.'

Geez, this guy was scary. As I walked from the bathroom, I saw the man from Paige's picture, short, round-faced, doe eyes watching me impassively. To his left was a young woman with spiked, burgundy hair and a snub nose adorned with a diamond chip stud. She kept her gaze on my chin as if not wanting to look higher. Both were seated in chairs that hadn't been in the room five minutes ago. Flanking them stood two guards, more military types. Like the guy accompanying me, they wore fatigues, had buzz cuts, carried guns, and looked buff enough to give WWF champs a good whupping. They stared at me with expressions so blank you'd think they were guarding the chairs instead of live people. I caught one's eye and gave a shy half-smile. He didn't even blink. So much for seducing the guards. Damn. And they looked so cute . . . in a GI Joe, molded-plastic, automaton kind of way.

Once I was seated, my escort secured me to the chair with arm restraints and leg irons.

Matasumi studied me for at least three full minutes, then said, 'Please do not use this opportunity to attempt escape.'

'Really?' I looked at the metal bands strapping my wrists

and ankles to the chair, then at the trio of armed guards behind me. 'There goes that plan.'

'Good. Now, Ms. Michaels, we will skip the denial phase and begin our discussion based on the premise that you are a werewolf.'

'And if I refuse that premise?' I asked.

Matasumi opened a teak box filled with bottles and syringes and tools, the uses of which I preferred not to ponder.

'You got me,' I said. 'I'm a werewolf.'

Matasumi hesitaed. The young woman lifted her pen from the pad, glancing at me for the first time. Maybe they'd expected me to resist. Or maybe they were just hoping for a chance to use their toys. Matasumi ran through some baseline lie-detection questions, the sort of things anyone who'd done the most basic research would know: my name, age, place of birth, current occupation. I wasn't dumb enough to lie. Save that for the big stuff.

'Let me begin by telling you that we already have a werewolf in custody. Your answers will be compared against information he has already provided. So I would suggest you tell the truth.'

Damn. Well, that changed things, didn't it? So much for wholesale prevarication. On the other hand, it was possible that Matasumi was lying about having a mutt. Even if he did, I could pepper my lies with enough truth to keep them guessing which of us wasn't being completely honest.

'How many werewolves are in this . . . Pack?' Matasumi asked.

I shrugged. 'It depends. It's not static or anything. They come and go. It's not a close-knit group. Kind of abitrary, actually, who the Alpha lets in and kicks out, depending on his mood. He's a very temperamental guy.'

'Alpha,' his assistant interjected. 'Like the Alpha in a wolf pack. You use the same terminology.'

'I guess so.'

'Interesting,' Matasumi said, nodding like an anthropologist who's just discovered a long-lost tribe. 'My knowledge of zoology isn't what it should be.'

Behind me, the door clicked and air whooshed out. I turned to see the woman who'd lured me into the car.

'Tucker told me you'd started early,' she said. She turned a pleasant smile on me, as if we were new acquaintances meeting for cocktails. 'I'm glad to see you're up and about so quickly. No lasting effects from the tranquilizers, I hope.'

'Feeling peachy,' I said, trying hard to smile without baring my teeth.

She turned back to Matasumi. 'I'd like Doctor Carmichael to check her out.'

Matasumi nodded. 'Tess, please call Doctor Carmichael from the hall phone. Tell her to bring her equipment down for a checkup at seven o'clock. That should give us sufficient time with the subject.'

'The subject?' the older woman laughed and glanced at me. 'Please excuse us. Our terminology isn't the most civil, I'm afraid. I'm Sondra Bauer.'

'So pleased to meet you,' I said.

Bauer laughed again. 'I'm sure you are. Hold on, Tess,' she said as the assistant headed for the door. 'No need to buzz Doctor Carmichael. She's expecting us in the infirmary.'

'Infirmary?' Matasumi frowned. 'I don't believe this subject—'

'Her name is Elena,' Bauer said.

'I prefer Ms. Michaels,' I said.

'I'd like Elena checked by Doctor Carmichael immediately,' Bauer continued. 'I'm sure she'd appreciate the chance to stretch her legs and have a look around. We can continue our discussion with her in the upstairs room. She'll get tired of these four walls soon enough.'

'May I speak to you privately?' Matasumi asked.

'Yes, yes. You're concerned about security. I can see that,' she said, lips twitching as she looked from my restraints to the guards. She slanted an eye-roll at me, as if sharing a joke. 'Don't worry, Lawrence. We'll make sure Elena is properly restrained, but I don't see the need for excess. Handcuffs and armed guards should be quite sufficient.'

'I'm not sure—'

'I am.'

Bauer headed for the door. My picture of the power structure here was developing fast. Research assistant, guards, half-demon, all roughly equal – the hired help. Scientists above them, mystery woman above scientist. And Ty Winsloe? Where did he fit in? Was he even involved?

My guard unstrapped me from the chair and removed the restraints from my arms and legs, then herded me into the corridor. My cell was the last one on the end, across from a recessed metal door with two red lights above it. At the other end was a matching door with matching red lights. Twin rows of one-way glass flanked the hall. I counted door knobs. Three more on my side, four opposite.

'This way, Elena,' Bauer said, walking right.

Matasumi gestured to the closer door. 'This route would be quicker.'

'I know.' Bauer gestured me forward, smiling encouragingly, like I was a toddler taking her first steps. 'This way please, Elena. I'd like to show you around.'

Really? A guided tour of my prison? Well, I couldn't argue with that, could I? I followed Bauer.

EXHIBITION

As I walked toward Bauer, I passed a chair facing my cell, presumably where Tess had been taking notes. When I glanced at the chair, it started to shake. I'd like to think it was scared of me, but I rarely invoked that response in living things, let alone inanimate objects.

'Earthquake zone?' I asked.

'Shhh!' Matasumi said, holding up his hand.

Matasumi crouched beside the chair and studied it. The chair rocked from one diagonal to the other, back and forth, faster, then slowing, then regaining speed, tilting almost to the point of tipping, then reversing.

Matasumi motioned me forward. When I didn't move fast enough, he waved impatiently. I stepped toward the chair. It kept rocking. Matasumi thrust his palm at me, telling me to move away. I did. No change. He crooked his finger to motion me back, eyes never leaving the chair. I walked beside it. The chair kept rocking, speed unaffected. Then it stopped. Bauer flashed me a wide, almost proud smile.

'What did you think of that?' she asked.

'I'm really hoping it doesn't mean this place is built on a fault line.'

'Oh, no. We chose the environment very carefully. You didn't feel a tremor, did you?'

I shook my head.

'You'll see that sort of thing quite often down here,' she said. 'Don't be alarmed if you wake up in the morning to find your magazines in the shower stall or your dining table upside down.'

'What's causing it?'

She smiled. 'You are.'

'Ms. Bauer means all of you,' Matasumi said. 'Our subjects. I doubt you personally would have much impact. Werewolves are known for physical, not mental powers. These events began several weeks ago, as our collection of subjects grew. My hypothesis is that they result from the high concentration of diverse psychic energy. Random spurts of energy causing equally random events.'

'So it just happens? No one's doing it?'

'There's no discernible pattern or meaning to the events. They're also quite harmless. No one has been injured. We're monitoring it closely, as there is always the possibility the energy could build to dangerous levels, but at this point, we can safely say you have no reason for concern.'

'If objects start flying, duck,' Bauer said. 'Now, let's resume the tour before we have any further interruptions.' She motioned to the ceiling. 'We're underground. The outer walls are several feet of reinforced concrete. Perhaps not impossible to break through – if you had a wrecking ball, plus a bulldozer to dig your way out. The second floor is also subterranean, so this level is more than fifty feet down. The ceiling is solid steel, as is the floor. The one-way glass is a special experimental design. It will resist – how many tons of pressure, Lawrence?'

'I don't know the precise specifications.'

'Let's just say "a lot," then,' Bauer said. 'The doors at either end are reinforced steel, at least as strong as the glass. The security system requires both hand and retinal scan. As you've already discovered, the walls between the cells are not quite so impenetrable. Still, there's not much to be gained by knocking peepholes into the next cell since, as you can see, it's currently unoccupied.'

She gestured at the adjoining cell. It was empty, as was the one across from mine.

'Our next guest might be familiar,' Bauer said, leading me farther and motioning left.

The man was watching television. Average height, trim and fit, dirty blond hair made several shades dirtier by a lengthy interval between showers, whisker shadow growing into a full-scale beard. Familiar? Only vaguely. By Bauer's introduction, I guessed he was a mutt, but I couldn't be sure without smelling him. Of the few dozen mutts in North America, I'd recognize about half by sight alone. For the others, I needed a scent to jog my memory.

'Werewolf?' I asked.

'You don't know him?'

'Should I?'

'I thought you might. He knows you quite well. By reputation, I suppose. Do you have any contact with the werewolves outside your Pack?'

'As little as possible.'

It was true. We didn't go out of our way to associate with

mutts. Unfortunately, that didn't mean we lacked contact with them. I'd probably had a run-in with this one before, but I'd had so many run-ins with so many mutts that I could scarcely separate one from the next.

Bauer moved on. Matasumi was right behind us now. Tess had resumed her note-taking, jotting down my every word. I'd have to start being more eloquent. If they were recording me for posterity, I wanted to sound at least moderately intelligent. 'Clever' would be good, but a stretch.

'Next on the right we have a Voodoo priest.'

'"Voodoo" is the common name,' Matasumi said. 'The correct terminology is "Vodoun."'

Bauer waved off the distinction, then tilted her hand like a spokesmodel toward the cell on the right. I knew I'd have nightmares about this, dreaming that I was sitting in my cage scratching my butt while Vanna White here conducted tours of the ward – 'And on the left we have a rare example of the female *Canis lupis homo sapiens*, common name "werewolf."'

The man in the cage had dark skin, short dreadlocks, and a close-cropped beard. He glared at the one-way glass as if he could see through it, but his eyes were focused a few feet left of our group. His lips parted and he muttered something. I couldn't make out the language, but I recognized the raspy voice as that of the man who'd been shouting earlier.

'He's cursing us,' Bauer said.

Matasumi made an odd chortling sound. Tess stifled a giggle. Bauer did one of her eye-rolls, and they all laughed.

'Voodoo priests have only the most negligible powers,'

Bauer said. 'They're a minor race. Are you familiar with that term?'

I shook my head.

Matasumi took over. 'We have the good fortune to have someone on staff who was able to supply us with the details of classification. Major and minor refer to the degree of power a race possesses. Major races include witches, half-demons, shamans, sorcerers, necromancers, vampires, and werewolves. These groups are relatively small. Minor races are much larger. In fact, it would be a misnomer to even call them "races" because they often have no blood ties. Typically, they are normal people who display a certain aptitude and may have been trained to hone these talents. These minor races include Vodoun priests, druids, psychics, and many others. To a layperson these people may appear to have great power, but in comparison to a witch or a werewolf—'

'There is no comparison,' Bauer cut in. 'Not for our purposes. This "priest" has no skills that the weakest witch or shaman couldn't top. Our first and last foray into the world of the minor races.'

'So for now you're keeping him here . . . ?' I prompted.

'Until we need the cell,' Bauer said.

Guess it would be too much to hope that they'd release subjects who proved unworthy.

'Trial and error,' Bauer continued. 'More often than not, we've made excellent choices. For example, take a look at the guest in the room next door.'

The next prisoner was another man, this one in his late thirties, small, with a compact build, light brown skin, and finely drawn features. He lifted his gaze from a magazine, stretched his legs, then resumed reading. As he'd looked up, I amended my age estimate to mid-forties, maybe closing in on fifty.

'Can you guess what he is?' Bauer asked.

'No idea.'

'Damn. I hoped you could tell us.'

Matasumi forced a pained smile. Tess gave an obligatory laugh. Obviously an old joke.

'You don't know what he is?' I asked.

'No idea,' Bauer said. 'When we picked him up, we thought he was half-demon, but his physiology is all wrong. Like most of the major races, half-demons have common physical traits, as we've learned in examining the three specimens we've acquired so far. Armen doesn't share any of them. His anatomical quirks are all his own. His powers aren't half-demon, either.'

'What can he do?'

'He's a human chameleon.' She waved off Matasumi's protests. 'Yes, yes, Doctor Matasumi will tell you that's not an accurate description, but I like it. Much more catchy than "unknown species with minor facial contortion abilities."' She winked at me, again as if sharing a private joke. 'Marketing is everything.'

'Minor facial contortion abilities?' I repeated.

'Mr. Haig can willfully alter his facial structure,' Matasumi said. 'Minor changes only. He cannot, for example, turn himself into you or me, but he could change his face enough so he would no longer resemble his passport photo.'

'Uh-huh.'

'It doesn't sound very useful for everyday life, but it is incredibly significant in the larger scheme of things. This particular power is completely undocumented in the annals of parapsychology. I'm postulating a new evolutionary shift.'

He smiled then, the first smile I'd seen from him. It shaved decades from his face, lighting his eyes with child-like excitement. He watched me and waited, lips twitching as if he could barely contain the urge to continue.

'Evolutionary shift?' I echoed.

'My hypothesis is that all supernatural races – the true races, the major races – are the result of evolutionary anomalies. For example, with the werewolves, somewhere in the very distant past one man somehow developed the ability to change into a wolf. A complete quirk of nature. Yet a quirk that improved his ability to survive and therefore was reflected in his hereditary DNA, which he passed to his sons. The minor powers of a werewolf – longevity, strength, sensory enhancement – may have been part of this initial change or may have evolved later, to make werewolves better suited for the lives they lead. Similar anomalies would explain the beginnings of all the major races.'

'Except half-demons,' Bauer said.

'That goes without saying. Half-demons are a reproductive hybrid. They rarely transmit their powers to their offspring. Now, back to Mr. Haig. If my theory is correct, these random evolutionary changes must happen with some frequency – not commonly, but more often than would explain the few existing major races. Perhaps some of these deviations are so recent that there aren't yet enough members to classify as a race. If that is true, then Mr. Haig may be the forefather of a new species. Over generations, his power could develop exponentially. Where Mr. Haig may only be able to fool a traffic officer, his great-great-grandson may be able to alter his physical structure enough to *become* the officer.'

'Uh-huh.'

Matasumi turned around and gestured to the last pair of cells across the hall. 'Here are two more interesting specimens. Look to your left first, please.'

In the cell beside the mutt, a woman lay on the bed, eyes open, staring at the ceiling. She was roughly my age, maybe five-six, 120 pounds. Dark red hair, green eyes, and enviably clear skin that looked like it had never sprouted a blemish. She radiated vibes of sturdy good health, the sort of woman I could imagine cheerfully manning some National Park outpost.

'Witch?' I asked.

'Half-demon,' Bauer said.

So half-demons could be female? No one had said otherwise, but I'd assumed they were all male, maybe because the only two I'd ever met were men or maybe because when I thought 'demon' I thought 'male.'

'What's her power?' I asked.

'Telekinesis,' Bauer said. 'She can move things with her mind. Leah is the daughter of an Agito demon. Are you familiar with demonology?'

'Uh – no. The shortcomings of a modern education.'

Bauer smiled. 'Not much call for it these days, but it's a fascinating subject. There are two types of demons: eudemons and cacodemons. Eudemons good, cacodemons bad.'

'Good demons?'

'Surprising, isn't it? Quite a common religious belief, actually. Only in Christian mythology do you find demons so thoroughly . . . demonized. In truth, both kinds exist, though only the cacodemons procreate. Within each of the two types there's a hierarchy based on the demon's relative degree of power. An Agito is quite high on the scale.'

'So I guess telekinesis is more than a parlor trick, then.'

'Much more,' Matasumi said. 'The implications and applications of such a power are infinite.'

'What can she do?'

'She can move things with her mind,' Matasumi said, parroting Bauer's earlier description.

In other words, they had no idea what the 'implications and applications' were either. Sure, telekinesis sounded fine, but what could you really do with it? Besides grab the salt from the counter without leaving the dinner table.

'Are there many female half-demons?' I asked.

'Males are more common, but females aren't unknown,' Matasumi said. 'We actually selected Leah for her gender. We've had some difficulties with our male subjects, so I thought females might be easier to manage. More passive.'

'Watch it,' Bauer said. 'You're surrounded by women here, Lawrence. Yes, women seem to make better subjects, but it has nothing to do with passivity. Women are better able to assess the situation and see the futility of resisting. Men seem to feel an obligation to fight back, no matter what the odds. Take our Voodoo priest. Rants and curses all day, every day. Does it help? No. But he keeps doing it. How does Leah react to the same situation? She stays calm and she cooperates.' She turned to me. 'Have you ever seen telekinesis?'

'Uh, no,' I said. 'I don't think so.'

She smiled. 'Time for a performance, then.'

SAVANNAH

Bauer reached for the intercom button on the half-demon's cage. Something in my gut tightened, and I opened my mouth to stop her, then bit back the protest. Why did I care if Bauer talked to this woman? Maybe I just didn't like the idea of my fellow captives knowing they were being watched and discussed like zoo animals.

'Leah?' Bauer said, leaning into the speaker.

'Hey, Sondra,' Leah said, rising from bed. 'Did my appointment get bumped up again?'

'No, I'm just passing by. Showing a new guest around. She's very interested in your powers. How about a demonstration?'

'Sure.' Leah turned to the small table. After a second, a coffee mug rose from the surface and spun around. 'How's that?'

'Perfect. Thank you, Leah.'

The woman smiled and nodded. If she had any objection to being treated like a trained monkey, she gave no sign of it, just stood there awaiting further commands.

'I'll see you later, Leah,' Bauer said.

'I'm not going anywhere. Say hi to Xavier for me. Tell him to stop by some time. Bring a deck of cards.'

'I'll do that.'

Bauer clicked off the intercom.

'Xavier is our other half-demon,' she said to me. 'You've met him.'

'Houdini.'

Bauer smiled. 'Yes, I suppose so. No books will hold that one, as we soon discovered. Lucky for us he was happy to cooperate with our questions and experiments for the right financial incentive. Quite the mercenary, our Xavier. A valuable asset to the team, though.'

'Like the sorcerer,' I said.

Bauer shot me a studiously blank look.

'I heard you hired a sorcerer, too,' I said.

Bauer hesitated, as if pondering whether to lie, then said, 'Yes, we have a sorcerer. He helps us find our supernaturals. You're not likely to encounter Mr. Katzen though, if that puts your mind at ease.'

'Should it?'

'Sorcerers have an . . . unsavory reputation among some supernatural races. Not entirely unwarranted.'

Matasumi coughed discreetly, but Bauer ignored him and rapped her nails against the Vodoun priest's cell wall. He glanced up, maybe sensing someone there, and cast a baleful glare at the mirrored glass.

'Untrustworthy egomaniacs, most of them,' Bauer went on. 'Our Mr. Katzen, I'm afraid, is no exception. As I said, though, you don't need to worry about him. He doesn't associate with what he considers the "lower" races. Now Xavier is much more sociable.'

'He keeps Leah entertained, I see.'

'Actually no. He's not likely to take her up on her offer. Sad, really. When Leah found out we had another half-demon here she was thrilled. I don't think she's ever met another of her kind. But Xavier won't have anything to do with her. He met her once and has since refused to go near her. We've even tried bribes. Keeping our guests happy is very important to us. Leah is a very gregarious young woman. She needs social stimulation. Fortunately we've found other ways to accommodate her. She's taken quite an interest in two of our other guests.'

'Curtis and Savannah,' Tess said.

Bauer nodded. 'Who are also our two guests most in need of companionship, someone to cheer them up. I think Leah has a knack for that. An innate sense of altruism. Curtis and Savannah both enjoy her company immensely. Which only makes Xavier's animosity all the more unfathomable. He won't even talk to her. It's causing some concern for us. We'd like to bring Leah on the team, but we can't afford the tension it would cause.'

'Have a lot of cap— guests joined "the team"?'

Bauer's eyes sparked as if I'd asked the million-dollar question. 'Not many, but it's certainly possible. Particularly for our more honored guests, like yourself. Once we're assured of a guest's cooperation, we're quite happy to make an offer. It's something to strive for.'

In other words, if I was a very, very good girl, I too could kidnap and torture my fellow supernatural beings. Oh, joy.

'Any idea why Xavier doesn't like Leah?' I asked.

'Jealousy,' Matasumi said. 'Within the half-demon hierarchy Leah has higher standing.'

'Are they aware of this hierarchy?' I asked. 'I thought half-demons didn't have much contact with one another. They don't have any central or ruling group, right? So how do they know who has what status?'

Silence.

After a moment Matasumi said, 'At some level, I'm sure they're aware of their status.'

'An Agito demon ranks over an Evanidus, Xavier's sire,' Bauer said. 'And an Exustio ranks over both. That's Adam Vasic's sire, right? An Exustio?'

'Never came up in conversation, surprisingly.'

Disappointment flashed across her face, then vanished in another false-hearty smile. 'We'll have Doctor Carmichael check those burns. I'm assuming Adam gave them to you.'

She paused. I said nothing.

'An Exustio half-demon is very powerful,' she continued. 'Right at the top. He'd be a first-rate catch. Maybe you could help with that. I'm sure those burns don't tickle.'

'They're healing,' I said.

'Still, we'd be very grateful—'

Matasumi interrupted. 'We don't even know if Adam Vasic's sire is an Exustio, Sondra. We only have one person's secondhand account on that.'

'But it's a very good account.' Bauer turned to me. 'One of our early captives was a shaman who served on Ruth Winterbourne's council back when Adam's stepfather started bringing him to the meetings. He's a Tempestras half-demon. The stepfather, that is. He's also supposedly an expert on demonology, and he was convinced Adam's sire was an Exustio.'

'Though he's never given any indication of having such an advanced degree of power,' Matasumi said. 'Skin burns are more likely the sign of an Igneus. An Exustio would have incinerated Ms. Michaels.'

'Still, even an Igneus half-demon would be quite a coup. And I'd love to get his stepfather. There's very little data on Tempestras demons.'

'I'd like to meet the mother,' Tess said. 'What's the chance that a woman is going to be chosen to bear a demon's offspring and end up marrying a half-demon? There must be something in her that attracts them. It could be very useful research. And interesting.'

This was creeping me out. How much did these people know about us? It was bad enough that they knew what we were, but to have delved into our personal lives like this was downright disturbing. Did they do this a lot, stand around discussing us like we were characters in some modern *Dark Shadows* soap opera?

'Why didn't you grab Adam instead of me?' I asked.

'Don't underestimate your own importance to us, Elena,' Bauer said. 'We're thrilled to have you with us.'

'And we couldn't find Adam,' Tess added.

Gee, thanks.

Bauer continued, 'And, beside Leah, our last, but certainly not least guest.'

I turned. In the cell behind me was a girl. No, I don't

mean a young woman. I mean a child, no more than twelve or thirteen. I assumed her youthful appearance was the manifestation of some unknown supernatural race.

'What is she?' I asked.

'A witch,' Bauer said.

'Does a spell do that? Make her look young? Handy trick, but if it was me, I sure wouldn't want to return to that age. Either long before or long after puberty for me, thank you very much.'

Bauer laughed. 'No, it's not a spell. Savannah's twelve.'

I stopped. If I'd been shivering before, I was frozen now, a block of ice lodged in my gut.

'Twelve?' I repeated, hoping I'd heard wrong. 'You captured a twelve-year-old witch?'

'The absolute best age,' Matasumi said. 'Witches come into their full powers with the onset of their first menses. Being on the brink of puberty, Savannah presents us with the perfect opportunity to study mental and physiological changes that might explain a witch's ability to cast spells. We had a remarkable stroke of luck finding her. An accident really. Savannah is the daughter of a former Coven witch we targeted several weeks ago. When our men picked up the mother, the daughter was unexpectedly home from school, so they were forced to bring her as well.'

I scanned the cell. 'You don't keep her with her mother?'

'We had some trouble with her mother,' Bauer said. 'Her powers were stronger than our sorcerer led us to believe. Dark magic, you might call it, which would likely explain her split with the Coven. Eve was . . . well, we had to—'

'We removed her from the program,' Matasumi cut in. 'The best thing, really. She proved much too difficult to be a useful subject, and her presence distracted the child.'

The ice expanded to fill my stomach. These people were holding a child in an underground cell, congratulating themselves on having found her, and extolling the advantages of killing her mother? I watched the girl. She was tall for her age, whip-thin, with a face that was all planes and sharp angles. Waist-length jet-black hair fell so straight it seemed weighted down. Huge dark blue eyes overpowered her thin face. An odd-looking child with the promise of great beauty. She stared intently at a crossword puzzle book, pencil poised above the page. After a moment she nodded and scribbled something. She held the book at arm's length, studied the completed puzzle, then tossed it aside, got up from the table, paced a few times, and finally settled for surveying the contents of a bookshelf behind the television set.

'She must get bored,' I said.

'Oh, no,' Bauer said. 'This isn't easy for Savannah. We know that. But we do our best to accommodate her. Anything she wants. Chocolate bars, magazines . . . we even picked up some video games last week. She's quite . . .' Bauer paused, seeming to roll a word on her tongue, then discarded it and said quietly, 'She's comfortable.'

So she knew how bad it sounded. 'Sorry we executed your mom, kid, but here's some Tiger Beats and a Game Boy to make up for it.' Bauer tapped her manicured nails against the wall, then forced a smile.

'Well, that's it,' she said. 'You're probably wondering what all this is for.'

'Perhaps later,' Matasumi murmured. 'Doctor Carmichael is waiting and this isn't really the place . . .'

'We've shown Elena around. Now I think it's only fair we offer some explanation.'

Matasumi's lips tightened. So this wasn't usually part of the tour? Why now? A sudden need to justify herself after showing me Savannah? Why did Bauer care what I thought? Or was she defending it to herself?

Before Bauer continued, she led me out of the cell block. I studied the security procedures. Once through, we passed two armed guards stationed in a cubbyhole beyond the secured door. Their eyes passed over me as if I was the cleaning lady. One of the advantages to hiring guards with some form of military background: Curiosity had been drilled out of them. Follow orders and don't ask questions.

'Some sort of military connection?' I asked. As long as Bauer was in a mood to answer questions, I should ask them.

'Military?' She followed my gaze to the guards. 'Using supernatural beings to build the perfect weapon? Intriguing idea.'

'Not really,' I said. 'They did it on *Buffy the Vampire Slayer*. A sub-par season. I slept through half the episodes.'

Bauer laughed, though I could tell she had no idea what I was talking about. I couldn't picture her lounging in front of a TV set, and even if she did, I was sure the only thing she watched was CNN.

'Don't worry,' she said. 'This is a completely private enterprise. Our choice of guards was merely practical. No governmental overtones intended.'

We walked through another set of doors into a long corridor.

'In our post-industrial society, science is constantly pushing the boundaries of technology,' Bauer said, still walking. I glanced overhead for speakers, half-certain I was hearing Bauer's voice on some prerecorded tour tape. 'The human race has taken great strides in the field of technology. Massive strides. Our lives get easier with each passing day. Yet are we happy?'

She paused, but didn't look back at me, as if not expecting an answer. Rhetorical question, dramatic pause. Bauer knew her public-speaking tricks.

'We aren't,' she said. 'Everyone I know has a therapist and a shelf of self-help books. They go on spiritual retreats. They hire yogis and practice meditation. Does it do any good? No. They're miserable. And why?'

Another pause. I bit my lip to keep from answering. It wouldn't have been the sort of reply she wanted.

Bauer continued, 'Because they feel powerless. Science does all the work. People are reduced to technological slaves, dutifully pumping data into computers and waiting for the great god of technology to honor them with results. When the computer age first arrived, people were thrilled. They dreamed of shorter work weeks, more time for self-improvement. It didn't happen. People today work as hard, if not harder, than they did thirty years ago. The only difference is the quality of the work they perform. They no longer accomplish anything of value. They only service the machines.'

Pause number three.

'What we propose to do here is return a sense of power to humanity. A new wave of improvement. Not technological improvement. Improvement from within. Improvement of the mind and the body. Through studying the supernatural, we can affect those changes. Shamans, necromancers, witches, sorcerers – they can help us increase our mental capabilities. Other races can teach us how to make immense improvements in our physical lives. Strength and sensory acuteness from werewolves. Regeneration and longevity from vampires. Countless other advances from half-demons. A brave new world for humanity.'

I waited for the music to swell. When it didn't, I managed to say with a straight face, 'It sounds very . . . noble.'

'It is,' Matasumi said.

Bauer pressed a button and elevator doors opened. We stepped on.

TRICK

The infirmary was exactly what one would expect from such a high-tech operation: antiseptic, white, and cold. Filled with gleaming stainless-steel instruments and digital machines. Not so much as a faded 'symptoms of a heart attack' poster on the wall. All business, like its doctor, a heavyset middle-aged woman. Carmichael covered all opening pleasantries with a brusque hello. From there it was 'open this, close that, lift this, turn that.' Zero small talk. I appreciated that. Easier to swallow than Bauer's unwarranted chumminess.

The examination was less intrusive than the average physical. No needles or urine samples. Carmichael took my temperature, weight, height, and blood pressure. She checked my eyes, ears, and throat. Asked about nausea or other tranquilizer aftereffects. When she listened to my heart, I waited for the inevitable questions. My heart rate was well above normal. A typical werewolf 'physiological anomaly,' as Matasumi would say. Jeremy said it was because of our increased metabolism or adrenaline flow or something. I didn't remember the exact reason. Jeremy was the medical expert. I barely passed high school biology.

Carmichael didn't comment on my heart rate, though. Just nodded and marked it on my chart. I guess they already expected that from examining the mutt.

After Carmichael finished with me, I rejoined my part in the waiting room. Only one of the three guards had accompanied me into the infirmary. He hadn't even sneaked a peek when I'd changed in and out of my medical gown. Serious ego blow. Not that I blamed him. There wasn't much to see.

Matasumi, Bauer, Tess, and the three guards led me down the hall away from the infirmary waiting room. Before we got to our destination, a guard's radio beeped. There was some kind of 'minor incident' in the cell block, and someone named Tucker wanted to know if Matasumi still needed the guards. It was dinner hour and most of the off-duty guards had gone into town. Could Matasumi spare the three accompanying us? Matasumi told Tucker he'd send them down in five minutes. Then we all trooped into an area Bauer referred to as the 'sitting room.'

The sitting room was an interrogation chamber. Anyone who'd seen a single cop show wouldn't be fooled by the comfortable chairs and art deco prints on the walls. Four chairs were arranged around a wooden table. A pool-table-sized slab of one-way glass dominated the far wall. Video cameras and microphones hung from two ceiling corners. Bauer could call it a goddamned formal parlor if she wanted. It was an interrogation room.

My escort led me to the near side of the room, facing the one-way glass. Once I was seated, he opened flaps in either side of the chair and pulled out thick reinforced straps, which he fastened around my waist. Though my wrists were still cuffed, he used another set of straps to bind my elbows to the chair arms. Then, from the floor he pulled a heavy buckle attached to chains that retracted under the carpet. This he affixed to my feet. All four chair legs were welded to the floor. Damn, we needed one of these for our sitting room at Stonehaven. Nothing like a steel-bonded restraint chair to make a guest feel at home.

Once I was secured, Matasumi released the guards. Wow, he was taking a big chance there. No armed guards? Who knew what havoc I could wreak. I could . . . Well, I could spit in his face and call him really nasty names.

As for the questioning, it was pretty boring. More of the same sort of questions Matasumi had fired at me in the cell. I continued to mix my truths and lies, and no one called me on it. About twenty minutes into the session, someone knocked at the door. A guard came in and told Matasumi and Bauer that this Tucker guy requested their presence in the cell block to advise on an 'issue.' Bauer balked, insisting Matasumi could handle it, but it involved some special project of hers, and after a moment's argument, she agreed to go. Tess followed Matasumi out, though no one had invited her. Guess she was afraid of being spit on. Bauer promised they'd be back as soon as possible, and they were gone. Leaving me alone. Hmmm.

My optimism faded fast. There was no way I was getting out of this chair. No adrenaline rush would give me the strength to break these bonds. With the way I was tied up, someone could perform open-heart surgery on me and I couldn't do more than scream. I couldn't even change into a wolf and hope to slip out. The straps and chains were tethered with a device that gobbled up slack like a seat belt. If I were to Change, I would only risk hurting myself.

As I examined my bonds, the door behind me opened. A man stumbled into the room, tripping over leg irons. Before I could see his face, a smell hit me and the hairs on my arms rose. A mutt. I twisted my neck to see the mutt from the cage downstairs. Patrick Lake. The name leaped to my consciousness at the first whiff of his scent. I'd only met him once, and not a memorable meeting at that, but a werewolf's brain categorizes smells with the efficiency of a top-notch filing clerk. With a few molecules of scent, the accompanying information is at our mental fingertips.

Patrick Lake was a drifter and a man-eater. He wasn't a profile killer – a body here, a body there, like most mutts, savvy enough to know each kill brought him closer to exposure, but unable or unwilling to quit. The Pack didn't bother much with mutts like Lake. Maybe that sounds bad, like we should be out there stopping every mutt who kills humans, but if we did that, we'd need to exterminate three-quarters of our race, and really, it wasn't our job. If humans were being killed, let other humans deal with it. Harsh but practical. We became concerned only when a mutt called attention to himself, thereby endangering the rest of us. Lake did that about four years ago by killing the daughter of a city official in Galveston, Texas. Clay and I had flown down to do our respective jobs. I'd investigated the status of the murder case. If Lake became a suspect, he had to die. Since it never got that far, Clay settled for beating the crap out of Lake as a warning, then making sure he caught the next plane out of Texas. Patrick Lake hadn't given us any trouble since.

When Lake staggered into the room, I jerked up in my seat, snapping the bonds tight. Houdini – Xavier – walked in behind him. Seeing me, he stopped and blinked, then looked around the room.

'All alone?' he asked.

I didn't reply. Unless there were half-demon guards with the power of invisibility, it was quite apparent I was alone. Still, Xavier leaned out the door to check the hall. Then, shoving Lake ahead of him, he crossed to the one-way glass, peered through, frowned, zapped into the next room, and returned.

'Alone,' he said, shaking his head. 'You gotta love this place. Military efficiency, high-tech security, the latest communication gadgetry. And for all that, as disorganized as my mother's kitchen cupboards. I can't believe they left you alone. It is eight o'clock, isn't it?'

'Let me check my watch,' I said.

He chuckled. 'Sorry. They sure have you tied down, don't they? Somebody's not taking any chances. But I'm sure it's eight, and I was supposed to bring Lake up here at eight. Now they can't even keep their scheduling straight. Someone's gotta hire a secretary.'

Lake stared at me. He'd never met me before, not officially anyway. In Galveston, I'd come close enough to smell him, but I'd stayed upwind and out of sight. That was a complication Clay hadn't needed. Mutts got a little . . . excited the first time they met me. A hormone thing. I'd been told that I smelled like a bitch in heat – not the most flattering description, but it explained a lot. After a mutt got to know me, his human brain usually kicked in and overroad the signals, but the first few meetings were always dicey. Sometimes I could use the reaction to my advantage. Usually it was just a major pain in the ass.

'Like her?' Xavier asked.

Lake muttered something and tried to wrench his gaze away, but he didn't succeed in breaking visual contact. He walked behind my chair, leg chains sparking static against the carpet. I stared straight ahead. Get it over with, asshole. Lake circled the table twice. When Xavier snickered, Lake paused only a second before instinct impelled him forward again, circling, eyes shunting back to me.

'I'll admit, she's a good-looking girl,' Xavier said. 'But don't you think you're overdoing it, buddy?'

'Shut up,' Lake growled and kept circling.

'Don't worry,' Xavier said, turning to me. 'If he tries to sniff your crotch, I'll snap a muzzle on him.'

Lake turned on Xavier, tensed as if to lunge at him, then thought better of it and settled for growling a string of epithets. The spell was broken, though, and when he wheeled back to face me, his eyes were still blazing, but with fury, not lust.

'You were there, weren't you?' he said. 'In Galveston. With *him*. When he did this to me.' He lifted his cuffed hands and thrust them out. His left palm was permanently fixed in handshake position, the rest of the forearm gnarled and wasted, the result of too many breaks and insufficient setting.

'Who's "he"?' Xavier asked.

'Clayton,' Lake spat, gaze still skewering mine.

'Oh, the boyfriend.' Xavier gave a mock sigh. 'Did you have to mention the boyfriend? I saw him in Vermont, and I'm still feeling pretty inferior about the whole thing. Please tell me that guy's got some nasty habits. Body odor. Picks his nose. Give me something.'

'He's a fucking psycho,' Lake snarled.

'Perfect! That's exactly what I wanted. Thank you, Pat. I feel much better now. Whatever my questionable mental status, no one has ever accused *me* of being a psychopath.'

Lake stepped closer and eyed my bonds.

'Don't be getting any uncivilized ideas,' Xavier said. 'You touch her and I'll have to let her touch you back. You don't want that. She's a strong girl.'

Lake snorted.

'You don't believe me?' Xavier said. 'She's been here a few hours and she's already put a hole in her cell wall. You've been here two weeks and haven't even dented yours. Could be she's stronger than you.'

'Not likely.'

'No, maybe not. You're bigger. More muscle mass. Male advantage. But she's definitely smarter. Figured out how to knock me down on her second try. You and I went ten times as many rounds and you never laid a finger on me. The female of the species is more deadly than the male. Who sang that?'

'It's from Kipling,' I said.

'See? She is smarter than us.'

'Better educated,' Lake said. 'Not smarter.'

'How about a bet then? A match. If she takes you, I get your diamond ring.'

'Go to hell,' Lake muttered.

'Sociable guy, isn't he? Brilliant conversationalist. No wonder you won't let him in your Pack.'

'Go to hell,' Lake enunciated more slowly now, turning his glare on Xavier.

'Touched a sore spot, did I? Oh, come on. Play my game. Show me what a big bad wolf you are. You want some comeuppance for that arm, don't you? How about it, Elena? Feel like a few rounds with Mr. Personality?'

'I don't fight on command,' I said.

Xavier sighed and rolled his eyes. Then he strolled over to me and undid the straps holding me to the seat, leaving only the handcuffs.

'Hey!' Lake said, striding toward us.

Xavier stopped him with an outstretched hand, knelt to undo Lake's leg irons, then unlocked his handcuffs. Lake shook the cuffs off and drew his arm back for a swing at Xavier. But his fist connected with empty space. Xavier was gone.

I'd stayed in my seat. No point in facing off with this mutt. Better to sit here, refuse to play the game and hope Matasumi and Bauer returned soon.

Lake stepped back and surveyed me. A grin tickled the corners of his mouth.

'Don't bother,' I said. 'It's been tried before under far more advantageous circumstances. You know what'll happen if you even try. Clay will ensure you can't ever try again.'

'Really?' Lake's eyes widened and he looked around. 'I don't see him here. Maybe I'm willing to take the chance.'

'Fine,' I said. 'Knock yourself out.'

I didn't move. Werewolf fights were seventy percent bravado. These days, Clay won most of his battles simply by showing up. His reputation was enough. At least it worked for male werewolves. I wasn't so lucky. No matter how many bouts I won, mutts still figured I was helpless without Clay to protect me.

Lake circled the chair. I didn't move. He grabbed my hair, wrapping the long stands around his fist. I set my teeth and still didn't move. He yanked my head back. I only glared up at him. With a growl, he released my hair, grabbed my shoulders and shoved me forward out of the chair. I twisted, trying to brace myself against the table, but, unlike my chair, it wasn't bolted to the floor. When I hit the table edge, it skidded out of reach and I collapsed to my knees, my manacled hands shooting forward to break my fall. Lake slammed a foot into my ass and sent me crashing onto my face. I stayed still, face against the carpet.

'Whoa,' Lake said. 'That was hard.'

'My hands are cuffed,' I muttered against the carpet pile.

'Yeah? Well, my left hand doesn't work so good, thanks to lover boy. Maybe I should do the same to you. Nah. Not the arm. The face. Maybe then he won't find you quite so appealing.'

'Face or arm, it doesn't matter. Touch me and you're a dead man.'

'I'm already a dead man, honey. With you here, these bastards don't want me anymore. Might as well get my kicks while I can.'

While we traded volleys, I kept my arms tucked under

me and concentrated. Sweat broke out across my forehead. Lake knelt in front of me and grinned.

'Looking a little pale there, honey. Not as tough as you pretend.'

I shifted, pulling my weight off my arms. Lake leaped to his feet and stomped one foot into the center of my back. Something cracked. Pain arced through me. Stifling a cry, I closed my eyes and focused on my hands. I eased my belly off the carpet and twisted my palm up. I felt the weight of Lake's foot on my back, resting there. Without warning, he pushed down, grinding me into the carpet. Five needles drove through my shirt and into my stomach. I gasped and smelled blood.

'Does that hurt?' Lake said. 'Geez, I feel sooo bad. Do you know how much this arm hurt? Do you have any idea? Unable to go to the hospital, to a doctor? Tracking down some quack who'd had his license revoked—'

I flipped over fast, catching Lake off guard. He stumbled backward. In a second, he'd regained his balance and drew his foot back, aiming at my chest as I twisted upright. I swung my right hand up and caught his leg. My nails tore through his jeans and sank into flesh. When I had a good grip, I yanked, ripping his leg open. Lake screamed and stumbled away.

'Fuck! What the fuck—?'

He looked at my hand. Only it wasn't a hand. It was a claw, the grip and fingers of a human hand, the fur of a wolf, nails long, razor-sharp, and rock-hard. The cuffs hung from my other hand. The partial Change had narrowed my hand enough to pull it through the bracelet.

'What the fuck!?' Lake repeated backing against the wall.

'Pack trick,' I said. 'Takes concentration. Too much for a mutt.'

I advanced on him. He hesitated, then launched himself at me. We went down. I clawed his back. He yelped and tried to wrestle free. I grabbed the back of his shirt with my left hand and flung him off me. As I scrambled to my feet, the door flew open. Bauer hurried into the room with Matasumi, Tess, and two guards at her heels. All five stopped inside the doorway and stared. Then Bauer strode across the room, barreling down on Lake.

'What the hell is going on here?' Bauer said.

'She started it,' he said.

'Oh, please,' I said, getting to my feet.

My hand was normal now. I'd even slipped it back through the cuff. Xavier strolled through the doorway.

'*He* started it,' Lake said.

'Just following orders,' Xavier leaned against the door-jamb, hands in pockets. 'The ring's mine, Pat. She whupped your ass.'

'Is it on tape?' Matasumi asked.

Xavier yawned. 'Of course.'

Bauer spun on both of them. 'Orders? Tape? What happened in here?'

I knew what had happened. I'd been set up, and I was furious for not seeing it earlier. Shouldn't I have wondered why security-paranoid Matasumi released my guards? Why he then left me in the room alone? Why Xavier was strolling around alone with another werewolf after Matasumi had argued over letting me leave my cell even under armed guard? Matasumi must have arranged everything while I was in the infirmary. As long as I was out of my cell, why not try a little experiment? Find out what happens when you put a Pack werewolf in the same room as a mutt.

Bauer started reaming out Matasumi, then stopped herself. She dismissed Xavier and Tess for the night, then asked the two guards to escort me back to my cell. Once we were out of normal earshot, she lit into Matasumi again.

CONTACT

I'd been back in my cell for about twenty minutes when Bauer brought my dinner. Ham, scalloped potatoes, baby carrots, cauliflower, salad, milk, coffee, and chocolate cake. Decent enough food to fend off any notion of a hunger strike – not that I would have done that anyway. No protest was great enough to warrant starvation.

Before I ate, Bauer showed me around the cell, pointing out the toiletries, demonstrating how the shower worked, and explaining the meal schedule. A nightgown and a single day's worth of clothing were kept in a drawer under the bed. Why only one change of clothes? Bauer didn't say. Maybe they were afraid if we had too much fabric, we'd rig up a way to hang ourselves from the nonexistent rafters. Or did they think there was no sense providing more when we might not live long enough to need it? Cheery thought.

Bauer didn't leave after conducting my cell tour. Maybe she expected a tip.

'I apologize,' she said after I sat down to eat. 'What happened upstairs . . . I didn't know they planned that. I don't believe in tricking our guests. This whole arrangement is difficult enough for you without having to worry about stunts like that.'

'It's okay,' I said through a mouthful of ham.

'No, it isn't. Please tell me if anything like that happens when I'm not around. Would you like Doctor Carmichael to look at your stomach wounds?'

'I'm fine.'

'There's clean clothing if you want to change out of that shirt.'

'I'm fine,' I said, then added a conciliatory 'Maybe later.'

She was trying to be nice. I knew I should reciprocate. Knowing and doing were two different things. What was I supposed to say? Thanks for caring? If she cared, she wouldn't have kidnapped me in the first place, right? But as she watched me eat, her look of concern seemed genuine. Maybe she didn't see the contradiction here, abducting me, then worrying about how I was treated. She stood there as if waiting for me to say something. Say what? I had little enough experience with other women. Making chitchat with someone who'd drugged and kidnapped me was well beyond my set of social skills.

Before I could think of suitable small talk, Bauer left. Relief mingled with my guilt. As much as I knew I should try to be friendly, I really wasn't in the mood for conversation. My back hurt. My stomach hurt. I was hungry. And I wanted to go to bed, which didn't mean I was tired, but that I wanted to talk to Jeremy. Jeremy could communicate with us mentally. The catch was he could only do it while we slept. After the incident with Lake, anxiety had begun oozing from behind my carefully erected barricades. I wanted to talk to Jeremy before my stress got out of control. He'd already be working on a rescue plan. I needed to hear it, to know that they were taking action. Even more than that, I needed his reassurance. I was scared, and I needed some comforting, someone to tell me everything would be okay, even if I knew that was an empty promise. I'd be friendly and polite to Bauer tomorrow. Tonight I wanted Jeremy.

Once I'd finished my meal, I took a shower. Definite privacy issues with the shower setup. The bathroom walls were see-through. The glass door on the shower stall was only slightly opaque, marring features but leaving very little to an observer's imagination. I fashioned a half-curtain by stretching the bath towel from the toilet to the shaving mirror over the sink. Waltzing around Stonehaven naked was one thing. I wasn't doing it in front of strangers. When I used the toilet, I draped the towel over my lap. Some things demand privacy.

After my shower, I put my clothing back on. They may have provided a nightgown, but I wasn't wearing it. Nor would I wear their fresh clothing tomorrow. I'd take another shower in the morning and hope nothing started to smell. My clothes were the only personal thing I had left. No one was taking them away from me. At least, not while the odor was bearable.

Jeremy didn't contact me that night. I don't know what went wrong. The only time I'd known Jeremy to be unable to contact us was when we were unconscious or sedated. I was sure the sedatives were out of my system, but I clung to that excuse. It was also possible that Jeremy was unable to contact me here, below ground, but I preferred not to consider that since it meant not only wouldn't I have Jeremy's help planning my escape, but he might assume I was dead and not try effecting any rescue. Deep down, I knew that last part was bullshit. Clay would come for me. He wouldn't give up until he saw a corpse. Still, there was always that insecurity, that nagging voice forever trying to destroy my faith, telling me I was wrong, he wouldn't risk his life to save me, no one could or would care for me that much. So, despite everything I knew to the contrary, I awoke in a cold sweat, certain I'd been abandoned. No amount of reassuring self-talk would help me. I was alone and I feared I would remain alone, forced to rely on my own wits to escape. I didn't trust my wits that much.

In the late hours of night, nearing dawn, someone did contact me. But it wasn't Jeremy. At least, I didn't think it was. I was dreaming that I was in a Mongolian yurt with Clay, arguing over who got the last red M&M. Just when I'd begun to consider giving in, Clay gathered his furs and stormed out into the howling wind, swearing never to return. The dream startled me up from sleep, heart thudding. As I tried to settle back to sleep, someone called my name: A woman's voice. I was sure it was a woman, but I was in that confused state between sleeping and waking, unable to tell if it was someone in my cell or a voice calling from a dream. I struggled to lift my head from my pillow, but plunged into a fresh nightmare before I could rouse myself.

The next morning, I stayed in bed as long as I could, stretching out sleep in the unlikely event that Jeremy was still trying to contact me and only needed a few more minutes. At eighty-thirty, I admitted defeat. I wasn't sleeping, only keeping my eyes closed and faking it.

I shifted my legs out of bed, doubled over, and almost collapsed to the floor. My stomach felt like someone had sliced open all the muscles while I slept. Who'd think five little puncture wounds could hurt so much? The fact that they were self-inflicted didn't help. One day into my captivity and I was already doing more damage to myself than to my enemies. Maybe Patrick Lake was in more pain that I was. Not likely. My back had seized up overnight from Lake's stomping, and as I struggled to stand straight, my body revolted from both sides, stomach, and spine. I hobbled to the shower. Steaming water helped my back but set my stomach afire. Cold water soothed my stomach but tightened my back again. Day two was off to a wonderful start.

My mood sank when Bauer brought my breakfast. No complaints about the meal, of course, and not really any complaint about Bauer bringing it, but one look at her sent my spirits plummeting. Bauer sauntered in wearing snug-fitting beige suede pants, a billowing white linen shirt, and knee-high boots, her hair artlessly swept up in a clip, cheeks flushed with pink that didn't come from a bottle, smelling faintly of horse, as if she'd just breezed in from a morning ride. I was dressed in a ripped and bloodstained shirt, my too-fine hair knotted from the harsh shampoo, and my eyes bloated from a rough night. When she called out a cheery good morning, I stumped over to the table, unable to stand fully erect or manage more than the most monosyllabic grunt in greeting. Even bent over, I was four or five inches taller than Bauer. I felt like Neanderthal woman – big, ugly, and none too bright.

When Bauer tried to entice me into conversation, I was tempted to thwart her efforts again, but a peaceful breakfast wasn't a luxury I could afford. If I had to plot my own escape, I needed to get out of this cell. The best way to get out of this cell would be to 'join' my captors. And the best way to join them would be to secure Bauer's favor. So I had to play nice. This was tougher than it sounded. Oddly enough, I had a problem sitting around chatting about the weather with the woman who'd thrown me into captivity.

'So you live near Syracuse,' she said as I tore into my bagel.

I nodded, mouth full.

'My family's from Chicago,' she said. 'Bauer Paper Products. Have you heard of it?'

'It sounds familiar,' I lied.

'Old money. Very old.'

Should I be impressed? I feigned it with a wide-eyed nod.

'It's odd, you know,' she said, settling back into her chair. 'Growing up with that kind of name, that kind of money. Well, not odd for me. It's all I know. But you see yourself reflected through other people's eyes and you know you're considered very lucky. Born with the proverbial silver spoon. You're supposed to be happy, and God help you if you aren't.'

'Money can't buy happiness,' I said, the cliché bitter on my tongue. Was that what this was about? Poor little rich girl? I'm rich and unhappy so I kidnap innocent strangers – well, maybe not so innocent, but unwitting nonetheless.

'But *you* are happy,' Bauer said. A statement, not a question.

I managed a half-genuine smile. 'Well, at this very moment, being held captive in a cell, I wouldn't exactly say—'

'But otherwise. Before this. You're happy with your life.'

'No complaints. It's not perfect. There's still that nasty werewolf curse—'

'You don't see it that way, though. As a curse. You say it, but you don't mean it.'

She stared at me now. No, not at me. Into me. Eyes blazing, leaning forward. Hungry. I pulled back.

'Some days I mean it. Trust me.' I polished off my bagel. 'These are great. Real New York bagels. I don't suppose there's any chance of seconds.'

She leaned back, flames in her eyes extinguished, polite smile back in place. 'I'm sure we can arrange something.' She checked her watch. 'I should be getting you up to Doctor Carmichael for your physical.'

'Is that a daily routine?'

'Oh, no. Yesterday was just a checkup. Today is the full physical.'

Bauer lifted her hand. The door opened and two guards walked in. So that's where they'd been hiding. I'd wondered, hoping maybe Bauer felt comfortable enough to forgo the armed entourage. Guess not. The appearance of trust, but a lack of substance. Or perhaps just a lack of stupidity. Damn.

I had a neighbor. When I stepped from my cell, I saw someone in the room across from mine. A woman seated at the table, her back to me. It looked like . . . No, it couldn't be. Someone would have told me. I would have known. The woman turned half-profile. Ruth Winterbourne.

'When . . . ?' I asked.

Bauer followed my gaze and smiled as if I'd uncovered a hidden present. 'She came in with you. We were in Vermont near the meeting hall that morning. When we saw you leave with the Danvers, Xavier and I decided to follow. The rest of the team stayed near the others. We knew someone would be alone eventually. Fortunately, it was Ruth. A very good catch. Of course, any one of them would have been good. Well, except her niece. Not much use in an apprentice witch of that age. Savannah is another matter, given her youth and what we know of her mother's powers.'

'How come I didn't see Ruth yesterday?'

'The trip was unusually . . . difficult for her. Her age. The very thing that makes her valuable is something of a liability. We overestimated the sedative dosage. But she's quite fine now, as you can see.'

She didn't look fine. Maybe someone who'd never met Ruth would mistake the dull eyes, yellow-hued skin, and lethargic movements for normal signs of aging, but I knew better. Physically, she seemed well enough. No signs of illness or broken bones. The damage was deeper than that.

'She looks pretty down,' I said. 'Depressed.'

'It happens.' Statement of fact. No emotion.

'Maybe I could speak to her,' I said. 'Cheer her up.'

Bauer tapped her long nails against her side, considering. If she saw an ulterior motive in my altruism, she gave no sign of it.

'Perhaps we could arrange something,' she said. 'You've been very cooperative, Elena. The others were worried, but other than the wall-punching, you've been surprisingly well behaved. I believe in rewarding good behavior.'

Without another word, she turned and left me to follow. Inwardly I balked, but outwardly I trailed along at her heel like a well-trained puppy. Trained puppy indeed. Forgive me, but 'well behaved' is not a term one ought to apply to a grown woman, yet Bauer said it without malice or insinuation. Be a good puppy, Elena, and I'll give you a treat. The temptation to show Bauer exactly what I thought of her reward system was almost overwhelming. Almost. But I did want to talk to Ruth. She was my only contact in this place, and I wasn't above asking for help. A spell had gotten us out of that doomed situation in the Pittsburgh alley. With her spells and my strength, we should be able to devise a way out of here.

So I was a good puppy. I suffered through the physical without protest. This time my visit to the infirmary wasn't nearly so unintrusive. They took X-rays, blood samples, urine samples, saliva samples, and samples of bodily fluids I didn't know I had. Then they attached wires to me and took readings of my heart and brain. Carmichael poked and prodded and asked questions I'd blush answering for my gynecologist. But I reminded myself that this was the price of talking to Ruth, so I ignored the intrusions and answered the questions.

The physical lasted several hours. At noon, someone knocked, then opened the door without waiting for a reply. Two guards walked in. They might even have been the ones who'd brought me up here, but I couldn't be sure. By this point, the crew cuts had blended into a nameless, faceless blob. Seen one, you seen 'em all. One of the guards – maybe one of these two, maybe not – had stayed in the infirmary with me earlier, but after an hour or so, he'd muttered something about a shift change and told Dr. Carmichael to call for backup. She hadn't. When these two arrived, I thought they were coming to take the place of that missing guard. Instead they escorted in the 'human chameleon,' Armen Haig.

'I'm running behind,' Carmichael said, not turning from a series of X-rays clipped to a lighted wall.

'Should we wait outside?' one guard asked.

'Not necessary. Please take the second table, Doctor Haig. I'll be right with you.'

Haig nodded and walked to the table. His guards promised to return in an hour, then left. Unlike me, Haig wasn't even manacled. I suppose his powers weren't any great security risk. Even if he made himself look different, the guards were bound to notice an apparent stranger prowling the compound. Escape wasn't likely.

For the next twenty minutes, Carmichael bustled around the infirmary, checking X-rays, peering through microscopes, jotting notes on a clipboard. Finally she stopped, surveyed the room, then snatched a tray of fluid-filled vials from a metal cart.

'I need to run a test in the lab before we finish up here, Ms. Michaels.'

Déjà vu or what? Bring another captive into a room with me, find an excuse for leaving that room, and see what fun and exciting chaos ensues. Couldn't these guys think up more than one ruse?

Carmichael headed for the exit, then stopped and looked from me to Haig. After a pause, she laid the tray on the counter and picked up the intercom phone. Though she turned her back and lowered her voice, her words were impossible to miss in the silent room. She asked someone in security whether there were any 'issues' with leaving Haig and me together for a few minutes, if I was manacled. There wasn't.

'Don't forget to turn on the camera,' Haig murmured as she hung up. His voice was rich and honey-smooth, with traces of an accent.

Carmichael snorted. 'I can't program my damned VCR. You think I can operate that thing?' She waved at the video camera mounted overhead. 'A word of warning, though. Don't think of leaving. I'll be locking the door behind me. There's a perfectly functioning camera in the waiting room and guards in the hall. They won't look kindly on an escape attempt.'

She took her tray of vials and left the room.

PARTY

After Carmichael left, I studied the video camera for signs of activity, but it stayed silent and still.

'So,' Haig said. 'What are you in for?'

'Raping and pillaging.'

The corners of his mouth turned up. 'That would have been my first guess. Are you finding the accommodation to your liking?'

'My kennel, you mean?'

Another quarter-smile. 'Ah, so you *are* the werewolf. I didn't know whether it was polite to ask. Emily Post doesn't cover circumstances such as this. Werewolf. Hmmm. I had a patient with lycanthropy once. Felt compelled to turn around three times before settling onto the couch. Quite trying. But he always brought in the paper from the front stoop.'

I remembered how Carmichael had addressed him. 'Doctor Haig,' I said. 'So you're a shr— psychiatrist?'

'A shrink, yes. My special abilities aren't very profitable in everyday life. I suppose they might help if I was to become an international assassin, but I'm a terrible shot. And please call me Armen. Formality seems rather out of place here.'

'I'm Elena. Psychiatry, eh? So did you know Matasumi? Before you came here?'

'I'd heard of him.' Dark lips curved in a moue of distaste. 'Parapsychology. With a reputation for skirting the code of research ethics.'

'Really? Go figure. You must have no shortage of people to analyze here, between the captives and captors.'

'Frighteningly enough, the ones in the cages would be more likely to earn my recommendations for early release.'

'Matasumi's got some definite issues,' I said. 'And Bauer?'

'One of the sanest, actually. Just sad. Very sad.'

That wasn't the impression I got, but before I could press for details, Armen continued. 'The one I'd most like to get on the couch is Tyrone Winsloe. Though once I had him there, I'd be sorely tempted to tie him to it and run like the devil.'

'What's wrong with him?'

'Where do I start? Tyrone Winsloe is—' Armen cocked his head toward the door; footsteps entered the waiting room, then stopped '—out of town on business at the moment.' He lowered his voice, 'If you need any help . . . adjusting, please ask. This isn't a very pleasant place. The sooner we can be out of it, the sooner we'll all feel much better.'

As he fixed me with a knowing look, I knew he wasn't offering help with my psychological adjustment.

'As I said, my special ability isn't very useful,' he murmured. 'But I'm very observant . . . as a psychiatrist. And like everyone, I can always use companionship. For moral support. Additional resources and strength. That, I believe, is your specialty. Strength.'

The doorknob turned. Carmichael bumped it open with fresh clipboard and walked in, flipping through pages.

'Off you go, then, Ms. Michaels,' she said. 'Your escort is in the waiting room.'

'A pleasure to meet you, Elena,' Armen said as I left. 'Do enjoy your stay.'

Bauer and the guards took me back to the sitting/interrogation room. One guard fastened me to the leg and torso restraints, and removed my wrist manacles, which pleased me until I realized they'd only left my hands free so I could eat lunch. Once I finished, on went the handcuffs and wrist straps. Then Matasumi and Tess joined us, and I endured round two of interrogation.

A couple of hours later, as Bauer walked me to my cell, I checked across the hall. The opposite cell was empty.

'Where's Ruth?' I asked.

'A slight setback. She's in the infirmary.'

'Is she okay?'

'There's no immediate danger. We're probably overreacting, but our guests' health is very important.'

'Can I see her when she comes back?'

'I'm afraid that won't be possible,' she said, reaching for the door to my cell. 'But I have arranged for company of a different sort.'

'I'd like to speak to Ruth.'

Pushing open my door, Bauer walked through as if I hadn't said anything. The guards prodded me forward. I stepped into my cell, then stopped. My hackles rose, and some ancient instinct warned me that my den had been invaded.

'You remember Leah, don't you?' Bauer said.

The red-haired half-demon sat at my table, pouring a glass of wine. She glanced up and smiled.

'Hey,' she said. 'Elena, right?'

I nodded.

'Welcome to the party,' she said, raising her glass in a toast. 'Can you believe this? Wine, cheese, fancy crackers. I don't eat this well at home. Are you joining us, Sondra?'

'If you don't mind.'

'The more the merrier.' Leah beamed a smile 100 percent sarcasm-free. 'May I pour you ladies a glass?'

'Please,' Bauer said.

I didn't answer, but Leah filled two more glasses. As Bauer stepped forward to take hers, I could only gape. A wine and cheese party? Please tell me they were kidding.

'Do you like white?' Bauer asked, extending my glass to me. 'It's a very good vintage.'

'Uh – thanks.' I took the wine and managed to fold myself into a chair, a task that seemed far more onerous than it should.

'Elena's a journalist,' Bauer said.

'Really? TV or radio?' Leah asked.

'Print,' I murmured, though it came out as a guttural mutter, dangerously close to a grunt.

'She does freelance work,' Bauer said. 'Covering Canadian politics. She's Canadian.'

'Oh? Interesting. You guys have a prime minister, right? Not a president.'

I nodded.

Leah gave a self-deprecating laugh. 'Well, there's the

extent of my knowledge of international politics. Sorry.'

We sipped our wine.

'Leah's a deputy sheriff in Wisconsin,' Bauer said.

I nodded, struggling to think of some germane comment to make and coming up blank. Oh, please, Elena. You can do better than this. Say something. Say anything. Don't sit there like a grunting, nodding idiot. After we'd touched on my career, I should have asked Leah about hers. That was how small talk worked. My experience socializing with other women was embarrassingly slight, but certain rules held true no matter who you were talking to.

'So you're a police officer,' I said, then winced inwardly. Duh. If I couldn't come up with something more intelligent than that, I should keep my mouth shut.

'Not as exciting as it sounds,' Leah said. 'Especially not in Wisconsin. Cheese, anyone?'

She cut wedges from a round of Gouda and proffered the cheese board. We each took one, along with a lacy cracker that crumbled most unbecomingly as I bit into it. As we munched, Bauer refilled our half-empty wine glasses. I downed mine, praying it might help, then noticed both women watching me.

'Thirstier than I thought,' I said. 'Maybe I should stick to water.'

Bauer smiled. 'Drink all you want. There's more where that came from.'

'So, do you live in Canada?' Leah asked.

I hesitated, but realized if I didn't answer, Bauer would. My life wasn't exactly a secret around here. 'New York State.'

'Her husband's American,' Bauer said. 'Clayton is your husband, isn't he? We couldn't find a marriage record, but when we were following you, I noticed he wears a wedding ring.' She glanced at my right hand. 'Oh, but you don't. That's an engagement ring you have, though, isn't it?'

'Long story,' I said.

Leah leaned forward. 'Those are always the best.'

I inched back in my chair. 'So, how about you two? Married? Boyfriends?'

'I've run through the marriageable material in my little town,' Leah said. 'I've put my name in for a transfer before the seventy-year-old widowers start looking good.'

'I've been married,' Bauer said. 'Youthful rebellion. Married him because my father forbade it and soon realized that sometimes Father does know best.'

'What does your husband do?' Leah asked me.

'Clayton's an anthropologist,' Bauer answered before I could deflect the question.

'Oh? That sounds . . . fascinating.'

Sipping her wine, Bauer gave a giggling laugh. 'Admit it, Leah. It sounds perfectly awful.'

'I didn't say it,' Leah said.

Bauer drained her glass and refilled everyone's. 'No, but you were thinking it. Trust me, this guy is no tweedy academic. You should see him. Blond curls, blue eyes, and a body . . . Greek god material.'

'Got a photo?' Leah asked me.

'Uh, no. So, how do you like—'

'We have some surveillance pictures upstairs,' Bauer said. 'I'll show them to you later. Elena is a very lucky girl.'

'Looks aren't everything,' Leah said, flashing a wicked smile. 'It's performance that counts.'

I studied the bubbles in my wine glass. Oh, please, please, please, don't ask.

Leah downed her wine. 'I have a question. If it's not too personal.'

'And even if it is,' Bauer said with a giggle.

Oh, please, please, please—

'You guys change into wolves, right?' Leah said. 'So, when you and your husband are wolves, do you still . . . you know. Are you still lovers?'

Bauer snorted so hard wine sprayed from her nose. Okay, that was the one question even worse than asking how Clay was in bed. This was a nightmare. My worst nightmare. Not only thrown into a wine-and-cheese party with two women I barely knew, but with two women who knew everything about me and were getting a wee bit tipsy. Let the floor open up and swallow me now. Please.

'This is really good cheese,' I said.

Bauer laughed so hard she started to hiccup.

The door whooshed open. A guard stuck his head inside.

'Ms. Bauer?'

In an eye blink, Bauer was sober. She coughed once into her hand, then straightened up, face as regal as ever.

'Yes?' she said.

'We have a situation,' he said. 'With prisoner three.'

'They're not prisoners,' she snapped, getting to her feet. 'What's the problem with Mr. Zaid?'

'His clothes are gone.'

Leah snorted a laugh and covered her mouth with her linen napkin.

'What's he done with them?' Bauer asked.

'He – uh – hasn't done anything, ma'am. He finished his shower and they were – uh – gone. Started raising a hel – ruckus. Cursing, ranting. All that voodoo stuff. Demanded we get you. Immediately.'

Annoyance flitted across Bauer's face 'Tell Mr. Zaid . . .' She stopped. Hesitated. 'Fine. I'll speak to him. Step inside. I'll be right back.'

Ghosts

Bauer wasn't gone long enough for Leah and I to exchange more than a few sentences. When she returned, she brushed past the guard she'd left in the cell with us. She didn't looked pleased.

'How's Curtis?' Leah asked.

Bauer blinked, as if distracted by her own thoughts. 'Fine,' she said after a moment's pause. 'He's fine. Just . . . unnerved by all this.'

'Where were his clothes?' Leah asked.

Another blink. Another pause. 'Oh, on his bookshelf.' She settled into her chair and refilled her wine glass. 'Neatly folded on the top shelf.'

'The spirits are at work,' Leah intoned, grinning mischievously.

'Don't start that,' Bauer said.

'Did you move—' I began. 'I mean, can you do things like that?'

Leah waved a cheese-topped cracker, scattering crumbs. 'Nah. It would be fun, though. Telekinesis is limited to a half-demon's range of vision. If I can't see it, I can't move it. My powers aren't very precise either. If I tried lifting a pile of clothes—' She turned and looked at my bed. The folded blanket at the end levitated, floated over the side, and fell in a heap on the carpet. 'Gravity takes over. I could throw it against the wall or toss it in the air, but when I let go, it would never fall nicely folded.'

'So it's that random psychic energy thing, then?' I asked Bauer.

'They're back,' Leah said in a high-pitched child's voice.

Bauer laughed, covering her cracker-filled mouth with one hand and wagging her free index finger at Leah. 'Stop that.' She turned to me. 'That's what I meant. Leah's pet theory. She thinks we have a poltergeist.'

'Poltergeist?' I repeated. 'Don't tell me you built this place over an Indian burial ground. After three movies, you'd really think people would learn.'

Leah laughed. 'There, see? Thank you, Elena. Sondra hasn't even seen the first *Poltergeist*. All my pop culture references are lost on her.'

'So you're kidding,' I said. 'About the poltergeist.'

'Uh-uh.'

'Don't get her started,' Bauer said.

'You don't really believe in ghosts,' I said.

'Sure,' Leah said, grinning. 'But I draw the line at were-wolves. Seriously, though, how much do you know about poltergeists?'

'I walked out during the second movie and skipped the third. That's it.'

'Well, I'm something of a self-taught expert. When I was in high school, I read everything I could find on polter-geists. Because of the similarities with my "condition." I

203

wanted to know more about myself and my kind and figured maybe so-called poltergeists were really manifestations of telekinetic half-demons.'

'Sounds plausible,' I said.

'It does, until you learn more about it. Poltergeists typically appear around children approaching puberty. Half-demons don't come into full powers until closer to adulthood. Poltergeists are also associated with noises and voices, which aren't part of my repertoire. Neither is stuff like rearranging furniture or neatly moving objects from one place to another, other marks of a poltergeist.'

'We haven't heard any strange noises,' Bauer said.

'But not all poltergeist manifestations involve sound. Everything else about these occurrences points to a poltergeist.'

'A poltergeist who just happened to appear here?' I said. 'Of all places?'

'It's *not* Savannah,' Bauer said, slanting a warning look at Leah.

'The young witch?' I said.

'Just another theory,' Leah said. 'Savannah is at the perfect age, and with her powers, she'd be an ideal conduit, especially under these strained circumstances.'

'You think she conjured up—'

'Oh, no, no,' Leah said. 'Savannah is a sweetheart. A total innocent, I'm sure. Now, her mother was a real piece of work, and I wouldn't have put anything past her, but I'm certain Savannah didn't inherit any of her darker powers.'

'If,' Bauer said, 'and I repeat, *if* Savannah has caused

some kind of poltergeist to materialize, which I doubt, I'm sure she isn't aware of it.'

'Certainly,' Leah said. 'She probably can't even control it. There's been no evidence to the contrary . . . well, except for . . .'

Bauer sighed. 'A few of the more alarming disturbances have revolved around Savannah. When she becomes upset, the activity increases.'

'If that poor guard hadn't ducked . . .' Leah said. 'But no, I still say it's beyond Savannah's control. More likely, her anger spurs the poltergeist to react. An unwitting emotional connection, though potentially, it could be quite dangerous if someone were to cross—'

'It's random psychic energy,' Bauer said firmly. 'Until Doctor Matasumi or I see anything to the contrary, that's the assumption.'

The door opened.

'Yes,' Bauer snapped, then turned to see Matasumi's assistant hovering in the doorway. 'I'm sorry, Tess. What is it?'

'It's nearly four-thirty. Doctor Matasumi thought I should remind you—'

'Oh, yes. The conference call. I'm sorry. I'll be right with you. Could you please send the guards in to escort Leah back to her room?'

'Party's over,' Leah said and chugged the rest of her wine.

After dinner, the voice I'd heard the night before called again. This time I was sure I was awake. Well, reasonably sure, at least. I still held out hopes that the whole wine-and-cheese party had been a nightmare.

'Who's there?' I said aloud.

'It's me, dear. Ruth.'

I hurried to the hole I'd punched between my cell and the next, crouched, and peered through. No one was there.

'Where are you?' I asked.

'Across the hall. It's a ranged communication spell. You can speak to me normally and I'll hear you as if I was there in the room. Thank goodness I finally got in touch with you. I've been having the devil of a time. First the sedatives. Then the blocking field. Just when I figured out a way around that, they whisked me out of here because my white blood cell count was low. What do they expect at my age?'

'Blocking field?' I repeated.

'I'll explain. Sit down and make yourself comfortable, dear.'

To ensure our privacy, Ruth cast a sensing spell that could detect anyone in the corridor. Useful things, spells. Not my cup of tea, but far more practical than I would have imagined.

Our captors had taken Ruth around the same time Bauer and Xavier had trapped me, so she hadn't known I'd been kidnapped, which meant she didn't know whether Jeremy and Clay had returned to the others or even if they knew what had happened to me. When I told her I hadn't been able to contact Jeremy, she was surprised to the point of shock, not that we couldn't make contact, but that any werewolf had telepathic abilities. We all have our stereotypes, I guess. Witches equaled mental power, werewolves equaled physical power, and never the twain shall meet.

'What happened when you tried to contact him?' she asked.

'I can't do that,' I said. 'He's the one with the powers. I have to wait for him to make contact.'

'Did you try?' she asked.

'I wouldn't know how.'

'You should try. It's very simple. Relax and pretend— Never mind. It won't work anyway.'

'Why won't it work?'

'They've put up a blocking field. Have you met their spell-caster?'

I shook my head, realized she couldn't see the motion and said, 'No. I've heard of him, though. Katzen, I think they called him.'

'Isaac Katzen?'

'You know him?'

'I know of him. He was with one of the Cabals, I believe. Oh dear, I hope they aren't involved. That would be the devil of a problem. Sorcerer Cabals are—' She stopped. 'Sorry, dear. Spell-casting business. You don't need to know anything about that.'

'What about his Katzen guy? Do I need to know anything about him? Bauer says I'm not likely to run into him. How'd she put it? He doesn't associate with "lower races"?'

A short chuckle. 'That is most definitely a sorcerer. No, dear, I shouldn't think you'd have to worry about Isaac Katzen. Sorcerers have little use for non-spell-casters. Little use for witches, too. Sorcerers aren't male witches. Completely different race. Nasty bunch, I'm sad to say. No sense of themselves as part of something greater. An absolute absence of altruism. They'd never dream of using their powers to help—' A sigh and a chuckle. 'Stop digressing, Ruth. Age, you know. It's not that the mind starts to wander; it's that it's so stuffed full of information that it's forever jumping off track and zipping down tangents.'

'I don't mind.'

'Time, my dear. Time.'

I turned toward the door. 'Is someone coming?'

'Not yet. If they have Isaac Katzen "on staff," as you'd say, then he has almost certainly cast a spell to block telepathy, among other things.'

'What other things?'

'Well, he could monitor communications, provide added security—'

'Monitor communications? You mean he could be listening to us right now?'

'No, dear. He'd need to be close by to do that, and I've already ascertained there's no one down here but our fellow captives. Do be careful, though. If he does visit the cells, he could listen without using the intercom system. For most spells, he'd need to be nearby, but he can block telepathy remotely.'

'But you've figured out a way around that. Can you contact someone outside the compound?'

'I believe I can, though I haven't had a chance. I will later. I'll get in touch with Paige and tell her you're here, so she can communicate with you. She's had the proper training. Never had the need to use it, but it should go well. She'll be a very powerful spell-caster someday. She has the potential and more than enough ambition. Some difficulty accepting her boundaries right now, so it may not go as smoothly as she'd like. Be patient with her, Elena. Don't let her become frustrated.'

'Why do I need to communicate with Paige at all? You can do that, right? You talk to her, I'll talk to you . . .'

'I have something else I need to do. I don't mean to be rude, my dear. I'm not abandoning you. With Paige's help, you'll get along fine without me. There's someone else who needs me more. They have another witch here. A child.'

'Savannah.'

'You've met her?'

'Seen her.'

'Horrible, isn't it?' Ruth's voice clogged with emotion. 'Just horrible. A child. How anyone could be so callous – but I can't dwell on that. I need to help her.'

'You can get her out of here?'

Silence. As it dragged past ten seconds, I wondered if someone had entered the hall. Then Ruth continued, 'No. Sadly, that's beyond my capabilities or I'd get you both out, along with every other poor soul in here. The best I can do is give the child the tools she'll need to survive. At her age, she has only the most rudimentary knowledge and can cast only very benign spells. I need to give her more. Accelerate her development. Not the path I'd choose under any other circumstances. It could be . . . well, it may not be the best thing, but given the choice between that and perishing . . . I'm sorry, my dear. I don't need to bother you with the details. Suffice it to say, I'll be busy with the child, though I'll contact you when I can. Now, here's what you'll need to do to help Paige communicate with you.'

Ruth told me how to prepare for Paige's telepathic spells. 'Be receptive' was the condensed version. Nothing terribly complicated. I might feel something like the grains of a tension headache. Instead of ignoring it, I had to relax and concentrate on clearing my mind. Paige would do the rest. Ruth would contact her tonight, let her know we were both safe, and give her some tips on how to work the spell so it would overcome the blocking field. Once I communicated with Paige, I could tell her how to contact Jeremy.

'Now,' Ruth said when she'd finished. 'One caution. You mustn't let Paige know about Eve's child. Savannah, I mean.'

'Did she know her?' I asked.

'Savannah? No. Eve left when she was pregnant. Paige probably doesn't even remember her. She was only a child herself then. No one was close to Eve. It doesn't matter. If Paige knows there's a young witch here, she'll insist on rescuing her immediately. If she couldn't get to her and something happened . . .' Ruth inhaled sharply. 'Paige would never forgive herself.'

'It won't matter. When we break out, we'll take Savannah.'

Ruth paused. When she spoke, there was a pain in her voice so deep I could feel it. 'No, you can't concern yourself with the child. Not now. I'll give Savannah what powers I can. You must concentrate on getting yourself out.'

'What about you?'

'It's of no consequence.'

'No consequence? I'm not leaving—'

'You'll do what you must, Elena. You're the important one now. You've met these people. You've seen this place.

That knowledge will be invaluable in helping the others fight this threat. As well, your escape will secure the aid of your Pack. If you don't get out – But you will. You'll get out, and your Pack will help the others to stop these people before they capture more of us. Then, when you return, you can worry about the child. If – when – you get her free, take her straight to Paige. That's important. After what I'm going to do for Savannah, only Paige will be able to control the damage. At least, I hope . . .' Her voice trailed off. 'I can't worry about it. Not now. The important—'

She stopped and fell silent. Then, 'Someone's coming, dear. I'll speak to you when I can. Be ready for Paige.'

'Expect the second ghost when the clock strikes two.'

Ruth chuckled. 'Poor Elena. This must be quite unsettling for you. You're doing fine, dear. Just fine. Now get some sleep. Good night.'

REJECTION

Bauer brought my breakfast the next morning, along with a coffee for herself. We settled at the table and, after getting the 'How's breakfast? How did you sleep?' formalities out of the way, I said, 'I'd really like to see Ruth. If it's possible.' I kept my eyes downcast, voice as near to groveling as I could manage. It stung like hell, but I had more important things than wounded dignity to consider.

Bauer was silent a moment, then laid her hand atop mine. I fought the urge to pull away and kept my gaze down so she wouldn't see my reaction.

'It isn't possible, Elena. I'm sorry. Doctor Matasumi and Colonel Tucker think it's a security risk. I can only push things so far before they start shoving back.'

'How is Ruth?' I asked. 'Still depressed?'

Bauer paused, then nodded. 'A bit. More adjustment problems than usual.'

'Maybe if she saw me. A familiar face.'

'No, Elena. Really, I can't. Please don't ask again.'

I picked up a slice of apple and nibbled at it, then said, 'Well, maybe she could have another visitor, then. What about Savannah? That might perk her up.'

Bauer tapped her nails against her mug. 'You know, that might not be such a bad idea. But, again, there's the security issue.'

'Is there? I thought Savannah hadn't come into her powers yet. Now with me, there's the danger that Ruth and I could plot something together. I understand that. But what kind of spells could Savannah cast that Ruth couldn't already do herself?'

'That's a good point. I'll mention it to Lawrence. Doctor Carmichael and I are worried about Ruth. A visit from Savannah might be just what she needs. Very thoughtful of you, Elena, to think of it.'

Hey, I'm a thoughtful kind of gal. No ulterior motives here. 'It might be good for Savannah, too,' I said. 'An older witch to talk to, now that her mother's dead.'

Bauer flinched at that. Good shot, Elena. Nice and low. I decided to pluck out the barb before it had time to fester. Continue my thoughtful ways . . . and keep worming into Bauer's good graces.

'I enjoyed meeting Leah yesterday,' I said. 'Thanks for arranging it.'

'I'll do what I can, Elena. I know this isn't . . . the best of circumstances.'

'Not as bad as it could be. Though I am going to miss a publication deadline if I'm not out by next week. I don't suppose there's any chance . . .'

Bauer gave a tiny smile. 'Sorry, Elena. No promises.'

'Worth a shot.' I finished my orange juice. 'So, when we were discussing careers yesterday, we forgot to ask you about yours. Do you work for the family business? Pulp and paper, right?'

'That's right. My father retired a few years back, so I head the business now.'

'Wow.'

A wan smile. 'There's very little "wow" about it. I'm only there because my father had the misfortune to sire only two children. My younger brother took over the company after my father retired. Actually, "took over" is a minor exaggeration. My father handed him the company. It proved to be too much for my brother. He killed himself in ninety-eight.'

'I'm sorry.'

'After that, I was the heir by default, much to my father's chagrin. If he hadn't had a stroke after my brother's death, he'd probably have taken the reins back rather than hand them to a woman. Like I said, old company, old family. A daughter's place is to marry well and bring fresh blood to the board of directors. Technically, I run the company, but in reality I'm only a figurehead, a woman still reasonably young and attractive enough to trot out at major functions, show the world how progressive the Bauer family is. CEOs, VPs, they do all the work. They think I can't handle it. It doesn't matter if I'm twice as smart as my brother was. Twice as ambitious. Twice as driven. But you must know what that's like.'

'Me? I don't really—'

'The only female werewolf? A bright, strong-willed young woman invading the last bastion of male exclusivity? Come on. This Pack of yours. They treat you like some kind of pet, don't they?'

'—They aren't like that.'

She was quiet. I glanced up from my breakfast to see her watching me with a smile of satisfaction, as if I'd said exactly what she wanted to hear.

'You get respect?' she asked.

I shrugged, hoping it would wipe the satisfaction from her smile. It didn't. Instead she inched forward in her chair. Her eyes burned with the same intensity I'd seen yesterday when she'd asked me about my life.

'You enjoy special status, don't you? The only female.'

'I wouldn't say that.'

She laughed. Triumph. 'I've talked to that other were-wolf, Elena. Patrick Lake. He knew everything about you. You speak for the Pack leader. You intercede with outside werewolves on his behalf. You can even make decisions in his stead.'

'I'm just a glorified mediator,' I said. 'When it comes to mutts, I do more housecleaning than policy-making.'

'But you are entrusted with the power to speak for the Alpha. Immense power in your world. The trusted aide of the most important werewolf and the lover of the second most important. All because you're the only female.'

She smiled as if unaware she'd just insulted me. I wanted to tell her that Clay and I fell in love before I became 'the only female werewolf' and that I'd *earned* any status I had with the Pack. But I wouldn't rise to the bait. I didn't need to. She only paused for breath before continuing.

'Do you know what's the worst thing about my life, Elena?'

I thought of rhyming off a list, but doubted she'd appreciate the effort.

'Boredom,' she said. 'I'm tied to a job no one will let me do, stuck in a life no one will let me lead. I've tried to take advantage of it, the spare time, the money. Mountain-climbing, alpine skiing, deep-sea diving. You name it. I've done it. The riskier and more expensive, the better. But do you know what? I'm not happy. I'm not fulfilled.'

'Huh.' A headache knotted behind my eyes.

Bauer leaned forward, 'I want more.'

'It must be difficult—'

'I deserve more,' she said.

Before I could try another response, she stood and sailed from the cell like a prima donna after her greatest performance.

'What the hell was that about?' I muttered after she'd left.

The headache tightened. Damn it, I was a mess. Trampled spine, punctured stomach, and now a headache. I thought about Bauer. Enough of your problems, lady, let's talk about mine. I chuckled to myself, then gasped as the laugh sent splinters of pain coursing through my skull. I rubbed the back of my neck. The pain only worsened. When I lay on the bed, the light overhead scorched my eyes. Damn it. I didn't have time for a headache. I had so much to do. Finish breakfast, shower, scrub the bloodstains off my shirt, plot how to escape this hellhole, and foil the villians' evil plans. A very busy timetable for someone confined to an underground cage.

I forced myself up from bed. The sudden movement felt like needles stabbing through my eyes. Tension headache? All things considered, I was entitled to one. Rubbing the back of my neck again, I headed for the shower.

'Elena?'

I turned and looked around. No one was there.

'Ruth?' I said, though the voice didn't sound like hers. It wasn't the way Ruth had communicated with me either. Ruth's voice had been audible. This one was more something I sensed or felt rather than heard.

'Elena? Come on!'

This time, I smiled. Though the voice was still a whisper, too faint to recognize, the exasperation was remarkably identifiable. Paige.

I closed my eyes, prepared to reply, and realized I had no idea what I was doing. It wasn't like talking to Jeremy. With Jeremy, communication took place in a dream state, where I imagined I could both see and hear him. It sounded and felt like natural conversation. This didn't. Paige's summons was the proverbial 'hearing voices in your head,' and auditory delusions weren't part of my normal psychopathology. How did I answer back? I tried mentally forming a response and waited.

'Come . . . ena. Answer . . . !'

Okay, she couldn't hear me and I was losing her. I concentrated harder, picturing myself saying the words. Silence returned.

'Paige?' I said, testing the words aloud. 'Are you there?'

No response. I called her again, mentally this time. Still nothing. The knot in my head loosened and I began to panic. Had I lost her? What if I couldn't do this? Damn it, concentrate. What had Ruth told me? Relax. Clear your head. My head was clear . . . well, excepting the frustration zipping through my brain. Concentrate, concentrate. No good. The harder I tried, the more I feared I couldn't do it. Now I was stressed. And Paige was gone. I took a deep breath. Forget this. Go have a shower. Dress. Relax. She'd try again . . . I hoped.

Paige's second attempt came about two hours later. This time I was lying in bed, reading a boring magazine article and half asleep. It must have been the perfect telepathy environment. When I heard her call, I responded without thinking, answering in my head.

'Good,' she said. '. . . there.'

'I can barely hear you,' I said.

'That's . . . you don't . . . experience.'

Although I couldn't hear the full sentence, I could guess at the missing content. I couldn't hear her because I was new at this. The problem had nothing to do with *her* inexperience. Naturally.

'. . . Ruth?'

'She's okay.'

'Good.' Louder, clearer, as if the reassurance added to the signal. 'How about you? Are you okay?'

'Surviving.'

'Good. Hold on then.'

'Hold—?'

Too late. The signal disconnected. I was alone. Again. Damn her.

Twenty minutes later, 'Okay, I'm back.'

Paige. Another easy contact, probably because, once again, I wasn't expecting it.

'You ready?' she asked.

'For what?'

The floor slid out from under me. I twisted to break my fall, but there was nothing there. No floor. No 'me.' The order to move came from my brain and went . . . nowhere. I was pitched into complete blackness, but I didn't lose consciousness. My brain went wild, issuing commands, move this, do that, look, sniff, listen, scream. Nothing. There was nothing to respond. I couldn't see, hear, speak, move, or smell. Every synapse in my brain exploded with panic. Absolute animal panic.

'Elena?'

I heard something! My mind scrambled back to sanity, clinging to that one word like a life raft. Who said that? Paige? No, not Paige. A man's voice. My heart leaped with recognition before my brain even figured it out.

'Jeremy?'

I said the word, didn't think it, but said it and heard it. Yet my lips didn't move and the voice I heard wasn't my own. It was Paige's.

I saw light. A blurred figure in front of me. Then a mental pop and everything became clear. I was sitting in a room. Jeremy stood in front of me.

'Jer?'

My words. Paige's voice. I tried standing. Nothing happened. I looked down and saw my hands resting on the arms of a chair, but they weren't my hands. The fingers were shorter, soft, bedecked with silver rings. I followed the line of my arm. Brown curls spilled over my shoulder, lying atop a dark green lily-of-the-valley print sundress. A sundress? This was definitely not my body.

219

'Elena?' Jeremy crouched in front of me – or not me. He frowned. 'Did this work? Are you there, sweetheart?'

'Jer?' I said again.

At the bottom of my field of vision, I saw my – the – lips move, but I felt nothing. Even my field of vision itself was skewed, the angle all wrong, like I was watching the scene though an oddly placed camera. I tried to shift upward, add some height to my position, but nothing happened. The sensation was unsettling to the point of panic. Was this what it was like to be paralyzed? My heart fluttered in my chest. I didn't feel it pounding, only perceived it in my mind, some gut-level awareness of my body's normal responses to fear, knowing that my heart should be fluttering, even if it wasn't.

'What—' I began. The voice was so alien in my ears that I had to stop. Swallowed. Mentally swallowed, I mean. If my throat moved, I wasn't aware of it. 'Where am I? *Who* am I? I can't move.'

Jeremy's face clouded. 'Didn't she?' He muttered something under his breath, then started again, calm. 'Paige didn't explain?'

'Explain what? What the hell is going on?'

'She's transported you to her body. You can see, hear, speak, but you won't have any sort of mobility. She didn't explain—?'

'No, she dumped me into limbo and I woke up here. Showing off.'

'I heard that,' a distant voice in my head said. Paige.

'She's still here,' I said. 'There. Somewhere. Eavesdropping.'

'I'm not eavesdropping,' Paige said. 'You have my body. Where am I supposed to go? I wasn't showing off. I knew you'd want to speak to Jeremy, so I wanted to surprise you. It should have been a smooth transition, but I guess your lack of experience—'

'My lack of experience?' I said.

'Ignore her,' Jeremy said.

'I heard that,' Paige said, quieter.

'How are you?' Jeremy asked. He laid his hand on mine. I saw it, but couldn't feel it and felt a pang of loss.

'Lonely,' I said, surprising myself. I lightened my tone. 'Not for lack of company, though. Seems I'm quite the popular "guest" around this place. But it's – I'm—' I inhaled. Pull yourself together, Elena. That was the last thing Jeremy needed, to hear me on the verge of an emotional breakdown. Where had this come from?

'I'm tired,' I said. 'Not sleeping well, not eating well, no exercise. So I'm touchy. Cabin fever, I guess. Physically, I'm fine. They aren't torturing me, beating me, starving me. Nothing like that. I'll be okay.'

'I know you will,' he said softly. He pulled up a chair. 'Do you feel up to talking about it?'

I told him about Bauer, Matasumi, rattled off some details on the guards and the other staff like Xavier, Tess, and Carmichael, giving him a rough picture of the situation. I explained as much as I could about the setup of the compound, then about the other captives, remembering Paige's silent presence and stopping myself before talking about Savannah.

'I'm only interested in getting you out,' Jeremy said

221

when I'd finished. 'We can't worry about the others.'

'I know.'

'How are you holding up?'

'Fi—'

'Don't say "fine," Elena.'

I paused. 'Is Clay . . . around? Maybe I could talk to him . . . Just for a few minutes. I know we have to keep this short. No time for socializing. But I'd like – if I could . . .'

Jeremy was quiet. Inside my head, Paige muttered something. Alarm zinged through me.

'He's okay, isn't he?' I asked. 'Nothing's happened—'

'Clay's fine,' Jeremy said. 'I know you'd like to speak to him, but it might not be . . . a good time. He's . . . sleeping.'

'Sleep—?' I began.

'I am not sleeping,' a voice growled from across the room. 'Not voluntarily, at least.'

I looked up to see Clay in the doorway, hair tousled, eyes dimmed by sedatives. He lumbered into the room like a bear awaking from hibernation.

'Clay,' I said, heart tripping so fast I could barely get his name out.

He stopped and fixed me with a scowl. My next words jammed in my throat. I swallowed them and tried again.

'Causing trouble again?' I asked, forcing a smile into my voice. 'What did you do to make Jeremy drug you up?'

His scowl hardened with something I'd seen in his face a million times, but never when he looked at me. Contempt. His lips twisted, and he opened his mouth to say something, then decided I wasn't worth the effort and turned his attention to Jeremy.

'Cl—' I began. My gut was solid rock. I couldn't breathe, could barely speak. 'Clay?'

'Sit down, Clayton,' Jeremy said. 'I'm talking to—'

'I can see who you're talking to.' Another twist of the lips. The briefest glare in my direction. 'And I don't know why you're wasting your time.'

'He thinks you're me,' Paige whispered.

I knew that. Deep down, I knew that, but it didn't help. I saw the way he looked at me, and it didn't matter who Clay *thought* was there, he was looking at me. Me.

'It's not Paige,' Jeremy said. 'It's Elena. She's communicating through Paige.'

Clay's expression didn't change. Didn't soften. Not even for a second. He turned his stare to me and I saw the disdain there, stronger now, hard and sharp.

'Is that what she told you?' he said. 'I know you want attention, Paige, but this is low. Even for you.'

'It's me, Clay,' I said. 'It's not Paige.'

He sneered, and I saw everything there that I'd never wanted to see in Clay's face when he looked at me, every drop of contempt he had for humans. I'd had nightmares of this, seeing him turn that look on me. I'd woken sweating, blood pounding, absolutely terrified, the way no childhood nightmare had ever frightened me. Now I looked at him and something snapped. The world went black.

REBIRTH

I awoke on the floor of my cell. I didn't get up. Had I been dreaming? I wanted to believe it, then chided myself for such a silly wish. Of course, I didn't want it to have been a dream. I wanted to believe I'd talked to Jeremy, conveyed all my observations to him, set the wheels of rescue in motion. Who cared about Clay? Okay, I cared. Cared more than I wanted to most times, but I had to put this thing in perspective. Clay hadn't looked at *me* that way. At least, he hadn't intended the look for me. Obviously he wasn't getting along with Paige, and frankly, that didn't surprise me. Where humans were concerned, Clay wasn't Mr. Congeniality at the best of times, and certainly not when said human was an overconfident, outspoken witch young enough to be one of his students. I lay on the floor and told myself all this, and it didn't help a bit. I felt . . . My mind clamped shut before the last word escaped, but I pried it back open. Admit it. I had to admit it, if only to myself. I felt rejected.

So what, right? I felt rejected. Big deal. But it was a big deal. Too big a deal. The second I owned up to the emotion, it engulfed me. I was a child again, taking the hand of a new foster parent, clasping it tight and praying I'd never have to let go. I was six, seven, eight years old, faces flipping before me like pages in a photo album, names I'd forgotten but faces I'd recognize if I saw them for a split second on a passing train. I heard voices, the drone of a television, my small body held tight against the wall, barely daring to breathe for fear of being overheard, listening to them talk, waiting for 'The Conversation.' The Conversation. Admitting to one another that it wasn't working out, that I was 'more than they bargained for.' Convincing themselves they'd been tricked by the agency, fooled into taking a blond-haired, blue-eyed doll, a broken doll. They hadn't been tricked. They hadn't listened. The agencies always tried to warn them about me, about my past. When I was five, I'd seen my parents killed in a car accident. I'd sat on the country road all night, trying desperately to wake them up, crying for help in the dark. No one found me until morning, and after that, well, I wasn't quite right after that. I withdrew into my mind, emerging only to throw fits of rage. I knew that I was spoiling things for myself. Every time a new foster family took me in, I swore to myself I'd make them fall in love with me; I'd be the perfect little angel they expected. But I couldn't do it. All I could do was sit in my head, watch myself scream and rant, wait for the final rejection, and know it was my fault.

I never tell that story. I hate it. Hate, hate, hate it. I refuse to let my past explain my present. I grew up, I grew stronger, I overcame it. End of story. From the time I was old enough to realize that my problems weren't my fault, I'd decided not to shift the blame to all those foster families, but to get rid of it. Throw it out. Move on. I could imagine no fate worse than becoming someone who tells the story of her dysfunctional childhood to every stranger on the bus. If I did well in life, I wanted people to say I did well, not that I did well 'all things considered.' My past was a private obstacle, not a public excuse.

Clay was the only person I'd ever told about my childhood. Jeremy knew bits and pieces, the parts Clay felt necessary to impart in those early days when Jeremy had to deal with me as a newly turned werewolf. I'd met Clay at the University of Toronto, where I was an undergrad with an interest in anthropology and he was giving a short lecture series. I fell for him. Fell hard and fast, not impressed by his looks or his bad-boy attitude, but by something I can't explain, something in him I hungered for, something I needed to touch. When he favored me with his attention, I knew that was something special, that he didn't open up to people any more than I did. As we grew closer, he told me about his own screwed-up childhood, glossing over details he couldn't impart without revealing his secret. He told me about his past, so I told him mine. As simple as that. I was in love and I trusted him. And he betrayed that trust in a way I'd never completely recovered from, as I would never recover from that endless night on the country road. I hadn't forgiven Clay. We'd moved past talk of forgiveness. It wasn't possible. And he'd never asked for it. I don't think he expected it. Over time, I'd learned to stop expecting myself to be able to give it.

Clay's motive for biting me was inexplicable. Oh, he'd tried to explain it. Many times. He'd brought me to

Stonehaven to meet Jeremy, and Jeremy had been planning to split us up, and Clay had panicked and bit me. Maybe it was true. Jeremy admitted he'd intended to end Clay's relationship with me. But I don't believe that Clay's bite had been unplanned. Maybe the timing was, but I think in some deep part of his psyche, he'd always been ready to do it if the need ever arose, if I ever threatened to leave him. So what happened after he bit me? Did we make up and move on? Not on your life. I made him pay and pay and pay. Clay had made my life hell, and I returned the favor tenfold. I'd stay at Stonehaven for months, even years, then leave without a moment's notice, refusing all contact, cutting him from my life completely. I'd sought out other men for sex and, once, for something more permanent. How did Clay react to this? He waited for me. He never looked for revenge, never tried to hurt me, never threatened to find someone else. I could be gone for a year, walk back into Stonehaven, and he'd be waiting as if I'd never left. Even when I'd tried to start a new life in Toronto, I'd always known that, if I needed him, Clay would be there for me. No matter how badly I fucked up or how badly fucked up I was, he'd never leave me. Never turn his back on me. Never reject me. And now, after more than a decade of learning that lesson, all it took was one look from him, one single look, and I was curled up on the floor, doubled over in pain. All the logic and reasoning in the world didn't change how I felt. As much as I wanted to believe I'd overcome my childhood, I hadn't. I probably never would.

* * *

Lunch came and went. Bauer didn't bring it, for which I was grateful. I didn't see her again until nearly six. When she opened my cell door, I double-checked the time, figuring either dinner was early or my watch had stopped. But she didn't bring food. And when she stepped through the door, I knew no early meal was forthcoming. Something was wrong.

Bauer walked in with none of her usual assertive grace. She half-tripped over an imaginary wrinkle in the carpet. Her face was flushed, cheeks bright spots of crimson, eyes glittering unnaturally bright, as if she had a fever. Two guards followed her in. She waved them toward me, and they bound me to the chair where I'd been reading a magazine. The whole time they were tying me up, Bauer refused to meet my eyes. Not good. Really not good.

'Go,' she said when they were done.

'Should we wait outside—' one began.

'I said go. Leave. Back to your posts.'

Once they were gone, she began to pace. Small, quick steps. Back and forth, back and forth. Fingers tapping her side, the mannerism changed now, not tapping with thoughtful slowness but fast. Manic. A mania to her pacing. To her eyes. To everything.

'Do you know what this is?'

She whipped something from her pocket and held it up. A syringe. Quarter-filled with a clear liquid. Oh, shit. What was she going to do to me?

'Look,' I said. 'If I did anything to upset—'

She waved the syringe. 'I asked if you knew what this was.'

The syringe slipped from her hands. She scrambled to retrieve it, as if the plastic would shatter upon striking the carpet. As she fumbled, I caught a whiff of a familiar smell. Fear. She was afraid. What looked like mania was a struggle for control, as she desperately tried to disown an emotion she wasn't accustomed to feeling.

'Do you know what this is, Elena?' Her voice rose an octave. Squeaked.

Was she afraid of me? Why now? What had I done?

'What is it?' I said.

'It's a saline solution mixed with your saliva.'

'My what?'

'Saliva, spit, gob.' Voice racing up the scales. Nervous giggle, like a little girl caught saying a bad word. 'Do you know what this can do?'

'I don't—'

'What will it do if I inject it into myself?'

'Inject—?'

'Think, Elena! Come on. You're not stupid. Your saliva. You bite someone. Your teeth piece their skin, like this needle piercing mine. Your saliva goes into their bloodstream. My bloodstream. What happens?'

'You'd turn— You could turn—'

'Into a werewolf.' She stopped pacing and went still. Completely still. A small smile tugged up her lips. 'That's exactly what I'm going to do.'

It took a moment for this to register. When it did, I blinked and opened my mouth, but nothing came out. I swallowed, fought for calm. Don't panic. Don't make it worse. Treat it as a joke. Diffuse the situation.

'Oh, come on,' I said. 'Is that the answer to your problems? You don't get respect at work so you'll become a werewolf? Get a good job with the Pack, knock some heads together, find yourself a handsome lover? 'Cause if that's what you're thinking, trust me, it don't work that way.'

'I'm not an idiot, Elena.'

She spat the words at me, spittle flinging from her lips. Ooops, wrong tactic.

'What I want is change,' she continued. 'To reinvent myself.'

'Becoming a werewolf isn't the answer,' I said softly. 'I know you're not happy—'

'You know nothing about me.'

'Then tell—'

'I came onto this project for one reason. For the chance to experience something new, something more dangerous, more exhilarating, more life-altering than scaling Mount Everest. Experiences all my money and influence can't buy. Spells, immortality, extrasensory perception, I didn't know what I wanted. Maybe a little of everything. But now I know exactly what I want, what I was looking for. Power. No more kowtowing to men, pretending I'm dumber than they are, weaker, less important. I want to be everything I have the potential to be. I want this.'

My brain still skidded, unable to find traction long enough to understand what Bauer was saying. The suddenness of it all overwhelmed me, almost convinced me I must be dreaming or hallucinating. Yet how sudden was it? Unbelievably so, from my perspective, but what about from hers? How long had she been watching the parade of inmates, waiting for the one who could give her the power she craved? Now, having found what she thought she wanted, perhaps she was afraid to hesitate, afraid she'd change her mind. I had to change it for her. But how?

Bauer held up the syringe. As she stared at it, she blinked, almost blanched. Fear so thick it clogged my nostrils unwittingly started my adrenaline pumping. When she looked back at me, the anger was gone. What I saw in those eyes stopped me cold. Pleading. Fear and pleading.

'I want you to understand, Elena. Help me. Don't make me use this thing.'

'You don't have to use it,' I said quietly. 'No one's going to make you.'

'Do it for me then. Please.'

'Do—?'

'Bite my arm.'

'I can't—'

'I have a knife. I'll cut the skin. You can just—'

Panic settled in my chest. 'No, I can't.'

'Help me do it right, Elena. I don't know how well the saline solution will work. I could only guess at the amount, the proportion. I need you—'

'No.'

'I'm *asking* you—'

I strained against my bonds, locking eyes with her. 'Listen to me, Sondra. Give me a minute and let me explain what'll happen to you if you use that. It isn't the way you think it is. You don't want to do this.'

Her eyes glittered then. All mania gone. Ice cold. 'I don't?'

She lifted the syringe.

'No!' I shouted, bucking in my chair.

She buried the needle into her arm, shoved the plunger down. And it was done. One second. One split second. As much time as it had taken Clay to bite me.

'Goddamn you!' I yelled. 'You stupid bitch— Call the infirmary. Now!'

Her face was preternaturally calm, lips curving in something like bliss. Blissful relief at having done it. 'Why, Elena? Why should I call the infirmary? So they can reverse it? Suck the gift from my veins like snake venom? Oh, no. We'll have none of that.'

'Call the infirmary! Guards! Where the hell are the guards?'

'You heard me send them away.'

'You don't know what you've done,' I snarled. 'You think this is some great gift. One prick of the needle and you're a werewolf? You did your research, didn't you? You know what happens now, right?'

Bauer turned her dreamy smile on me. 'I can feel it coursing through my blood. The change. It's warm. Tingling. The beginnings of metamorphosis.'

'Oh, that's not all you're going to feel.'

She closed her eyes, shuddered, reopened them, and smiled. 'Seems I've gained something tonight and you've lost something. You're no longer the only female werewolf, Elena.'

Her eyes widened then. Bulged. Veins in her neck and forehead popped up. She gasped, choked. Hands going to her throat. Body jerking upright. Spine snapping rigid. Eyes rolling. Rising to her toes, pitching forward and back, like a convict on the end of a hangman's noose. Then she collapsed, pooling to the floor. I screamed for help.

WINSLOE

'**W**hat did you do to Ms. Bauer?' Matasumi asked. Guards had collected Bauer soon after I started shouting. Twenty minutes later, they'd returned with Matasumi. He now stood there accusing me without a trace of accusation in his voice.

'I told the guards.' I sat on the edge of my bed, trying to relax, as if this sort of thing happened every day. 'She injected herself with my saliva.'

'And why would she do that?' Matasumi asked.

'The bite of a werewolf is one way of becoming a were-wolf.'

'I realize that. But why—' He stopped. 'Oh, I see.'

Did he? Did he *really* see? I doubted it. None of them could understand what was coming. I could, and I was trying very, very hard not to think about it.

Matasumi cleared his throat. 'You claim Ms. Bauer injected herself—'

'The syringe is on the floor.'

His eyes flickered to the needle, but he made no move to pick it up. 'You claim she used this syringe—'

'I don't *claim* anything. I'm telling you what happened.

She injected herself in the arm. Look for the needle mark. Test the contents of the syringe.'

The door opened. Carmichael hurried inside, lab coat billowing behind her.

'We don't have time for this,' she said. 'I need to know what to do for her.'

Matasumi waved Carmichael aside. 'First, we must establish the exact nature of Ms. Bauer's ailment. It's all very well for Ms. Michaels to claim—'

'She's telling the truth,' Carmichael said. 'I saw the needle mark.'

It would have been hard to miss. Even as the guards had carried Bauer from the cell, I'd seen the injection point, swollen to the size of a ping-pong ball. A memory of my own bite leaped to mind, but I shoved it back. Cold, clinical observation. That was the only way I could deal with this. Take notes from Matasumi.

Carmichael turned to me. 'I need to know how to deal with this. Sondra's unconscious. Her pressure's dropping. Her temperature's sky-rocketing. Her pupils won't react to stimuli. Her pulse is racing and becoming erratic.'

'There's nothing I can do.'

'You've been through this, Elena. You lived through it.'

I said nothing. Carmichael advanced on me. I eased back on the bed, but she only came closer, pushing her face into mine until I could smell her frustration. I turned my head. She grabbed my chin and wrenched my face back to hers. 'She's dying, Elena. Dying horribly.'

'It'll only get worse.'

Her fingers tightened, digging into my jaw muscles. 'You

are going to help her. If it was you up there, I wouldn't stand by and watch you die. Tell me how to help her.'

'You want to help her? Put a bullet through her head. Skip the silver variety. Regular lead will do.'

Carmichael flung my chin aside and stepped back to stare at me. 'My God, you are cold.'

I said nothing.

'This isn't helping,' Matasumi said. 'Treat the symptoms as you see them, Doctor Carmichael. That's the best we can do. If Ms. Bauer inflicted this misfortune on herself, then all we can do is treat the symptoms and leave the rest to fate.'

'That's not the best we can do,' Carmichael said, her eyes boring into mine.

I didn't want to defend myself. I really didn't. But the weight of that glare was too much.

'What exactly do you think I can do?' I asked. 'I don't run around biting humans and nursing them back to health. Do you know how many newly bitten werewolves I've met? None. Zero. It doesn't happen. I've never even been around a hereditary werewolf who's come of age. I don't know what to do.'

'You've been through it.'

'You think I took notes? Do you know what I remember? I remember Hell. Complete with fire and brimstone, demons and imps, red-hot pinchers and bottomless pits of lava. I remember what I saw up here.' I smacked my palm against my forehead. 'I remember what I imagined, what I dreamed. Nightmares, delirium, that's all there was. I don't know shit about temperatures and blood pressure and pupil response.

Someone else dealt with that. And when it was all over, I didn't want to know what he did. All I wanted was to forget.'

'These visions of Hell,' Matasumi said. 'Perhaps you could describe them for me later. The connection between the supernatural and Satanic ritual—'

'For God's sake, leave it alone,' Carmichael said. 'For once. Leave it alone.'

She strode from the room. Matasumi bent for the syringe, then stopped, motioned for a guard to pick it up and followed Carmichael.

Would I have helped Bauer if I could? I don't know. Why should I? She kidnapped me and threw me in a cage. Did I owe her anything? Hell, no. If the woman was stupid enough to turn herself into a werewolf, that wasn't my problem. Did I do or say anything to make her embrace such unbelievable folly? Did I regale her with stories of the wonderful, fun-filled life of a werewolf? Anything but. Did I seek revenge by encouraging her to plunge that needle into her arm? Absolutely not. Yes, she was my enemy, but she'd brought this on herself. So why did I feel responsible? I wasn't. Yet part of me wished I could help, at least alleviate her suffering. Why? Because I understood that suffering. This was another woman who'd become a werewolf, and as different as our circumstances were, I didn't want her to suffer. The outcome would almost certainly be death. I hoped it came quickly.

At midnight, Winsloe walked into my cell. Through the shadows of an impending nightmare, I heard the door open, subconsciously realized the sound came from the real world, and forced myself awake, grateful for the diversion. I rolled out of bed and stood, to see Tyrone Winsloe standing in my cell doorway, framed by the hallway light, presenting himself, waiting for my acknowledgement. A disconcerting surge of awe ran through me. It was like having Bill Gates show up on my doorstep – no matter how much I wanted to be *not* impressed, I couldn't help myself.

'So this is the female werewolf.' He stepped inside, flanked by two guards. 'A pleasure to make your acquaintance,' he said with a mock bow. 'I'm Ty Winsloe.'

He introduced himself, not with modesty, as if I might not recognize him, but with a smarmy self-importance, an introduction as phony as the bow. When I didn't respond fast enough, a tremor of annoyance unsettled his features.

'Promethean Fire,' he said, prompting me with the name of his world-famous company.

'Yes, I know.'

His face rearranged itself back into a gratified smirk. Motioning the guards to stay put, he stepped farther into the cell. His gaze inched over me, walking around, giving my backside a slow once-over, scrutinizing me without embarrassment, as if I were a potential slave in a Roman marketplace. When he circled back to my front, his gaze paused at my chest, lips curving downward in a disappointed frown.

'Not bad,' he said. 'Nothing a couple of implants couldn't fix.'

I narrowed my eyes. He didn't seem to notice.

'Ever thought of that?' he asked, circling back to my front, gaze settling on my chest.

238

'I don't plan to have kids, but if I ever do, I'm sure they'll find this set quite adequate.'

He threw back his head and laughed as if this were the funniest thing he'd ever heard. Then he leaned around me and swept his gaze over my rear again.

'Great ass, though.'

I sat down. He only smiled and continued studying my lower half. Then he tossed a bundle of clothes on the table.

'You can leave the jeans on,' he said. 'I brought a skirt, but I like the jeans. That ass was made for jeans. I don't like big, flabby asses.'

He liked women with little butts and big tits? Someone had played with one too many Barbie dolls as a kid. I glanced at the pile of clothes but made no move to take it.

'The shirt has to go,' he said. 'There's a halter top there. Skip the bra.'

I stared at him, unable to believe what I was hearing. This was a joke, right? Billionaires were supposed to be eccentric, so this must be Winsloe's warped idea of a practical joke. Yet as I stared, his lips compressed, not in a smile but in pique.

'Take the clothes, Elena,' he said, all joviality draining from his voice.

Behind him, the two guards stepped forward, fingering their guns as if to remind me of their presence. Okay, maybe it wasn't a joke. What was with the people in this place? Within several hours I'd seen an intelligent woman turn herself into a werewolf and met a billionaire with the maturity and mind-set of an adolescent boy. Compared to this bunch, I was downright normal.

Still, I reminded myself, Tyrone Winsloe was in charge here, and he was a man accustomed to getting what he wanted when he wanted it. But if he thought I was changing into a halter top so he could leer at my substandard breasts – well, a girl's gotta set limits, right? I'd been treated this way by mutts, though I knew how to handle them. If they talked like that, I told them off. If they touched me, I broke their fingers. They wouldn't want it any other way. As Logan always said, mutts liked their women with balls. Ty Winsloe wasn't a mutt, but he was a guy with his hormones in overdrive. Close enough.

'My arms are still burned,' I said, turning away from the clothing. 'They look like shit.'

'I don't mind.'

'I do.'

One long moment of silence.

'I asked you to put on the top, Elena,' he said. He looked down at me, lips twisted in a humorless, teeth-baring grin that any wolf would have recognized.

I glanced from him to the guards, snatched the halter top from the pile, killed the urge to return Winsloe's warning snarl, and settled for stalking into the bathroom.

Going into the bathroom to change was a waste of time, considering the see-through wall, but I could still turn my back to him as I switched shirts. The halter top would have fit a prepubescent girl – a short prepubescent girl. It rode up to my rib cage and cut furrows in my shoulders. Looking down, I saw that it left absolutely nothing to the imagination. First, it was skintight. Second, it was white.

Twin dark circles pressed against the fabric. If I caught even the slightest breeze, that wasn't all that would be pressing against it. A wave of humiliated fury flooded me. After everything that had happened in the last twelve hours, this was the pinnacle. The proverbial straw. I would not take this. I would – I stopped. I would do *what?* I remembered the look in Winsloe's eyes when I'd challenged his command to change. I remembered Armen Haig's comments on Winsloe's mental state. What would Winsloe do if I refused? Was I willing to take that risk over something as ultimately trivial as not wanting to wear a revealing shirt? I rubbed my hands over my face, resisted the urge to cross protective arms over my chest, and marched back into the cell.

Winsloe studied my chest for two whole minutes. I know because I counted the seconds, struggling not to spend the time fantasizing about retaliation. This was nothing, I told myself. Nothing. But it was. Somehow, being forced to parade my tits in front of this man was worse than any torture Matasumi could have devised with his box of toys. I realized then that this juvenile farce had nothing to do with getting me into a halter top. It was about power. Winsloe could make me put on this halter top and there wasn't a damn thing I could do about it. He wanted to make sure I knew it.

'At least they're firm,' Winsloe said. 'Not bad, really, if you like them small. I think implants are still our best bet, though.'

I bit my lip. Bit it hard enough to taste blood and wish it was his.

'Amazing tone,' he said circling me. 'Lean and tight, but no bulk. I was worried about bulk. Muscles on a girl are downright creepy.'

'Oh, I have muscles,' I said. 'Wanna see them?'

He only laughed. 'That hole in the wall tells me all I need to know. Plus I saw the video of you and Lake, though I guess that wasn't so much strength as cunning. Quick wits. Very quick.'

'How's Ba— Ms. Bauer?' I asked, hoping to change the subject.

'You know about that?' He wriggled his butt onto my dining table and perched there. 'I guess you would. Bizarre, huh? No one saw it coming. Sondra's always been so together. Uptight, even. Guess it's the rigid ones that snap the hardest, huh? About that video—'

'How is she?' I repeated. 'What's the prognosis?'

'Shitty, last I heard. Probably won't make it through the night. Now, speaking of that video, I have some news you'll like.' He smiled, his partner's impending death already forgotten. 'Wanna guess what it is?'

'I couldn't begin to imagine.'

'Tonight I'm sending your fellow combatant to his final reward. The great doggie bone in the sky – or the other direction. We're gonna have ourselves a hunt.'

'A . . . hunt?'

He jumped off the table. 'A hunt. A big ol' wolfie hunt. Tonight. Larry's done with your "mutt" and we're gonna give him a proper send-off.' Winsloe snapped his fingers at the two guards, whose presence at this debacle I'd been trying hard to ignore. 'Chop-chop, boys. Get on the horn and tell your buddies to prepare the guest of honor. We'll meet them at the lookout.'

I'd spent most of the last half-hour gaping at Winsloe. Now my disbelief was mingled with something else. Dawning horror. Did he mean what I thought he meant? He was going to hunt Patrick Lake? Release him and hunt him down like the prize quarry at some big-game reserve? No, I must be mistaken. I had to be mistaken.

'Well?' he said, turning to me. 'Grab that jacket from the table. It's getting cold out there. Wouldn't want you to catch pneumonia.'

'I'm going outside?' I said slowly.

Winsloe laughed. 'We sure as hell can't hunt him in here.'

He threw back his head, barking a laugh, slapped me on the rear, and waltzed from the cell.

GAME

The night was cold for late summer. It was still August, wasn't it? I calculated back. Yes, still August. It only seemed like I'd been gone longer.

If I'd hoped to pick up any clues to our location by going outside, I was disappointed. We took an elevator two flights up to ground level, exited through a secured door, and emerged a dozen feet from a forest that could have existed anywhere from Cape Breton to northern California. Maybe if I'd known my regional fauna better, I could have narrowed the possibilities, but examining trees was the furthest thing from my mind.

My wrists were manacled. Winsloe walked in front of me. The two guards, guns now drawn, followed behind. A path wove through thick forest to a clearing where a lookout stand towered a hundred feet in the air. Patrick Lake stood at the base of a wooden pillar, stamping his feet against the cold, both hands cupped around a lit cigarette.

'Hey,' he said as we neared. 'What's going on? It's fucking cold out here.'

'Finish your smoke,' Winsloe said. 'You'll be plenty warm soon enough.'

'I asked—'

One of Lake's guards jabbed him with a rifle butt.

Lake snarled, lifted a hand to swat the guard, then stopped himself. 'I was only asking—'

'It's a surprise,' Winsloe said, grabbing the ladder railing. 'Finish your smoke.'

'What's she doing here?' Lake waved his cigarette at me.

Winsloe was twenty steps up. He leaned over the railing. 'It's a surprise,' he repeated. 'We'll start as soon as you're ready.'

Lake pitched his cigarette to the ground and stomped it. 'I'm ready now.'

'Then we begin.'

'Release point two?' a guard asked.

'As planned,' Winsloe said. 'Everything as planned.'

Winsloe continued his ascent. I followed, with our two guards close behind. By the time we reached the top, Winsloe was puffing. I surveyed the forest below. Lake and his guard duo had disappeared into the darkness.

'Over there,' Winsloe panted, waving to the east. 'Release point two. Release point one just below. Release point three by the river.'

Not only was there a predesignated release point, but there was more than one. Why? I opened my mouth to ask, then realized I might not want to know.

'The choice of release point depends on the quarry,' Winsloe continued. 'So far I've done a witch and a half-demon.'

'You – hunted them?'

He made a face. 'Not much of a hunt. Especially the

245

witch. You'd think she'd have been more of a challenge, casting spells and all that. In RPGs the magical races can be your strongest players once they gain enough experience. But in real life? She fell apart. Couldn't take it. Cast a few penny-ante spells and quit. Found her curled up under a bush. No survival instinct. Like that old lady they picked up with you. First sign of trouble and she sinks into depression. Can't take the pressure.'

I eyed the ground below. Wondered if it was hard enough to kill Winsloe if he took a tumble.

'The half-demon was a minor improvement. At least he tried. I didn't hunt him, though. That was an escape. We fixed the problem soon enough, so don't let that give you any ideas. He didn't get far anyway. Dogs took care of him. From what I hear, he was even worse than the witch. Ran full out until he collapsed.'

'So now—' I cleared my throat, forced calm. 'So now you're going to hunt Lake.'

'A werewolf.' Winsloe lowered his binoculars to grin at me. 'Cool, huh? The hunter becomes the hunted. That's the trick, the challenge. All that "Most Dangerous Game" bullshit is just fantasy crap. Put your average modern guy in the woods and he freaks. Take away his tools and his weapons and you might as well go deer hunting. At least deer have some experience eluding hunters. Humans have nada. But wolves? They *are* the hunters. They have their own tools, their own weapons. They know the forest. Combine that with human intelligence and bingo: You've got yourself the ultimate big game.' He held out the binoculars. 'Want to have a look?'

I shook my head.

'Go on. They're night vision. Not that you'd need them, I guess. I hear you guys can see in the dark. That's why I'm doing this at night. Added challenge. Of course, I have all the latest toys, like these. Wouldn't want it to be *too* much of a challenge.'

I lifted the binoculars to my eyes. Looking out, all I saw was forest. Endless forest. Then a flash of orange light.

'The flare,' Winsloe said, voice rising with excitement. 'They've stunned Lake. Now they'll take off. In ten, maybe fifteen minutes he'll wake up all alone in the woods. If he has half a brain, he'll realize it's a trick, but he'll run anyway. My guess is he'll smell the river and run west. Better be careful, though. If he takes the easy route, he'll find himself in a bear pit.' Winsloe laughed, the sound taking on a grating edge. 'Traps everywhere. Here, here, over here.'

I turned to see him pointing at places on a laminated map. When I stepped closer, he whisked it out of sight and waggled a finger at me.

'Uh-uh. Can't have you learn all my secrets. You like those binoculars?'

'They . . . work well.'

'Of course they do. I wouldn't buy them otherwise. Wait until you see the rest of my gadgets. And the weapons.' He rolled his eyes in near lust. 'The weapons. Unbelievable what they come up with these days. I have lockers of them scattered all over the playing field, so I'll have variety. Only thing missing is a nail gun. That's the pisser. The nail gun's always my favorite.'

'You hunt with a nail gun?'

'Not out here. In games, of course. The nail gun is the absolute best. The shredding factor can top grenades.'

'Games,' I repeated. 'You mean video games.'

'What other kind is there?'

I looked out at the forest beyond. The playing field, he'd called it. A giant, custom-designed playing field stocked with high-tech gadgets, booby traps, and an arsenal of weapons.

'That's what this is,' I said slowly. 'A video game. A real-life video game.'

'One step up from virtual reality. Actual reality. What a concept.' He grinned and slapped me on the rear again. 'Let's move. The game is afoot.'

We met Lake's two guards before we reached the main path. They confirmed that the release had gone smoothly, then they took up position in front of Winsloe, guns drawn, flanking him for protection. I walked behind Winsloe. The other two guards followed, side by side, at my rear. Everyone except me wore night-vision goggles. Even I could have used a pair. The darkness was nearly complete, a weak crescent moon darting between clouds and treetops, no stars in sight. My vision faded in and out with the moon. Not that there was much to see. Nothing but trees, trees, and more trees.

Despite the ball of dread nestled in my gut, my heart began tripping with anticipation as we moved deeper into the woods. Even while my brain knew what I was doing here, my body refused to believe it. It took in the stimuli – the crisp night air, the scent of rotting leaves and damp earth, the sounds of voles and mice scampering from our path – and formed its own interpretation, based on years of experience. I was walking through the woods at night, ergo I must be going for a run. Ignoring all commands to the contrary, my body reacted like an excited puppy straining at its leash. My skin prickled. My blood drummed. My breathing quickened. On the plus side, my senses sharpened, letting me see, hear, and smell twice as well. On the minus side, there was that niggling worry about contorting body parts and unsightly hair growth.

Before quashing my body's reaction, I used my heightened awareness to get a better sense of my surroundings. Sight-wise, it didn't help much. No matter how well I could see, I didn't have X-ray vision, so I couldn't see through the damned trees. My other senses were more helpful. A few minutes of listening convinced me there was nothing to hear. Well, there was plenty to hear – creaking branches, whispering breezes, predators and prey hooting, squealing, bolting, and diving – but that wasn't what I wanted. I hoped for some distant sound of civilization, and the only ones I detected were the chugs and wheezes of the machinery that kept the compound running. I switched to smell, my best sense. Again, I searched for human life and found only the stink of the main building and the gravel road that led to it. The odor of the road was faint, indicating it ran south of the compound. Unfortunately, the forest was to the north, which was the direction I'd run if I escaped the compound. While there might be an easy way out to the south, it was safer to stick with what I knew, and right now all I'd seen was this forest.

Beyond the compound, the wilderness gave off only its

own scents. Nature reigned here. Even the path bore mere traces of human scent, as if nature fiercely wiped it clean the moment human trespassers were gone. Again, my brain and body vied for interpretation. My body thought it was in heaven, a natural paradise as pristine as that at Stonehaven and – even better – a fresh paradise ripe for exploration. My brain decided it was in hell, an endless forest with no civilization in sight. If I escaped, I had to go somewhere. Somewhere meant a house, a town, a public place where my pursuers might fear to follow.

Escaping now was out of the question. Even if I made it past the armed guards, I'd only become an added attraction on Ty Winsloe's hunt. I'd have to wait, but I still hoped to break out of the compound at some point, preferably before my captors got bored with me as they had with Patrick Lake. If I – no, *when* I – escaped, where would I go? There was nothing out here but forest. Endless forest. I could run and run for hours and— Wait a second. What the hell was I saying? I'm a wolf. Half-wolf, at least. Gee, what's a wolf going to do in the wilderness? Duh. Survive, of course. Here I could escape my pursuers better than I could in any concrete jungle. This was my element. Even now, in human form, I was at home here, able to see in the near-dark, able to smell water and food, able to hear the quietest owl swoop overhead. I didn't need the safety net of civilization. Well, eventually, I would need to find a way back to the others, but I could outlast any human that tried to recapture me – night-vision goggles, high-powered telescopes, and all. I'd need to be careful, but the only danger I'd face would come from my pursuers. I certainly didn't need to worry about dying of starvation, dehydration, or exposure.

'Where's his clothing?' Winsloe snapped.

I skidded to a halt before I ran into Winsloe's broad back. Surfacing from my reverie, I blinked and looked around. We stood beside a tree bedecked with strips of fluorescent orange plastic.

'This is release point two,' Winsloe said.

'Yes, sir,' said one of the front guards, pulling a map from his pocket and holding it out.

Winsloe smacked the map to the ground. 'I wasn't *asking*. I was *telling*. I know this is release point two. I want to know if you morons know it. Is this where you released Lake?'

The guard's jaw tightened, but his voice remained deferential. 'Of course, sir.'

Winsloe spun on me. 'He has to undress to change into a wolf, doesn't he? Either that or he'd rip his clothes, right?'

I nodded.

'So either way, there should be clothes here. Where are they?'

I made a show of looking around, though I could tell with a single sniff that Lake hadn't left anything behind. 'If they're not here, then he hasn't changed forms.'

Winsloe wheeled to one of the rear guards. 'Pendecki. Checkpoints.'

The guard to my left rear wore a black bandolier covered in gadgets, with looping wires connecting them to a battery pack. He calmly pulled one from its holster and flicked a switch. The device blipped, red LED lights blinking, like one of those early handheld video games.

'The target has passed checkpoints five and twelve, sir.'

'We have visual at five,' Winsloe said.

'Yes, sir. Checkpoint five has a motion-sensor camera and—'

'I'm not *asking*! I'm telling!' Winsloe said. 'Show me the fucking tape!'

Still unruffled, Pendecki unclipped another gadget, unfastened its connecting wire, and held it out to Winsloe, who snatched it with a curse. Pendecki's expression didn't change. Either he was accustomed to dealing with Winsloe or he'd worked with men like him before. The other three guards weren't nearly so cool under pressure. One of the foreguards had begun to sweat. The other kicked his toes against the earth as if trying to stay warm. Pendecki's partner stood motionless, tensed for trouble.

Winsloe held a small back-and-white screen. Out of the corner of my eye, I watched as he pounded tiny buttons. A tape rewound and played, showing a few seconds of infrared video. An arm and leg appeared on screen, then vanished. Winsloe hit buttons and watched it again.

'He's not a wolf,' he said, lifting his head. 'Can someone tell me why he isn't a wolf?'

Of course, no one could. Except me. I waited until all eyes turned my way, then said, 'A lot of non-Pack werewolves can't Change on demand.' Even as the words left my mouth. I regretted them. They led to a painfully obvious next question.

'Non-Pack,' Winsloe said. 'So Lake can't shape-shift when he wants. But you can.'

'It depends on—'

'Of course you can,' Winsloe said. 'I saw the tape.'

I realized then why I was here. I'd assumed Winsloe had invited me along to impress me with his game, one hunter showing off to another. Maybe that was part of it. But there was a deeper reason why he'd told me about his gadgets and traps and weapons but hadn't let me near his map. He was warning me. If I screwed up, if I displeased him, this would be my fate. Matasumi might not be done with me, but Winsloe wouldn't care. He was young and rich and powerful. Delayed gratification wasn't in his vocabulary. Right now, he wanted a hunt. If Lake couldn't provide it, I could.

I felt my lips move, heard words come out. I tried to persuade myself that what I said next was born of my will to survive. But it didn't feel that way. It felt like cowardice. No, worse than cowardice. It felt like treason.

'He'll Change if he's frightened.'

Winsloe smiled, all teeth. 'Then let's frighten him.'

FAILURE

'Checkpoint eight four minutes ago,' Pendecki said. Winsloe glanced over his shoulder at me, boyish excitement back in his eyes. 'Just so you know, I don't use checkpoint tracking when I hunt. Not terribly sporting, old chap. The camera setup wasn't even my idea. Tucker insisted on it. You know Tucker? Head guard?'

I nodded, teeth chattering. I told myself it wasn't that cold, but I couldn't stop shivering.

'Old-style military. So rigid you couldn't shove a dog tag up his ass. After the shaman got loose, he figured we needed these trip-wire cameras. Later, when we got Lake, I decided the cameras might come in handy for my hunts. Like I said, not to use them for tracking, but to make sure he stays within the perimeter of the playing field. We have miles to go until we reach the edge of the property, but I figure werewolves are the one monster that might be able to run that far.'

'What if he does get that far? Will you let him go?'

'Oh, sure. A hundred yards beyond the perimeter is home free. That's my rule. Of course with these cameras, we pretty much ensure he'll never make it that far.'

'Checkpoint twelve, sir. Sorry to interrupt, but we're close enough that there's no delay on the signal.'

'He just passed it?'

'Affirmative.'

Winsloe grinned. 'Pick up the pace, then.'

As a group, we jogged along the path.

'Checkpoint twelve again, sir.'

'Circling,' Winsloe crowed. 'Perfect. Good doggie. Wait right there.'

'We're coming up to twelve—'

Winsloe raised his hand for us to stop. His head bobbed in the darkness. Then he pointed to the northeast, where I could smell Lake about seventy feet away. Undergrowth crackled. Winsloe's grin broadened. He reached into his jacket. With his other hand, he waved a complex series of motions. The guards nodded. The front two lifted their rifles. The rear two silently laid theirs on the ground and pulled pistols from beneath their coats. Winsloe withdrew a grenade from his jacket. He turned to me with a grin and a wink, as if he hadn't been contemplating my death only minutes before.

Winsloe pulled the pin from the grenade and pitched it through the air. The moment he released it, the rear guards took off, each circling in opposite directions around the grenade's path. The front guards pointed their rifles farther afield. As the grenade detonated, the guards fired. The forest exploded with firepower.

'Run, fucker, run,' Winsloe chortled. He grinned back at me. 'Think that'll scare him?'

'If it didn't kill him.'

Winsloe waved aside my pessimism, then paused and grinned. 'Hear that? He's on the move. Fall out, boys. We have a runner.'

Chaos ensued. At least to me it was chaos. Six humans running half-blind through thick forest after a panicking werewolf was not my idea of graceful pursuit. The more we ran, the more racket we raised, the more we spooked Lake, the more he ran. A vicious circle that ended only when Winsloe stopped, panting and leaning against a tree for support.

'Gotta give him a chance to change forms,' Winsloe wheezed.

'Good idea, sir,' Pendecki said, darkness hiding the sarcastic glint in his eyes from all but me.

Winsloe bent double at the waist, gasping for breath. 'Is the air thinner up here?'

'Could be, sir.'

Had we run up a hill? Hmmm, can't say I noticed it.

'So, he'll change forms now?' Winsloe asked me.

'He should,' I said.

If he's not worn out, I thought. With any luck, after the initial run and this chase, Lake would be too exhausted to Change. Why did I hope this? Because I didn't want Winsloe to get his hunt. I wanted this game to be as disappointing as the others. If Lake didn't give Winsloe the adrenaline rush he wanted, Winsloe would abandon werewolves as his theoretical 'ultimate' prey and look elsewhere, as he had after hunting a witch and a half-demon.

If Lake fulfilled Winsloe's expectations, he'd soon be scouring the cells for another victim and, seeing as how I was the only remaining werewolf, it wasn't hard to guess where his attention would fall. He might like to tart me up and concoct a few jerk-off fantasies, but I suspect Ty Winsloe got off on his hunting conquests more than he did with the sexual variety.

A moan shivered through the trees. Winsloe stopped panting and lifted his head. Another moan, deep, drawn out. The hairs on my arms pricked.

'Wind?' Winsloe mouthed.

Pendecki shook his head.

Winsloe grinned and motioned us toward the noise. We crept through the forest until one fore-guard lifted his hand and pointed. Through the brush, something pale flickered. I inhaled, then choked on a sudden gasp. The stink of fear and panic flooded the clearing, the scent so strong I wondered if Lake had lost control of his bowels.

Winsloe hunkered down and inched forward.

'No,' I hissed, grabbing the back of Winsloe's jacket. 'He's Changing.'

Winsloe only grinned. 'I know.'

'You don't want to see that.'

The grin broadened. 'Oh yes, I do.'

One of the nameless guards butted his rifle against my arm, knocking my hand from Winsloe's jacket. I turned to glare at him, but he was already past me, overtaking Winsloe. I crouched and waited for him to stop Winsloe. Instead, the guard circled past him and tugged a sheaf of greenery from Lake's hiding spot.

'Jesus Christ!' the guard yelled, leaping to his feet. 'What the fuck—!'

As he'd jumped up, he'd torn the fern from its roots, exposing the clearing. A blur of pale flesh flashed from within, then a shriek that set my teeth on edge. Lake rolled to the ground, legs up, protecting his underbelly. For a moment, he moved too fast for anyone to see more than skin. Then he lay still and everyone saw more. Much more.

A hairless, lipless muzzle protruded from the middle of Lake's face, his still-human nose grotesquely stuck on top, nostrils flared wide. His eyes were on the sides of his head where his human ears should have been. His ears had grown, bat-like now, stopped midway on their ascent to the top of his skull. Sparse fur webbed his fingers and toes. A naked stump of tail batted the ground between his legs. The slice I'd cut in his leg pulsated bright pink where his stretching skin had ripped the scabs free. His back was hunched and twisted, swallowing his neck and pulling his head into his chest.

'What the fuck happened to him?' the guard shouted, still falling back, hand going to his gun.

Fury filled me. This was not something anyone should see, the absolute most private part of a werewolf's life. This was a werewolf at his most vulnerable, naked and hideous, a true monster, but one stripped of even the most basic means of self-protection. Mutt or not, at that moment, Lake was closer to me than these gaping, stinking humans.

'He's Changing,' I snarled. 'What the hell did you think it looked like?'

'Not like that,' Winsloe said, staring like a kid at a carnival freak show. 'Holy shit. Can you believe that? That is the most disgusting—'

Lake's lipless muzzle contorted in a bellow of pain. The guard poked his rifle into the clearing and prodded Lake.

'Stop that!' I shouted, turning on the guard. 'Back off and let him finish.'

Lake writhed on his back, clubbed hands crossed to protect his vital organs. The guard pushed his gun forward again. Pendecki lunged and grabbed the barrel.

'She's right,' Pendecki said. 'If you want your hunt, sir, I'd suggest we do as she says. Back off and let him finish . . . whatever he's doing.'

Winsloe sighed. 'I suppose so. But sometime I've gotta see this.'

'Wait a few days,' I said. 'You can watch Sondra Bauer go through it.'

'If she lives.' He sighed, not at the prospect of his colleague's death, but at the thought that her imminent death might ruin his chance to see a werewolf Change. 'Okay. Stop teasing the brute, Bryce. About face, boys. Fall back.'

Pendecki and the two other guards backed out of the clearing. Bryce ignored the command, but Winsloe didn't notice, his attention engrossed in the spectacle before us. As Lake lay still curled in the fetal position, his flesh began to writhe, as if snakes were trapped under his skin. Hair sprouted like reverse dominos, leaping up in a straight line from his wrist to his shoulder.

'Jesus!' Winsloe said.

The hair retracted and Lake convulsed, moaning.

'Get back,' I hissed. 'He can't—'

Winsloe waved me into silence and inched forward. Lake's head spun wildly, trying to watch Winsloe from both skewed eyes at once. His back arched and twin rows of muscles sprang from his neck, thickening it to twice its width. The tendons pulsated, grew, shrank, grew, shrank. The Change stopped there, only the neck muscles moving from human to wolf and back again.

'What's wrong?' Winsloe asked, not taking his eyes from Lake.

Lake was stuck between forms. I didn't say that to Winsloe. I didn't dare open my mouth for fear that, if I moved at all, it would be to grab Winsloe by the shoulders and fling him into the bushes beyond, which would earn me a certain bullet from the guards. As I watched Lake, I prayed the seizure would end. Let him become a wolf or a human. Something. Anything. He was doomed, but to die like this? My guts went cold at the thought. Every werewolf's subconscious nightmare was to become stuck between forms, caught in this monstrous, misshapen body, unable to change either way. The ultimate horror.

Lake rolled from side to side, panting and sweating and making ghastly mewling sounds. Muscles jerked and spasmed at random. Only his neck changed forms, tendons growing and shrinking. He gave one huge, gagging convulsion and flipped onto his other side. Looking straight at me. I turned away.

'Shoot him,' I said quietly.

'What the fuck?' Winsloe scrambled up to glare at me.

'Who's giving the orders around here? You don't tell me what to do. Not ever.'

'He's caught,' I said. 'He can't finish and he can't change back.'

'We'll wait.'

'I won't—'

'I said, we'll wait.'

'Then move back.' I forced myself to add, 'Please. Give him some privacy.'

Winsloe grunted and shot me another lethal glare, but waved the others back, though the other three guards were already ten feet from the thicket. Bryce couldn't resist one last prod. As he pushed his rifle forward, Lake's hands flew to his sides.

'Watch—!' I began.

With an inhuman shriek, Lake pushed off on his arms and flung himself at Bryce. The guard fired. Lake squealed and tumbled backward, hit the ground, and skittered into the undergrowth, trailing blood in a slug's path behind him.

'What the hell are you doing?' Winsloe bellowed. 'You shot him!'

'He attacked—'

'Get back!' Winsloe shouted, spittle flying. 'All of you. Get back. Now!'

The undergrowth rustled. Everyone jumped. Bryce and another guard lifted their weapons.

'Guns down!' Winsloe said. 'Put the fucking guns down!'

We all froze and listened to the silence. Lake's smell was everywhere. I swiveled my head, honing in on it.

'Okay,' Winsloe said, inhaling deeply. 'Well, that was a

royal fuckup. Now, here's what we're going to do, and if I hear one more goddamn gunshot, it better be from me. Is that—'

The bushes exploded. Bryce raised his rifle.

'Don't you fucking dare!' Winsloe screamed.

Lake's misshapen body sailed through the air. Two shots rang out. I dropped. The ground shuddered once, then twice. A moan. A very human moan. I lifted my head to see Bryce beside me on the grass, his head to the side, eyes locked with mine. His mouth opened. Bloody foam bubbled out. He coughed once. Then he went still. I tore my gaze from his dead eyes and looked around. Lake lay on my other side, a bloody hole in his forehead.

I struggled to my feet, trying to figure out how Lake could have killed Bryce so quickly. As I stood, I saw the bullet hole in Bryce's chest. Behind him, Winsloe flung his pistol to the ground.

'Can you believe it?' he shouted. 'Can you fucking believe it? I ordered him not to fire. A direct order. He killed my werewolf. He fucking shot my werewolf.'

Only Pendecki moved, but his limbs wouldn't coordinate. He dropped awkwardly, knelt beside Bryce's corpse, fingers trembling as he felt for a pulse.

'Dumb fuck!' Winsloe shouted to the sky. He clenched his fists at his sides, face purple with rage. Stepping forward, he kicked Bryce's body. 'I ordered him not to fire. Did anyone hear me order him not to fire?'

'Y – yes, sir,' Pendecki said.

Winsloe spun on me. My heart stopped.

'Get her out of here,' he said. 'Take her back to her

fucking cage. Go. All of you. Get out of my fucking sight before I—' He strode to where his pistol lay in the grass.

We were out of his sight before he turned around.

NURSE

I was next.

When the guards returned me to my cell, I sat on the edge of my bed and didn't move for three hours. Winsloe's hunt had been a bigger disaster than I could have dreamed. That was what I'd wanted, right? In the forest it had seemed so clear to me. If the hunt failed, I'd be safe. But I wasn't safe. I was next.

I'd reasoned that if Winsloe didn't get what he wanted from Lake, he'd move on. I'd been wrong. Tonight hadn't been a minor disappointment for Winsloe. It had been failure. Abject failure. How would he react to that? Get pissed off, stomp his feet, murder a guard, and move on to a new source of amusement? Sure. That was just the kind of reaction to failure that would have helped Winsloe build one of the biggest corporations in the computer industry. No, this 'setback' wouldn't stop Winsloe. To people like Tyrone Winsloe failure wasn't an obstacle simply to be overcome, but to be blown into the stratosphere, destroyed so thoroughly that it wouldn't leave even as much as a scorch mark on his pride. Having failed – and failed before an audience of inferiors – he'd step back, analyze the situation, hone in on the source of his defeat, fix it, and start over. When he'd determined what had gone wrong and ensured it wouldn't happen again, he would come for me. I couldn't wait around to be rescued. I had to act.

Now, this made perfect sense, this talk of action. But I'd hardly spent the last three days lounging around my cell ignoring perfectly good avenues of escape. If I knew how to get out, I'd damned well have done it. My one and only plan had been to ingratiate myself with Bauer. Great plan, really, barring the small matter of her turning herself into a werewolf and dying. Okay, she wasn't dead yet, but even if she recovered, she'd be in no shape to help me. Or would she? I hadn't lied to Carmichael when I'd said I couldn't help Bauer. But Jeremy could. If I could communicate with him, maybe I could save Bauer's life, and if I saved her life, maybe she'd feel indebted enough to help me. Way too many ifs and maybes in that plan, but it was all I had.

I formulated my course of action with a logical detachment that half-impressed and half-scared me. Sitting on the bed, watching the digital clock flip past minutes, then hours, I felt nothing. Absolutely nothing. I remembered Clay's rejection and felt nothing. I remembered Bauer plunging the syringe into her arm and felt nothing. I remembered Lake caught in his Change, the guard lying dead beside me, Winsloe's frustrated rage. Still I felt nothing. Two-thirty, three, three-thirty. The passage of time engrossed every particle of my attention. At four o'clock I came up with my plan. At four-thirty I looked at the clock and realized a half-hour had passed. Where had it gone? What had I done? It didn't matter. Nothing mattered, really. Jeremy and Paige would be sleeping. I shouldn't bother them. Five o'clock. Maybe I should try contacting Paige. Be ready with Jeremy's advice when the guards brought my breakfast. Still, it took effort. So much effort. Much easier to watch the clock and wait. All the time in the world. Five-thirty. Perhaps Jeremy would be up now. I wouldn't want to wake him. It wasn't really that important. I could try, though. It might take a while to get hold of Paige. No sense delaying. Six o'clock. Six—? Where—? Never mind. Give it a try.

I tried. Nothing happened. Of course nothing happened. What made me think it would? I wasn't the one with the telepathic abilities. Yet this thought never occurred to me. I mentally called for Paige, and when she didn't answer, I thought, 'Huh, that's strange,' and kept trying. Okay, so my brain wasn't working on all cylinders. In the last twelve hours I'd been rejected by my lover, watched my only hope for freedom turn herself into a werewolf, and discovered that the leading investor in this project was a psycho with a fetish for athletic women and monster hunting. I was entitled to blow a few mental circuits.

Eventually I accepted that I couldn't contact Paige. So I waited for her to contact me. And I waited. And waited. Breakfast came. I ignored it. Breakfast went.

At nine-thirty, Paige tried to contact me. Or I think she did. It started with a headache, like the day before. On the first twinge of tension, I'd leaped into bed, stretched out, closed my eyes, and waited. Nothing happened. The headache decreased, vanished, then returned a half-hour later. I was still in bed, afraid even to change position for fear I'd screw up Paige's transmission. Again, nothing

266

happened. I relaxed. I imagined opening myself up, imagined talking to Paige, imagined every possible bit of conducive imagery I could. Not so much as the barest whisper rewarded my efforts.

What if Paige couldn't contact me? What if she wasn't strong enough, if the last time had been a fluke? What if I'd screwed things up when I'd inadvertently severed the connection? What if, even now, some deep part of my psyche resisted contact, terrified of further rejection? What if the damage was permanent? What if I was on my own . . . for good?

No, that wasn't possible. Paige would be back. She'd find a way, and I'd talk to Jeremy and everything would be fine. This was temporary. Maybe she hadn't even been trying to contact me. Maybe I just had a headache, completely understandable given the circumstances.

Paige would be back, but I wouldn't sit around waiting. Action was the only true cure for panic. I had a plan. Yes, it would be easier if I had Jeremy's advice, but I could start on my own. All I needed to do was remember my own transformation by reaching into the deepest, most carefully suppressed crevices of my psyche and dredging up memories of Hell. No problem.

Two hours later, drenched in sweat, I tore free of my memories. For the next twenty minutes, I sat on the edge of my bed, collecting myself. Then I went and had a shower. I was ready.

At lunch I told the guards I wanted to see Carmichael. They didn't respond. They never spoke to me more than necessary. A half-hour later, as I'd begun to suspect they'd ignored my request, they returned with Matasumi. That complicated my plan. While Matasumi seemed to want to help Bauer, he was not inclined to do so at the cost of letting me out of my cage. If he had his way, I don't think captives would set foot outside their cells from the moment they were captured until someone came to dispose of the carcass.

Eventually I persuaded Matasumi to take me upstairs, provided I was manacled, in leg irons, and accompanied by a cadre of guards to prevent me from getting within ten feet of Matasumi. At the infirmary, Matasumi left to find Carmichael. Three guards escorted me inside while the others blocked the exit through the waiting room.

Bauer lay on the first bed. Beside her, Tess read a paperback mystery and worried a cuticle. When Tess saw me, she jerked up in alarm, then noticed the guards and settled for scooting her chair back six inches before she resumed reading.

Lying on the hospital bed, Bauer looked even more regal and composed than she had in life. Her dark blond hair fanned out across a pristine white pillow. The fine lines around her eyes and mouth had vanished, smoothed into the face of someone half her age. Her eyes were closed, lashes lying against flawless white skin. Her full lips curved in the faintest of smiles. Absolutely still, composed, and ethereally beautiful. In short, she looked dead.

Only the graceful rise and fall of her chest told me I wasn't too late, that they hadn't laid Bauer out for a viewing. Still, the urge to compliment the mortuary cosmetician was almost overwhelming. Almost. I kept my comments to myself. Somehow I doubted my audience would appreciate them.

'Peaceful, isn't she,' Carmichael's voice said from behind me.

'She's not restrained,' I said as Carmichael walked around the bed and waved Tess out.

'The sides of the bed are high enough to prevent accidents.'

'Not the type I'm thinking of. She needs arm and leg restraints. The best you can find.'

'She's sleeping soundly. I'm not—'

'Restrain her or I leave.'

Carmichael stopped checking Bauer's pulse and looked up sharply. 'Don't threaten me, Elena. You've admitted to Doctor Matasumi that you can help Sondra, and you will, with no conditions. At the first sign of a violent reaction, I'll restrain her.'

'You won't be able to.'

'Then the guards will do it. I want her to be comfortable. If that's all I can do, that's good enough.'

'Noble sentiments. Ever wonder how comfortable we are in the cell block? Or don't we count? Not being human and all, I suppose we aren't covered under the Hippocratic oath.'

'Don't start that.' Carmichael resumed her survey of Bauer's vital signs.

'You have your reasons for doing this, right? Good, moral reasons. Like everyone else here. Can I guess yours? Let's see . . . discover unimaginable medical breakthroughs that will benefit all of humankind. Am I close?'

Carmichael's mouth tightened, but she kept her eyes on Bauer.

'Wow,' I said. 'Good guess. So you justify imprisoning,

torturing, and killing innocent beings in the hopes of creating a human super-race? Where'd you get your license, Doctor? Auschwitz?'

Her hand clenched around her stethoscope, and I thought she was going to hurl it at me. Instead, she gripped it until her knuckles whitened, then she inhaled and looked past me to the guards.

'Please return Ms. Michaels to her—' She stopped and swiveled her gaze to mine. 'No, that's what you want, isn't it? To be sent back to your cell, relieved of your obligations. Well, I won't do it. You're going to tell me how to treat her.'

Bauer's body went stiff. One tremor shuddered through her. Then her arms flew out, ramrod straight. Her back arched against the bed, and she started to convulse.

'Grab her legs,' Carmichael shouted.

'Restrain her.'

Both Bauer's legs flew up, one knee knocking Carmichael in the chest as she leaned over to hold her down. Carmichael flew back, air whooshing from her lungs, but she rebounded in a second and threw herself over Bauer's torso. The guards jogged across the room and fanned out around the bed. One grabbed Bauer's ankles. Her legs convulsed, and he lost his grip, sailing backward and toppling a cart to the floor. The other two guards looked at one another. One reached for his gun.

'No!' Carmichael said. 'It's only a seizure. Elena, grab her legs!'

I stepped away from the table. 'Restrain her.'

Bauer's upper body shot up, hurling Carmichael to the floor. Bauer sat straight up, then her arms flew up, windmilling in a perfect circle. When they passed her head, they didn't veer from their course to allow for the normal range of motion. Instead they went straight back. There was a dull double snap as her shoulders disconnected.

Carmichael grabbed the slender straps that hung from the bedsides. I was about to say that Bauer needed to be restrained with something ten times stronger, but I knew I'd already gone too far, turning this into a battle of wills that the doctor wouldn't forfeit. The guard who had grabbed Bauer's legs earlier took a tentative step forward.

'Get back!' I snarled.

I walked toward the end of the bed, ignoring Carmichael's frantic efforts to attach the bed restraints, paying attention only to the movements of Bauer's legs. As I passed the spilled cart, I picked up two rolls of bandages. I counted the seconds between convulsions, waited for the next one to subside, then grasped both of Bauer's ankles in one hand.

'Take this,' I said, throwing one bandage roll at the nearest guard. 'Tie one end to her ankle, the other to the bed. Don't make it tight. She'll break her own legs. Move fast. You have twenty seconds left.'

As I talked, I tied Bauer's left leg to the bedpost, leaving enough room for her to move without hurting herself. Carmichael picked up another bandage roll from the floor and reached for Bauer's arms, ducking as one flailed awkwardly.

'Count off—' I began.

'I know,' Carmichael snapped.

We managed to get Bauer's arms, legs, and torso loosely tied to the bed, so she could convulse without hurting herself. Sweat poured from her in musky, stinking rivulets. Piss and diarrhea added their own stench to the bouquet. Bauer gagged, spewing greenish, foul-smelling bile down her nightgown. Then she started to seize again, torso arching up in an impossibly perfect half-circle off the bed. She howled, closed eyes bulging against the lids. Carmichael ran across the room to a tray of syringes.

'Tranquilizers?' I asked. 'You can't do that.'

Carmichael filled a syringe. 'She's in pain.'

'Her body has to work through this. Tranquilizers will only make it harder the next time.'

'So what do you expect me to do?'

'Nothing,' I said, collapsing into a chair. 'Sit back, relax, observe. Maybe take notes. I'm sure Doctor Matasumi wouldn't want you to ignore such a unique educational opportunity.'

Bauer's seizures ended an hour later. By then her body was so exhausted she didn't even flinch when Carmichael fixed her dislocated shoulders. Around dinnertime we had another mini-crisis when Bauer's temperature soared. Again, I warned Carmichael against any but the most benign first-aid procedures. Cool compresses, water squeezed between parched lips, and plenty of patience. As much as possible, Bauer's body had to be left alone to work through the transformation. Once her temperature dropped, Bauer slept, which was the best and most humane medicine of all.

When nothing else happened by ten o'clock, Carmichael let the guards return me to my cell. I showered, put my clothes back on, and left the bathroom to find I wasn't alone.

'Get off my bed,' I said.

'Long day?' Xavier asked.

I hurled my towel at him, but he only teleported to the head of the bed.

'Touchy, touchy. I was hoping for a more hospitable greeting. Aren't you bored with talking to humans yet?'

'The last time we spoke, you tossed me – handcuffed – into a room with a very pissed-off mutt.'

'I didn't toss you in. You were already there.'

I growled and grabbed a book from the shelf. Xavier vanished. I waited for the shimmer that presaged his reappearance, then launched the book.

'Shit,' he grunted as the book hit his chest. 'You learn fast. And you carry a grudge. I don't know why. It wasn't like you couldn't handle Lake. I was right there. If something had gone wrong, I could have stopped him.'

'I'm sure you would have, too.'

'Of course I would. I was under strict orders not to let anything happen to you.'

I grabbed another book.

Xavier held up his arms to ward it off. 'Hey, come on. Play nice. I came down here to talk to you.'

'About what?'

'Whatever. I'm bored.'

I resisted the urge to pitch the book and shoved it back on the shelf. 'Well, you can always turn yourself into a werewolf. That seems to be the common cure for ennui around here.'

He settled farther back on the bed. 'No kidding. Can you believe that? Sondra, of all people. Not that I can't imagine a human wanting to be something else, but she must have a few screws loose to do it like that. It's bound to happen, though. All the exposure. Inferiority complexes are inevitable.'

'Inferiority complexes?'

'Sure.' He caught my expression and rolled his eyes. 'Oh, please. Don't tell me you're one of those who thinks humans and supernaturals are equal. We have all the advantages of being human plus more. That makes us superior. So now you get these humans who, after a lifetime of thinking they're at the top of the evolutionary ladder, realize they aren't. Worse yet, they discover they *could* be something better. They can't become half-demons, of course. But when humans see what the other races can do, they'll want it. That's the rotten core of this whole plan. No matter how high-minded their motives, they'll all eventually want a piece. The other day—'

He stopped, glanced at the one-way glass as if checking for eavesdroppers, then vanished for a second and reappeared. 'The other day, I walked into Larry's office, and you know what he was doing? Practicing a spell. Now, he says he was conducting scientific research, but you know that's a pile of horseshit. Sondra is only the beginning.'

'So what are you going to do about it?'

'Do?' His eyes widened. 'If the human race is intent on destroying itself, that's its problem. So long as they pay me big bucks to help, I'm a happy guy.'

'Nice attitude.'

'Honest attitude. So tell me—'

The door clicked and he stopped. When it whooshed

open, two guards walked in, led by an older uniformed man with a grizzled crew cut and piercing blue eyes.

'Reese,' he growled at Xavier. 'What are you doing here?'

'Just keeping our inmates happy. The female ones at least. Elena, this is Tucker. He prefers Colonel Tucker, but his military discharge was a bit iffy. Borderline court martial and all that.'

'Reese—' Tucker started, then stopped, pulled himself upright, and turned to me. 'You're wanted upstairs, Miss. Doctor Carmichael asked for you.'

'Is Ms. Bauer okay?' I asked.

'Doctor Carmichael asked us to bring you up.'

'Never expect a direct answer from ex-military,' Xavier said. He hopped from the bed. 'I'll take you upstairs.'

'We don't need your help, Reese,' Tucker said, but Xavier had already hustled me out the door.

As I passed Ruth's cell, I noticed it was empty.

'Is Ruth okay?' I asked.

'No one told you?' Xavier said. 'I heard you made a suggestion to Sondra before she flipped out.'

'Suggestion? Oh, right. For Ruth to visit with Savannah. They let her?'

'Better yet. Come take a look.'

Xavier headed down the row of cells.

CRISES

'**D**octor Carmichael wants her upstairs now,' Tucker said.

Xavier kept walking, so I followed. I glanced in each cell as we passed. Armen Haig sat at his table reading a *National Geographic*. Leah napped in bed. The Vodoun priest's cell was empty. Had Matasumi 'removed' him from the program? I shivered at the thought, yet another reminder of what happened when captives outlived their usefulness.

When we came to Savannah's cell, Xavier reached for the door handle.

'Don't you dare,' Tucker hissed, striding toward us.

'Relax, old man. You'll give yourself a heart attack.'

'I'm in better shape than you'll ever be, boy. You're not taking this . . . young lady into that cell.'

'Why? Afraid of what'll happen? Four supernatural beings in one place. Imagine the incredible concentration of psychic energy,' Xavier said in a passable imitation of Matasumi.

Xavier pushed open the door. Savannah and Ruth sat at the table, heads bent together as Ruth drew imaginary lines on the tabletop. As the door opened, they jerked apart.

'Oh, it's just you,' Savannah said as Xavier stepped inside. 'What's the matter? Can't zap through walls anymore? That'd be a shame, losing your one and only power.'

'Isn't she a sweetheart?' Xavier said, looking back at me as Ruth shushed Savannah.

Ignoring the older woman, Savannah stood and craned her neck to see behind Xavier.

'Who's with you?' she asked.

'A guest,' Xavier said. 'But if you're not going to be nice—'

Savannah dodged past him and looked up at me. She smiled. 'You're the new one, the werewolf.'

'Her name's Elena, dear,' Ruth said. 'It's not polite—'

'A werewolf. Now that's a *real* power,' Savannah said, shooting a look at Xavier.

'Come in, Elena,' Ruth said. When I did, she embraced me. 'How are you, dear?'

'Surviving.'

'I heard the most awful thing about that poor Miss Bauer—'

'So what happens when you change into a wolf?' Savannah asked. 'Does it hurt? Is it gross? I saw this movie once, about werewolves, and the muzzle came right through this guy's mouth and ripped his head—'

'Savannah!' Ruth said.

'It's okay,' I said, smiling. 'But we don't have much time. They're taking me upstairs.' I glanced at Ruth. 'Is everything going well?'

Ruth looked at Savannah. A beam of pride penetrated her exasperation.

'Very well,' Ruth said.

'Tucker's getting restless,' Xavier said. 'We should go.'

'Bring her back sometime,' Savannah said, returning to her seat. 'I'm out of Mars bars, too.'

'And remind me what should compel me to do you these favors?' Xavier said. 'Your boundless charm?'

Savannah gave a mock sigh, eyes twinkling with a cunning that was half-child, half-woman. 'Fine. Get me some candy bars and I'll play Monopoly with you. Since you get so bo-o-o-red.'

'I don't think that's such a good idea, dear,' Ruth whispered.

'It's okay,' Savannah said. 'He's a really shi— crappy player. We can both beat him.'

There was still something I needed to say to Ruth, but I had no idea how to do it without Xavier overhearing. I didn't dare ask to speak to Ruth in private. Even if I could, where would we find privacy in a glass cube?

'You're having trouble contacting Paige,' Ruth said.

I jumped and glanced over at Xavier. He was still bantering with Savannah.

'He can't hear me,' Ruth said. 'Don't answer aloud, though. The spell only works for me. Just nod.'

I nodded.

Ruth sighed. 'I was afraid of that. I spoke to her yesterday, but when I tried this morning, I couldn't contact either you or her. Perhaps it's because I'm concentrating too much of my energy on the child. I had no idea how powerful Savannah would be. Her mother had great potential, but she never lived up to it. Too undisciplined. Too inclined toward . . . darker things. With the proper training, this one could be—' She stopped. 'But that's witch business. I won't bore you with it. Just please make sure you get her to Paige. After what I'm doing, Savannah must not be left on her own. As for renewing contact, try to relax, dear. It will come. If my energy returns, I'll communicate with Paige myself and get a message to you.'

'—poker?' Savannah was asking me.

'Hmmm?' I said.

'Do you play poker,' she said. 'Xavier says he won't play because we need a fourth person, but I think he's just scared he'll get beat by a girl.'

'Good night, Savannah,' Xavier said, ushering me out of the cell.

'Not the dark Mars bars,' Savannah called after him as the door closed. 'They give me zits.'

Xavier chuckled and pulled the door shut. Tucker still stood in the hall, arms crossed.

'So?' Xavier asked him. 'See any unidentified flying objects? Did the walls come crumbling down?'

Tucker only glared. Xavier grinned and led me toward the exit.

'You don't believe that psychic energy explanation?' I asked as we walked. 'What do you think it is? A poltergeist?'

'Polt—?' he started, then his lips curled. 'Leah.'

'She seems to think—'

'I know what she thinks.' Xavier opened the security door. 'Her poltergeist theory.'

'There you are!' a voice called.

I looked to see Carmichael bearing down on us.

'You,' she said to Xavier. 'I should have guessed. I asked for Elena over twenty minutes ago.'

'If it was an emergency, you'd have come yourself,' Xavier said.

'It's an emergency now.' She waved him off. 'Go make yourself useful for once. Maybe you can help—'

Xavier vanished. Carmichael sighed and shook her head, then grabbed my elbow and propelled me onto the elevator. As we headed down the corridor to the infirmary, I caught a few snatches of conversation from behind a closed door. Soundproofing muffled the voices nearly to the point of obscurity, even for me. One sounded like Matasumi. The other was unfamiliar, male with undertones of a lilting accent.

'Vampires?' the unfamiliar voice said. 'Who gave him permission to capture a vampire?'

'No one needs to give him permission,' Matasumi said, his voice a near-whisper, though nobody except a werewolf could possibly hear through the soundproofed walls. 'With Sondra incapacitated, he's starting to throw his weight around. He wants you to tell us where we can find a vampire.'

'He' had to be Winsloe. And the second man? Bauer said the sorcerer was helping them find potential captives. Was this the elusive Isaac Katzen? I slowed to listen as we passed the door.

'You're wasting your time with this, Lawrence,' the man said. 'You know you are. You have to put your foot down. Tell him no. I gave him two werewolves. That's enough. We have to stick with the higher races, the spell-casters and half-demons. Werewolves and vampires are common brutes, driven entirely by physical needs. They have no higher purpose. No higher use.'

'That's not entirely true,' Matasumi said. 'Though I agree that we should concentrate on the spell-casters, the were-wolves are providing invaluable insights into the nature of physical and sensory power. A vampire might be useful for—'

'Goddamn it! I don't believe this! You're as bad as Sondra! Seduced by . . .'

His voice trailed off as Carmichael propelled me down the hall. I pretended to stumble, giving myself time to hear more, but the voices hushed until I couldn't stall any longer and followed Carmichael into the infirmary.

There was no emergency. The spot where Bauer had injected herself was gushing a thick, stinking, blood-streaked pus and had swollen to the size of a golf ball, which threatened to cut off circulation to her lower arm. Okay, maybe that would normally seem like a cause for alarm, but in the meta-morphosis from human to werewolf it was only one of several dozen potentially life-threatening hurdles. Again, I advised Carmichael against fancy medical cures. The transforma-tion had to run its course. Simple, almost primitive medi-cine was the only solution. In this case, that meant draining the wound, applying compresses to reduce the swelling and watching for temperature spikes. During it all, Bauer stayed asleep. She hadn't once regained full consciousness since collapsing in my cell. Nature had taken over, shutting the brain down to divert all resources to the body during this crucial period.

Once the crisis passed, Carmichael decided I should move permanently into the infirmary. Hey, I wasn't arguing. Anything to be out of my cell and one level closer to freedom. Naturally, Matasumi wasn't fond of the idea. He argued with Carmichael and, as usual, lost. I was given a cot in the infirmary and round-the-clock guards, one in the room and two outside the door. Then I made a demand of my own. I wanted my manacles removed. If Bauer regained consciousness, I needed to be able to defend myself. The three of us argued over this, but Matasumi and Carmichael finally relented, agreeing to remove my handcuffs in return for posting a second guard inside the room.

Still convinced I'd hear from Paige, I mentally compiled a list of questions to ask Jeremy. There were so many things I couldn't recall from my own transformation. I remembered him explaining that he couldn't give me anything for the pain, constantly reiterating the 'nature must run its course' line, but on one occasion he'd administered sedatives. Why? I couldn't remember, but it meant there must be exceptions to the 'no drugs' rule. So what were they? How bad did things have to get before *not* drugging Bauer would be more dangerous than drugging her? What about the restraints? How tight was too tight? How loose was too loose? Madness added strength, but did that make Bauer stronger than an experienced, physically fit werewolf like myself? And what about the saliva transfer? A bite injected a limited amount of saliva. Bauer had overdosed. Was that a problem? Would the fact that she'd injected the saliva instead of receiving it through a bite cause problems? I was sure Jeremy would know. All I needed to do was talk to him.

It didn't happen. I lay awake as long as I could, but after thirty-six stress-filled, sleepless hours, I couldn't fend off slumber for long. Paige never contacted me.

The next day began with back-to-back medical crises. First, more seizures. Then, before Bauer recovered from that, she stopped breathing. Her throat swelled and the muscles thickened as she started to change from human to wolf. Her underlying anatomy wasn't ready yet for the transformation, so while her neck altered, the inside of her throat – windpipe, esophagus, whatever – remained human. Don't ask me for specifics. I'm no doctor. Even Carmichael seemed baffled. The point was that Bauer stopped breathing. If we spent time wondering why, she would have suffocated. I tilted her head back, straightening her windpipe, and massaged her neck, pressuring it back into human form. That worked, but too slowly. Carmichael began worrying about oxygen deprivation, and I had to agree. So she performed an emergency tracheotomy. Lots of fun. Once Bauer was breathing, we could relax. For a while.

Being in the infirmary had more advantages than I'd imagined. Not only was I closer to freedom, but after the first day people treated me much the same way they did Tess. I became not an inmate, but Carmichael's assistant, unimportant enough in the overall hierarchy that my presence was ignored. In other words, people talked around me as though I was part of the furnishings. Matasumi talked to

Carmichael, the guards talked to one another, Tess talked to the cute janitor. Everyone talked. And I listened. Amazing what I could pick up, not only tips about the compound and its organizational structure, but petty things like which guards had a reputation for slacking off. Fascinating stuff.

Later that day, I even got to see Armen Haig again and the Vodoun priest, Curtis Zaid, who was still very much alive. I didn't have much luck with Zaid. If, as Bauer had implied, Leah had befriended the Vodoun priest, she had even better social skills than I thought. When I tried talking to Zaid, he blocked even such pleasantries as 'good morning' with baleful glares and silence. Definitely not a potential ally. Armen, on the other hand, was a very promising prospect. He not only wanted to escape – and wanted help – but he'd been doing his homework. He knew the security system, the guards' rotations, and the compound layout. Better yet, he managed to convey this information to me right in front of Carmichael, working it into such banal conversation that she never even noticed. Observant, canny, and extremely bright. My kind of guy . . . for an escape partner, that is.

EXIT

The next crisis was another bout of seizures. After we'd subdued Bauer, I couldn't sit still. I prowled the infirmary, touching this, playing with that, until my knee banged a steel cart and Carmichael finally looked up from her paperwork.

'Would you sit down?' she snapped. 'Before you break something.'

I walked to the chair, looked at it, then paced to Bauer's IV.

'Don't—' Carmichael began.

'What's in there?'

'It's a general solution, mostly water with—' Carmichael stopped, seeing that I'd already moved on, my attention now caught by the beeping heart-rate monitor. 'Is it close to your time to Change?'

I considered it. I'd last Changed early Monday morning, almost five days ago. Like most werewolves, my cycle ran weekly. That meant, although I could Change as often as I liked, I needed to Change at least once a week, or risk having my body force a Change. Already I could feel the restlessness coursing through me. Soon my muscles would start to twinge and ache. For now, though, I could control it. I had a few days left. If I had to Change in this place, they'd probably put me in a secure cell with a full audience and a videographer. I'd endure a whole lotta aches and pains before I let that happen.

'No, not yet,' I said. 'I'm just restless. I'm not used to being in such a confined space.'

Carmichael capped her pen. 'I could probably arrange for you to take a walk through the compound. Under sufficient guard. I should have recommended some exercise in your program.'

'Exercise?' said a voice from the door. 'Don't be talking like that in my compound.'

'Hello, Tyrone,' Carmichael said without turning to face him. 'Did you need something?'

Winsloe sauntered into the room and grinned at me. 'Just what you've got there. Thought I'd keep Elena company for a while, let you do your work.'

'That's very . . . considerate of you, Tyrone, but I'm afraid you'll have to wait if you need to speak to Ms. Michaels. I was about to call for some additional guards to take her for a walk. She's restless.'

'Restless? Is she ready to Change?'

'No, she is not.' Carmichael thumped her clipboard onto the counter and headed for the intercom.

'It should be soon. Maybe she needs—'

'She doesn't.'

Carmichael hit the intercom button. Winsloe walked behind her and clicked it off.

'You said she needs exercise?' Winsloe said. 'What about

the weight room? Get some extra guards and I'll escort her myself.'

Carmichael paused, looked from Winsloe to me, then said, 'I don't think that's such a wise idea. A walk—'

'Won't be enough,' Winsloe said, grinning his little-boy grin. 'Will it, Elena?'

I considered it. While I'd rather walk and explore the compound, I also had to ingratiate myself with Winsloe, to give him a reason to keep me alive. 'A weight room would be better.'

Carmichael's eyes met mine, conveying the message that I didn't have to go with Winsloe if I didn't want to. When I glanced away, she said, 'Fine,' and punched the intercom button.

We left my two in-room guards at the infirmary, gathered the two at the door, and added three more, meaning I was guarded by more than double the firepower and muscle they'd left with Bauer. Skewed priorities, but nobody asked my opinion, and I'd only waste my breath offering it. I was surprised Carmichael didn't send all the guards with me and cover Bauer by herself.

The weight room wasn't any larger or better equipped than the one at Stonehaven. It was little more than fifteen feet square with a multiuse weight machine, free weights, a punching bag, a treadmill, a ski machine, and a StairMaster. We didn't have any cardio equipment at Stonehaven. No matter how bad the weather, we'd rather be jogging outside than running on an indoor hamster wheel. As for the StairMaster – well, buns of steel weren't high on any werewolf's priority list, and from the looks of the dust on this machine, the guards didn't think much of it either.

Three guards were working out when we arrived. Winsloe ordered them to leave. One did. Two stuck around for the show. A girl lifting weights. Wow. What a novelty. Obviously they hadn't been to a public gym in a very long time.

I didn't pump iron for long. Every time I sat down, Winsloe was there, checking my weight load, asking how much I could manage, generally annoying the hell out of me. Since dropping a fifty-pound barbell on his foot didn't seem a wise idea, I abandoned the weights. I tried the treadmill but couldn't figure out the programming. Winsloe offered to help and only succeeded in jamming the computer. Obviously his technical know-how didn't extend beyond PCs. It didn't matter. I didn't want to jog anyway. What I really wanted to do was hit something – hard. The perfect outlet for that was in the far corner. The punching bag.

As I strapped on hand guards, the onlookers edged closer. Maybe they hoped I was going to pummel Winsloe. I strode to the punching bag and gave it an experimental whack. A collective inhalation went up from the crowd. Oooh, she's going to fight. Wow. If only it was another girl standing there instead of a punching bag. But you can't have everything, can you?

I knocked the bag a few times, getting the feel of it, reminding myself of the stance, the motions. A few slow jabs. Then faster. Slowing. A right hook. Winsloe sidestepped close enough so I could see him in my field of vision, and if I scrunched up my eyes just right, I could shift his image in front of the punching bag. Bam-bam-bam. Three lightning-fast punches. Out of the corner of my eye, I saw him staring, lips parted, eyes glowing. Guess it was as good for him as it was for me. All the better. I danced back. Pause. Inhale. Ready. I slammed my fist into the bag, once, twice, three times, until I lost count.

Thirty minutes later, sweat plastered my hair to my head. It dripped from my chin, it stung my eyes, the smell of it wafted up stronger than anything the best deodorant could disguise. If Winsloe noticed the stink, he gave no sign of it. His eyes hadn't left me since I'd started. Every few minutes my gaze dropped to the bulge in his jeans and I hit the bag harder. Finally, I couldn't take it any longer. I wheeled around and slammed a roundhouse kick into the bag, crashing it into the wall. Then I turned to Winsloe, letting the sweat drip from my face.

'Shower,' I said.

He pointed to a door behind the StairMaster. 'In there.'

I strode toward it. He followed, along with two guards he waved forward. I stopped, turned on my heel, and glared at them. Winsloe only watched me, lips twitching with the anticipation of a ninth-grader sneaking into the girls' locker-room. I met his gaze and something in me snapped. Grabbing my shirt, I ripped it off, then hurled it into the corner. My bra followed. Then my jeans, my socks and finally my underwear. Pulling myself straight, I glared at him. This what you want to see? Fine. Get your fill. When he did – and all the guards did – I stormed into the shower room.

Now, at this point, you'd think even the most callow voyeur would rethink his actions, maybe experience a twinge of embarrassment. If Winsloe felt any such twinges, he probably mistook them for indigestion. Still grinning, he followed me into the communal shower room, gesturing for the two guards to follow, and proceeded to watch me bathe. When he offered to wash my back, I slapped his hand away. Winsloe lost his grin. He stomped to the faucets and turned off my hot water. I made no move to defy him by turning the hot back on and finished my ice-cold shower. That placated him enough to hand me a towel when I was done. A lesson here. Winsloe liked me tough, so long as that toughness wasn't directed at him. Like those women pictured on a certain type of fantasy paperback – long-limbed, lean-muscled, and wild-haired . . . with jewel-studded slave collars. His personal Amazonian love-slave.

When we emerged from the shower room, a guard told Winsloe that Carmichael had been calling. She needed me. Winsloe walked me to the infirmary. After he left, I discovered there was no real crisis, just a mild spell of seizures. If Carmichael had used the excuse to rescue me from Winsloe, she gave no sign of it, her demeanor as curt as ever, commands interspersed with bouts of annoyance at my medical ineptitude. After two days together, though, we'd established a routine of tolerance and borderline courtesy. I respected her. I can't say she felt the same about me – I suspected she saw my refusal to defy Winsloe as a sign of weakness – but at least she treated me as if I was an actual person, not a scientific specimen.

That evening there was a disturbance in the cells. A guard came to the infirmary with head wounds, and since I was there with Bauer, I was privy to all the excitement and discussion that ensued.

The guard had been retrieving the dinner dishes from Savannah and Ruth. When he'd opened the door, a plate had flown at his head. He'd ducked, but it struck the door frame with such force that pieces of exploding china had embedded themselves in his scalp and one side of his face, narrowly missing his eye. Carmichael spent a half-hour picking shards from his face. As Carmichael stitched up the longest slice, she and Matasumi discussed the situation. Or, more accurately, Matasumi explained his theories and Carmichael grunted at appropriate intervals, seeming to wish he'd take his hypotheses elsewhere and let her work. I guess with Bauer gone, Matasumi didn't have anyone else to talk to. Well, he could have talked to Winsloe, but I'd gotten the impression no one really discussed anything important with Winsloe – he seemed to exist on another level, the dilettante investor who was indulged and obeyed, but not included in matters of compound operation.

Apparently the level of paranormal activity in the cells had increased recently. Leah, whose cell was next to Savannah's, complained of spilled shampoo bottles, ripped magazines, and rearranged furniture. The guards were another favored target. Several had tripped passing Savannah's cell, all reporting that something had knocked their legs from under them. Annoying, but relatively benign events. Then, that morning, the guard who'd brought Savannah's and Ruth's daily change of clothing had rebuked Savannah for spilling ketchup on the shirt she'd worn the previous day. As he'd left the cell, the door had slammed against his shoulder, leaving a nasty bruise. Matasumi suspected this rash of activity was caused by having Ruth and Savannah together. Yet even after the potentially serious accident with the flying plate, he didn't consider separating the two. And lose such a valuable opportunity to study witch interaction? What were a few scarred or crippled guards compared to that? As he expounded on the situation's 'potential for remarkable scientific discoveries,' I thought Carmichael muttered a few epithets under her breath, but I may have been mistaken.

That night, curled on my cot, I tried to contact Ruth. Okay, maybe I was in denial about my lack of psychic abilities. I guess I figured if I tried hard enough, I could do anything. Supremacy of the will. The incident with the guard worried me. If the 'psychic events' in the cell were increasing, I suspected it was related to Ruth's training of Savannah. I wanted to warn her: Tone it down or risk separation. After an hour of trying, I gave up. This failure only reminded me of my inability to contact Paige, which reminded me that I was out of contact with Jeremy, which reminded me that I was on my own. No, I admonished, I was not on my own. I was temporarily out of contact. Even if I was cut off from Jeremy, I was quite capable of plotting my own strategies. Last year I'd single-handedly planned and executed Clay's rescue. Of course, there'd been a few bugs . . . well, more than a few, actually, and I'd almost gotten myself killed . . . but, hey, I'd saved him, hadn't I? I'd do better this time. Live and learn, right? Or, in this case, learn and live.

* * *

'Not that – no, the *left*-hand drawer. Your *other* left hand!'

I tossed in my sleep, dreaming of Carmichael barking orders.

'The crash cart. Goddamn it! I said the *crash* cart, not that one.'

In my dream, a dozen identical carts surrounded me as I stumbled from one to the next.

'Give— No, just move. Move!'

Another voice answered, male, mumbling an apology. My eyelids flickered. Fluorescent light stabbed my eyes. I clenched them shut, grimaced, and tried again, squinting this time. Carmichael was indeed in the infirmary, but for once I wasn't the object of her frustration. Two guards scrambled around the room, grabbing this and that as she snatched an instrument tray from the counter. My two in-room guards watched, stupefied, as if they'd been half-asleep.

'Can I do anything?' one said.

'Yes,' Carmichael said. 'Move!'

She thrust him out of the way with the crash cart and pushed it out the door. I tumbled from bed and followed, my drowsiness making me either brave or stupid. Either way, it was the right move. Carmichael didn't notice me tagging along. When she was this preoccupied, I'd have to stab her with the scalpel to get her attention. The guards didn't say anything either, maybe assuming that I was now Carmichael's assistant in all matters and, if she didn't want me, she'd have stopped me herself.

By the time the guards and I arrived at the elevator, the doors were closing behind Carmichael. We waited and got on when it returned. I hoped we'd head up to the surface.

No such luck. We went down. To the cells.

'What's happened?' I asked.

Three guards ignored me. The fourth paid me the courtesy of a shrug and a muttered 'Dunno.' When the elevator opened on the lower level, the guards remembered their job and flanked me as we headed down the hall. Once through the secured door, I heard Savannah's voice.

'Do something! Hurry!'

The door to Ruth and Savannah's cell was open, letting voices stream into the hall.

'Calm yourself, Savannah,' Matasumi said. 'I need the guards to explain what happened.'

I winced. Another guard accident? So soon? Now Ruth and Savannah would definitely be separated. I tried to hurry, but the guards blocked my path and kept me at their pace.

'I didn't do anything!' Savannah shouted.

'Of course you didn't,' Carmichael snapped. 'Now get out of the way. All of you.'

'There's no need for all this equipment,' Matasumi said. 'There weren't any vital signs when I arrived. It's too late.'

'I'll say when it's too late,' Carmichael said.

No vital signs? That sounded bad. When I wheeled into the room, Savannah launched herself at me. Reflexively, my hands flew up to ward off an attack, but she wrapped her arms around my waist.

'I didn't do anything!' she said.

'I know,' I murmured. 'I know.'

I touched her head awkwardly and stroked it, hoping I wasn't petting her like a dog. Consoling distraught children wasn't one of my strengths. Actually, I could say with some certainty that it was something I had never been called on to do before in my life. I scanned the room for Ruth. The cell was filled to capacity. Carmichael and three guards huddled over the bed as the doctor worked on a prone figure. The four guards that had accompanied me all crowded in for a better look, shoving Savannah and me into the corner. I craned my neck to see over their heads.

'Where's Ruth?' I asked.

Savannah stiffened, then pulled back. My gut tightened. I looked at the bed. Carmichael and the three guards still blocked my view, but I could see a hand dangling over the side of the bed. A small, plump, liver-spotted hand.

'Oh no,' I whispered.

Savannah jerked away. 'I – I didn't do it.'

'Of course not,' I said, pulling her back to me and praying she hadn't seen my initial reaction.

Matasumi turned on the four guards who'd come down with me. 'I want to know what happened.'

'We just got here,' one said. He motioned to the guards surrounding the bed. 'They were on the scene first.'

Matasumi hesitated, then stepped toward the bed and tapped one guard's arm. As the guard turned, a commotion erupted in the hallway. Two more guards burst in, guns in hand.

'Please!' Matasumi said. 'We didn't call for reinforcements. Return to your posts.'

Before they could move, another guard entered, accompanied by Leah.

'What—' Matasumi sputtered. He stopped and regained

his composure with a quick intake of breath. 'Why is Ms. O'Donnell here?'

'When I passed her cell, I noticed she was quite agitated,' the young guard said, traces of color blossoming on his cheeks. 'I – uh – used the intercom to inquire and she – uh – asked if she could see what was going on.'

'You do not release a subject from a cell. Ever. Return her immediately.'

Leah pushed past Matasumi, edging through the group until she was right at the bedside. When she saw Ruth, she gasped and wheeled to face Savannah and me.

'Oh,' she said, hands flying to her mouth, eyes fixed on Savannah. 'I am so sorry. How – What happened?'

'As I've been asking for the past ten minutes,' Matasumi said.

The guard he'd tapped stepped away from the bed. 'I was walking past on my rounds and I saw the old – Miss Winterbourne on her bed. The kid was leaning over her. I thought something was wrong, like maybe she'd had a heart attack, so my partner and I opened the door. We found the clock beside them on the floor. Blood splattered on it. Miss Winterbourne's skull bashed in.'

Savannah tensed in my arms, heart pounding.

'Oh, you poor thing,' Leah said, hurrying toward us. 'What a horrible accident.'

'It – it wasn't me,' Savannah said.

'Whatever happened, it's not your fault, hon.'

Leah reached for Savannah. The girl hesitated, still clinging to me. After a moment, she reached for Leah's hand and held it tight, her free arm still around me. A flash of disappointment crossed Leah's face. Then she nodded, as if realizing this wasn't a popularity contest. Leah squeezed Savannah's hand and stroked the back of her hair.

After a moment, Leah turned to the group surrounding the bed. She cleared her throat and said loudly, 'Can I take Savannah to my cell? She shouldn't be here.'

Carmichael glanced up from her work, sweat streaming down her broad face.

'What's she doing here?' she said, waving at Leah. 'Put her back in her cell.'

The guards jumped to obey, as they hadn't for Matasumi. Two hustled Leah out. Savannah watched her go with such sadness that I wanted to implore Carmichael to let Leah stay, but I was afraid if I did, I'd be kicked out too. Savannah needed someone. While Leah would have been preferable, Savannah would have to make do with a not-so-empathic female werewolf. When Leah was gone, Savannah deflated and leaned against me. She was quiet for several minutes, then she glanced around at the others. Everyone was busy with Ruth.

'I think—' she whispered.

She stepped closer. I laid a tentative hand on her shoulder and she melted against me. I patted her back and murmured wordless noises that I hoped sounded comforting. It seemed to calm her, probably not so much because of any consolation I offered, but because she saw me as her only remaining ally in a roomful of enemies. After a minute, she looked up at me.

'I think,' she whispered again, 'I think I might have done it.'

'You couldn't—' I began.

'I wasn't sleeping. I was thinking about things – things Ruth told me. My lessons. Then I saw it. The clock. It flew – like the plate with the guard. I think I did it. I'm not sure how, but I think I did.'

The impulse to deny her culpability sprang to my lips, but I bit it back. The look on her face wasn't that of a child begging to be consoled with well-meaning lies. She knew the truth and trusted me with it.

'If you did, it wasn't your fault,' I said. 'I know that.'

Savannah nodded, brushed back streaks of tears, and leaned her head against my chest. We stood like that, not speaking, for at least five minutes. Then Carmichael stepped away from the bed. Everyone stopped what they were doing. The only sound in the room was the tripping of Savannah's heart.

'Time of death—' Carmichael began.

She lifted her arm, but she must not have put on her watch when summoned from bed. For a long moment, she stared at her wrist, as if expecting some magical timepiece to appear. Then she dropped her hand, closed her eyes, exhaled, and walked from the cell.

It was over.

CHANGES

Once everything quieted down, Matasumi realized I was there. Of course, he'd seen me there earlier, but he hadn't realized what it meant, namely that I was someplace I definitely should not have been. He bustled me back to the infirmary with four of the remaining guards.

I spent the next few hours lying on my cot, staring at the lights blipping on Bauer's machines. Ruth was dead. Could I have done something to prevent that? Should I have? She'd known the risks. That didn't make me feel any better. Now she was dead and Savannah blamed herself. I should have been more comfort to Savannah. I should have known the right gestures, the right words. Ruth's death would be a turning point in her life, and all I'd been able to manage were the most awkward solaces. Shouldn't I have been able to dredge up some deeply rooted maternal instincts and known what to do?

Of course, Savannah hadn't intended to kill Ruth. But had she done it? I feared so. More than that, I was afraid it hadn't been an accident. No, I didn't think Savannah had sent that clock flying on purpose. Absolutely not. Her pain at Ruth's death had been too raw, too real. Yet I was afraid that some unconscious part of Savannah had killed Ruth, that something in her nature, in her genes, something she couldn't help, had made her unwittingly attack those guards and kill Ruth. Maybe I'd seen too many 'demon child' horror movies. I hoped that was it. I prayed that it was. I liked Savannah. She had spirit and intelligence, an engaging mix of childish innocence and preteen sass. She was a normal kid, part angel, part devil. Surely there was no more to it than that. But the psychic events revolved around Savannah. As Ruth had trained Savannah, the events had rapidly escalated from harmless to lethal. What had Ruth said about Savannah? Great power, incredible potential . . . and a mother inclined toward the 'darker side' of magic. Was there such a thing as a genetic predisposition to evil? Had Ruth overlooked it? Had she refused to see anything bad in someone so young? In giving Savannah more power, had she signed her own death warrant? Please, let me be wrong. For Savannah's sake, let me be wrong.

With morning came breakfast. I didn't touch it. Carmichael arrived at her usual time, shortly before eight, a brusque 'How are you?' the only indication that anything had happened the night before. When I said I was fine, she studied me for an extra second, grunted, and began her paperwork.

I spent the early morning dwelling on Ruth's death, how it changed things, how I could have prevented it. I spent a lot of time on the last one. Maybe I shouldn't have. Life and death was beyond our control here. At any moment,

Matasurni could have decided Ruth was no longer a viable subject or Winsloe could have strolled into her cell and taken her on one of his hunts. Still, I shouldered part of the blame, maybe because it gave me some sense of control in an uncontrollable situation.

Around mid-morning a soft moan roused me from my thoughts. I glanced up. Bauer moaned again. She dug her head back into the pillow, face contorting in pain.

'Doctor?' I said, standing. 'She's coming to.'

As Carmichael strode across the floor, I leaned over Bauer. Her eyes flew open.

'Hello, Sondra,' I said. 'We—'

She bolted upright, thin restraints snapping, and slammed against my shoulder. As I fell back, I caught Bauer's gaze, saw something hard and blank there. Before I could react, she grabbed my shoulders and flung me into the air. For a moment, everything slowed, and there was that split second of suspension before gravity took over and I hurtled across the room and crashed into the wall.

Carmichael helped me stand and shouted for the guards. Bauer struggled to get out of bed, sheets twisted around her legs. Her face was contorted with rage, eyes were blank, lips moving soundlessly. When the sheets didn't give way, she roared in frustration and jerked her legs sideways, tearing through the cloth. I scrambled to my feet, ran to the bed, and threw myself across Bauer.

'Keep your fucking hands off me!' Bauer roared. 'All of you! Get back! Don't touch me!'

'Delirium,' Carmichael panted as she raced to the bed with stronger restraints. 'You said it was one of the steps.'

'Right,' I said, though at that moment, lying atop Bauer as she flailed beneath me, a medical diagnosis wasn't exactly a priority. 'Where the hell are the guards?'

The guards were right there, doing what they did best – holding their guns and waiting for the signal to fire. Carmichael threw the restraints at them.

'Tie her!' she said. 'Now!'

Before they could move, Bauer bucked and sent me flying again. This time I stayed on the floor an extra moment to regain my breath. Let the damned guards handle it. Let Carmichael handle it. She was the one who'd refused to properly restrain Bauer.

Bauer stopped struggling and sat still as a statue. The four guards surrounded the bed, tensed, restraints in hand, looking like animal-control officers waiting to throw a net on a rabid dog, none wanting to make the first move. Sweat streamed down Bauer's face and her mouth hung open, panting. She moved her head from side to side, eyes scanning the room. Wild and blank, they passed the guards, me, Carmichael. They stopped at an empty spot to her left, and she lunged forward, held back only by the ripped sheets.

'Get the fuck out of here!' she yelled.

No one was there.

I crawled to my feet, keeping my movements careful as if trying to avoid the notice of a wild animal.

'We have to restrain her,' I whispered.

No one moved.

'Give me those,' Carmichael said, reaching to snatch the restraints from the nearest guard.

'No,' I said. 'Let them do it. I'll get closer and run interference if she attacks. You get a sedative ready and stand
back.'

Oh, sure, give myself the life-threatening job. And for
what? No one would notice. No one would care. Still, the
job had to be done. If I didn't do it, one of these yahoos
would fire his pistol at the first sign of trouble. Then where
would my plans be? Dead and buried with Bauer.

Carmichael turned to the guards. 'Wait until Elena is
beside the bed. Then move quickly, but carefully. Sondra
doesn't know what she's doing. We don't want to hurt her.'

Which, of course, was easier said than done. While I
crept across the room, Bauer kept still, staring and cursing
at unseen intruders. Yet the moment the guards touched
her, she exploded, summoning up the unexpected strength
of delirium. All of us working together could barely wrestle
her onto the bed.

Once Bauer was down, I helped the nearest guard fasten
his restraint. As my fingers worked at the clasps, Bauer's
arm seemed to shimmer and contract. I shook my head
sharply, feeling the pain inside it bounce around like a red-
hot coal. My vision blurred.

'Elena?' Carmichael grunted as she fought to tie Bauer's
other arm down.

'I'm okay.'

As I worked on the knot, Bauer's arm convulsed, the
wrist narrowing, the hand twisting and contorting into a
knot. It hadn't been a trick of my eyes. She was Changing.

'Elena!'

At Carmichael's shout, I jumped. Bauer's hand flew from

its bindings and tore at the empty space where my throat had been. Webbed fingers and misshapen claws swung through the air. I threw myself over Bauer's chest as she bolted upright again.

A snarl of rage erupted and she shoved me off of her. Both hands now free, Bauer grabbed a guard and threw him across the room. He collapsed, unconscious, against the wall. Bauer's back shook and contorted, great lumps moving under the skin. She howled and fell onto her side.

'Sedate her!' I shouted.

'But you said—' Carmichael begun.

'It's too soon! She's not ready! Sedate her! Now!'

Hair sprouted from Bauer's back and shoulders. Bones lengthened and shortened, and she cried out, half-howling, half-whimpering. Her whole body convulsed, clearing the bed, me still clinging atop her. Her face was unrecognizable, a hellish mask of writhing muscles that was neither wolf nor human. Fangs jutted over her lips. Her nose had stopped midway on the transformation to muzzle. Hair sprouted in tufts. Then there were the eyes. Bauer's eyes. They hadn't changed, but they were bulging and rolling, agony pouring out in waves. She met my gaze, and for a second I saw recognition. Some part of her had passed the delirium and was conscious, trapped in that hell.

Carmichael jabbed the syringe into Bauer's arm. Bauer flew upright and hung there, with me draped over her lap. Her body jerked several times, then she gave a low snuffle, and her eyes widened as if in surprise. She blinked once. Then she slid down onto the bed.

I tensed, waiting for the next round; then the Change

reversed. This time there was no violence or pain to the transformation. She melted peacefully back into human form, like a computer-generated morphing. When she was fully human again, she curled into semi-fetal position and fell asleep.

Armen made another visit to the infirmary. Yesterday had been his regular checkup. Today he feigned a migraine headache with such finesse that even Carmichael never doubted his symptoms, though I suppose that wasn't surprising, considering he was a psychiatrist and therefore had a medical degree himself. We picked up our conversation where we'd left off. He had a plan for escaping that involved another medical ruse, thereby bringing him up to the second floor with me, which was much easier to escape from than the well-secured cell block. Again, he worked this into such ordinary small talk that I had to keep my own brain revving to keep up with the subtext interpretation.

The more I talked to Armen, the more I viewed my ploy with Bauer as a backup plan. Armen was an ally far more to my liking. First, he was conscious, which was a definite advantage over the comatose Bauer. Second, he reminded me of Jeremy, which increased my comfort level tenfold. He was quiet, courteous, and even-tempered, an unassuming exterior disguising a strong will and razor-sharp mind, someone who took charge instinctively, yet tempered that authoritarianism with enough grace and wit that I didn't mind letting him take the lead. I trusted Armen and I liked him. An ideal combination.

* * *

The rest of the day passed quietly, but the night made up for it, plaguing me with strange and disturbing dreams. I started the night at Stonehaven, playing in the snow with Clay and Nick. We were in the middle of a snowball fight when a new dream overlapped that one, cutting in like a more powerful radio station. In the other dream, I was lying in bed while Paige attempted to contact me. The two dreams spliced together: One minute I'd feel icy snow dripping down my neck, the next I'd hear Paige calling me. Some part of me chose the snowball dream and tried to block the other, but it didn't work. I lobbed two last snowballs at Nick, then a wave of snow engulfed me, swallowing that dream and spitting me into the other.

'Elena? Damn it, answer me!'

I struggled to return to my winter games, but to no avail. I was stuck in the dream of Paige. Wonderful.

'Elena. Come on. Wake up.'

Even in my dream, I didn't want to answer, as if I knew that imagining myself speaking to Paige would only depress me more, reminding me that I'd been out of contact with her for three days, a situation that now seemed permanent.

'Elena?'

I mumbled something unintelligible even to myself.

'Ah-ha! You *are* there. Good. Hold on. I'm going to bring you into my body. Fair warning this time. Jeremy's here. Now, on the count of three. One, two, three, ta-da!'

Five seconds of silence. Then, 'Oh, shit.'

Paige's curse faded behind me as I tumbled through bits and pieces of dreams, like someone was flipping channels, refusing to pause long enough for me to see what was on.

When it stopped, I was a wolf. I didn't need to see myself; I could feel it in the way my muscles moved, the perfect rhythm of each stride. Someone ran ahead of me, a shape flickering through the trees. Another wolf. I knew that, though I couldn't get close enough to see anything but shadow and blurred motion. Although I was the pursuer, not the hunted, fear strummed through me. Who was I chasing? Clay. It had to be Clay. That degree of panic, of blind fear, fear of loss and abandonment – I could only associate it with Clay. He was there, somewhere, ahead of me, and I couldn't catch up. Each time my paws struck the ground, a name echoed through my skull, a mental shout. But it wasn't Clay's name. It was my own, repeated over and over, beats matching the rhythm of my legs. Glancing down, I caught sight of my paws. They weren't my paws. Too large, too dark – a blond nearly gold. Clay's paws. Ahead a bushy tail flashed in the moonlight. A white-blond tail. I was chasing myself.

I started awake and bolted upright in bed. Leaning forward, chest heaving, I ran my hands through my hair, but it wasn't my hair, not a long, tangled mess, but close-cropped curls. I dropped my hands to my lap and stared at them. Thick, squared hands, nails clipped back to the quick. Workman's hands, yet ones that rarely handled a tool larger than a pen. Uncallused, but not soft. Bones broken more times than I could count, each time meticulously reset, emerging unmarred except for a road map of minute scars. I knew each one of those scars. I could remember nights lying awake, asking, 'Where'd you get this one? And this one? And – whoops, I gave you that one.'

A door opened.

'It didn't work, did it?' Clay's angry drawl, not from the doorway, but here, from the bed.

Jeremy shut the door behind him. 'No, Paige wasn't able to make contact. She thought she did, but something went wrong.'

'And aren't we all shocked to hell. You're entrusting Elena's life to a twenty-two-year-old apprentice witch. You know that, don't you?'

'I know that I'm willing to use any tool possible to find Elena. Right now, that apprentice witch is our best hope.'

'No, she's not. There's another way. Me. I can find Elena. But you won't believe it.'

'If Paige is unable to reestablish contact—'

'Goddamn it!' Clay grabbed a book from the nightstand and whipped it across the room, denting the far wall.

Jeremy paused a moment, then continued, voice as unruffled as ever. 'I'm going to get you something to drink, Clayton.'

'You mean you're going to sedate me again. Sedate me, shut me up, keep me quiet and calm while Elena is out there – alone. I didn't believe it was her talking through Paige and now she's gone. Don't tell me that wasn't my fault.'

Jeremy said nothing.

'Thank you very much,' Clay said.

'Yes, you're to blame for us losing contact that time, though it probably doesn't explain why we can't recontact her. We'll keep trying. In the meantime, perhaps we can discuss this other idea of yours in the morning. Come see me if you change your mind about that drink. It'll help you sleep.'

As Jeremy left, the dream evaporated. I tossed and turned, thrown back into the channel-surfing world again. Snap, snap, snap, bits of dreams and memories, too scattered to make any sense. Then darkness. A knock at the door. I was seated at a desk, poring over a map. The door was behind me. I tried to turn or call out a welcome. Instead, I felt my pen move to scratch a few words on a pad. I looked at the writing and, with no surprise, recognized Clay's scrawl.

The room swirled, threatening to go dark. Something tugged at me with the gentle insistence of the tide, reaching out to pull me back. I fought it. I liked where I was, thank you very much. This was a good place, a comforting place. Just sensing Clay's presence made me happy, and damn it, I deserved a bit of happiness, illusory or not. The tide grew stronger, swelling to an undertow. The room went black. I wrenched myself free and slammed back into Clay's body. He'd stopped writing now and was studying a map. A map of what? Someone knocked again at the door. He didn't respond. Behind him, the door opened, then shut.

'Clayton.' Cassandra's voice, butter-smooth.

He didn't answer.

'A grunt of greeting would suffice,' she murmured.

'That would imply a welcome. Don't you need to be invited into a room?'

'Sorry. Another myth shot to hell.'

'Feel free to follow it.'

Cassandra chuckled. 'I see Jeremy inherited all the

manners in the Danvers family. Not that I mind. I've always preferred honesty and wit over polish.' Her voice drew closer as she crossed the room. 'I noticed your light on and thought you might care to join me in a drink.'

'Love to, but I'm afraid we don't share the same taste in fluids.'

'Could you at least look at me when you turn me down?'

No answer.

'Or are you afraid to look at me?'

Clay turned and met her eyes. 'There. Piss off, Cassandra. How's that?'

'She's not coming back, you know.'

Clay's hand clenched around the pencil, but he said nothing.

I felt the tugging at my feet again and braced myself against it. Somewhere in my head Paige called my name. The undertow surged, but I held firm. This was one scene I definitely wasn't leaving.

'They won't find her,' Cassandra said.

'According to you, we should stop trying.'

'I only mean that it's a waste of our time. Better we concentrate our efforts on stopping these people. Save all our lives, not just Elena's. If, in stopping them, we rescue her, that's wonderful. If we don't . . . it's hardly the end of the world.'

The pencil snapped between Clay's fingers. Cassandra stepped closer. When the undertow threatened again, I kicked and fought with all my might.

Cassandra took yet another step toward Clay. I felt him tense and start to step back, then stop and hold his ground.

'Yes, you love her,' Cassandra said. 'I can see that and I admire that. Really, I do. But do you know how many men I've loved in all these years? Loved passionately? And of those men, do you know how few names I remember? How few faces?'

'Get out.'

'I'm asking you to join me for a drink. One drink. Nothing more.'

'I said, get out.'

Cassandra only smiled and shook her head. Her eyes gleamed now with the same look I'd seen her give the server at the restaurant, only stronger now. Hungrier. Her fingers grazed Clay's forearm. I wanted to scream for him to look away, but I was powerless to do anything but watch.

'Don't pull that shit, Cassandra,' Clay said. 'It doesn't work on me.'

'No?'

'No.'

Clay looked Cassandra squarely in the eyes. She went completely immobile, only her eyes working, glowing brighter as she stared at him. Several minutes passed. Then Clay stepped toward Cassandra. Her lips curved in a triumphant smile. My heart stopped.

'Get out, Cassandra,' Clay said, his face only inches from hers. 'Ten seconds or I throw you out.'

'Don't threaten me, Clayton.'

'Or you'll do what? Bite me? Think you can sink your teeth into me before I rip your head off? I hear that's a good cure for immortality. Five seconds, Cassandra. Five . . . four . . .'

The scene went black. No swirling, no tugging. Just a sudden stop. I blinked. Harsh light blinded me. I squeezed my eyes shut. Through my lids, I saw the light swing away. Fingers gripped my shoulder and shook me.

'Rise and shine, sleepyhead.'

A voice. Unfortunately, not Clay's voice. Not Cassandra's voice. Not even Paige's. This was worse. Ten times worse. Ty Winsloe. From pleasant dreams to unsettling visions to outright nightmares. I clenched my eyes shut.

'Whaddaya think, boys?' Winsloe said. 'Does our sleeping beauty need a kiss to wake her up? Of course, in the original fairy tale, she needed more than a kiss . . .'

My eyes snapped open and I bolted upright. Winsloe chortled and beamed a flashlight in my face, then skimmed it over my body.

'You always sleep with your clothes on?' he asked.

'This isn't exactly a private suite,' I said, snarling a yawn. 'What time is it?'

'Just past three. We need your help. There's been a breakout.'

I sat on the edge of my cot, blinking, brain struggling to get past visions of Clay and Cassandra. Three o'clock? In the morning? Breakout? Did he mean someone had escaped? Who? Why did they need my help? Had there been an accident? Did Carmichael want me?

'Huh?' I said. So much for intelligent and articulate questions. What do you expect at three A.M.?

Winsloe prodded me from bed. 'I'll explain on the way.'

BLOODHOUND

Armen had escaped. When Winsloe told me, my breath caught, and for a long moment I couldn't breathe. Armen had escaped . . . without me. On the heels of my panic came a flash of hurt, then the realization that Armen must have been presented with an opportunity that he couldn't ignore. Could I blame him? Of course not, though that didn't make things any better. My escape partner was gone, taking our plan with him. Worse still, Winsloe wanted me to stop him.

'You want me to track him down?' I said.

'That's what I said. Use your nose. Sniff him out.'

'Like a bloodhound.'

Winsloe glanced over sharply at my tone. 'Yes, like a bloodhound. Is that a problem?'

Of course that was a problem. I was a person, not an animal, not a sideshow attraction. I didn't perform for anyone's amusement. I wanted to say so, but the edge in Winsloe's voice dared me to defy him. I didn't have the guts. Or, more accurately, my instinct for self-preservation was too strong. I remembered Winsloe's reaction when I'd slapped his hand away in the shower and knew I couldn't afford another show

313

of defiance. That didn't mean I'd betray Armen. I might have to track him, but I didn't have to find him.

Flanked by guards, I followed Winsloe downstairs to the cell block. Two more guards waited outside Armen's cell. Inside, Tucker knelt beside a guard, who sat on the floor, cradling his head. The guard looked familiar, but I couldn't put a name to him. The only time I ever bothered to note a guard's name was when he'd done something to distinguish himself from the others. Most hadn't.

'Did you find out what happened?' Winsloe asked, in a voice that implied he didn't give a damn what had happened, he only wanted to get on with the hunt.

'Seems like Haig made himself a weapon,' Tucker said. 'Something sharp, like a knife. Caused a commotion when my men were doing their rounds, then pulled this weapon on them when they opened the door. Knocked Ryman here out cold. Must have taken Jolliffe along to get past security. Ryman's okay, but we'd better move if we want Jolliffe alive. We'll need to track him. I've sent Pendecki to get the tracking—'

'No need,' Winsloe interrupted. 'I've got a world-class tracker right here.'

Tucker looked at me and frowned. 'That's one of my men out there, sir. With all due respect, I don't think we should fool around—'

'Fool around?'

Tucker's jaw clicked as if biting something back. 'I didn't mean it that way . . . sir. I'm concerned about—'

'Of course you are. So am I. That's why I brought Elena. Ryman, feeling up to joining us?'

Ryman struggled to his feet. 'Yes, sir.'

'I don't think—' Tucker began.

'Don't think,' Winsloe cut in. 'That's not what I pay you for. Come on, Ryman, and we'll see if we can't get this bastard. Maybe get you a little payback for that goose egg on your head.'

Outside the compound, Winsloe dismissed the two guards accompanying me, leaving only the injured Ryman. I wondered at this, knew it wasn't a good sign, but was still too sleep-drugged to make sense of it. Other thoughts clogged my tired brain. Armen had made a weapon? He'd attacked a guard? Knocked him unconscious? Was this the same Armen who'd been looking to me to provide the brute force for an escape?

As we headed into the woods, someone shouted 'Hey!' behind us. Ryman whirled, gun poised, reflexes unhampered by any lingering effects from his head injury. No one was there. Dead grass crackled farther up the path, and we all spun back around to see Xavier twenty feet away.

'Easy, soldier,' Xavier said, hands in the air. 'Don't be shooting the friendlies.'

'I should,' Ryman muttered. 'Teach you a lesson.'

'What's up?' Xavier asked, sauntering toward us. 'I hear Haig made a break for it. We doin' the search-and-rescue thing? Or the search-and-destroy thing?' He saw me and stopped. 'Whoa, what's wolf-girl doing out of her cage?'

I glowered at him. He sidestepped fast, as if ducking my glare, then bobbed back grinning.

'That's one lethal look you have there. Deadlier than

315

Ryman's bullets.' He turned to Winsloe. 'So what's the deal? Fun and games time? Can I play?'

'Maybe next time,' Winsloe said.

'Oh, come on. Don't be a spoilsport. I wanna play.'

'Yeah?' Ryman said. 'How about you be the practice target?'

Winsloe waved Ryman to silence. 'That's enough. Back inside, Reese. I said, next time.'

'Fine.' Xavier rolled his eyes, then vanished. Obviously someone else who knew enough not to push Winsloe.

'Are we still on track, Elena?' Winsloe asked.

'Hmmm? Oh, right.' I sniffed the air. 'Yes, Ar – Haig was here. With someone else.'

'Jolliffe,' Winsloe said. 'Good. Tucker will be pleased. Lead on, then. Ryman, stay behind her.'

We head into the woods.

'Are you sure this is the way?' Winsloe asked ten minutes later.

It wasn't. I'd branched away from Armen's true path ten yards back. Winsloe shone his flashlight on my face. I swallowed a quick assertion and made a show of sniffing the air. Out of the corner of my eye, I watched him, gauging his credulity, and decided to test the water before making a potentially fatal leap.

'I thought it was,' I said slowly. 'The trail seemed to turn this way.'

'Undergrowth looks pretty dense,' Winsloe said.

Did it? It appeared passable to me, but maybe I was looking as a wolf, not a panicked human running for his life, captive in tow. I hunkered down and inhaled close to the ground. Behind me, Ryman snickered.

'You're right,' I said. 'They didn't come this way. I must have been picking up their scent on the breeze. Better retrace our steps.'

'Maybe you should stay on all fours,' Ryman said. 'Keep your nose to the trail.' He smirked.

'That's okay, Elena,' Winsloe said. 'Take it slow. Don't feel pressured.'

Me? Feel pressured? Why on earth would I feel pressured? Just because I was being asked to hunt down a fellow captive, with a loaded pistol at my back and a psychotic megalomaniac calling the shots?

'Maybe I am a little nervous,' I said. 'Sorry.'

Winsloe beamed a magnanimous smile. 'That's okay. Just take it easy.'

Sure, boss. No problem. I inhaled, backtracked to the real trail, and started again. About fifty yards farther along, Armen's trail veered east. I decided to keep heading south. I didn't get three steps.

'You sure that's the right way?' Winsloe called from behind me.

I froze.

'Seems to me they went east,' he said. 'There's some bent branches here.'

I turned to look at the bushes surrounding the wide gap Armen had gone through. Not a single twig was broken. There was no way Winsloe could tell Armen had turned here. Unless he already knew. The warning tingle I'd felt since we'd begun this expedition surged to an Arctic chill.

Winsloe knew exactly where Armen had fled to, probably had him tracked and captured before he even came to the infirmary. He was testing me – my abilities and my honesty. Had I already failed?

Quelling the urge to stammer excuses, I looked from the bushes to the path I'd chosen, pinched the bridge of my nose and tried to look exhausted, which wasn't much of a stretch. I crouched and sniffed the ground, then crept over and smelled the bushes, then stood and sampled the air. With a sigh, I rubbed the back of my neck.

'Well?' Winsloe said.

'I'm smelling a trail both ways. Give me a sec.'

I rolled my shoulders and took a deep breath of chilly night air. Then I got down on all fours, ignoring Ryman's snickers, and followed both potential paths for several yards.

'That one,' I said, pointing at the real trail as I got to my feet. 'He took a few steps the other way, then backed up and turned down that gap between the bushes.'

Plausible, and impossible to refute unless you had a were-wolf's nose. Winsloe nodded. It worked for him. Good.

As I followed the trail, I wondered how Winsloe planned to end this charade. They'd obviously recaptured Armen already. Would we bump into the troop of guards holding him? Or would the trail loop back to the compound? What was the point? To amuse himself by making me perform like a circus dog? Humiliate me while testing my trustworthiness? Was he hoping I'd screw up or make a run for it, giving him an excuse to hunt me? I wouldn't give him the satisfaction. If he wanted a loyal two-legged hound, that was exactly what he'd get.

I didn't try to trick him again. What was the use, if he already had Armen? We trekked another half-mile into the forest. The scent grew stronger, until I could pick it up in the wind.

'They're close,' I said.

'Good,' Winsloe said. 'Slow down then and—'

Ahead, a clump of bushes exploded with crackles and curses. Two figures flew out of the shrubbery, Armen atop a guard, hands grappling against the man's throat. Winsloe raced forward, yanking a gun from under his jacket. Ryman fired a warning shot. Armen froze. Winsloe launched himself at Armen and knocked him off Jolliffe.

Anger flared in my gut, white hot. I clenched my fists to keep from acting on it. I wanted to scream at Winsloe, denounce his 'tracking exercise' for what it was. A game. Another juvenile game choreographed right down to leaping on Armen *after* the poor man was paralyzed by the sound of gunfire. You trying to impress me, Tyrone? Oh, I'm impressed. I'd never seen such a pathetic performance.

'There,' I said, barely able to unhinge my jaw enough to force words out. 'You have him. Good job. Can we go now?'

Everyone ignored me. Winsloe had Armen spread-eagled on the ground and was patting him down looking for weapons. Jolliffe sat in the shadows, as if too stunned to move. Ryman walked over and extended a hand, helping his partner to his feet.

'What happened here?' Winsloe said.

'He had a weapon, sir,' Jolliffe said. 'He forced me from the cell, took my gun, and made me open the doors, then dragged me into the woods. He tried to kill me. I escaped a ways back, followed, and caught up to him here.'

At which time you held him until we arrived, I thought. After having probably been in radio contact with Winsloe since you escaped from Armen.

'He was hiding in those bushes,' the guard said, continuing his story. 'He shot at me. I disarmed him and we fought, then you showed up.'

'Wh – what?' Armen said, struggling to lift his head from the ground. 'I didn't – you came to my cell. You brought me out here. You—'

Winsloe slammed Armen's face back into the dirt. Again, it took every ounce of restraint not to fly at him. Then the impulse vanished and I couldn't have moved if I'd wanted to. My legs turned to cold lead as I saw the look on Armen's face, the confusion and disbelief beneath a layer of blood and bruises. Jolliffe said something. My gaze swiveled to him. I saw his face, really saw it, and recognized it, as I'd earlier recognized Ryman. Watching them together, I knew where I'd seen them. At the hunt. The two nameless men with Pendecki and Bryce the night we'd hunted Patrick Lake. That wasn't the last time I'd seen them, either. They'd been the two who'd accompanied me into the shower with Winsloe. His pet guards. Handpicked for another special mission.

Armen hadn't escaped. It made no sense. Armen was a thinking man, not the sort who'd take such a risk on a sudden impulse. He wouldn't know how to fashion a makeshift prison weapon. And he certainly wouldn't attack two armed guards, each twice his size. No, he hadn't escaped. He'd been brought here. Beaten and dragged into the forest. For what? To play a role in Winsloe's latest game? Winsloe wanted me to track someone, so he'd gone to the cell block, chosen a target, and enlisted his pet guards to help build the scenario. Was it worth it, you sick bastard? Did you get your rocks off this time?

'Can we go now?' I asked again, raising my voice to be heard over their conversation. 'We have him. We should head back.'

Winsloe shifted so he was sitting sideways atop Armen, leaning back like he was in a comfortable chair. 'Can't do that, Elena. Wish we could, but we can't. We aren't done yet.'

He glanced at Ryman and Jolliffe. The two guards grinned back, and my gut turned to ice.

'We can't have prisoners escaping, can we, boys? Escaping their cells, then escaping punishment. No siree. We have to set a standard. No one escapes my compound and lives.'

I struggled for breath. 'But – but I thought Haig was an important subject. Doctor Matasumi said—'

'Larry will understand. A prisoner escapes, we hunt him down, we try to bring him back alive, but . . . well, things happen. Capturing a prisoner is a delicate matter. So much could go wrong, and of course, we can't risk letting anyone get away and put the project at risk.'

I could not let this happen. I'd felt sick enough over hunting Patrick Lake, and he'd been a vicious killer. Armen Haig was no monster. He was a decent man, an innocent in a world where most of us, myself included, had forfeited our innocence when we became something other than human. The monsters here were the three with no excuses for their behavior.

What did Winsloe see when he looked at Armen, at me, at Patrick Lake, at the guard he'd killed, or anyone else who inhabited his world? Did he see people, conscious beings? Or did he see cardboard cutouts, actors, characters in some grand game designed for his amusement?

'You can't kill him,' I said, keeping my voice as neutral as possible.

Winsloe stretched his legs, settling his weight onto Armen. 'You're right. I can't. Well, I *could*, but I won't.'

'Good. Now can we—'

'I'm not killing him. You are.'

SACRIFICE

I stopped short, words jamming in my throat. 'I – I—'
'That's right. You're killing him. You're going to change into a wolf and hunt him.' Winsloe stood and put a foot on Armen's back. 'Is that a problem, Elena?'

For one brief second, I was certain Winsloe knew about my collaboration with Armen, that this was his way of foiling our plans, killing my ally, and letting me know that he knew, but I quickly realized that Winsloe couldn't know. Armen had been too shrewd, had kept our discussions well disguised. We hadn't progressed far enough in our plans for even the most quick-witted listener to realize what we were plotting. If someone had been listening, they would have only heard two people carrying on a conversation. With an icy jolt, I wondered if that had been enough. Had Winsloe overheard me with Armen and detected a blossoming friendship? Did that explain why he'd chosen Armen from all the other captives, risking Matasumi's displeasure? Why not take Leah or, better yet, Curtis Zaid, the useless Vodoun priest? Because it wouldn't hurt me enough. It wouldn't be sadistic enough.

Winsloe stepped closer. 'I said, is that a problem, Elena?'

'Yes, it's a goddamned problem,' I snarled. 'I will not kill a man for your amuse—'

I reeled back. Felt the imprint of his hand burning my cheek. Stumbled. Recovered. Spun around, fist barreling toward his jaw. A bullet seared my side. Threw me off-balance, half-impact, half-surprise. Grabbed a tree. Broke my fall. Stood there, facing the trunk, chest heaving, a serpent of rage whipping through my body. I gripped the tree hard enough to puncture bark holes in my palms. Closed my eyes. Inhaled. Fought for control. Found it. Took deep breaths and stepped back. I dropped my fingers to my side and felt the wound. Straight through, nicking a rib and nothing more.

'One more time, Elena,' Winsloe said, walking up behind me. 'Is that a problem?'

I turned slowly, keeping my eyes off his. Winsloe gave a grunt of satisfaction, interpreting my lack of eye contact as a sign that I was cowed, not that I didn't dare look at him for fear I'd rip his face off if I did.

'Answer the question, Elena.'

'I can't.' Inhaled. Forced apology into my tone. 'I can't do—'

I saw his hand go up, this time with the gun in it. Saw the pistol careering toward my face. I backpedaled but too late. The gun glanced off the side of my skull. Lights flashed. Then went dark. When I recovered, I was lying on the ground with Winsloe standing over me.

'This is how it's going to work, Elena,' he said, leaning down into my face. 'You're going to change into a wolf. Right here. Right now. Then you're going to hunt Mr. Haig.

324

When you capture him, you will hold him until I arrive. Then you will kill him. Any deviation from this plan and you will both die. Understood?'

I tried to sit. Winsloe's foot landed on my stomach, forcing me down and knocking the breath from my lungs.

'It's – it's not that easy,' I gasped between gulps of air. 'I might not be able to Change. Even if I do, I won't be able to control myself once I catch him. It doesn't work that way.'

'It will work any way I say it will work.' Winsloe's voice held all the emotion of a golf pro explaining the rules of the course. 'If you fail, you will answer to me. And when you're done answering to me, my boys will take their turn, and when they've tired of you, you die. Is that incentive enough, Elena?'

I started to shake. No anger now. Just fear. Uncontrollable terror. Killing Armen would be an act of cowardice I would never forgive myself for, even if I could do it. But if I didn't? Rape and death. To me, the idea of being raped was more terrifying than that of dying. Ghosts of my childhood filled my brain, voices that said I'd promised such a thing would never happen again, that I was too strong, that I could never again be forced to submit to anyone.

'I can't,' I whispered. 'I just can't.'

I saw Winsloe's foot fly back. Squeezed my eyes shut. Felt his boot connect with my side, landing square atop the bullet wound. Heard a woman's scream. My scream. Hated myself. Hated, hated, hated. I would not die this way. Not raped. Not forced to kill an innocent man. If I had to die, I'd do it my way.

I flung myself up, throwing Winsloe clear. He landed on his back. I scrambled to my feet and turned on him.

'No!' A shout. Armen.

I whirled, saw Ryman raise his gun. Armen lunged at me. The gun spat a stream of bullets. Armen's body stopped in midair, chest exploding, body jolting with the impact. As he hit the ground, I dropped beside him.

'More merciful. For both of us.' His voice was paper thin, too low for anyone's ears but mine. Bloody froth bubbled from his lips.

'I'm sorry,' I whispered.

'Don't—' His eyelids fluttered once. Twice. Then closed.

I hung my head, felt tears clog my throat. In the silence that followed, I braced myself for what was to come. Winsloe would kill me for this. For attacking him. For ending his game. When I finally turned to face him, though, I saw only satisfaction in his eyes. He hadn't lost at all. The outcome was still the same. Armen was dead. It was my fault. I knew it and I'd suffer for it.

'Take her back to her cell,' Winsloe said, brushing off his jeans. 'Then get someone out here to clean up this mess.'

As he glanced down at Armen, his mouth tightened and he skewered me with a glare. The outcome may have been the same, but his game had been ruined. I'd pay for it. Not tonight. But I would pay.

Ryman and Jolliffe led me into the forest. We were about halfway to the compound when Ryman suddenly shoved me hard. I tripped. As I steadied myself and turned to glare at him, I found myself glaring into the barrel of his gun. I clenched my jaw, wheeled around, and continued walking. I'd gone about five feet when a kick from Jolliffe cut my legs from under me. I stumbled against a tree and took a moment to compose myself before turning. Both men trained their guns on me.

'What do you want?' I said. 'An excuse to shoot me?'

'We don't need one,' Ryman said. 'We just tell Tyrone that you made a break for it and we had to take you down.'

'Like a rabid dog,' Jolliffe said.

Both men laughed. Rage shot through me. What had happened back in that grove made me sick with guilt and self-loathing. I wanted nothing more than to find another target for that anger, someone else I could blame for Armen's death. These two morons were screaming for the job. I sized them up. Could I bring them down without getting shot? I estimated my odds at five to one. When those odds struck me as reasonably good, I knew I was in trouble. My rage was fast consuming my common sense. I tore my gaze away from the two guards and continued walking.

Ryman strode up beside me and grabbed my arm. As he slammed me against a tree, I started to lash out, then felt the cold metal of a gun barrel at my temple.

'Don't ever turn your back on me, bitch,' he breathed in my face. 'Cliff and I were looking forward to some fun tonight. You ruined it. Maybe Ty's willing to overlook that, but we aren't. Who the hell do you think you are anyway? Defying Tyrone Winsloe? Attacking him? Spoiling our game?'

'Take your hands off me.'

'Or what?' he jammed his knee into my crotch. 'What are you going to do if I don't?'

327

Someone chuckled to our left. 'How about . . . rip out your fool throat, tear off your testicles, and carve you up like a Thanksgiving turkey. Not necessarily in that order.'

We turned to see Xavier leaning against a tree, puffing on a cigarette. He threw down the stub, strolled over, and tugged me out of Ryman's grasp.

'You don't wanna be messing with this gal,' Xavier said. 'Did you see what she did to that other werewolf? Ripped his leg open . . . while wearing handcuffs. Now you boys might have guns, but I wouldn't want to see how much damage she could do before she went down.'

Before either guard could open his mouth, Xavier hooked his arm around my waist and led me back to the open path, heading for the compound.

'She seems to tolerate you just fine,' Jolliffe muttered as he walked up behind us. 'Something we should be telling Ty about, Reese?'

'I'm not crazy enough to trespass on the big man's territory,' Xavier said. 'Can I help it if the poor girl's got a thing for me?'

He grabbed my ass. I whirled to slug him, but he vanished, reappearing on my other side.

'It's one of those love-hate things,' he called back to the guards. Under his breath he murmured. 'Play nice, Elena. You don't want me to take my marbles and go home.'

He was right. As much as I hated being indebted to Xavier, he was the only thing standing between me, the two guards, and a potentially nasty situation.

Xavier rested his arm around my waist again and glanced over his shoulder. 'Think Tyrone will let me have her when he's done? We could run away together, build a hut on some deserted island, live off coconuts, sunshine, and sex. What do you say, Elena? We'd make beautiful babies. Think about it. We could single-handedly turn wolves into a vanishing species.'

'Ha-ha,' I said.

Xavier paused, cocked his head. 'No laughter from the peanut gallery. Guess they don't get the joke. Want me to explain it to you, guys?'

'We want you to fuck off, Reese,' Ryman said. 'Like right now.'

'In front of you guys? I'm a demon, not an exhibitionist.' Xavier walked a bit faster, propelling me alongside him. 'Anyway, we're almost at the compound. Larry was wondering what happened. Getting pretty worried about his star subject. I volunteered for the search party. Think I'll win a prize?'

'Not when Matasumi finds out what happened to that star subject,' I murmured.

Something flashed across Xavier's face, but before I could decipher the expression, it did its own disappearing act, hiding behind his usual cocky nonchalance. He kept up a running monologue until we arrived at the compound. Then Xavier took me through the security door, letting it bang shut on the two guards. We almost made it into the elevator without them, but Jolliffe grabbed the doors at the last moment. They got on and pushed the button for the cell block. When the car stopped on the middle floor, Xavier tried to lead me off. Ryman snatched my arm.

'Ty said return her to her cell.'

Xavier sighed. 'He meant the infirmary. That's where she sleeps now. He must have forgotten.'

'He said the cell.'

'He made a mistake.'

The two men locked gazes. Then Xavier straightened up and leaned out the elevator door. Carmichael's voice and footsteps echoed down the hall.

'Doc?' Xavier called. 'I have Elena here. These guys tell me Tyrone wants her taken back to her cell.'

'He must have made a mistake,' Carmichael said as she approached.

'That's what I told them.'

Carmichael stopped in front of the open elevator doors. 'Cliff, Paul, take Ms. Michaels to the infirmary. I'll be right there.'

Xavier accompanied me to the infirmary and didn't leave until Carmichael showed up. He tried to stay longer, but she shooed him out, grumbling that my sleep had been interrupted enough and she needed my help in the morning. As he left, Xavier mouthed, 'You owe me.' I did. And I was sure he wouldn't let the IOU go unpaid.

As I settled onto my cot, Carmichael bustled around the room, prepping equipment and checking Bauer. Once she asked me if there was anything I'd like to talk about. There was, but I couldn't do it. I didn't want to see my guilt reflected in another person's face. A good man had died that night. He'd been shot by a vicious guard, after being sentenced to death by a sadistic tyrant, but ultimately the weight of his demise lay on my shoulders. I couldn't share that with Carmichael. The one person in the world I could have unburdened myself on was hundreds of miles away, fighting his own battles in a motel room. Thinking about that only reminded me how alone I was. Before Carmichael left, she fixed me a cup of tea. From the medicinal smell, I knew it contained a sedative, but drank it anyway. That was the only way I was going to fall asleep that night and I desperately wanted to sleep, to sleep, to forget . . . if only for a few hours.

EXILE

fter breakfast the next day, Bauer awoke.

I was sitting beside her bed, absorbed in my thoughts, as I had been all morning. When she first opened her eyes, I thought it was a reflexive action. Her eyes opened, but she didn't move, just stared at the ceiling, expressionless. Then she blinked.

'Doctor?' I said.

Carmichael made a noise and glanced up from her paperwork. A split second later, she was at the bedside. It took a while for Bauer to rouse herself. I guess if you've been out cold for days, you don't exactly jump up screaming – at least, we should be thankful she *didn't* jump up screaming, all things considered.

It took about twenty minutes for Bauer to awaken enough to move. She tried shifting onto her side, but the restraints held her back. She glanced down sharply, frowning, saw the bonds, and shot a glare at Carmichael. Her mouth opened, but only a whisper came out, so faint even I couldn't distinguish words. Carmichael got the message, though, and quickly loosened the arm restraints.

'Uh, that's not such a good idea,' I said.

'She's too weak to talk, much less move,' Carmichael said.

Bauer's eyes went from me to Carmichael, following our exchange. She searched my face with no flicker of recognition. Then I saw the flash. She remembered me. Her eyes narrowed.

'Wh—' She stopped and swallowed. 'Wh— why's she here?'

'Elena's been helping me, Sondra. Since your . . . mishap.'

'Mi—?' Bauer swallowed again, tongue flicking over her dry lips. 'What mishap?'

'Grab Sondra a glass of water, Elena.'

Again Bauer's gaze settled on me. 'Wh— why's she here?'

'Get the water and then have the guards take you for a walk. I need to speak to Sondra.'

I retrieved the water and tried to ignore the second half of the request, but Carmichael shooed me away. I knew I shouldn't leave Carmichael alone with Bauer. I also knew there was no sense arguing with the doctor. So I settled for leaving with the in-room guards and advising the door guards to take up posts inside. To my surprise, they obeyed. It would have been a heartening sign of my growing power and position if I hadn't suspected they were hightailing it into the infirmary so they could regale their colleagues with tales of being the first to see the new werewolf awake.

After my walk, Tucker met us outside the infirmary.

'Drop her off with Peters and Lewis inside,' Tucker said. 'Then get down to the cells and escort Miss O'Donnell into Zaid's cell.'

'I thought Doctor Matasumi canceled all visits,' one of my guards said.

'Katz— Doctor Matasumi changed his mind.'

'But I thought he said—'

'He changed his mind. Miss O'Donnell will visit Zaid for one hour, followed by a one-hour visit with Miss Levine.'

'How is Savannah?' I asked.

Three pairs of eyes turned on me, as if the walls had spoken. For a moment it seemed no one was going to answer me, then Tucker said brusquely, 'She's fine.'

'You know, I wouldn't mind seeing her myself,' I said. 'Maybe cheer her up a little.'

'Miss O'Donnell can do that,' Tucker said, then turned and headed down the hall.

The two guards led me into the room. Bauer still lay on the bed. Carmichael sat beside her, holding her hand. I assumed Bauer had fallen back asleep, then noticed her eyes were open. Carmichael motioned me to silence.

'I know it's a shock,' Carmichael murmured. 'But you're in good health and—'

'Good health?' Bauer spat, turning to skewer Carmichael with blazing eyes. 'Do you know what I feel like right now? This – this—' Her left hand tried to punch the air, but only succeeded in a weak flutter before collapsing back at her side. 'This *isn't* my body. It's not me. It's – it's wrong. Horribly, disgustingly wrong. And the dreams.' She gave a choking gasp. 'Oh, God. The dreams.'

Carmichael touched Bauer's brow. Bauer closed her eyes and seemed to relax. Then she opened her eyes and saw me.

'Get her out of here,' Bauer said.

'I realize Elena might not be the person you most want to see right—'

'Get her out of here.'

Carmichael squeezed Bauer's hand. 'I know she's a reminder of what's happened, but you need her, Sondra. She understands what you're going through, and she can help us. Without her—'

'Without her?' Bauer looked at me and pulled back her lips in a snarl. 'Without her, I wouldn't be here.'

'I understand your anger, Sondra. If it hadn't been for Elena coming here, this would never have happened. But you can't blame her—'

'Can't blame her? Can't blame her?' Bauer's voice rose. 'Who the hell do you think did this to me?'

An hour later, I was back in my cell.

After everything I'd done, every risk I'd taken, one accusation from a newly turned, half-mad werewolf and I was in my goddamned cell. I'd nursed Bauer back to health. I'd prevented Carmichael from administering potentially life-threatening medicines. I'd thrown myself between Bauer and the gun-happy guards. How did she repay me? She blamed me, and not just in a figurative sense – because she'd used my saliva – but literally accusing me of turning her into a werewolf. Madness, right? What about the syringe? The needle mark? The evidence exonerated me. What did they think, that I'd stolen a syringe from the infirmary during my physical, filled it with my spit, and jabbed it into Bauer's arm? That was exactly what they thought. Or what Matasumi thought. Carmichael seemed to have the sense to realize this was preposterous. She hadn't said so outright, but she'd argued to keep me in the infirmary, and when I'd been forced to leave, she'd walked me to the door and promised to 'get things straightened out.'

How much good would Carmichael be as an ally? She was an employee with no real authority. When only Matasumi and Winsloe had been in charge, Carmichael's strong will had metamorphosed into true power. In battles of personality, Matasumi was defenseless. Winsloe had the requisite willpower to challenge anyone, but he kept out of the day-to-day running of the compound. So, in Bauer's absence, Carmichael had little trouble getting me into the infirmary against Matasumi's wishes. But now Bauer was back. Where did that leave Carmichael? I weighed the personalities of both women, assessing their chances.

There was one more factor to consider. How hard would Carmichael fight for me? She made little secret of her contempt for Winsloe and Matasumi but seemed fond of Bauer. Would she subject her weakened patient to a battle of wills? It depended on one thing: Bauer's convalescence. If Carmichael felt she needed me to help Bauer, she'd fight. But if Bauer recovered without relapse, I was shit outta luck. My best hope was for something horrible to happen, for Bauer to lose control, and for Carmichael and Matasumi to realize they needed my help. Knowing what a newly turned werewolf was capable of, it was an awful thing to wish for.

I had truly been cast out of favor. If there'd been any doubt, it soon vanished. The guards brought my breakfast two hours late, dropped it off, and left. Then they brought my lunch. Nothing happened in the interim. Absolutely nothing. Carmichael didn't summon me for a checkup. Matasumi didn't come down to question me. Xavier didn't pop by for a visit. Even Tess didn't take up observation duty outside my cell. I was left with my thoughts, consumed by memories of the night before. Alone with my fears, my self-recriminations, and my grief, reflecting on Armen's death, then Ruth's, then my own situation, which was growing bleaker with each passing hour.

Around mid-afternoon my door opened, and I leaped from my seat so fast you'd have thought Ed McMahon stood there with a Publishers Clearing House check. Okay, so it was only a guard, but at this point, any face was welcome. Maybe he was coming to take me upstairs. Maybe he was coming to deliver a message. Hell, maybe he was just coming to *talk* to me. Six hours of exile and I already felt as if I'd spent a week in solitary confinement.

The guard walked in, laid a bouquet of flowers on the table, and left.

Flowers? Who'd be sending me flowers? Carmichael trying to cheer me up? Right. Matasumi apologizing for sending me back to the cell? Oh, yeah. Bauer thanking me for all my selfless work on her behalf? That's gotta be it. With a bitter laugh, I turned the flowers around and read the card.

Elena,
Sorry to hear what happened.
I'll see what I can do.
    Ty

I slammed the vase off the table and clenched my fists, seething with fury. How dare he! After last night, how did he dare send me flowers, feign concern over my exile. I scowled at the flowers strewn across the carpet. Was this his idea of a joke? Or was he trying to fool me into thinking he still cared? Was he taunting me? Or did he, in his twisted way, really still care? Goddamn it! I snarled and kicked the vase across the room. When it didn't shatter, I strode over, scooped it up in one hand, and whirled to pitch it into the wall. Then I froze in mid-throw, fingers still wrapped around the vase. I couldn't do this. I couldn't afford to incur Winsloe's anger. The impotent fury that swept through me was almost enough to make me hurl the vase into the wall, damn the consequences. But I didn't. Giving into the rage would only give him an excuse to hurt me again. He wanted to play mind games? Fine. I dropped to my knees and began gathering the flowers, obliterating all signs of my anger. Next time Tyrone Winsloe stepped into my cell, he'd see his flowers nicely displayed on the table. And I'd thank him for his thoughtfulness. Smile and thank him. Two could play this game.

At seven o'clock that evening, the door opened. A guard walked in.

'They need you upstairs,' he said.

Elation rushed through me. Yes! And not a minute too soon. Then I saw his face, the tightness of his jaw failing to conceal the anxiety in his eyes.

'What's happened?' I said, getting to my feet.

He didn't answer, only turned and held the door. Two more guards waited in the hall. All had their guns drawn.

My stomach plunged. Was this it, then? Had Bauer ordered my death? Had Winsloe tired of toying with me and decided to hunt me? But that wouldn't make the guards anxious. Some, like Ryman and Jolliffe, would be fairly licking their chops at the prospect.

As I stepped through the door, the first guard poked me in the back with his gun, not a hard jab, more of an impatient prod. I picked up speed and we quick-marched through the security exit.

The infirmary waiting room was jam-packed. I counted seven guards, plus Tucker and Matasumi. As I stepped through the door, time slowed, giving me a montage of visual impressions bereft of smell and sound, like a silent movie cranking through one frame at a time.

Matasumi seated, face white, eyes staring at nothing. Tucker at the intercom barking silent orders. Five guards clustered around him. One guard sat beside Matasumi, head in his hands, palms over his eyes, chin damp, a wet smear staining one shirt sleeve. The last guard faced the far wall, bracing himself with arms outstretched, head bowed, chest heaving. As I shifted my weight forward, my shoe slid. Something slick on the floor. I glanced down. A thin puddle of opaque yellowish brown. Vomit. I looked up. The infirmary door was closed. I stepped forward, still in slow motion. Faces turned. The crowd parted, not giving me room but stepping away. Nine pairs of eyes on me, expressions ranging from apprehension to disgust.

'What's going on here?' Winsloe's voice behind me shattered the illusion.

I could smell now: vomit, sweat, anxiety, and fear. Someone muttered something unintelligible. Winsloe shoved past me to look through the infirmary door window. Everyone paused, collectively holding their breath.

'Holy shit!' Winsloe said, his voice filled not with horror but with wonder. 'Did Elena do – oh, shit, I see. Jesus fucking Christ, would you get a look at that!'

Almost against my will, my feet moved toward the infirmary door. Winsloe sidestepped to give me room and put his arm around my waist, pulling me in.

'Can you believe that?' he said, then laughed. 'I guess you can, right?'

At first, I saw nothing. Or nothing unusual. Beyond the window was the counter, shining antiseptic white, stainless-steel sink gleaming like something in a kitchen showroom. A row of bottles stood at attention along the back of the counter. Carmichael's binder lay at a perfect ninety-degree angle beside the sink. Everything ordered and spotless, as always. Then something along the base of the counter caught my eye. An obscenity amid the pristine cleanliness. A star-shaped splatter of blood.

My gaze traversed the floor. A smear of blood six inches from the counter. Fat drops zigzagging to the crash cart. The cart upended, contents scattered and broken. A puddle of blood. A shoe print in the puddle, edges razor perfect. Then another smear, bigger, the bloodied shoe sliding across the floor. The filing cabinet. The hundred-pound steel cabinet toppled over, blockading the far corner as if someone had tipped it and hidden behind its imperfect barricade. Papers scattered across the floor. Blood spattered over them. Beneath the bed, a shoe with a bloodied bottom. Above the shoe, a leg. I whirled to face the others, to tell them someone was in there. As I turned, my gaze traveled up the leg to the knee, to a pool of bright crimson, to nothingness. A severed leg. My stomach leaped to my throat. I spun away, fast, but not fast enough. I saw a hand lying a few feet from the bed. Closer to the door, half-obscured under a spilled tray, a bloody hunk of meat that had been human.

Something hit the door, reverberating so hard I stumbled back with the impact. A roar of fury. A flash of yellowish-brown fur. An ear. A blood-soaked muzzle. Bauer.

'Tranquilizers,' I wheezed as I regained my balance. 'We need to sedate her. Now.'

'That's the problem,' Tucker said. 'It's all in there.'

'All of it?' I inhaled, blinking, struggling to get my brain working again. I rubbed a hand across my face, straightened up and looked around. 'There must be a backup supply. Where's Doctor Carmichael? She'll know.'

No one answered. As silence ticked by, my guts heaved again. I closed my eyes and forced myself to look through the window, back at the foot under the bed. The shoe. A sensible, sturdy black shoe. Carmichael's shoe.

Oh, God. That wasn't fair. It was so, so, so not fair. The refrain raced through my head, chasing out all other thoughts. Of everyone in this goddamned place. Of all those who I'd gladly see die. Of those few I'd even be happy to see die a death as horrible as this. Not Carmichael.

Rage surged through me. I clenched my fists, gave into

the anger for a moment, then shoved it back as I turned to face the others.

'She's fully Changed,' I said. 'You have a fully Changed, half-mad werewolf in there, and if you don't act fast, she'll come right through this door. Why's everyone standing around? What are you going to do?'

'The question is,' Tucker said, 'what are *you* doing to do?'

I stepped away from the door. 'This is your problem, not mine. I warned you. I warned and warned and warned. You used me to help her recover, then you threw me back in my cell. Now things have gone wrong and you want me to fix it? Well, I didn't screw it up in the first place.'

Tucker waved at the guards. One moved to the door, checked through the window and turned the handle.

'You'll find sedatives in the cupboards along the far wall,' Tucker said.

'No way,' I said. 'No fucking way.'

Four of the remaining guards lifted their guns. Trained those guns on me.

'I will not—'

The door opened. Someone shoved me. As I stumbled in, the door slammed shut, catching my heel and knocking me to the floor. Scrambling to my feet, I heard nothing but silence. Then a sound vibrated through the room, more felt than heard. A growl.

RAMPAGE

till on all fours, I looked up slowly. A 120-pound wolf
stared back, yellow-brown fur on end, making Bauer
seem as big as a mastiff. She stared me in the eyes,
ears forward, teeth bared, curled in a silent snarl.

I looked away and stayed down, holding myself a few
inches lower than Bauer. The submission rankled, but my
life was worth more than my pride. And yes, at that moment,
I was very worried about my life expectancy. Even Clay
would avoid tackling a werewolf who was in wolf form when
he was not. As a wolf, Bauer had the advantage of teeth
and claws. Moreover, the human shape itself is awkward for
fighting an animal – too slow, too tall, too easily thrown
off-balance. The only superior weapon humans have is their
brain, and that doesn't help much against something with
an animal body and a human brain. Against a newly turned
werewolf, the human brain is actually a disadvantage. Our
minds are fundamentally logical. We assess a situation,
devise possible strategies, and pick the one that represents
the best compromise between likelihood of success and likelihood of survival. If I'm late for work, I can floor the gas
pedal all the way to the office, but considering the risk of

personal injury, I'll choose instead to drive ten or fifteen miles over the speed limit and arrive at work slightly late but alive. A new werewolf in wolf form loses that ability to reason, to assess the consequences. It is like a rabid beast, fueled by instinct and fury, ready to destroy everything in sight, even if it kills itself in the process.

I could fight Bauer only if I Changed into a wolf. But even under ideal conditions that took five to ten minutes. Like Lake, I'd be completely vulnerable during that interim, too deformed even to stand and run away. Bauer would tear me apart before I sprouted fur. Yet no one was letting me out of here until I stopped Bauer. The only way to do that would be to sedate her.

To knock Bauer out, all I had to do was run across the room, grab a sedative-filled syringe from the cupboard, and jab it into her. It sounded so easy. If only there wasn't a blood-crazed wolf between the cupboard and me. Even if Bauer didn't pounce on me before I ran past, she'd attack the second my back was to her. I inhaled. First step: I had to find the proper mix of submission and self-confidence. Too submissive and she'd see me as easy prey. Too assertive and she'd see me as a threat. The key was to not show fear. Again, it sounded so easy . . . if you weren't in a room littered with bloody body parts, reminding you that with one false move your limbs and vital organs would join them.

I inched forward, keeping my gaze focused below Bauer's eyes. As I moved, I scrutinized her body for signs: bunched muscles, tense tendons, all the signals that preceded an attack. In five steps, I was parallel to her, about six feet to her left. Sweat stung my eyes. Did it stink of fear? Bauer's nose twitched, but the rest of her remained motionless. As I sidestepped past, I swiveled, keeping my face to her. Her eyes followed me. I kept moving sideways. A dozen steps to go. Bauer's hindquarters shifted up, the first sign of an impending leap. With that early sign, I thought I'd have time to react. I didn't. By the time my brain registered that she was about to lunge, she was airborne. There was no time to turn and run. I dove past her, hit the ground and rolled. Behind me, Bauer hit the floor, all four legs skidding. As I watched her slide, I realized I did have an advantage here. Like a new driver plunked behind the wheel of a Maserati, Bauer was unprepared for the power and precision handling of her new body. If I could take advantage of her mistakes and inexperience, I could survive.

As I lurched to my feet, Bauer was veering around. I sprinted past her and vaulted onto the counter. Throwing one cupboard open, I grabbed the wooden partition between the doors to balance myself and spun around. Bauer flew at me. I kicked her under the jaw and she somersaulted backward, skidding across the floor. As I flipped to face the cupboards, I saw faces crowding the infirmary window. Were they enjoying the show? Damn, I hoped so.

While Bauer recovered, I threw open the second cupboard door and searched both sides for syringes filled with sedative. Instead, I saw a box of plastic-encased syringes and rows of labeled bottles. A do-it-yourself job. Shit! Were these the right syringes? Which bottle did I need? How much should I fill it? I pushed my questions aside, grabbed a syringe, and started scooting down the counter toward the bottles. Then I stopped, plucked a second packaged syringe from the box and shoved it into my pocket. Klutz insurance. When I reached the bottles, I scanned them for a familiar name. Behind me, Bauer struggled to her feet. Move, Elena! Just grab one! I saw pentobarbital, recognized it from Jeremy's medical bag, and reached for it. Bauer leaped at the counter but miscalculated and crashed into it. The whole structure shook as my fingers grazed the pentobarbital. My hand knocked the bottle. I fumbled for it, but it toppled from the cupboard, bounced off the countertop, and rolled across the linoleum. As Bauer circled for another attack, I reached for a new bottle of sedative. There wasn't another one. Frantically, I scanned the shelf, but saw nothing I recognized. Bauer leaped. I swung around to kick her again, but missed by a hair's breadth. This time I hadn't braced myself, and the motion propelled me off-balance. I pitched forward and jumped from the counter before I fell. Bauer grabbed my left leg at the knee. Her fangs sank in. Pain clouded my vision. Blindly I swung my fist at the source of the pain, connected with her skull, and sent her reeling, probably more from surprise than pain. When she jerked away, her fangs ripped through my knee. My leg buckled as soon as I put weight on it. Gritting my teeth, I stumbled to the bottle of pentobarbital on the floor, found it – unbroken – snatched it up and sailed awkwardly over the first bed. As Bauer leaped after me, I thrust the bed at her and knocked her off her feet.

I tore the seal off the bottle and filled the syringe. Did I use too much? Did I care? If it stopped Bauer – temporarily or forever – that was good enough. Bauer flew over the bed. I scrambled over the second bed, but Bauer caught my foot.

Her fangs scraped my ankle as my shoe came free in her mouth. The shoe snagged on her teeth and she tumbled back to the floor, shaking her head wildly to free herself from this new enemy. Still atop the second bed, I lifted the syringe over Bauer and plunged it down, feeling a momentary elation as the needle penetrated the deep fur behind Bauer's head. Now all I had to do was hit the plunger. But I'd put so much force into the downswing that I wasn't prepared for the next step. I released the syringe to get a better grip and Bauer twisted away, leaving the needle stuck harmlessly in her shoulder.

As Bauer lunged at my legs, I jumped to the floor. At this rate, I was fast running out of obstacles. I raced around the end of the bed as Bauer hurtled over it. I shoved the bed, trying to hit her again, but she'd leaped high enough this time and cleared it easily. While she circled around, I sprinted across the room. Could I get close enough to depress the syringe plunger? Not without getting close enough for Bauer to rip out my throat.

I grabbed a metal cart and flung it at Bauer as she came at me. It knocked her back. I turned to find some new weapon. At my feet lay a bloodstained piece of white cloth. With a gnawed torso inside it, and a head atop it, neck bitten through almost to decapitation, eyes wide, disbelieving. Carmichael. Her eyes paralyzed me. I could have saved her. If they'd brought me up here earlier. . . . How long did they wait? How long was Carmichael in here with Bauer? Running for her life? Feeling teeth rip through her flesh? Knowing it was over but still hoping, praying for rescue? Had she been dead before Bauer began ripping her apart? Before Bauer started to eat her? Oh, God. I doubled over, faintly registering a blur of motion to my left, knowing Bauer was coming but unable to move, unable to wrench my gaze or my thoughts from Carmichael. Out of the corner of my eye, I saw Bauer leap. That broke the spell.

I dove out of Bauer's path, but she caught my pant leg in her teeth and I tripped, crashing to the floor. As I flipped over, she leaped onto my chest, jaws wide, slashing down at my throat. I brought my fists up into the underside of her jaw, skewing her aim. Wrapping both hands in her neck fur, I fought to keep her head away from mine. Her jaws snapped so close a rush of hot air hit my throat. The stink of her breath enveloped me, the stench of blood and rage and raw meat. I arched my head up to meet her eyes, trying to assert my superiority with a glare. It didn't work. It would never work. She was too far gone to recognize a dominant wolf. Grappling with her, I managed to get both my legs up and thrust them into her stomach. She fell back. As I scrambled from under her, something moved to my left. Xavier. He waved his arms.

'Here doggy, doggy,' he called. 'Time for a new chew-toy.'

Bauer kept coming at me. Xavier lunged and grabbed a handful of tail fur. When she whipped around, he vanished and reappeared a few feet away. She charged. He popped to the other side of the room.

'Over here, doggy,' he called. 'Come on, Elena. You have to hit the plunger for the stuff to work.'

'I know that,' I snarled.

Bauer wheeled and charged Xavier again. This time, I tore after her. Xavier waited until the last second, then disappeared. Bauer tried to stop but had built up too much speed and plowed into the wall. I jumped on her back and slammed the syringe plunger down. Relief flooded me. Then I realized Bauer was twisting around, jaws open. What had I expected? That she'd drop the second the sedative went in? I whacked my open hand against the sensitive top of Bauer's muzzle. Then I ran like hell. Behind me, I heard a thud, but I didn't turn around until I'd leaped onto the countertop. Bauer lay crumpled on the floor. For a moment, I stood there, rigid, heart pounding. Then I slumped onto the counter.

An hour later I was back in my cell. I sensed a pattern here – save the day, get thrown into solitary confinement. Great motivation.

Though Bauer had only scraped my foot, she'd done a bang-up job on my knee. Without Carmichael, there was no one to tend to my wounds. Matasumi had examined my leg and pronounced that the muscles and tendons may or may not have been torn. Gee, thanks. Tucker had stitched up the two longest tears. He hadn't used anesthetic, but I'd been too exhausted to care.

Once inside my cell, I went into the bathroom, undressed, and sponge-bathed with a facecloth. A shower would have been heaven, but I couldn't get my bandages wet. As I scrubbed blood from the tear in my jeans, I remembered the blood splatters in the infirmary and, remembering the blood, remembered the mangled pieces of Carmichael scattered across the floor. I stopped and inhaled. Damn her. Why hadn't she listened to me? If she'd heeded my warnings,

349

if she'd properly restrained Bauer, if she'd kept Bauer under guard, if she'd fought harder to keep me in the infirmary . . . So many ifs.

I closed my eyes and inhaled again. I didn't even know Carmichael's first name. As that thought skittered guiltily through my brain, I realized it didn't matter. I'd known enough about her to know that, however misguided the aspirations and dreams that brought her to this place, she hadn't deserved to die like that. She'd been the only person who'd given a damn about Bauer, and Bauer's first act as a werewolf had been to slaughter her. How do you like your new life now, Sondra? Is it everything you imagined?

The door of my cell opened. I glanced up to see Xavier, for once using the conventional method of entering a room. He closed the door behind him and waved a bottle of Jack Daniel's.

'Thought you could use this,' he said. 'Probably not up to your standards, but Winsloe keeps moving his stash of the good stuff.'

I wrung out my jeans over the sink and tugged them on. Xavier could see my state of undress through the glass wall but didn't comment on it. Maybe the tragedy upstairs had shaken him. Or maybe he was just too tired for one-liners.

When Xavier had come to my rescue in the infirmary, I'd assumed Matasumi or Tucker had sent him in, but later, when the two of them discussed the situation while examining my knee, I'd learned Xavier had acted on his own. Of course, with his powers, he'd never been in any real danger from Bauer, but at least he'd put himself out enough to help. So, for once, I didn't tell him get the hell out of my cell. Besides, I really did need a drink.

While I dressed, Xavier filled the two tumblers he'd brought. He handed me one as I walked from the bathroom.

'How did that happen?' I asked. 'Where were the guards?'

'They'd decided guards weren't necessary. Sondra was still partially restrained last time I saw her. Either she broke free or the good doctor released her. A guard stopped by at six-thirty and found Sondra chowing down on her first wolf meal.'

'No one heard anything?'

'Hey, they bought the best soundproofing on the market, remember? I'd bet Carmichael hit the intercom buzzer but didn't have time to stand around and chat. Of course, no one in central security admits he heard the buzzer.'

I downed my whiskey and shook my head.

'I've saved your ass twice now,' Xavier said. 'With Ryman and Jolliffe yesterday and now with Sondra.'

'Sorry, but they confiscated my checkbook when I arrived. You'll have to bill me.'

He grinned, unoffended. 'Money isn't everything. Or so they keep telling me. This seems a good time to test the theory and try an even more time-honored method of commerce. The barter system. A tax-free exchange of services.'

'Uh-huh.'

'Oh, don't give me that look,' he said, tipping another few ounces into my glass. 'I'm not talking about sex. You'd eat me alive.' He paused and made a face. 'Bad choice of words. My apologies to the good doctor. What I meant is

351

that you owe me big-time, and someday I will collect.'

'I'm sure you will.'

'And so long as you're running a tab, here's a bit of advice you can add to it. You've overstayed your welcome, Elena. We both have. The big man is plenty pissed with both of us right now.'

'Winsloe.' I closed my eyes and winced. 'Now what did I do?'

'Enough. I know you must be making escape plans, so I'd suggest you bump them up before he erupts.' He lowered his voice to a near-whisper. 'Now, two things you have to be careful of when you break out. First is Katzen—'

'The mysterious sorcerer. I haven't even met the guy.'

'Neither have I. He's a paranoid son of a bitch. Won't deal with anyone except—'

My cell door opened. Winsloe walked in with Ryman and Jolliffe.

'Too late,' Xavier murmured around the rim of his glass. He took a slug, then waved the empty glass at Winsloe. 'See what I have to resort to? Jack Daniel's. Barely drinkable. You get me hooked on the good stuff, then keep hiding it on me. Sadistic bastard.'

Xavier grinned, and I detected more than a hint of satisfaction in that grin, the pleasure of being able to call Winsloe that to his face and get away with it.

'You owe me a bottle of cognac anyway,' Xavier continued. 'I like the Remy Martin XO, not the VSOP. You can have someone drop it off at my room later.'

Winsloe arched his brows. 'And how do you figure that?'

'I saved your girl. Twice now, actually.' He grinned at

Ryman and Jolliffe. 'But we won't get into that first time, will we, guys? I'm no tattletale. Besides, that wasn't a big deal. But upstairs there? Whew. Another minute and she'd have been a goner.'

'You think?' Winsloe said.

'Oh, yeah.' Xavier slapped my back. 'No offense, Elena, but you were in way over your head.'

'Thanks,' I said, and managed to almost sound like I meant it.

'So you owe me, Ty. Drop off that bottle anytime.'

Winsloe laughed. 'You've got balls, Reese. Fair enough then. I owe you. You'll get your cognac. Stop by my room in about an hour and pick it up. Maybe I can rustle up a few glasses of the Louis XIII for us, make that XO taste like bad moonshine.'

'Sounds like a plan.'

Under Xavier's quick grins and Winsloe's easygoing camaraderie thrummed a current of tension so strong you could almost see it. Xavier had been right. He was in deep shit. Yet both men chatted away as if nothing was wrong, as if they were just two old buddies planning to get together later for a few drinks. Masters of bullshit, both of them.

'So I'll see you in my room?' Winsloe said. 'In an hour?'

'You bet,' Xavier said. And I knew he had no intention of keeping that appointment, just as I knew that when he bade me good night he was really saying good-bye and that if he ever collected on that IOU, it wouldn't be within these compound walls. Like all successful gamblers, Xavier knew when to take the money and run.

After Xavier zapped from the room, Winsloe's gaze slithered over me and he pursed his lips.

'That's the same clothing you arrived in,' he said. 'They've given you other stuff to wear, haven't they? What about that shirt I brought you?'

Actually, I'd tried using it as a spare washcloth, but there wasn't enough fabric to get decent sudsing action. Be nice, I reminded myself. If Xavier was right, I was already on Winsloe's bad side. Again. I couldn't afford to make things worse. No matter how badly I'd been torn up that night, physically and emotionally, I had to play nice. Had to. Whatever he said. Whatever he did. I could not fight back. It would be a greater game of wit and fortitude than my match with Bauer, but I could handle this. I really could.

'It's a werewolf thing,' I said, injecting apology into my tone. 'Laundry soaps, fabric softeners – the smell's too strong.'

'You should have said so. I'll tell the staff to get unscented detergent. Don't bother with the clothes Sondra supplied. I'll order new things for you.'

Oh, joy.

Winsloe plopped onto my bed. I stayed standing, back to the bookshelf, trying hard not to feel concerned.

'Can you believe what Sondra did to the doc?' Winsloe asked, eyes glinting like a little boy who's seen his first NHL blood-on-ice brawl.

'It . . . happens.'

'You ever do stuff like that?'

'I'm a Pack werewolf.'

He hesitated, as if this was a non sequitur. Then he

leaned forward. 'But you could do it. Obviously. You're stronger and *much* younger.'

When I didn't answer, he hopped to his feet and rocked on his heels. 'You did a helluva job of evading Sondra. Better than the doc, that's for sure.' He laughed. The sound grated down my spine. 'Too bad Xavier interfered. I'd hoped you'd fight Sondra.'

'Sorry.'

I should have explained why I hadn't fought, but I couldn't. My exhaustion was too great. An apology would have to suffice. Maybe if I was polite but not encouraging, he'd take the hint and leave.

'You should have fought her,' Winsloe said.

I shook my head, eyes downcast, and slumped into a chair.

'I would have liked it if you'd fought her,' he continued.

How 'bout you fight her next time, Ty? Now I'*d* like that. I kept my eyes down so he wouldn't see the flare of contempt.

'I would have liked that, Elena,' he repeated, ducking his head to look at me.

'Why didn't you say so?' Damn! Too sharp. Retreat, retreat. 'I guess I got the impression you guys wanted Bauer alive. I should have asked.'

Silence. Had that still sounded sarcastic? Damn it! Change tack, double-time. I yawned and rubbed my hands over my face.

'I'm sorry, Ty. I'm so tired.'

'You didn't look tired when I walked in. Standing around, chatting it up with Xavier. You two seem pretty tight.'

'I was just thanking him. He did me a big favor, jumping in—'

He snapped his fingers, pique vanishing in an eye blink. 'Favor. That reminds me, there's something I need to ask you about. Hold on and I'll be right back.'

I wanted to ask if it could wait until morning. I really did. But after last night, I desperately needed to get back into his good graces. I couldn't deny him a favor. Besides, he seemed to be in a chipper mood. That was a good sign. So I summoned my last bits of strength, managed a clumsy half-smile, and nodded. Not that my consent mattered. Winsloe and his guards were already gone.

TORTURE

When Winsloe returned I was dozing in my chair. He burst into the cell waving a manila envelope. 'Devil of a time finding these buggers,' he said. 'Larry had already filed them in his to-do box. Way too efficient.'

I roused myself. Tried to look interested. Accidentally yawned.

'Am I boring you, Elena?' Winsloe asked. The edge in his voice twisted his grin into a teeth-baring grimace.

'No, no.' Bite back another yawn. 'Of course not. What do you have there?'

'Surveillance photos of a werewolf I'd like you to identify.'

'Sure' – Damn it, Elena. Stop yawning! – 'if I can, but my memory for faces is pretty bad.'

'That's okay. This one doesn't have a face.' Winsloe chortled. 'Not a human face, I mean. He's a wolf. If you ask me, all wolves look the same, which is why Larry didn't bother asking you for an ID. But then I thought, maybe that kind of thinking is too race-centered. You know, like those witnesses who get on the stand and finger the wrong black guy because all black men look the same to them?'

'Uh-huh.' Get to the point. Please. Before I drift off.

'So, I thought, maybe all wolf faces don't look the same to a wolf. Or to a part-time wolf.' Another chortle that set my nerves on edge.

'I'll do my best,' I said. 'But if I've seen this mutt before, I've probably only seen him as a human. A scent would be better.'

'Scent.' Winsloe snapped his fingers. 'Now why didn't I think of that. See? Race-centered again. I think I'm sharp if I can identify the smell of pepperoni pizza.'

I reached for the envelope. He thumped onto the bed and tossed it beside him, as if he hadn't noticed me reaching for it.

'Could I see—' I began.

'A team spotted this guy late last night. No, I guess that'd be early this morning. The wee hours anyway.'

I nodded. Please, please, please get to the point.

'Very bizarre circumstances,' Winsloe mused. 'Ever since we snatched you and the old witch, we've had a team trying to find the rest of your group. We could always use another werewolf, and Larry's pretty keen on getting that fire-demon guy. We lost track of them after we grabbed you two. That's not exactly a secret, though I'd rather you didn't tell Larry I told you. He's not too pleased about the whole thing, but I'm sure it makes you feel better, knowing your friends got away.'

Winsloe paused: And waited.

'Thanks,' I said, 'for telling me.'

'You're welcome. So, we've had this team scouting the area, picking up tips, most of them useless. Yesterday Tucker recalled that group and sent a fresh one to replace them. Keeping up morale and all that. The first team was heading back and spent the night in some backwater motel. Next morning, they get up for a pre-dawn start, go outside and what do you think they see there, on the edge of the woods?'

'A – uh—' Come on, brain, wake up. 'A – umm, a wolf?'

'Glad to see you're paying attention, Elena. Yes, it was a wolf. A big fucker of a wolf. Standing right there, watching them. Now either this is the biggest coincidence in the universe or this werewolf had been following them. Searching for the search party.'

Brain kicking in now. 'Where was this?'

'Does it matter?'

'All werewolves are territorial. Technically mutts can't hold territory, but most stick to a familiar piece of ground, like a state, just moving from city to city. If I knew where this took place, it would help me figure out who it might have been.'

Winsloe smiled. 'And help you figure out where *you* are. None of that, Elena. Now let me tell my story. So, the guards see this wolf and they figure out that it's a werewolf. One grabs a camera and snaps some photos. The other two go for the tranquilizer guns. Before they can unpack them, though, the wolf vanishes. So they gear up and head into the woods. And do you know what? He's right there, like he's waiting. They get close, he runs, then stops and waits. Luring them in. Can you believe that?'

'Werewolves retain human intelligence. It's not that strange.' But it was. Why? Because luring prey was an animal tactic and mutts didn't use animal tactics. No, I corrected quickly. They *rarely* used animal tactics. Of course they *could*. Some did.

'Wait,' Winsloe said, grinning. 'It gets weirder. You know what this wolf does next? He separates them. Takes a commando team, including a former Navy Seal, and figures out how to separate them. Then he starts picking them off. Killing them! Can you believe that?' Winsloe laughed and shook his head. 'Man, I wish I'd been there. One werewolf turning those military goons into blithering idiots, wandering around the woods, getting picked off like blonds in a horror flick. The wolf kills two and goes after the third. And what do you think he does?'

My heart was pounding now. 'Kills him?'

'No! That's the topper. He doesn't kill him. He runs him ragged. Like he's trying to exhaust him, like he wants to keep him alive but too weak to fight. Okay, maybe I'm reading too much into this, attributing human motivations to an animal. Anthro— what do they call that?'

'Anthropomorphism,' I whispered, feeling as if all the air had been knocked from my lungs, knowing this was no accidental segue.

'Right. Anthropomorphism. Hey, that's what your boyfriend studies, right? Anthropomorphic religions. Boring as hell if you ask me, but people say that about computers, too. Each to his own. Now where was I?'

'The wolf,' I whispered. 'Running down the last survivor.'

'You don't look so good. Maybe you should come over here and lie down. Plenty of room. No? Suit yourself. So the wolf is running circles around this last guy. Only something goes wrong.'

360

I wanted to stop up my ears. I knew what was coming. There was only one way Winsloe could have the photos in that envelope, only one way he'd know this story. If the last team member had survived. If the wolf—

'Somehow that canny fucker screwed up. Miscalculated a turn or a distance maybe. He got too close. The guard fired. Pow! Dead wolf.'

'Let – let me see the photos.'

Winsloe tossed the envelope at me. As it tumbled to the floor, I scrambled after it, ripping it open and yanking out the contents. Three photos of a wolf. A golden-haired, blue-eyed wolf. I felt a whimper snake up my throat.

'You know him?' Winsloe asked.

I crouched there, clutching the photos.

'No? Well, you're tired. Keep them. Get some rest and give it some thought. Xavier's probably waiting for me upstairs. I'll come back in the morning.'

Winsloe left. I didn't see him go. Didn't hear him. All I could see was the photographs of Clay. All I could hear was the pounding of my blood. Another whimper crept up from my chest, but it died before reaching my mouth. I couldn't breathe. Couldn't make a sound.

Suddenly my body convulsed. A wave of agony blinded me. I toppled, photos fluttering the carpet. My leg muscles all knotted at once, like being seized by a thousand charley horses. I screamed. The waves hit in rapid succession and I screamed until I couldn't breathe. My limbs flailed and jerked as if being wrenched from their sockets. Some dim part of my brain realized I was Changing and told me to get control before it tore me apart. I didn't. I gave into it, let the agony rip through me, welcomed each new torment even as I screamed for release. Finally it was over. I lay there, panting, empty. Then I heard something. The faintest scratch from the hallway. Winsloe was there. Watching. I wanted to leap up, charge the wall, and batter myself against it until it broke or I did. I wanted to tear him apart, mouthful by mouthful, keeping him alive until I'd wrenched every last shriek from his lungs. But grief crushed me to the floor, and I couldn't even find the energy to stand. I managed to pull my belly off the ground and hauled myself into the narrow crevice between the foot of the bed and the wall, the one place where Winsloe couldn't see me. I wedged into the tiny space, tucked my tail under me, and surrendered to the pain.

I spent the night replaying Winsloe's words, fighting against my grief to recall each one. Where had the guards seen the wolf? Behind the motel or beside it? Exactly when did it happen? What did Winsloe mean by 'pre-dawn'? Had it been light out yet? As I asked these questions, part of me wondered if I was just allowing my mind to stutter through inanities rather than confront the soul-numbing possibility of Clay's death. No. These questions held clues, minute clues that would reveal the lie in Winsloe's words. I had to find that lie. Otherwise, I feared my breath would jam up in my throat and I'd suffocate on my grief.

So I tortured myself with Winsloe's story, his hated voice invading and filling my brain. Find the lie. Find the inconsistency, the misspoken word, the detail so obviously wrong. But no matter how many times I replayed his story, I couldn't find a mistake. If Clay found the search party, he'd have done exactly what Winsloe claimed he did: lure them into the forest, separate them, and kill them, leaving one alive to torture for information. There was no way Winsloe could make up something so true to Clay's character. Nor was there any way Winsloe could have guessed what Clay would do in that situation. So he'd told the truth.

My heart rammed into my throat. I gasped for breath. No, it had to be a lie. I'd know if Clay was dead. I'd have felt it the moment the bullet hit him. Oh, God, I wanted to believe that I'd know if he was dead. Clay and I shared a psycho-physical connection, maybe because he was the one who had bitten me. If I were hurt and he wasn't around to see it, he'd feel it, knowing something was wrong. I'd experience the same twinges, the same floating anxiety and unease if he were hurt. I hadn't felt anything that morning. Or had I? I'd been asleep at dawn, drugged by Carmichael's sedative. Would I have felt *anything*?

I stopped myself. There was no sense dwelling on vagaries like premonitions and psychic twinges. Stick to the facts. Find the lie there. Winsloe said the last guard killed Clay, then returned with the photos and the story. If I could talk to that guard, maybe he wouldn't be as accomplished a liar as Winsloe. Maybe – I inhaled sharply. The guard had brought back the photos and the story. What about the body?

If that guard had killed Clay, he'd have brought back his body. At the very least, he'd have taken photos of it. If there'd been a corpse or photos of one, Winsloe wouldn't have settled for showing me pictures of Clay alive. He'd known exactly who the wolf was and he'd told me the story to torture me, to punish me. This was my comeuppance for disobeying him the night before. One small misstep and he'd lashed out with the worst punishment I could imagine. What would he do if I really pissed him off?

Eventually, after I'd persuaded myself that Clay was alive, the exhaustion took over and I fell asleep. Though I'd fallen asleep as a wolf, I awoke as a human. It happened sometimes, particularly if a Change was brought on by fear or emotion. Once we relaxed into sleep, the body morphed painlessly back to human form. So I awoke, naked, with my head and torso sandwiched between the bed and the wall and my legs sticking out.

I didn't get up immediately. Instead, I thought of ways to catch Winsloe in a lie, so I'd be certain about Clay. I had to be certain. Winsloe had left the photos. Maybe if I studied them I'd see something—

'Open this fucking door now!' a voice shouted.

I bolted upright, knocking my head against the bed. Dazed, I hesitated, then wriggled from my hiding place.

'Let me out of here!'

A woman's voice. Distorted, but familiar. I winced as I recognized it. No. Please no. Hadn't I suffered enough?

'I know you hear me! I know you're out there!'

With great reluctance, I moved to the hole in the wall between my cell and the next. I knew what I'd see. My new neighbor. I bent to peer through. Bauer stood at the one-way glass wall, banging her fists soundlessly against it. Her hair was snarled and matted, face still streaked with blood.

Someone had dressed her in an ill-fitting gray sweat suit that must have belonged to one of the smaller guards. No more meticulously groomed heiress. Anyone seeing Sondra Bauer now would take her for a middle-aged mental patient coughed up from the bowels of some gothic asylum.

After last night's rampage, they'd put Bauer in the next cell. The last wisp of hope in my dream of escape evaporated. Bauer was now as much a prisoner as I. She couldn't help me one whit. More than that, I now had a crazed, man-killing werewolf in the next cell, with a hole through the wall that separated us. Was this Winsloe's doing? Wasn't last night's torture enough? I realized it would never be enough. As long as I was in this compound, Winsloe would find new ways to persecute me. Why? Because he could.

I wanted to crawl back into my hidey-hole and go to sleep. I wouldn't sleep, of course, but I could close my eyes and blot out this whole nightmare, dredge up some happy fantasy world in my mind, and live there until someone rescued me or killed me, whichever came first.

Instead, with great effort, I plunked onto my bed and surveyed the room. My Change had shredded my clothing. So much for my wardrobe rebellion. I exhaled. No time for brooding. I'd have to wear whatever they'd given me. First step: Get presentable. Then I'd find out why Bauer was in the next cell.

When I emerged from the bathroom, clean and dressed, I returned to the hole and peeped through, in case Bauer's presence there had been a sadistic twist of my imagination. It wasn't. She lay huddled at the foot of the door, whimpering and scratching the glass like a kitten caught in the rain. I might have felt sorry for her, but I was fresh out of pity.

I sensed someone in the halls. Maybe it wasn't so much 'sensing' as assuming Tess or Matasumi would be observing the new werewolf. I raked my fingers through my hair, straightened my shirt, and walked to my own one-way glass wall.

'Could I please speak to someone?' I asked, calmly and clearly, hoping to set myself apart from the lunatic next door.

Moments later, two guards entered my cell.

'Could someone please tell me why Ms. Bauer is next door?' I asked.

They looked at one another, as if debating whether to answer. Then one said, 'Doctor Matasumi felt it was necessary to confine her. For security reasons.'

No shit. 'I certainly understand that. But could you tell me why she's in *that* particular room? There's a hole in the wall joining our cells.'

'I believe they are aware of that.'

'They?' I asked, all wide-eyed innocence.

'Doctor Matasumi and Mr. Winsloe.'

'Ah.' I inhaled softly. My teeth ached from all this saccharin. 'So they are aware they've given Ms. Bauer a cell with access to mine?'

'Mr. Winsloe felt it fulfilled all necessary security requirements.'

With as sweet a smile as I could muster, I thanked them for their time and they left. So I'd been right. This was Winsloe's idea. Put Bauer in the cell next to mine, leave the gaping hole unrepaired, and see what happens.

Once they were gone, I checked the hole. I'd torn it open nearly to the steel bracing, and it was less than a foot square. So there was no real risk of Bauer breaking through. The most we could do was communicate.

Without warning, Bauer leaped to her feet and slammed her fists against the glass. 'Open this door, you fucking bastards! Open it or I'll rip out your goddamned hearts! I'm the big bad wolf now. I can huff and I can puff and I'll blow you to smithereens.' Her voice trailed off in a high-pitched hiccuping laugh.

Well, *theoretically* we could communicate.

I examined the photos of Clay for clues as to when and where they were taken. The date stamp on the back said August 27. I mentally counted days. August 27 had been yesterday. So Winsloe's story had been true – at least the part about someone taking these pictures of Clay the morning before. I still refused to believe he was dead. Judging by the realism of Winsloe's tale, I assumed Clay really had killed several members of a search party. That made sense. If Jeremy discovered these guards were following the group, he'd have sent Clay after them with instructions to bring one back alive for questioning. But the last time I'd seen Clay, he'd been in no shape for high-risk missions.

'Do you recognize him?'

I whirled to see Winsloe and his two guards in my cell.

Winsloe smiled. 'Werewolf hearing not up to par this morning, Elena?'

Come to see what damage your sadistic ploy has wrought, Ty? Well, last night's breakdown was all the reward you're going to get. I was back and ready to play the game.

'Sorry,' I said. 'I was busy studying these pictures. He looks vaguely familiar, but I'm not coming up with a name.' Eyes still riveted on the photos, I asked. 'So, how did Xavier like the cognac?'

A split second of hesitation. I peeked out of the corner of my eye and saw Winsloe's mouth tighten. Score one for me. I bit my cheek to keep from grinning. Winsloe rolled his shoulders and crossed the room. When he looked my way again, he'd replaced his smile.

'Bastard never showed up,' Winsloe said. 'Probably passed out somewhere sleeping off that Jack Daniel's.'

Oh, yeah. Sleeping it off in a five-star hotel somewhere with a wallet full of Winsloe's cash.

'Probably,' I said. 'Now, about this wolf you want me to ID, like I said last night, a scent would be better. Get me a scent and, if I've met the guy, I'll know it.'

'You're that good?'

I smiled. 'The best. If you had an article of clothing or—' I jerked my head up. 'I know. The body. You have the body, right? Doctor Matasumi wouldn't leave the body in the woods for anyone to find. Take me to it and I'll give you that ID.'

Winsloe pulled out my dining chair and lowered himself onto it, buying a few extra seconds. Come on, asshole. Think fast.

'Well, that's a problem,' Winsloe said. 'The guard was really shaken up after he shot the brute. Hightailed it back here. Larry and Tucker lit into him like you wouldn't believe. Leaving a werewolf corpse in the woods? We didn't hire these guys for their brains, that's for sure. Tucker rounded up a new team yesterday afternoon and sent them out to retrieve the body. Only they couldn't. Guess why.'

'It was gone.'

Winsloe laughed and tilted his chair back. 'A fellow horror-flick buff. You got it. They found the spot and they found the blood, but no body. Now Larry's furious, thinking the project's in jeopardy because someone found the body. But there's another possibility, isn't there? That the werewolf is still alive.' Winsloe hummed the theme to *Halloween*. 'So I ordered another team to start looking for our mystery immortal. But don't worry.'

'About what?'

Winsloe grinned. 'I know what you're thinking, Elena. Don't put on the tough-chick face for me. You're worried that we'll find him. Am I right?'

'I really don't care—'

'Sure you do. You're worried that we'll bring this "mutt" back here and he'll try to hurt you, like Lake did. Or, worse yet, that he'll usurp your position here, that we'll find him a more interesting specimen and dispose of you. But that won't happen. I won't let that happen, Elena. You're too important to me. No other werewolf will take your place. I've made sure of that. Before that last team left, I took them aside and promised a hundred-thousand-dollar bounty for the guy who brings me the head. Just the head. I made that clear. I don't want the live werewolf.'

He stood to leave. I clenched my fists, nails digging into my palms until I smelled blood. Winsloe took five steps. Ryman smirked at me, then pulled open the door for

369

Winsloe. Before stepping through, Winsloe snapped his fingers, pulled a smaller envelope from his pocket, and tossed it at my feet.

'Almost forgot. New surveillance photos. Fresh from late night. Seems Tucker was using his brains, sending a new team to find your friends. They found them. For a few hours at least. They've lost track since, but I'll keep you posted. I know you're concerned.'

I gritted my teeth. Daggers of fury threatened to split my skull.

'Seems they're looking for someone,' Winsloe continued.

'Me,' I managed to say.

'Oh, I assume that, but now someone else has gone missing. Our team managed to capture some bits of conversation. Someone's jumped ship. Someone important. Problem is, we're having trouble figuring out who it is. Larry's working on it, comparing these new pictures with our old ones. Maybe you can see who's missing. You don't have to tell me, though. I wouldn't ask you to rat out your friends.'

Winsloe left. I closed my eyes, felt the pain stab through my skull and palms. It took several more minutes before I was ready to look at the photos. When I did, I found pictures of the group conferring and milling about. I didn't need to figure out who was missing. One look at Jeremy's expression told me. Clay was gone. He hadn't been acting under Jeremy's command the morning before, when he'd tracked down the former search team. He was on his own. Alone.

Clay was coming after me.

*　*　*

I spent the rest of the morning racking my brain for a new escape plan. I had to get out. Not eventually, not soon, but now, immediately, before Winsloe tired of this latest game and upped the ante yet again. The harder I struggled to come up with an idea, the more I panicked, and the more I panicked, the harder it was to come up with an idea. I had to calm down or I'd never think of anything.

Bauer settled down later that morning. When I was sure she was lucid – which I determined by the fact that she'd stopped screaming and started eating her cold breakfast – I went to the hole and tried to talk to her. She ignored me. When she finished her meal, she rummaged a pencil and paper from a drawer and wrote a two-page letter, then walked to the door and politely asked someone to deliver it. I could guess the contents: a plea for release, a more reasonable version of what she'd been ranting about for the last few hours.

So Bauer wanted out. Well, so did the rest of us. Did she feel like a 'guest' now? As I thought this, a plan formed in the back of my brain. Bauer wanted out. I wanted out. When I'd first gone to nurse her, I'd hoped that in her gratitude she'd help me escape. Gratitude was out of the question now. But what about escape? What if I offered to take her with me? Bauer knew the compound's weaknesses and its security system – that is, if she was sane enough to remember. Combine my strength and experience with her knowledge and we could be a formidable team. Not exactly a complete and foolproof plan, but it was a start.

One remaining problem – well, okay, there were lots of

remaining problems – but a big one was how to escape the cells. I pondered the possibility of staging something that would get me out of my room. Sure, I could probably do it, but could I get Bauer out at the same time? Unlikely. When the guards brought my lunch, I studied the door as it opened, seeing how it operated, looking for a weakness. Then I noticed something so blatant I kicked myself for not seeing it before. The guards didn't completely shut the door. They never did. Why? Because the door opened only from the outside and they never brought an extra guard to stand in the hall and let them out, as Bauer and Matasumi had always done. When they entered, they left the door a half-inch ajar, giving them finger room to pry it open. How could I use this to my advantage? Well, I could knock out one guard while the other pulled his gun and shot me – okay, bad idea. I could say, 'Hey, what's that crawling down the wall?' and make a break for it when they turned away. Umm, no. Better give this one some thought.

ALLIANCE

The guards dropped off my lunch at one. When they opened the door to leave, I sneaked a peek into the hallway. Tess wasn't there. Lunchtime for everyone. Good. While Bauer was lucid and no one was listening in, I could broach the subject of escape with her. Was it safe? She could try to garner favor with Matasumi by selling me out, but I doubted she was desperate enough to grovel. Not yet. Besides, given her circumstances and animosity toward me, no one would believe her if she did tattle.

Listening for telltale noises from the hall, I moved my chair close to the hole, sat, and peered through. Bauer was pacing.

'Feeling any better?' I asked.

She kept pacing.

'I don't want to make things worse,' I said. 'But you know they won't let you out of that cell. To them, you've switched sides.'

Pace to the door, to the TV, back to the door.

'If you want out, you'll have to get yourself out.'

Still no response. Not so much as an eye flicker in my direction.

'You have to escape,' I said.

Bauer wheeled on me. 'Escape?' A harsh laugh. 'To what? Life as a monster?'

I could have reminded her who chose that monstrous life, but I didn't. 'I know it's bad now, but it'll get easier—'

'I don't want it to get easier!' she snarled, striding toward the hole. 'I want it gone! That's what I want them to do for me. Get rid of it. Suck this curse from my veins and make me normal again.'

'They can't do that,' I said softly. 'Nobody can do that.'

'Bullshit!' Spittle flew from her lips. 'You want me to suffer, don't you? You're enjoying this. "Sondra got what she deserved." Ha-ha-ha. Well, I didn't deserve this. You never said it would be like this. You tricked me!'

'Tricked you? I warned you not to do it.'

'You didn't tell me everything.'

'Oh, well, excuse me. When you barged in here like a madwoman waving a syringe and ranting about starting an exciting new life, I should have whipped out my handy "So You Wanna Be a Werewolf" disclaimer form and made you sign on the dotted line.'

Bauer grabbed a chair, hurled it at the hole, then stomped into the bathroom.

I had to work on my approach.

A few hours later, Bauer's sanity made another guest appearance. I was ready. Plan two: Be more empathetic. While I found it hard to work up much sympathy for someone who'd done this to herself, somewhere deep in me there was a faint, fluttering urge to empathize. Bauer was another female werewolf, likely the only one I'd ever meet. Remembering the horror of my own transformation, I understood what she was going through. Winsloe had asked if I'd ever done anything like Bauer did to Carmichael. My reply hadn't been entirely honest. Back when I'd escaped from Stonehaven, my already demon-plagued brain had plummeted into uncontrolled madness and rage. I'd killed two people before Jeremy rescued me. Unlike what Bauer had done with Carmichael, I hadn't known my victims and I hadn't tormented them or torn them to pieces. Yet I had done one thing I would never forget. I'd eaten my victims. Was I that different from Bauer? I hadn't shot myself up with werewolf spittle, but I'd fallen in love with a man I suspected was dangerous. I hadn't killed a friend, but I had killed innocent people. As much as I resisted, I understood Bauer. And I wanted to empathize.

The question was: *Could* I empathize? As my awkward episode consoling Savannah had proven, I was not a naturally empathic person. Pushing past my doubts, I stationed myself by the hole and looked into Bauer's cell.

'How're you doing?' I asked.

Bauer spun to face me. 'How the fuck do you think I'm doing?' She inhaled sharply, eyes closing as if in pain. 'This isn't me. This body, this personality. It's not me. I don't use this language. I don't throw tantrums. I don't plead for my life. But do you know what's worse? *I'm* still here, trapped inside, looking out.'

'Your brain is still accepting the transformation. It'll get—'

'Don't tell me it'll get easier.'

I knew what I had to say, what I had to share, but the words caught in my chest. Biting back my pride, I forced them out.

'When I was first bitten, I—'

'Don't.'

'I just wanted to say—'

'Don't compare yourself to me, Elena. We have nothing in common. If I gave you that impression before, it was only because I wanted something from you.'

'Maybe so, but we have something in common now. I'm—'

Her voice went cold. 'You're nothing, Elena. A nobody who became a somebody by accident. Becoming a werewolf was the defining accomplishment in your life, and you didn't even take a hand in it. Your money, your youth, your strength, your position, your lover, they're all yours only because you were the only female werewolf.'

'I—'

'Without that, what are you? A no-name part-time journalist whose annual salary wouldn't cover my wardrobe.'

With that, she wheeled around, stomped into the bathroom, and started the shower.

You know, empathy really is a two-way street.

At seven the guards brought my dinner. As usual, one carried the tray while the other stood watch, gun at the ready. I ignored them, having given up hope of bringing a guard over to my side or gaining any valuable information from them. Best to treat them as deaf-mute waiters. I had other things to worry about.

When they came in, I was on my bed, thinking up escape plans. After a moment, I noticed the tray-bearing guard lingering at my table, looking at the photos of Clay. He nodded at his partner and nudged his attention to the pictures. 'It's him,' he mouthed.

'You know him?' I asked.

The guard started, as if the bed had spoken.

'You know him?' I repeated. 'The wolf in the photos?'

Both men looked at me as if I'd joined Bauer in her private asylum, probably thinking *I* should be the one who'd recognize a werewolf, not them.

'Tyrone dropped those off,' I said, still on my back, feigning all the nonchalance I could muster. 'He figured I might be able to ID the guy, but I couldn't. Seems he caused some hoopla at a motel.'

Now they were definitely looking at me like I was ready for a strait-jacket.

'You don't recognize him?' the one by the door asked.

I stifled a half-yawn. 'Should I?'

'Isn't this your mate?'

'Clay? No. He'd never leave the Alpha – our leader.'

'Then why—' The guard stopped, turned to his partner and lowered his voice. 'Does Matasumi know this?'

'Why?' the other guard said, not bothering to whisper. 'It doesn't matter who the werewolf is. If anyone sees him around here again, we kill him. That's the order.'

My hands clenched, but I forced myself not to make a noise, not to say a word, not to ask a question. The second guard shrugged, and they left without so much as a glance in my direction.

Clay was nearby. I'd been right. He was coming for me. I couldn't let him do that. There was too much he didn't know, too much he was unprepared for. Clay had bested Tucker's search party easily enough, but here there were at least five times as many guards, plus a fortified underground building with a top-notch security system, all surrounded by a forest laced with Ty Winsloe's traps. I had to stop Clay before he tried to rescue me. To do that, I needed to escape – fast. I glanced at Bauer's cage. Time to throw off the kid gloves.

It was nearly midnight before Bauer was lucid again. For the past two days, I'd been honing my ability to judge when someone was in the hall. Part of it was hearing, part of it was sensing. Though it was difficult to know if someone was watching us, there was a definitive way to tell if they were listening in. The intercom. When turned on, it gave an audible click, then hissed softly until someone turned it off. After Bauer regained her senses, I waited until the guards passed on their hourly tour, listened carefully for the intercom buzz, then reclined onto my bed.

'You still think they're going to let you out, don't you?' I called.

Bauer didn't answer, though I knew she could hear me.

'You know,' I continued, 'there was someone who would have let you out. Who probably wouldn't have let you get thrown in that cell in the first place. Unfortunately, you tore her to pieces.'

Bauer inhaled but didn't reply.

'I know you remember,' I said. 'It's like you said, part of

you is still there, a sane part, watching. Do you remember what it was like? Chasing her? Seeing her confusion? Her disbelief? Listening to her plead for her life? You can still picture it, can't you – the look on her face when you tore out her throat.' I paused. 'Do you remember what she tasted like?'

A clatter from the other cell. Then retching. I waited. Bauer stayed in the bathroom.

'Who's going to let you out, Sondra?' I called. 'Who's going to risk becoming your next meal? Who out there gives a damn? Only one person did and now she's in a garbage bag . . . or several garbage bags.'

'Stop it.' Bauer's voice was quiet, almost quavering.

'Maybe you plan to escape by yourself. Then what? Where will you go? Back home, snack on Mom and Dad?'

'Stop it.' Stronger, but still shaky.

'That's what'll happen. You won't be able to end the hunger and the Changes. Eventually you might gain enough control to survive, but at what cost? How many will die first? You'll start killing because you have to, then keep doing it because you can, because after a while you develop a taste for it, the power and the meat. That's what happens to mutts.'

I paused before continuing, 'Speaking of mutts, the first one you meet will kill you. Of course, he'll probably rape you first, as it will be his only chance to screw a female of his own species.'

'Shut up.'

'I'm foretelling your future here, Sondra. Free of charge. Only one person can help you avoid all that. The Pack

Alpha. The question is, how do you get his help? Well, if you escape by yourself, you could show up at his doorstep, plead for mercy. He'll be very nice about it. Invite you in, take your coat, show you to the parlor, offer you coffee. Then he'll introduce you to Clayton. And that handsome face you admire will be the last thing you see. That is, if I'm still alive. If I die here, I really wouldn't recommend you go anywhere near New York State. The hell you're going through now is nothing compared to what Clay will do to you if I die.'

The bathroom door slammed. 'You're trying to scare me.'

I laughed. 'You know better, Sondra. You met Patrick Lake. You know what mutts are like. You know Clay's reputation. I'm offering you a way out. Help me escape and I'll make sure Jeremy helps you.'

'Why should I believe you'd keep your word?'

'Because I'm a Pack wolf, and I wouldn't degrade myself by lying to a mutt. To me, that's what you are. A useful mutt, but a mutt nonetheless.'

Bauer didn't reply. For an hour we stayed silent in our respective cells. Then quietly, her voice barely above a whisper, Bauer agreed. And we went to sleep.

BREAK

We spent the next day planning, working around the observation schedule, the guards' cell-block tours, mealtimes, and Bauer's recurring bouts of madness. The last was the most troubling. What if Bauer flipped out in the midst of our escape? Her lucid periods were growing longer, but would they be long enough?

According to Bauer, Winsloe's security system was hard-wired with the identities of all compound staff. This hand-writing ensured it was almost impossible for a captive to tamper with the computer, adding his own retinal and finger-print scan. Of course, that meant it was equally difficult to remove an ID. What did this mean for us? Bauer's ID would still work. Since she had top clearance, she could enter and exit all levels of the compound with one unauthorized guest.

Would Bauer be leaving with only one companion? I still hadn't decided. As bad as I felt for Leah and Curtis Zaid, I couldn't take them with me. Ruth had been right. The more people I added to my escape plan, the greater the like-lihood of failure. Better to assuage my conscience with a personal commitment to free them when I returned with the others. But what about Savannah? Ruth had told me to leave her. Should I? Could I? Two very different questions. Given Savannah's certain link to Ruth's death and the other incidents, was it safe to set her free? I feared that Ruth's teachings had only intensified Savannah's powers, made her more dangerous. Was it wise to take Savannah out of here and dump her into the care of an apprentice witch like Paige? Or should I leave her here, where her powers could be safely contained, until we could make arrangements with the other Coven witches? Perhaps Ruth had anticipated the danger and that was why she'd told me not to take Savannah when I escaped. So I should leave Savannah.

But *could* I? Could I abandon a child here, knowing something could happen to her before I returned? Granted, that child might be capable of evil, but through no fault or will of her own. She was innocent. I was certain of that. So how could I leave her behind? I couldn't. Bauer could get us both through the exits simply by taking one person at a time. It would slow us down, but that didn't justify abandoning Savannah. If possible, I'd take Savannah. I just wouldn't tell Bauer about it. Not yet.

We planned to escape that night, when the guards brought my bedtime snack at ten-thirty. Were we ready? Probably not, but I didn't dare wait any longer. I had to stop Clay. We needed tomorrow as a backup day, in case I couldn't get out of my cell that night.

I spent the early part of the evening resting in bed. Of course, I didn't really rest – not mentally, at least. I lay awake worrying about everything that could go wrong.

Before the guards arrived, I would pick off the scabs on my torn knee, inducing it to bleed again, then use this distraction to kill them and get free. What if the bleeding-knee trick failed to incite the guard's concern? What if I wasn't fast enough, if the second guard pulled his gun while I killed the first? I had to kill them. I couldn't risk them recovering consciousness before we escaped—

Whoosh.

I froze, recognizing the sound before my brain registered it. My cell door had opened. Instead of jumping up to see who was there, I lay still, tensed and waiting. What time was it? Nine-twenty. Too late for Matasumi. Too early for my snack. Xavier was gone. That left Winsloe. Please, no. Not tonight. I stayed still, listening and smelling the air, hoping I'd misheard the noise.

A full minute passed with no word of greeting, no scent of an intruder, no whoosh of the door closing. I lifted my head from the pillow and turned toward the door behind me. No one was there. I shifted onto my elbows for a better look. The door was closed. No, wait. Not closed. Open a half-inch, maybe less. Again, I braced myself. Was Winsloe in the hall, giving last minute instructions to Ryman and Jolliffe? Yet I heard and smelled nothing. I counted off sixty seconds, then eased my legs over the side of the bed, and crept to the door. Leaning toward the open crack, I inhaled. Only old scents answered. How was that possible? Someone had opened the door only minutes before. Why couldn't I smell him?

Shifting into a semi-crouch, I edged the door open an inch, then another, then a full foot. I stretched my hamstrings, rolled onto the balls of my feet, and peered out the door. Someone was in the hall. I jerked back, then realized who I'd seen and leaned out again. Bauer stood outside her cell, looking one way, then the other. When she saw me, she straightened.

'Did you—?' she whispered.

I shook my head and stepped into the hall. Before I could say anything, a door opened at the opposite end of the hall and Savannah came out, half-stumbling with sleep, hair a dark tangle, one thin shoulder peeping from a red plaid nightgown. Seeing us, she rubbed a hand over her face and yawned.

'What happened?' she asked.

I motioned for silence and beckoned her closer. Since I couldn't smell anyone else in the hall, the doors must have opened automatically, some kind of mechanical malfunction. Too coincidental? Maybe, but I wasn't going to ignore the opportunity. Yes, it could be a trap, but to what purpose? To see whether we'd try to escape? That would be more of an intelligence test – anyone who'd stay in prison when the doors were open clearly lacked a few brain cells. It could be one of Matasumi's research experiments, like when he'd put me in that room with Patrick Lake. Worse yet, it could be another of Winsloe's sick games. So should I sit in my cell and do nothing? Maybe I *should*, but I couldn't. If this was real, I had the chance to save the three people whose safety concerned me most: Savannah, Bauer, and, of course, myself.

'We're leaving,' I whispered, leaning down to Savannah's ear. 'Bau— Sondra can get us out. Sneak back to your cell and get your shoes.'

'We're going now?' Bauer whispered.

'We're out, aren't we?'

As Savannah scampered back to her cell, Bauer hesitated, confusion clouding her eyes. I told myself she was only sleepy, but feared worse. Bauer's addled mind wouldn't respond well to changes in routine. She'd thought we were leaving in a few hours, and even this small deviation from the plan might throw her brain off track. I smiled as encouragingly as I could and steered her toward her cell.

'Just grab your shoes,' I said.

Bauer nodded and reached for the door handle. She turned it, frowned, glanced over her shoulder at me, then jangled the handle, and pushed against the door. It wouldn't open. Prodding her aside, I wrenched the handle and slammed my shoulder against the door. It didn't budge.

'It should open,' Bauer said, panic creeping into her voice. 'It *has* to open. There's no external lock.'

'I can't get back in my cell,' Savannah said as she ran back to us. 'The door's stuck.'

'So is this one,' I said. 'I guess if a mechanical malfunction can open them, it can jam them shut, too. We'll have to leave as we are.'

'What about Leah and Mr. Zaid?' Savannah asked. 'Shouldn't we get them out?'

'If we can.'

We couldn't. I started with Curtis Zaid. The Vodoun priest lay huddled atop his bedcovers, fast asleep. His door was shut tight.

'Jammed,' I said.

Savannah raced across the hall and tried Leah's door. 'Same here.'

'They'll have to stay behind for now,' I said. 'Sondra, the exit by Savannah's cell is the one with the guard station, right? The one by mine only has a camera linked to the station.'

Bauer nodded.

'Good.'

I headed for the exit on Savannah's side. Bauer grabbed my arm.

'That's the guarded one,' she said.

'I know.'

'But you can't— we can't— they'll shoot us!'

I disengaged her hands from my arm and met her wild eyes. 'We discussed this, remember, Sondra? Both doors link to a common hall with the elevator at the midpoint.' I chafed at the extended explanation, but I knew this was what Jeremy would do, how he'd calm Bauer's mounting hysteria. 'If we go out the camera-monitored door, the alert will notify the guards. They'll see us through the camera and meet us before we can get on the elevator. With the other door, the guards will be right on the other side. They'll have only seconds to react before I burst through. They won't have time to call for help. I'll ki— disable them and we can sneak upstairs.'

I nudged Bauer forward and motioned for Savannah to follow me. As Bauer walked to the door, something fell from the ceiling. I lunged forward, knocking her out of the way. The object hit the floor with a sharp pop and tinkling of glass.

'Just a lightbulb,' Savannah said. 'You sure moved fast.'

As Bauer recovered, I glanced up. Overhead was a row

of six bulbs, the first now only an empty socket. A tiny squeak caught my attention, and I noticed the second bulb in the line move. As I watched, the bulb twisted slowly, unthreading from the socket.

'Wow,' Savannah said. 'It almost looks like—'

Crack, crack, crack! The whole row of lightbulbs smashed to the floor, plunging us into darkness. Bauer yelped.

'It's okay, Sondra,' I said. 'Your eyes will adjust. You have night vision now. The light from the security door will be enough. Move toward it and—'

Savannah shrieked. I whirled and reached into the darkness to calm her. Something tickled my left arm. I slapped my right hand over the spot and felt blood welling beneath my palm. Bauer screamed. A white blur flew at my face and slashed my cheek. As I snatched it, razor-sharp glass bit into my palm. Another piece struck my scalp. My eyes adjusted then, and I saw a whirlwind of broken glass flying around us.

'The door!' I yelled. 'Sondra! Grab the door!'

Dimly I saw her outline huddled against the far cell, arms pulled in, head tucked down against the onslaught. Shards of glass pricked and sliced my bare arms and face as I pitched toward her. I grabbed her arm and yanked her to the exit, positioning her in front of the retina camera. As I reached for the button, I noticed her eyes were squeezed shut.

'Open your eyes!' I shouted.

She clenched them tighter, pulling her chin into her chest.

'Open your goddamned eyes for the scanner!'

I was reaching up to pry them open when she blinked.

I hit the button. The first red light flickered, then died and the whole panel went black. I smacked the button again. Nothing happened. I jabbed it over and over, eyes skimming the panel for any sign of life. Nothing. No lights. No sound. It was dead. I spun around. At the other end of the hall, a dim red glow reflected around the corner.

'The other door still has power,' I said. 'Let's go.'

'I can't,' Bauer whispered, cradling her head against the flying glass. 'I can't.'

I ignored her. 'Savannah, run to my cell. I didn't shut my door. Get inside while we unlock the other exit.'

I grabbed Bauer with both hands, and half-carried, half-dragged her down the corridor. The maelstrom of glass followed, whirling around us, biting like a thousand wasps.

In the darkness and my haste, I passed Savannah, and arrived at my cell ahead of her. With a spasm of relief I saw my door was still open. I remembered I needed my shoes and darted inside to grab them. As I turned, the foot of my bed moved. It bounced a half-foot off the ground, then shot straight up in the air and hurtled toward me. I barely had time to backpedal out of the cell before the mattress struck the back of the door, slamming it shut.

'What – what—' Bauer stammered.

I shoved her toward the other exit. A staccato series of pops rang out. Expecting gunfire, I dropped to my knees. The hall filled with deafening static, as if someone had cranked every intercom up full blast. Savannah brushed against me. I squeezed her shoulder and tried to tell her everything would be okay, but the static drowned me out. Giving Savannah one last reassuring pat, I grabbed Bauer and propelled her to the security door. This time, perhaps realizing it was her only escape from the flying glass, Bauer positioned herself in front of the retinal scanner and hit the button. The red light flickered out, and for a moment everything went dead. Then a green light flashed. Bauer grasped the handle and the second light changed from red to green. She yanked open the door and flew into the hall. I knew that Bauer's security pass only allowed one other person, so as soon as Savannah and I both went through, an alarm would sound somewhere. I couldn't worry about it. The guards would see us through the camera anyway.

I slammed the door behind us. A few stray shards of glass fell harmlessly to the floor.

'What happened in there?' Savannah whispered.

'I don't know,' I said. 'Are you both all right?'

Savannah and Bauer nodded. Yes, every inch of our bare skin seemed to be bleeding, but no one had taken a piece to an eye or a major artery, so we seemed to realize that made us 'all right.'

Voices echoed from the other end of the hall. Savannah's head jerked up.

'We aren't going to make it,' she whispered.

'Yes, we are,' Bauer said. She straightened, brushing a trickle of blood from over her eye. 'I am not going back in there. I'm out now and I'm staying out. Elena will take care of the guards. We'll stay here where it's safe.'

From whimpering jellyfish to group leader in sixty seconds flat? Nice to see Bauer regain her poise, but this wasn't the sort of change I'd have wished for. Never mind. At least she wasn't cowering in a corner. Besides, I *was* the one who should go after the guards. Bauer would only get in my way.

As I started forward, Savannah grabbed my shirt.

'I'll help,' she whispered. 'I'll cast a spell.'

I hesitated, wanting to tell her not to bother, but realized that giving Savannah a chance to feel useful might calm her fears. Besides, she was only a twelve-year-old neophyte witch. She'd only know the simplest sort of spells.

'Okay,' I said. 'As long as you can cast it from here. Keep down and quiet.'

As I crept forward, a crash shook through the hallway. Then another. Then smashing glass, louder than the falling lightbulbs. Then pitch dark. Yes! This time I welcomed the blackness. It would give me an advantage . . . so long as the broken glass didn't start flying again.

'Goddamn it!' a voice – presumably a guard's – hissed. 'First exit one dies, then the camera at exit two, now this. A fucking power failure.'

'I'll grab the flashlight,' a second voice said.

'We both will. I'm not standing around in the dark.'

So there were only two guards? Better and better. I quickened my pace to a lope, rounded the corner, and hit the elevator button. Then I headed for the guard station. Partway there, I stumbled over something and looked down to see a fluorescent light cover. I sidestepped and brought my stockinged foot down squarely on a shard of glass. Biting my cheek against a yelp, I brushed my foot left and right, clearing the path as I eased forward. Light darted from around the corner. The guards had found their flashlight. Damn.

Behind me, the elevator doors creaked open. A voice

called out, not in front of me, but from the rear. I froze in mid-step. The guards rounded the corner, flashlight beam bouncing off the walls. Someone behind me shouted. I whirled, saw a gun, and dropped to the floor. Shots rang out from front and back. A bullet grazed my leg. I gasped and crawled to the side of the hall. A scream. A shout of rage. A curse. I glanced up. The guards were shooting at one another, the two from the station firing at three by the elevator. Two more lay on the floor, one screaming and writhing. Bullets whizzed past me. I got up on my hands and knees, pitched forward and ran doubled-over to the others. I raced right past the second group of guards. They didn't even notice.

'Go back!' I yelled to Savannah and Bauer. 'Get inside!'

CORNERED

auer pushed past Savannah and flew through the security sequence. The exit opened and all three of us clambered through. I slammed the door behind us. Savannah shouted that the door was now open to the empty cell across from mine. We dove inside.

'I was peeking around the corner,' Savannah said as I gulped air. 'When the guards came with the flashlight, I saw the other ones get off the elevator. I cast a confusion spell so you could get past them. It worked pretty good, huh?'

'Very good,' I said, not mentioning that I'd been nearly caught in the crossfire. What the hell had Ruth taught this kid? A twelve-year-old witch should be casting spells to calm frightened kittens, not making armed men blast one another to bits.

'Hey,' a voice said from the doorway. 'Did I miss my party invitation?'

We all jumped. Leah stepped inside, yawning and raking her fingers through her sleep-mussed hair.

'Don't close that!' Bauer said, grabbing the cell door.

Did it matter now? Though I said nothing, I certainly didn't foresee another breakout attempt in our near future.

While the opened cells may not have been a trap, they hadn't been a lucky break either. The opposite, in fact. My great escape plan had vanished in that hailstorm of bullets outside. Even if we got through this mess, Winsloe would only need to check the computer logs to realize I'd used Bauer to get past security. He'd make sure it never happened again. I tried not to think of the multitude of ways he could ensure that.

Leah walked to the chair and slumped into it. 'Cut my damned foot walking down here. There's glass all over the floor. And how come the doors are open? Not that I'm complaining but— Whoa, what happened to you guys?'

'Flying glass,' I said.

'Geez. Not sorry I missed it. Is anyone hurt? I know first aid.'

'We're fine,' Bauer said, moving to the bed.

While we talked, Savannah leaned out the doorway. 'I don't see anyone. Are they all dead?'

'Dead?' Leah repeated as I yanked Savannah away from the open door. 'Who's dead?'

I explained what had happened. As I spoke, Leah kept shooting discreet glances at Savannah, who'd collapsed onto the carpet and didn't seem to notice.

'. . . we should stay in here,' I said. 'Remain calm and hope they do the same. No sudden moves. Nothing to set them off.'

Savannah pushed herself up from the floor. 'I know this calming spell—'

'I'm sure you do, hon,' Leah said. 'But maybe that's not such a good idea.'

Savannah's face fell. Leah put her arm around the girl's shoulders and gave her a squeeze.

'Elena and I can handle the guards,' Leah said. 'We'll find a safe place for you, hon, in case there's trouble when the guards arrive.'

Slanting a look sideways, Leah directed my gaze from Savannah to the stray lightbulb pieces on the floor. My heart sank. Savannah. Who else could have been responsible for the whirlwind of flying glass? There'd been only three of us in that hallway and only one who'd been known to propel dangerous objects through the air. It was a big step up from hurling plates, but I'd already seen a demonstration of Savannah's increased powers with that lethal confusion spell. Of course, she hadn't done it deliberately – she'd been hurt as badly as any of us – but that wasn't the point. Whether she intended it or not, Savannah was dangerous. Put her under emotional stress and she reacted with violence.

'Good idea,' I said. 'We should get Savannah someplace safe.' Safe for her and safe for us.

'Sondra, how about you go with Savannah?' Leah said. 'My cell's open. Hide in there.'

Bauer sat on the bed, knees pulled up, staring at the wall. Back to whimpering jellyfish.

'I'm fine,' she whispered.

'You've had a rough go of it,' Leah said. 'Elena and I can handle this. How about you take Savannah and—'

'I'm fine!' Bauer snarled, head jerking up, lips curling. Then she froze, as if realizing what she'd done. She closed her eyes and shuddered. 'I'm fine,' she said firmly. 'I want to help.'

'Maybe we can talk to the guards,' I said. 'Explain what happened. Is there an intercom, Sondra? Some way we can communicate with them?'

Bauer shook her head.

Outside the cell, something thudded against the exit door. We all stopped to listen. Two more thuds in quick succession, then silence.

'They can't get in,' Bauer whispered. 'The exit door must have lost power or jammed.'

'So much for hoping they were all dead,' Leah said. 'How many guards are there in total?'

'Three doz— no, thirty,' Bauer said. 'We— they started with thirty-six, but there have been casualties.'

'Lousy odds. Well, let's get Savannah out of here before things get bad.'

Leah reached for Savannah, but she ducked and ran to me.

'I want to help,' she said, looking up at me.

As if I didn't feel guilty enough just suspecting Savannah of causing the flying glass. But if Leah and I were going to fight this, we had to get Savannah someplace safe where she could calm down.

'We aren't trying to shut you out, Savannah. I know you could help. That confusion spell' – I managed a wry smile— 'well, I was impressed, I'll tell you that.'

'But . . .' Savannah sighed, with the weary resignation of a child who could hear 'but' coming a mile away.

'But if you stay, Leah and I will be too worried about you to concentrate on the danger.'

'We'd be *very* concerned if you stayed,' Leah said,

sneaking me a look. 'We'd all feel *much* better if you were someplace else . . . safe. I'll take you to my cell.'

'Fine,' Savannah said, in a voice that said our decision was anything but fine.

Leah reached for Savannah's hand, but the girl brushed her off and stalked out the door. Leah jogged after her.

Several minutes later, Leah hurried back. The guards were still beating at the exit door.

'She's in my cell,' Leah said. 'Hidden under the bed. I closed the door.'

I started to nod, then stopped. 'You closed the door? What if it jams? How will we get her out?'

'Right now I'm more worried about Savannah getting herself out. If I didn't lock her in, she'd be down here in two minutes flat, trying to help us. We don't need that kind of help.' She glanced at the broken glass. 'She's helped quite enough already.'

'If Savannah made the glass fly, it wasn't intentional.'

Leah shrugged. 'You're probably right. Anyway, it's not her fault. What can you expect, with a mother like Eve.'

'You think that's it. Just because her mother was into black magic doesn't necessarily mean—'

'Eve wasn't just a witch, Elena. Her father was a demon, meaning she was a half-demon/witch hybrid. A brutal combination. Now, I'm pretty laid back. I don't scare easily. But Eve scared the crap out of me. Sondra, remember when she first got here—'

Bauer whirled to face us. 'Who the fuck cares, Leah? We have God knows how many armed guards pounding at the

396

exit door and you're discussing Savannah's genealogy!'

'Chill out, Sondra. Elena and I have everything under control. We're used to this kind of stuff. All I'm saying, Elena, is to be careful around Savannah. Remember, she's a preteen girl, hormones kicking in and all that shit. It only makes things worse. Who knows—'

'Goddamn it!' Bauer shouted. 'They're breaking down the fucking door!'

'You think they'll get in?' Leah asked me, calmly, as if Bauer were some lunatic screaming inside a padded room.

'Eventually,' I said.

She sighed. 'Okay, then. Time to prepare the welcoming party.'

When we'd finished planning, we turned off the light. With our night vision, Bauer and I would be fine, and Leah had decided that the overall advantages of darkness outweighed the personal disadvantage of limited vision.

We slipped into the hall, staying behind the corner in case the guards broke through, guns blazing.

'Hello!' Leah shouted. 'We're trapped in here! Some of us are hurt! What's going on out there? Can you hear us?'

No one replied. As Bauer had warned, the door was soundproof. Leah tried a few more times, then I motioned her to silence and listened. I could hear only snatches of muffled voices.

'—when's that – getting here?'

'—other door – power out—'

'—radio – again—'

'—off-duty guys? – Matasumi, Winsloe?'

Leah leaned against my shoulder. 'Can you tell how many there are?'

I shook my head. 'Three, maybe four voices, plus those that aren't talking. Wait, I hear something else.'

A loud hissing sounded from the other side of the exit. As I tried to identify the noise, it suddenly rose to a grating whir, loud enough even for a non-werewolf to hear.

'Blowtorch,' Leah said. 'That'll work. We'd better get ready.'

We never got a chance to put our plan into motion. As I swung into the empty cell, the exit door suddenly opened. The guards' shouts of surprise broke into a barrage of commands. Leah darted into the first cell with me. As I wheeled to close the door, I realized Bauer wasn't with us.

'She bolted,' Leah said.

'Shit!'

I threw open the door. Bauer was running down the hall.

'Sondra!' I shouted.

She stopped. Instead of turning around, though, she started pounding on the cell door to her right.

'Open up!' she yelled. 'Goddamn you! Let me in!'

At first, I thought she'd lost it. Then I realized she was at the one remaining occupied cell, that of the Vodoun priest. Of course, Zaid couldn't hear her. The wall was soundproof. Despite everything happening out here, the poor guy was probably sound asleep. I leaned out the doorway to tell her to hide, but she was already gone, vanishing into Armen Haig's former cell.

As I closed the door, I realized a problem. Leah and I were hiding behind a one-way pane of glass. Any guards in the hall could see us, but we couldn't see them. Not good. I scanned the cell for a hiding spot, knowing I wouldn't find one. We were exposed. Any second now the guards would come around that corner – I stopped. Why hadn't they come around the corner already? When I cracked open the door, I heard frantic shouts, then a scream, an inhuman shriek that made my hackles rise.

I motioned Leah back. 'I'm taking a look.'

'Crouch,' she said. 'Stay below eye level.'

We both hunkered down. I eased the door open. A flash of light ricocheted off my eyes and I jerked back, only to see the beam skitter from wall to floor to ceiling, like someone wildly brandishing a flashlight. Over the screaming, I heard a male voice; then a high-pitched alarm swallowed all sound. I sniffed and smelled something so unexpected I doubted my own senses. The acrid stench of burned meat filled the air. As I inhaled again, second-guessing myself, a guard rocketed by so fast I didn't have time to retreat into the cell. It didn't matter. He flew past, mouth open in a scream swallowed by the siren. Something flapped at his side. I squinted in the near dark, then shuddered. It was his arm, almost severed above the elbow, swinging back and forth as he ran.

The flashlight beam continued to bounce around the walls. Shapes flickered, casting contorted shadows on the wall. The siren wavered and gave one last coughing blip. As it died, sound filled the air: the hissing of the blowtorch, shouts from the guards still hidden around the corner, the endless screams of the guard with the severed arm. Another guard stumbled around the corner, the blowtorch flickering beside him. As he passed our cell, he slid on something, his legs flying out. The blowtorch sailed into the air. Then it stopped. Stopped eight feet above the ground and hovered there, spitting blue flame. The fallen guard sprang to his feet. The blowtorch flew down and sliced him across the back. His arms shot up and he pitched forward, screaming as his shirt ignited. The stink of charred flesh and fabric filled the air.

'Open the fucking door!' a guard yelled from around the corner. 'Get us out of here!'

'They're trapped,' I whispered to Leah. 'I can't see what's going on. The blowtorch—'

Bang! A gunshot. Then three more in quick succession. Four loud metallic clangs.

'They're shooting the door,' Leah said. 'We should stay put.'

'Trust me. I'm not going anywhere.'

A sudden roar overlapped the screams and shouts.

'What's that?' Leah asked.

I knew. Even as I squinted down the hall, I knew what I'd see. Bauer had changed into a wolf. She charged the guards. I threw open the door. Leah grabbed my arm.

'The guards are still around the corner,' I said. 'I can stop Sondra before they see her.'

'Then what?'

Bauer reared as she collided with the fiery guard. Yelping, she backed up and skittered away from the flames. Then human instinct overtook animal. Wheeling around, she skirted the burning body and continued charging down the hall.

'Just let me—' I began.

'No. Think, Elena. You can't help her.'

Bauer barreled past us and rounded the corner. A guard screamed. He raced into the main stretch of hall, blood spattering from his torn shoulder. Bauer ran after him. Before they even reached our cell door, she pounced, landing on his back. As they fell, she sank her teeth into the back of his neck, tearing out a mouthful. Blood and gore sprayed.

'I'll use the distraction to run down to the other exit,' Leah said. 'Maybe it's open now.'

'What—?' I began, then realized she couldn't see what was happening, wasn't affected by it.

Leah brushed past me.

'Watch out!' I yelled, but she was gone and Bauer was too engrossed in her current victim to chase down another.

Bauer ripped chunks from the guard's shoulders and back, throwing them into the air. The guard's body convulsed. His face was stark white, eyes impossibly wide and blank. A guard around the corner shouted, as if just realizing his comrade was missing.

I couldn't watch any longer. I threw open the door and leaped out, no plan in mind other than somehow saving Bauer. Did she deserve saving? Was her life worth risking mine? It didn't matter. She was a werewolf, a female were-wolf born from my genes. I had to protect her.

As I tore from the cell, another guard came around the corner, gun raised. He fired. The shot blazed through the darkness and hit Bauer in the left haunch. She lunged at him. He lifted the gun, but she was on him, teeth ripping

401

at his throat. As I ran toward them, two shapes sprang from the darkness. Gunfire resounded down the hall. I dove, twisting around just in time to see the bullets hit Bauer, blasting her in the chest and head.

In that second, even as blood and brain exploded from Bauer's shattered skull, even before her body collapsed to the floor atop the dead guard, I saw the exit door swing open. I saw it and I saw my chance. My only chance. I felt my feet move, my body turn. Savannah flashed through my mind. I couldn't leave without her. Yet even as I thought this I felt my body diving for the open door. I didn't have time to go back for Savannah. Even if I could, should I? Who knew what she was capable of if things got really bad? With Savannah in tow, I might never escape, might die trying. Better to leave her here, underground, where her powers could be controlled, where she was too important to be killed. I'd come back for her later with the others.

I was already in the hall, my body having made the decision even as my brain floundered. What about Leah? Was I abandoning her, too? Coward! But my feet kept propelling me toward the elevator. Once there, I pounded my fist against the button, slamming it over and over, feeling the pain course down my arm and only hitting it harder, punishing my cowardice.

The elevator doors opened. I stepped in.

GONE

'**E**lena!'

Leah's voice. I grabbed the elevator door before it closed. Leaning out, I saw Leah jogging from the opposite exit.

'I couldn't get to Savannah,' I called.

'Me neither. Shit! All hell's broken loose in there. We'll never get back.'

'Hurry then.'

As she ran, the elevator door jerked, as if trying to close. I shoved it back, but it kept moving, pushing harder and harder until I had to lean against it, straining to hold it open.

'Come on!' I yelled. 'Something's wrong with the doors.'

When Leah was less than five feet away, the door jolted violently, slamming into my shoulder. I stumbled. Leah reached to grab me, but I fell backward into the elevator car. The doors clanged shut. I jumped up and pounded on the button to reopen the elevator.

'It won't open!' I yelled. 'Hit the call button!'

'I am!'

The elevator lurched suddenly. It heaved upward,

rocking and jerking so hard I nearly lost my balance. As I grabbed the side rail, a shrill grinding noise split the air. I white-knuckled the rail, brain scrambling to remember what to do in an elevator crash. Bend my knees? Get on the floor? Pray? The elevator slowed, then ground to a halt. I barely dared to breathe, waiting for the floor to give way beneath me. Then the doors opened.

I found myself staring at a waist-high wall. No, not a wall. A floor. The elevator had stopped between levels. As I stepped forward to look out, the elevator jerked again. Machinery groaned in the shaft overhead and the car began sinking. The floor inched from my waist to mid-chest. My window of escape was vanishing – literally. Grabbing the edge of the floor, I vaulted up, lost my grip, and fell back into the car. I clambered to my feet and tried again. This time I managed to keep my hold and wriggle through just as the elevator vanished down the shaft.

As I looked around, I recognized the top floor. So the elevator had brought me all the way up. Praise be. If I'd been let off on the middle level, I wouldn't have had a clue where to find a staircase.

I took a moment to compose myself and remember where the exit was. To my left, at the end of the hall. As I turned, voices echoed through the corridor, coming toward me from the rear. I looked about for a hiding place. There was a door about twenty feet down the hall. I sprinted for it, threw the door open, and was jumping inside when I realized the voices had stopped. The guards were back at the elevator. As I listened, they argued over what to do about the broken elevator, then unanimously decided to hand the decision to someone else – namely Tucker. A minute later, they were gone.

I waited until the sound of their boots receded into silence, then I eased from my hiding spot, looked both ways and ran. The corridor ended in a small room. Inside was the door to freedom. All I had to do was open it. And to open it, all I needed was the retina and handprint of an authorized person. Goddamn it! Why hadn't I thought of this? Getting *to* this level was only half the problem.

The voices near the elevator returned. Back already? I raced for the closet again. Once inside, I listened. Only two voices this time. They were waiting for their companions to return with Tucker. I didn't have time to think up a fool-proof plan, or much of any plan at all. I didn't stand a chance against more than two guards. If I hesitated, I'd be trapped in this closet until someone found me.

Pushing open the door, I checked the hall and made sure I couldn't see the guards – meaning they couldn't see me. As quietly as possible, I hustled toward the elevator. I stopped at the corner, crouched, and peered around it. The guards faced the opposite wall, one peering into the elevator shaft, the other bitching about the delay. I took one breath, then launched myself at the first guard, knocking him into the elevator shaft. His arms windmilled once, and he plunged out of sight. I nearly stumbled in after him and managed to avoid it only by using the momentum to twist and spring at the second guard. His hand went for his gun. As he yanked out the pistol, I snatched it from his hand and flung it down the elevator shaft. Then I slapped my palm over the guard's mouth and shoved him forward.

When he resisted, I heaved him off the ground and carried him. His feet kicked frantically. One struck my torn kneecap, sending such a jolt of pain through my leg that I pitched forward. A hair's breadth from dropping him, I regained my grip and started to run, half-stumbling, half-loping toward the exit.

I dragged the guard to the door. The security panel was the same as those on the cell-block exits. I hit the button Bauer had used and jammed the guard's chin upward. As the camera whirred, the guard realized what I was doing and shut his eyes. But it was too late. The first light flashed green. I grabbed the guard's hand and wrenched open his fist. Bones snapped. I forced his broken fingers around the door handle. The second light turned green. Placing my hand over his, I yanked open the door. Then I snapped his neck. I didn't hesitate, didn't wonder whether I had to kill him, if there wasn't some other way. I didn't have time for a conscience. I killed him, dumped his body on the floor, grabbed his boots, and bolted.

I raced into the forest, eschewing the network of paths and heading for the thick brush. No one came after me. They would. The question was how far I'd get before they did. How many miles to the nearest town? Which direction? I pushed back the first tendrils of panic. Finding civilization couldn't be my first priority. Getting someplace safe was more important. While the residual human in me equated public places with safety, I knew that any hiding place far enough from the compound would suffice. Run far, take cover, and recuperate. Then I could concentrate on finding a telephone.

It was another night like the one when Winsloe had hunted Lake: cold, damp, and overcast, the moon dimmed by cloud cover. A beautiful night for a prison break. The darkness would cover me, and the cold would keep me from overheating. As I soon discovered, though, body temperature wasn't a problem. I couldn't move fast enough to work up a sweat. Off the paths, the woods were rain-forest thick. Every ground-level inch was clogged with vines and dead vegetation. Every above-ground inch was covered with bushes and spindly trees, all vying for pockets of sunlight unclaimed by the towering old-growth forest. Here and there I stumbled onto paths trodden by deer, but I kept losing them as they petered out into thin trails already reclaimed by wilderness. A place for animals, not humans. Now, unlike most prison escapees, I had the option of turning into an animal, but I couldn't spare ten minutes to Change. Not while I was still so close to the compound. Any pursuing guards would be on foot so, for now, I could afford to share their disadvantage.

As I barreled through the forest, I realized I had one – or several – physical disadvantages not shared by the guards. First, I was wearing a pair of men's size twelve boots on women's size ten feet. More important, I was injured. Cuts covered my arms and face, stinging each time a branch whipped back against me. I ached from the zillion other still-healing wounds accumulated in the past week. I could live with that, though. Grit my teeth and be a big girl. My knee was another matter. Since Bauer had ripped it open in the infirmary, the fire had died to a dull, constant burning. The guard's kicks had reignited the flames, and running through the forest was only adding oxygen to blaze. After twenty minutes, I was limping. Limping badly. Hot blood streamed down my shin, and raw flesh rubbed against my pants, telling me Tucker's sewing job had come apart. I had to Change. Simple arithmetic: One bum leg out of four was twice as good as one out of two.

I slowed, moving more carefully now so I wouldn't leave an obvious trodden path. After I zigzagged for five minutes, I found a thicket, crawled inside, and listened. Still no sound of pursuers. I pulled off my clothes and Changed.

I was still straining with the final stages of my Change when something knocked me to the ground. Leaping up, I twisted to face my attacker. A rottweiler stood three feet away, growling, a stalactite of drool quivering from his curled upper lip. To his left was a large bloodhound. A tracking dog and a killer. These two hadn't strayed from a neighboring farm. They'd come from the compound. Damn it! I hadn't even realized they had any dogs. The kennel must have been outside. If I'd paused before bolting into the woods, I would have smelled the dogs and have prepared. But I hadn't taken the time.

My Change finished, I pulled myself up to my full height. The hound wheeled and ran, not so much intimidated as confused, seeing a canine and smelling a human. The rottweiler stood his ground and waited for me to take the next step in the dance of ritualized intimidation. Instead, I leaped at him. Screw ritual. Now was no time to stand on ceremony. Tracking dogs meant pursuing guards, and pursuing guards meant guns. I preferred to take my chances with the rottweiler.

My sudden attack caught the dog off-guard, and I sank my teeth into his haunch before he tore away. He twisted to grab me, but I darted out of reach. When I lunged again, he was ready, rearing to meet me in mid-jump. We crashed together, both struggling for the crucial neck hold. His teeth grazed my lower jaw. Too close for comfort. I broke away and sprang to my feet. The rottweiler scrambled up and leaped at me. I waited until the last second, then feinted left. He hit the ground, all four legs flying out to stop his slide. I dashed behind him and vaulted onto his back. As he fell, he twisted, jaws snapping onto my foreleg. Pain shot through me, but I resisted the urge to jerk away. I slashed at his unprotected throat, teeth ripping through fur and flesh. The rottweiler convulsed, bucking to throw me free. My head shot down again, this time grabbing his mangled throat and pinning him to the ground. I waited until he stopped struggling, then let go and ran.

Already the baying of a hound reverberated through the night air. The ground vibrated with running paws. Three dogs, maybe four. The hound had rediscovered his courage in a backup team. Could I fight four dogs? No, but experience had taught me that one or two would run from a werewolf, as the hound had. Could I handle those that remained? As I wondered this, someone shouted, making the decision for me. In the time it would take me to challenge and fight the dogs, the guards would be on us. My options narrowed to two: Throw the hound off my trail or lead the dogs away from their handlers. Either way, I had to run.

The best way to lose the hound would be to run through water. Winsloe had mentioned a river. Where was it? The night air was so damp, everything smelled like water. I'd run about a half-mile when the humidity content in the westerly wind tripled. As I veered west, I found a path and took it. Speed was not a bigger concern than laying a difficult trail. On the open path, I ran full tilt, head low, eyes narrowed against the wind. I dashed across a spongy patch of ground, covering it in three strides. As my front paws hit firmer earth, the ground beneath my back legs suddenly gave way. Grappling for a hold, I dug my front claws into the soil as my back legs pedaled air. Behind me, my hindquarters disappeared into the darkness of a deep hole. I recalled what Winsloe had said about Lake running for the river: '. . . if he takes the easy route, he'll find himself in a bear pit.' Why couldn't I have remembered that five minutes ago?

The hound's baying crescendoed, then split into two voices. Two hounds. Both getting very, very close. My right rear paw struck something on the side of the pit, a stone or a root. I pushed off it, getting enough leverage to launch my hindquarters almost out of the pit. Cursing my lack of fingers, I gripped the earth with my front nails, sank my rear claws into the side of the pit, and managed to wriggle my backside out. A dog yipped behind me. I didn't turn to see how close it was. Better off not knowing.

I ran for the river. An earsplitting yowl sounded to my left, so close I felt the vibration. I veered right and kept going. The thunder of running paws shook the ground. I hunkered down and picked up speed. I was faster than any dog. All I had to do was keep out of their reach long enough to outpace them. So long as I didn't hit any more traps, I could do it. The sound of running water grew until it drowned out the panting of the dogs. Where was that river? I could smell it, hear it . . . but I couldn't see it. All I could see was the path extending another fifty yards. And beyond those fifty yards? Nothing. Meaning the ground dropped off to the river. How much of a drop? A small riverbank or a hundred-foot cliff? Was I willing to take the risk, keep running until I fell off the edge? The water sounded close, so it couldn't be too steep a drop. I had to take the gamble. Not slowing, I raced toward the trail's end. Then, less than thirty feet away, a shape flew from the forest's edge and landed in my path.

GETAWAY

All four of my legs shot out, like brakes on a car careering out of control. I caught a glimpse of fur, a flash of canines, and braced for the attack. A tawny underbelly sailed over me. Stupid dog. They never did have any sense of aim. I wheeled around to meet my assailant on the backlash and saw only a flicker of tail fur as he raced away. Huh. Well, that was easy. As I began to run for the riverbank, a roar of fury split the night air, and I again skidded to a stop. I knew that roar. Inhaling, I caught my assailant's scent and realized why he hadn't attacked me.

Wheeling, I saw Clay fly at a pack of five dogs. I tore after him. Before I could cover the fifty feet between us, both hounds and one rottweiler turned tail and ran. That meant we each had to fight only one dog, a rottweiler and German shepherd. Perfect! Hey, wait a minute – Clay was running after the cowards, leaving me with both remaining dogs. Goddamn it! Couldn't he just let them go? Of all the egotistical— The rottweiler turned on me, cutting short my mental tirade. As I spun to face him, the shepherd lunged at my haunch. The rottweiler sank its teeth into my shoulder. I toppled backward, trying to knock him off. The shepherd leaped at my throat, but I saw the flash of teeth and snapped my head down to protect my neck. As the shepherd pulled back, I grabbed his ear between my teeth and wrenched, shredding it. He yelped and stumbled away. The rottweiler grabbed my shoulder again and shook me. My legs struggled for a foothold. Pain ripped through my shoulder. My traitorous knee joint flared, doubling the agony. As my good rear leg scuffed the ground, I dug in, got some leverage, and rolled, jerking the rottweiler off his feet. We tumbled down, somersaulting together, snapping at anything within biting distance. Then, in mid-roll, the rottweiler flew off me. Literally flew. One second his teeth were plunging into the thick fur around my neck, then next he was hurtling skyward. Blood sprayed my eyes. Blinded, I lurched to my feet, tossing my head to clear my vision. The first thing I saw was the rottweiler hanging from Clay's jaws. Then I noticed a movement to my right. The shepherd. It dove at Clay. I spun, catching it in mid-flight, and tore out its throat before we even hit the ground. Its body was still twitching when I heard the shouts of the guards.

I ran for the riverbank. Clay cut me off and shoved me toward the woods. As I snapped at him, I saw the bodies of both hounds lying farther up the path and I understood. Clay had gone after the fleeing hounds to ensure they couldn't double back and pick up our trail. With the hounds dead, we didn't need to head for the water.

We dove into the underbrush and circled north, coming within thirty feet of the guards as they jogged toward the river. They didn't stop, nor did the rottweiler loping beside them. They were making enough noise to cover ours, and the southeasterly wind kept our scent from the dog.

I followed Clay through two miles of forest, heading northeast. When he stopped, I sniffed for the stink of a road but smelled only forest. As I searched the breeze, he brushed along my side, rubbing close enough for me to feel the heat of his body through his fur. He circled me, then paused at my injured shoulder, licked it twice, and circled again. This time he stopped at my left back leg and nudged it out from under me, forcing me to my haunches. He snuffled my torn knee cap, then started to lick it. I jerked up, straining forward, motioning that we had to keep running, but he knocked my rear legs out again, less gently this time, and went back to work on my knee before moving his attention to my shoulder. Every few minutes, he'd move his muzzle to my cheek, breath whooshing hot against my face, nuzzle me, then return to cleaning my injuries. As he worked, my ears pivoted constantly, listening for the guards, but they didn't come. Finally, Clay prodded me to my feet, brushed along my side one last time, then headed northeast at a slow lope. I followed. A half-hour later, I picked up the distant scent of a road. Time to Change.

Even after I'd Changed back, I stayed in my hiding place. While Clay paced beyond the thicket, I crouched there, listening to the crunch of dead leaves under his feet and wondering what the hell I was doing. For nine days, I hadn't known whether I'd ever see Clay again. For one endless night, I'd even thought he might be dead. The moment my Change ended, I should have run to him. Instead I knelt close to the ground, heart thudding, not with anticipation, but something closer to fear. I didn't know how to face Clay. It was like a stranger was waiting for me and I wasn't sure how to react, wanting nothing more than to huddle here until he went away. Not that I wanted Clay to go away. I just . . . I wished Jeremy were there. Wasn't that awful? Wanting a buffer to protect me against a reunion with the man I loved? Clay was the only person with whom I ever felt completely comfortable. And now I felt as if I were confronting a stranger? What kind of bullshit was that? Yet even as I railed at my lunacy, I couldn't bring myself to go to him. I was afraid. Afraid I'd see something missing from his eyes, see traces of the look he'd given me when he'd thought I was Paige.

Clay stopped pacing. 'Elena?' he said softly.

'Ummm – I don't have any clothing.'

Of all the idiotic things I could say, that topped the list. I expected Clay to fall over laughing. He didn't. He didn't make a sound, just reached into the thicket and held out his hand. I closed my eyes, took it, and let him pull me out.

'Lousy time for joking, eh?' I said.

But he wasn't smiling. Instead he stood there, eyes searching my face, hesitant, almost uncertain. Then he pulled me against him. My knees gave way, and I stumbled into his arms, burying my face against his shoulder, inhaling his smell as a sound frighteningly close to a sob burst from my lips. I breathed in his scent, filling my brain with it, crowding out everything else. My body shuddered, then started to shake. Clay hugged me tight, one hand entwined in my hair, the other rubbing my back.

When I stopped shaking, I bent my knees, lowering us to the ground. His hands slid behind my back, cushioning it

415

against the cold earth. I touched my lips to his, tentatively, as if there was still a chance he'd pull away, reject me. His lips moved against mine, soft, then harder, increasing in pressure and intensity until I couldn't breathe and didn't care. I guided my hips up to his and pulled him into me.

Afterward, as we lay on the dew-damp ground, I listened for human sounds and heard only the tripping of Clay's heartbeat, slowing with each breath. It would be just my luck to have the guards find us now, lying in the grass twenty feet from freedom, having postponed our getaway to make love. Was that the ultimate in balls, recklessness, or plain stupidity? Probably a combination of all three. Never let it be said that Clay and I ever did anything as conventional as actually completing an escape from near-death before indulging in a quick round of reunion sex.

'We should go,' I said.

Clay chuckled. 'You think?'

'Probably. Unless you brought food. Then maybe we could squeeze in a picnic before we leave, watch the sun come up.'

'Sorry, darling. No food. There's a town about ten miles from here. We'll grab breakfast there.'

'No sense rushing things. Sex. A relaxing meal. Hell, maybe we find time for some sight-seeing before we go.'

Clay laughed. 'I'm afraid the only local sight we'll be seeing is the nearest restaurant drive-thru. I was in kind of a hurry to get away and I didn't grab a change of clothes. We'll have to share what I've got. Of course, that'll make it easier if we decide to stop for more sex after breakfast.'

'Just take me home,' I said.

'I wish I could, darling.'

'I meant, take me wherever Jeremy and the others are.'

He nodded and retrieved his clothes from behind a nearby tree. Then he handed me his shirt, boxers, and socks, leaving him with his jeans and shoes. Once we'd dressed – or half-dressed – he carried me to the waiting car. No, it wasn't some great romantic gesture. The ground was wet and I'd have drenched my socks if I walked. Plus my knee still throbbed when I put any weight on it. So maybe it was romantic after all. Practical romance. The kind we did best.

We were in Maine. Not seaside, vacation-land Maine, but the middle of the remote northern section. Before Clay had left Jeremy to look for me, the others had narrowed my location to upper Maine. In Clay's absence, Jeremy had moved everyone to New Brunswick, deeming it the safest location from which to search for both of us. Clay learned this by calling Jeremy from a roadside pay phone. Jeremy still had my cell phone and was able to give him directions.

On the way to New Brunswick we stuck to the back roads for as long as we could, but in that part of Maine, the non-highway roads were often so insignificant we couldn't find them on the map. We soon turned onto I-95. Forty minutes later we arrived at the Houlton–Woodstock border crossing. As usual, crossing the border into Canada was a snap. Pull up to the booth and answer a few simple questions. Citizenship? Destination? Length of stay? Bringing any firearms/liquor/fresh produce? Enjoy your stay. I hoped we would.

Jeremy had taken the others to a motel a few miles off the Trans-Canada Highway, near Nackawic. Why had Jeremy chosen western New Brunswick for their base camp? Two reasons. First, it was outside of the United States. Tucker and his guards were American and knew all of us – except me – were American, so they'd assume we'd stay in the States, even if Canada was a few scant hours away. Second, western New Brunswick was primarily French-speaking. That might seem like an obstacle – and Jeremy hoped it would – but in reality the language barrier was as easily crossed as the international border. Jeremy and I both spoke French, and even if we hadn't, most locals would be bilingual. It was difficult to live in Canada and not speak at least some English, despite our official national bilingualism. If Tucker even thought to send a search party across the border, he'd gravitate toward English-speaking regions in eastern New Brunswick. So, although we were less than two hundred miles north of the compound, we were safer here than if we'd run all the way down the coast to Florida.

Throughout the trip, Clay and I barely spoke. Anyone else would have peppered me with queries about my captors, the compound, my escape. Eventually I'd have to answer these questions, but right then, I wanted nothing more than to lean back in my seat, watch the scenery pass, and forget what I'd left behind. Clay let me do that.

We reached the motel at nine-thirty. It was an old but well-kept motor lodge with a huge roadside sign proclaiming 'Bienvenue/Welcome.' Only a half-dozen cars dotted the parking lot. Come evening, it would fill with vacationers making the trek from Ontario and Quebec to the Maritimes, but for now everyone was gone, up early and on the road by breakfast.

'Is this the right place?' I said. 'Do you recognize any of the rental cars?'

'No, but they'd have traded them for new ones. I do recognize that guy by the fence, though.'

Jeremy stood before a caged pen of grouse and pheasant, his back to us. I threw open the door and leaped out before the car stopped rolling.

'Hungry?' I called as I jogged toward Jeremy. 'They look fat enough.'

Jeremy turned, giving me a half-smile, as unsurprised as if I'd been standing behind him the entire time. He'd probably seen us drive in and stood here, watching the birds. At one time, not even so long ago, I'd have taken this as a snub, spent hours agonizing over why he hadn't come to greet me. But I knew Jeremy hadn't been ignoring me. He'd been waiting. Jeremy would no more come running out to welcome me back than he'd scoop me up in a bear hug and tell me he'd missed me. Anyone else in the Pack would, but that wasn't Jeremy's way, never would be. Yet when I threw my arms around him and kissed his cheek, he hugged me back and murmured that he was glad to see me. That was enough.

'Have you eaten?' he asked. Again, typical Jeremy. I'd spent nine days locked in a cell and his first concern would be that they hadn't fed me properly.

'We grabbed breakfast,' Clay said as he approached. 'But she's probably still hungry.'

'Starved,' I said.

'There's a restaurant a mile down,' Jeremy said. 'We'll get a proper meal there. First, though, I suggest you put on more clothing. Both of you.' He steered me toward the motel. 'We'll take my room. My kit's in there. Judging by the look of that knee we'll need it.'

A room door opened and Paige emerged, but Jeremy continued leading me toward the opposite end of the motel. I managed a quick smile and wave before Jeremy ushered me into his room.

'They're eager to see you, but it can wait,' he said.

'Preferably until after I shower,' I said.

'First, medical attention. Then a shower, food, and rest. There's no rush to talk to anyone.'

'Thanks.'

'Her knee's the worst,' Clay said as I sat down. 'The shoulder looks bad, but it's all surface tearing. The knee damage goes deeper. Partially healed and torn open again. The arm and facial cuts are superficial, but they need to be cleaned up. Same with the slice on her hand and the powder burns on her shoulder and side. There's also some healed puncture wounds in her stomach you should check.'

'Should I?' Jeremy said.

'Sorry.'

I knew Clay was apologizing not so much for giving Jeremy medical instructions but for the last few days, for taking off on his own. No one spoke as Jeremy examined my wounds. While he bent over my knee, my stomach growled.

Jeremy glanced over his shoulder at Clay. 'The restaurant is on the east side of the highway. Head south around the bend. They should have pancakes.'

'*Et le jambon, s'il vous plaît,*' I said.

'They speak English,' Jeremy said, lips twitching as Clay hesitated by the door. He gingerly pulled a half-dozen broken threads from my kneecap before adding, 'She said she wants ham as well. *Naturellement.*'

'Right,' Clay said. And left.

RECUPERATION

After examining and cleaning my myriad wounds, Jeremy restitched my leg. Now, one might wonder how he *happened* to have a surgical needle and thread on hand, but Jeremy was more likely to go on a trip without his toothbrush than his medical kit – and he was very conscientious about oral hygiene. From past experience, Jeremy had learned to take his kit pretty much every time he stepped out with Clay or me. We had a habit of turning even the most innocuous events into medical emergencies, like the time we went to the opera and I ended up with a fractured collarbone – my own stupidity really, but Clay had started it.

I persuaded Jeremy to forgo binding my wounds. A hot shower was more important. Once he'd tied off my stitches and warned me against getting them 'too wet,' I bolted for the bathroom. I waited for the water temperature to hit scalding before I stepped into the shower. For several minutes I stood motionless, letting the hot water cascade over me, sloughing away all remnants of the last week. When the shower door opened, I didn't turn. Sure, I'd seen *Psycho*, but no knife-wielding intruder would get past Jeremy, and I knew it wasn't Jeremy opening the door – a knife-wielding intruder would be more likely to interrupt my shower. Cool skin brushed against my bare legs. As the shower door slid closed, fingers tickled down my hip. I closed my eyes and leaned back against Clay, feeling his body slide into the contours of my back. I felt him lean forward, reaching for the shampoo. As I tilted my face up to the pelting water, his hands went to my hair, fingers tugging through the tangles, the sharp smell of soap perfuming the steam. I stretched my head back into his hands, nearly purring with contentment.

When he'd finished my hair, he shifted away for a moment, then returned. Soapy hands caressed my arms, then slid down to the outside of my legs, tracing circles there before gradually moving to the inside of my thighs. I parted my legs and Clay chuckled, the sound reverberating against my back. He ran his fingertips in slow zigzags up and down the inside of my thighs, teasing, then slipped inside me. I moaned and arched against him. His free hand went around my waist, pulling me closer, his erection pushing against the small of my back. I shifted onto my tiptoes and wriggled, trying to guide him into me. Instead he turned me around to face him and lifted me onto him. I bent my head back into the water, pulling Clay along as he kissed me. The water had cooled to chill pellets that beat down on my face. Reaching up, I entangled my fingers in Clay's drenched curls, feeling rivulets of water tickle along the insides of my wrists. He made a noise deep in his throat, half-groan, half-growl, and pushed into me, nearly toppling us into the tub. Then he shuddered and pulled out.

'Please don't tell me you're done,' I said, still hanging backward over his arms.

Clay laughed. 'Would I do that to you? I'm fine, but your breakfast is getting cold.'

'Trust me, I'm not worried.'

I reached to pull him back into me, but he eased away, got a better grip on my waist, opened the shower door, and carried me out. Once in the bedroom, he tossed me onto the bed and was inside me before the mattress stopped bouncing.

'Better?' he asked.

'Ummm, much.'

I closed my eyes and arched into him. As I moved, the smell of breakfast on the nightstand wafted between us. I hesitated a split second. My stomach growled.

'Upstaged by ham and pancakes,' Clay said. 'Again.'

'I can wait.'

Clay thrust into me with mock growl. 'You're too kind, darling.'

I moved my hips against his. My stomach chortled and wheezed. Clay shifted up and forward. I reached out to pull him back, but he didn't withdraw, instead reaching for something over my head. As I closed my eyes again, grease dripped onto my cheek, and a slice of ham pressed against my lips. I opened my mouth and chomped it down in a few bites, then sighed, and lifted my hips to meet Clay.

'Mmmm.'

'Is that for me or the ham?' he whispered against my hair.

Before I could assuage his ego, he pushed another slice of ham into my mouth, then bent his head to lick the dripped grease, his tongue tracing circles across my cheek. We moved together for a few minutes and I forgot the food. Honest. Then Clay reached up again, this time returning with a folded pancake. I sank my teeth into the bottom half and pushed the rest up to his mouth. He laughed and took a bite. When I finished, I lifted my head and licked the crumbs from his lips. He took another pancake and dangled it above me. I jerked my head up to snatch it. My teeth sank into something he hadn't been offering.

'Yow!' he said, shaking his injured finger.

'Don't be dangling the food, then,' I mumbled through a mouthful of pancake.

Clay growled and lowered his face to the side of my neck, nibbling a sensitive spot. I yelped and tried to wriggle away, but he pinned me down and thrust into me. I shuddered and gasped. Then I really did forget the food.

Twenty minutes later, I was curled up beside Clay, one arm draped over his back, tracing designs in the sweat between his shoulder blades as he nibbled the hollow between my neck and shoulder. I yawned, stretched my legs, then wrapped them around his.

'Sleep?' he asked.

'Later.'

'Talk?'

'Not yet.' I buried my face in his chest, inhaled, and sighed. 'You smell so good.'

He chuckled. 'Like ham?'

'No, like you. I missed you so much.'

His breath caught. One hand went to my hair, stroking

it back from my ear. I didn't usually talk like that. If I said I missed him, there was usually a punch line. If I said I loved him, it was almost always in the middle of making love, when I couldn't be held accountable for anything I said. Why? Because I was afraid, afraid that by admitting how much he meant to me, I'd give him the power to hurt me even worse than he had by biting me. Which was stupid, of course. Clay knew exactly how much I loved him. The only person I was fooling was myself.

'I was scared,' I said. Another thing I hated to admit, but as long as I was on a roll . . .

'So was I,' he said, kissing the top of my head. 'When I realized you were gone—'

Someone knocked on the door. Clay swore under his breath.

'Go away,' he murmured, too low for the visitor to hear.

'It could be Jeremy,' I said.

'Jeremy wouldn't bother us. Not now.'

'Elena? It's me,' Paige called.

Clay lifted himself onto his forearms. 'Go away!'

'I just wanted to see how Elena—'

'No!'

Paige's sigh fluttered through the door. 'Stop shouting, Clayton. I'm not going to harass her. I know she's been through a lot. I only wanted to—'

'You'll see her when everyone else does. Until then, wait.'

'Maybe I should talk to her,' I whispered.

'If you open that door, she won't go away until she's pestered every iota of information from you.'

'I heard that, Clayton,' Paige said.

He snarled at the door and muttered under his breath. Something told me Clay and Paige hadn't become fast friends in my absence. Fancy that.

'Ummm, Paige?' I called. 'I'm kind of tired, but if you'll give me a minute to dress—'

'She won't go away,' Clay said. 'You need time to relax. You don't need to be answering questions for a bunch of strangers.'

'I'm *not* a stranger,' Paige said. 'Could you be a little less rude, Clayton?'

Clay was right. If I let Paige in, she'd want to know everything. I wasn't ready for that. Nor did I want to lie here while Clay and Paige argued through a closed door.

I crawled from the bed and tossed Clay his jeans. When he opened his mouth to protest, I jabbed a finger at the window, then lifted it to my lips. He nodded. As I slid into Clay's T-shirt and boxers, he eased the window open and unhooked the screen. Then, while Paige patiently waited for us to open the door, we escaped into the surrounding forest.

'That probably wasn't very nice,' I said as we tramped deeper into the woods.

Clay snorted. 'Won't catch me losing any sleep over it.'

'I know Paige can be difficult, but—'

'She's a pain in the ass, darling. And that's being generous. The kid is barely out of school and she thinks she's a leader, pushing her way into everything, arguing, second-guessing Jeremy. Until she met you in Pittsburgh, she'd never been within screaming distance of real danger and suddenly she's an expert.' He shook his hands. 'Don't get me started.'

'Seems I already did.'

'Nah, that's nothing, darling. Give me a few hours and I'll tell you what I really think of Paige Winterbourne. *Nobody* talks to Jeremy that way, especially not some little girl with an overinflated sense of her own importance. If I had my way, Paige would have been sent packing last week. But you know Jeremy. He doesn't put up with her crap, but he won't let it get to him, either.' He pushed through a tangle of tree branches. 'Where're we going?'

'How about a run? Even Paige wouldn't pester a wolf.'

'Don't count on it.'

After our run, we made love. Again. Afterwards we lay in the grass, soaking up the late summer sun that pierced the canopy of trees overhead.

'You smell that?' Clay asked.

'Hmmm?'

'I smell food.'

'Dead or alive?'

Clay laughed. 'Dead, darling. Dead and cooked.'

He heaved himself up, looked around, then motioned for me to wait and vanished into the woods. A half-minute later he returned with a picnic basket. Well, a cardboard box actually, but the smells drifting from it were definitely of the picnic variety. Laying it on the grass, he unpacked cheese, bread, fruit, a covered plate of chicken, a bottle of wine, and assorted paper and plastic eating tools.

'Picnic fairies?' I asked, then caught a whiff of scent that answered my question. 'Jeremy.' I grabbed a drumstick and tore a chunk from it. 'I'm spoiled.'

'You deserve it.'

I grinned. 'I do, don't I?'

We polished off the meal and the wine in under ten minutes. Then I reclined onto the grass and sighed, content and sated for the first time in nearly two weeks. I closed my eyes and the first seductive tug of sleep washed over me. Sleep. Uninterrupted sleep. The perfect cap to a perfect day. I rolled against Clay, smiling drowsily, and let the waves of slumber pull me under. Then I bolted awake.

'We can't sleep out here,' I said. 'It's not safe.'

Clay's lips brushed my forehead. 'I'll stay awake, darling.'

As I opened my mouth to argue, Jeremy's voice drifted from the distance. 'You can both sleep. I'm here.'

I hesitated, but Clay pulled me back down, entwining his legs around mine and cushioning my head with his arm. I wrapped myself in his warmth and fell asleep.

It was late afternoon when Jeremy nudged us awake. Clay grunted between snores but didn't move. I yawned, rolled over, and kept rolling until I was lying on my other side, whereupon I promptly fell back asleep. Jeremy shook us harder.

'Yes, I know you're still tired,' he said as Clay grumbled something unintelligible. 'But Elena needs to speak to the others today. I can't postpone it until morning.'

Clay muttered under his breath.

'Yes, I know I *could*,' Jeremy said. 'But it would be rude. They've been waiting all day.'

'We need—' I began.

'I brought your clothing.'

'I need to brush—'

'There's a comb and mouthwash with the clothes. No, you're not going back to your room or I suspect I won't see either of you until morning. We're meeting in fifteen minutes. I'll keep it short.'

The meeting was to be held in Kenneth and Adam's room. As we crossed the parking lot, I saw Paige pacing the crumbling sidewalk. Her arms were crossed, probably against the cool night air, but it looked as if she was holding in a barrage of questions she'd been waiting half a day to fire at me. Just what I need— No, that wasn't fair. Of course, Paige was anxious to speak to me. I'd been in the enemy camp. I'd seen what we were up against. It was understandable that she'd be bursting with questions about the compound, my captors, the other prisoners— Oh, God. Ruth. Paige didn't know about Ruth. The past week was such a jumble that I'd completely forgotten Paige had contacted me *before* Ruth died. The last she'd heard, her aunt was alive. Damn it! How could I have been so insensitive? Paige had been waiting for news of her aunt. She'd held off while Jeremy treated my wounds, given me time to shower, then came to ask about Ruth. And what had I done? I'd snuck out the bedroom window.

'I have to talk to Paige,' I said.

'Stay in sight,' Clay called as I jogged away.

As I approached, Paige turned and nodded, acknowledging my presence, but saying nothing. Her face was expressionless, any annoyance hidden under a veneer of good manners.

'How are you feeling?' she asked. 'Jeremy says your wounds aren't too bad.'

'About earlier,' I said. 'I'm— I wasn't thinking – it's been a hell of a day.' I shook my head. 'Sorry, that's a lousy excuse. You wanted to know about your aunt. I never thought— I shouldn't have—'

'She's gone, isn't she?'

'I'm so sorry. It happened the day after we lost contact, and I forgot you didn't know.'

Paige's eyes moved from mine, turning to stare over the parking lot. I struggled for something to say, but before I could think of anything, she spoke, her gaze still fixed on some far-off point.

'I knew,' she said, her voice as distant as her gaze. 'I sensed she was gone, though I'd hoped I was wrong.' She paused, swallowed, then shook her head sharply and turned back to me. 'How did it happen?'

I hesitated. Now wasn't the time for the truth. Not until I'd spoken to Jeremy first.

'Heart attack,' I said.

Paige frowned. 'But her heart—'

'Welcome back!' Adam shouted from across the parking lot.

I turned to see him running toward me, grinning.

'You look good,' Adam said. 'Well, except for those cuts. We'll get them back for that. How are your arms? The burns, I mean. I never got a chance to explain. I didn't mean it, which I guess you figured, since Clay didn't kill me for it.

Anyway, I'm sorry. Really sorry.'

'To be honest, I'd forgotten all about it.'

'Good. Then forget I mentioned it.' He turned as Clay reached us. 'How come you didn't take me along? I could have helped with the rescue.'

'There was no rescue,' Clay said, looping his arm around my wait. 'While I was trying to find a way inside, Elena escaped. All I did was provide the getaway car.'

'See?' Cassandra said as she joined us. 'I told you Elena was a resourceful girl.'

Paige rolled her eyes at the use of 'girl,' but Cassandra ignored her.

'Congratulations, Elena,' she said, laying a cool hand on my arm. 'I'm glad to see you out and looking well.'

She sounded as if she meant it. I stopped myself. Why wouldn't she mean it? Because I'd dreamed that she'd counseled the others to abandon me and made a play for Clay? A dream, I reminded myself. A manifestation of my own insecurities. Cassandra's welcoming smile was genuine enough. If Clay's arm seemed to tighten around me, well, that was probably coincidence. Or my imagination.

'We should get this meeting started,' Paige said. 'We'll keep it brief. I'm sure you're exhausted, Elena. We won't pester you for details tonight. I promise.'

LOYALTIES

At the meeting, Jeremy summarized what my escape added to our knowledge. By combining my info with Clay's, we had a good picture of the internal and external geography of the compound. Perhaps most important, we knew where to find our enemies. Given the size and complexity of the operation, it was unlikely they'd move camp anytime soon. So, Jeremy reasoned, we could take the time to plan an infiltration strategy, end the threat permanently, and release Ruth and the others.

As Jeremy said this, I realized everyone assumed Ruth was still alive. Why wouldn't they? I hadn't said otherwise.

'Ruth – uh – didn't make it,' I said.

'What?' Adam's gaze darting to Paige. 'You mean she—'

'She's gone,' Paige said, her voice hollow and small.

'Shit.' Adam walked over to Paige and put his arm around her shoulders, then looked at me. 'What happened?'

Now I was trapped. Would I lie in front of the entire group, knowing they'd learn the truth after I explained everything to Jeremy? Or would I be honest and have Paige wondering why I'd lied only minutes before? How did I get into these scrapes? Better make a clean breast of it before I dug myself in any deeper.

'It's – uh – complicated,' I began.

'They murdered her, didn't they?' Paige said. 'I know the kidnapping must have been stressful, but she was in excellent health.'

In other words, Paige hadn't bought my heart-attack story. I mentally thanked her for giving me a graceful way out and not calling me on my lie.

'Actually, no,' I said. 'They didn't kill her. Not the people who kidnapped us, anyway. It was one of the other captives. But it wasn't her fault.'

Paige frowned. 'An accident?'

'Umm, kind of, but not exactly.' I inhaled. 'Ruth didn't tell you everything when she contacted you. There was another witch there. A young girl.'

I told the whole story: Ruth's training of Savannah, the unexplained events in the compound, the attacks on the guards, Ruth's death, and the mayhem Savannah caused during our escape attempt.

'So you're saying this kid's evil,' Adam said.

'No. She's not,' I said. 'She just does—'

'—evil things,' Cassandra finished. 'I'm sorry, Elena, but that sounds like evil to me. Whether it's intentional or not is hardly the point. We have to consider the wisdom of freeing a child with this capacity for destruction. From what I've heard, I seriously doubt any of us is capable of controlling her. Especially the Coven.'

Cassandra slanted a look at Paige. The young woman's

434

cheeks burned, and she opened her mouth as if to argue, then closed it.

'It's settled, then,' Cassandra said. 'We can't worry about the girl—'

'Savannah didn't do these things,' Paige said quietly.

Cassandra sighed. 'I understand why you'd like to think that, Paige. No one wants to believe a child capable of evil, much less condemn her to death, but the fact remains—'

'She didn't do it,' Paige said, stronger now. 'A witch can't do things like that. We just can't. A spell for moving an inanimate object? Yes. For moving the object with enough force to crush someone's skull? Absolutely not. The best a witch could do would be to knock a plate off the table, not hurl it across a room.'

'But Eve was also a half-demon,' Adam said. 'We were only kids when she left, but I remember that.'

'Her father was an Aspicio,' Paige said. 'That means Eve's power was limited to vision. She had enhanced sight and could cause temporary blindness. That's it. Besides, powers from a half-demon aren't transmitted to an offspring. You know that.'

A long minute of silence passed.

'Look,' Paige said. 'Cassandra's right. I don't want to believe there's something wrong with this girl. But would I lie to save her if it meant endangering others? Of course not. Give me credit for a little common sense. If Savannah could kill Ruth, she could kill me too.'

'There was another theory,' I said. 'Some people thought it was a – uh – poltergeist.'

'A what?' Clay said.

I scowled at him. 'I'm just repeating what I heard, okay?'

'It wasn't a poltergeist,' Paige said. 'And yes, Clayton, such things do exist, but this isn't how they manifest themselves. Someone inside that compound was responsible. What other supernaturals were there?'

'On the opposite side?' I said. 'The teleporting half-demon we met in Pittsburgh, but he left a few days ago. Plus they supposedly had a sorcerer named Isaac Katzen on staff, though I never met the guy.'

'A sorcerer could do it,' Adam said.

'Some of it,' Paige said. 'Opening the cell doors, playing with the intercom system, jamming the exits. All possible sorcerer spells. But hurling objects and unscrewing light-bulbs? No way. That requires a very specific talent.'

'Telekinesis,' I murmured.

'Exactly,' Paige said. 'Several races have varying degrees of telekinetic power, such as—'

'Such as a telekinetic half-demon,' I said. A lump of ice settled in my stomach. 'But she said— Damn it!' I inhaled sharply. 'There was one at the compound. A captive. She said she wasn't capable of stuff like that. And I believed her. I know that sounds incredibly stupid, but *everyone* believed her. Besides, she wasn't even around when most things happened.'

'That doesn't matter,' Paige said. 'A Volo, the highest level of telekinetic half-demon, wouldn't need to be present to exercise her powers. I remember hearing about one case where a Volo could find an arrow in an adjoining room and fire it into a bull's-eye with enough force to shatter the shaft into matchsticks.'

I closed my eyes. 'How could I have been so stupid?'

'It's not your fault,' Paige said. 'Like you said, everyone believed her. When people think of telekinesis, they picture a person bending a spoon, but in reality Volos might well be the most dangerous type of half-demon. They could throw a person out a tenth-floor window without lifting a finger.'

I cursed myself for having bought into Leah's whole girl-next-door routine, the displays of concern, the offers of help, the overtures of friendship. I'd believed Leah. I'd listened as she wove a web of lies and deceit around an innocent child, spreading the tendrils of doubt until Savannah herself believed she was guilty. Had Leah known about Ruth's training? Had she killed her to stop it? Whatever Leah's agenda, it involved Savannah. And I'd left them together.

Suddenly, I couldn't breathe. I staggered to my feet and ran from the room.

I heard Clay behind me. Not slowing, I loped around the motel and headed for the forest. He didn't call for me to stop or wait, just jogged up beside me as I walked into the forest.

'Paige is right,' he said after a few minutes. 'It wasn't your fault.'

'Yes, it is. I wanted to get Savannah out. But I didn't. The moment came and I choked. I told myself that I was doing the best thing, leaving her in there, but deep down I knew better. I saw my chance to escape and I took it. To hell with everyone else.'

'I don't believe that. If you left her behind, it's because you had to. We'll get her out when we go back.'

'But it doesn't sound like we're going back anytime soon.'

Jeremy stepped up behind us. 'We'll return as soon as we're ready, Elena. You're safe, so I won't rush.'

'But Savannah—'

'Our main objective is to stop these people, not to rescue anyone.'

'But you were planning to go in for me.'

'That's different. Clay and I were willing to take the risk. Everyone else was free to make their own decision. I won't risk your life or Clayton's by rushing in to rescue a stranger. Even a child.'

'What if I decide to take that risk myself?'

'You're not free to make that decision, Elena. So long as you're part of the Pack, I can make it for you, and I am forbidding you to return.'

'That's not—'

'Not fair,' Jeremy finished. 'Yes, we've been through this before. But it's Pack law. And don't threaten to leave the Pack because I will make certain you don't go back to that compound alone, no matter what rights to self-determination you claim. I take the responsibility for this decision. We'll make every effort to save this child when we return. If anything happens to her before we get there, blame me, not yourself.'

I started to argue, but Jeremy was already walking away.

I didn't chase Jeremy down to pursue the matter. After ten years of living under his roof and his rules, I knew what worked and what didn't. Hounding him didn't. Once Jeremy made up his mind, the only way to change it was to erode the obstacles with logic and persuasion. Bring out the battering rams and he only doubled the fortifications. I'll admit, patience isn't one of my virtues, but I resolved to give the matter some time. A few hours at least. Maybe overnight.

'So the security system requires both a fingerprint check and a retinal scan?' Jeremy asked.

He was seated at the tiny dining table in our room. Clay and I were sprawled across the bed, Clay dozing, me trying hard not to join him.

'Uh, right,' I said.

He jotted something onto his papers. 'Index finger?'

'Huh? Oh, no. Sorry. It's a handprint, not a fingerprint. You grab the handle and it reads your handprint.'

'We don't have to do this tonight. We'll have plenty of time later.'

Not if I had anything to say about it. 'I want to do it now, while it's fresh in my mind.'

'Have we had dinner?' Clay's muffled voice floated up from the pillows.

'What?'

He rolled onto his back. 'I'm counting meals. We had breakfast in Maine, then another breakfast here. Or was that brunch? If so, was the picnic lunch of dinner?'

'I'm counting it as lunch,' I said.

'Good. Then let's go get dinner.'

* * *

Jeremy insisted on being polite and inviting the others to join us. As Clay knocked at Kenneth and Adam's room, the neighboring door opened and Adam stepped out, turning to say a few words to someone inside. When Kenneth opened his door, Clay want in. I waited outside for Adam.

'We're going to dinner,' I said. 'Have you eaten?'

'Nope. I was just about to ask you guys the same thing. Let me grab my car keys.'

'Was that Paige?' I said, nodding to the next room.

'Yeah. She's pretty upset.'

'Should I ask her to join us?'

He shrugged. 'You can ask, but I don't think she's feeling up to it. If not, tell her I'll bring something back.'

I'd rather Adam asked Paige himself, but he vanished into his room, leaving me to it. I was probably the last person Paige wanted to see. Her aunt was dead and I hadn't even had the decency to tell her straight off. I inhaled, walked to her door, and rapped lightly, half-hoping she might not hear me. After a second's pause, I turned to leave. Then I heard the clank of the chain lock and the door opened.

'Hey, there,' Paige said, managing a wan half-smile. 'You still up? How are you feeling? I've got some sleeping teas if you're having trouble.'

How was I feeling? Oh, about two inches tall. Paige's eyes and nose were splotched red, as if she'd spent the last couple of hours crying, and she was worried that I might not be able to sleep?

'I'm really sorry,' I said. 'About your aunt. I don't mean

440

to intrude, but we're heading out for dinner and I was wondering if you felt like joining us.'

'No,' she said. 'Thanks, but no thanks.'

'Adam said he'd bring something back for you.'

She gave a distracted nod, paused, then said quickly, 'Could you— I don't mean to be a pain. Really. I know you're tired and sore, and I hate to pester you, but could you stop by when you come back? I have—'

She stopped and looked over my shoulder. I heard Clay's footsteps behind me. Paige paused, then straightened up, as if bracing herself, and went on, 'Clayton, I was just asking Elena if you could spare her for a while tonight. Thirty minutes tops. I promise.'

'You're not coming to dinner?' he asked.

'I'd rather not.'

'No one stays alone,' he said. 'That's Jeremy's rule.' I shot him a glare, warning him to be more sensitive, but he didn't catch it and continued, 'Cassandra will stay with you.'

'Oh, she'll love that,' Paige said.

'If she doesn't like the rules, she can leave.'

'We should all be so lucky,' Paige murmured under her breath. 'Seriously, though. You don't need to leave someone behind with me. I have plenty of protection spells.'

'Those are the rules,' Clay said. 'No one stays alone. It's not like Cassandra eats anyway.' He started to leave, then added, 'If Elena's feeling up to it, she can stop by with your dinner. Twenty minutes. Then she needs her rest.'

'Gee, does that mean I have your permission?' I called after him.

'I'm not answering that,' he said without turning.
'Smart man.' I looked at Paige. 'I'll pop by afterward.'
'Thanks. I appreciate it.'

CORONATION

At ten I returned to Paige's room, her still-warm dinner in hand. I found her alone.

'Where's Cassandra?' I asked.

'Out. Trolling for dinner or companionship. I refuse to be the former and I don't qualify to be the latter. Wrong gender.'

'No one is supposed to be alone. Does Jeremy know she's taking off on you?'

'No, and I'm not tattling, so let's keep it between us. Personally, I feel safer when she's gone. A vampire isn't exactly my ideal choice for a roommate. One attack of the midnight munchies and I'm a goner. I was bunking up with Adam, but sharing a room with Cassandra was putting a definite strain on Kenneth's nerves, so we switched.'

'So you and Adam are . . . together?'

She frowned, then caught my meaning and laughed. 'Oh, God, no. We've been friends since we were kids. Trust me, we know each other too well for anything else.' She walked to the mini-fridge. 'Can I get you something to drink? I have bottled water, diet soda. Nothing stronger, I'm afraid.'

'That's okay.'

'Just get on with it, right?'

'I didn't mean—'

She waved a hand. 'Don't worry. I know you're tired and, again, I apologize for bugging you. It's just, well, I'm working on specs, blue-prints, and such for the compound. I know we don't need them right away but, well, I want to keep busy. It's easier—' She nibbled at her lower lip, looked away. 'Easier if I have something to do, keep my mind occupied.'

I knew what she meant. Last year when two of my Pack brothers died, only action had assuaged my grief. I'd thrown myself into plotting against the mutts who'd killed them, partly for revenge and partly to keep from dwelling on their deaths. In preparing for our onslaught against those who'd killed Ruth, Paige was doing the same. I understood that.

'I've got most of it done already,' she said, passing me a notebook from the table. 'All I need is for you to fill in a few blanks.'

I flipped through her notes. 'Actually, Jeremy has most of this. You could—'

'Get it from him. Right. Sure.' She turned, but not before I saw disappointment flicker across her face. 'Guess I should have known he'd be two steps ahead of me. Okay, then, well, that's all I wanted. Sorry about that. I wasn't thinking.'

'Oh, wait. There's a couple of things here Jeremy hadn't asked,' I lied. 'Tell you what. I'm not tired yet. How about I fill in everything you're missing. Even if I've already told Jeremy, it never hurts to have two copies.'

'Oh?' For the first time since I'd arrived, her smile touched her eyes. 'That's great. Thanks.'

Like I said, I knew how she felt. Well, I didn't know

exactly how she felt, having no idea how close she'd been to her aunt, but I understood that she needed something to do, something to make her feel that she was taking action. Providing that was the least I could do.

When we finished, I offered to spend the night in Paige's room, arguing that Cassandra seemed in no rush to return and that Jeremy was sharing our room, so no one would be alone even if I stayed. Paige refused. She assured me her lock spells would keep out most intruders and her protection spells would warn her if anyone bypassed the locks. I suspected she wanted to be alone with her grief, so I didn't push the matter.

That night I dreamed of escaping the compound. Over and over. Each time the circumstances differed, but one element remained the same. I left Savannah behind. Sometimes I forgot about her until I was outside and it was too late. At other times my guilt was more obvious. I ran past her cell and I didn't stop. I heard her calling my name and I didn't stop. I saw Leah reach out to grab her . . . and I didn't stop. Finally, as the dream replayed for the umpteenth version, I was running for the open exit door. Then Savannah appeared on the other side, urging me on. I stopped. I turned around. And I ran the other way.

I bolted upright, gasping for breath. Clay was awake, holding me, brushing the sweat-sodden hair from my face.

'Do you want to talk about it?' he asked.

As I shook my head, his arms tightened, but I didn't look at his face. Didn't want to. This wasn't something I could discuss with him. He'd only try to convince me that I'd

445

done the right thing getting myself out safely. If the situation were reversed, would I want Clay risking his life to save a stranger? Of course not. But the point would be moot because Clay would never take any risk to save a stranger. He'd throw himself in front of a bullet to protect his Pack, but he wouldn't stop to help an accident victim. If I was there, he'd do it to please me, but if he was alone, the thought would never cross his mind.

I didn't expect Clay to care about Savannah. Well, maybe I still held out hope that he'd develop a social conscience, but I'd learned that such a change ranked alongside world peace on the scale of well-meaning but naïve wishes. Clay cared about his Pack and only his Pack. How could I expect him to understand my guilt over Savannah?

As I eased back into Clay's arms, I noticed Jeremy across the room, propped on his elbow, watching me from the cot. He lifted his brows in unspoken question. Did I want to talk to him instead? I gave a small shake of my head and lowered myself onto the bed. I could sense them both watching me, but closed my eyes and feigned sleep. Eventually the room went still. When it did, I slipped onto my back and lay there in the dark, thinking.

Had I jumped to conclusions earlier, when I decided it had been Leah causing the trouble and framing Savannah? What if I persuaded Jeremy to strike early, then discovered I'd been mistaken? What if people died because of that mistake? And what if I did nothing and Savannah died because of *that* mistake? I had to find a middle ground. If we had enough information, acting swiftly would be to our advantage. Did we know enough? Or, more accurately, what were our chances of learning more? Pretty slim. We had the data I'd gathered from inside the compound, plus what Clay had learned from scouting the site, plus what the others had uncovered in their research. Whatever we didn't know by now, we'd likely never find out. We had to concentrate on formulating a plan—

Outside, a neighboring door clicked. I tensed and listened. Our group occupied all the rooms at this end. Was someone going out? No, wait. It was probably Cassandra returning. I checked the clock. 2:35. Oh, that's great. We ask her to keep an eye on Paige and she takes off for half the night. Paige might not want to tattle, but I would. Jeremy needed to know we couldn't rely on Cassandra to back up Paige.

As I reclined onto the pillow, I heard shoes scuff against pavement outside. I glanced at Clay and Jeremy. Sound asleep. I eased out of bed and tiptoed to the window. Lifting a drapery corner, I peered out to see Paige stealing across the parking lot, suitcase in one hand, notebook in the other. Shit!

Being careful not to wake the guys, I tugged on my jeans and shirt and crept out the door. Paige rounded the bird pen and vanished into the darkness beyond. Barefooted, I scampered after her, one eye on my target, the other on the pavement, watching for broken glass. When I reached the bird pen, a pheasant roused itself, opened one sleepy eye, then squawked and jetted into the air. Damn it! Sometimes there were serious disadvantages to being a werewolf. Even as I lunged away from the cage, several other birds awoke and added their voices to the din. So much for a stealthy

447

approach. I raced through the grove of trees where I'd last seen Paige and found her in an auxiliary parking lot. She stood beside a car, frowning in the direction of the panicking birds. When she saw me, she fumbled with the keys, barely getting the door open before I arrived.

'Uh, hi,' she said, faking a bright smile. 'You're out late.'

'Going somewhere?' I asked.

'Ummm, just out for something to eat.' She backed into the driver's seat. 'The stuff Adam brought got cold so I thought I'd go see if I can find a 7–11 or something.'

'You won't mind if I join you then,' I said, snapped the passenger door lock and slid inside. I gestured to her suitcase. 'Hell of a purse you've got there.'

She laid her hands on the steering wheel spokes, paused, then glanced at me. 'I'm leaving, Elena. I know this is a bad way to do it, but I was afraid someone would try to stop me. It's too much for me. I'm backing out.'

'I'm sorry about your aunt.'

'She—' Paige looked out the windshield. 'She wasn't my aunt.'

'Oh, well, your Coven sister or whatever you—'

'She was my mother.'

'Your—?'

'That's how it works in the Coven,' Paige said, keeping her eyes on the windshield. 'Or how it used to work. The old way, from my mother's time. Witches didn't marry, so they avoided the stigmatism of single-motherhood by raising their daughters as nieces. No one outside the Coven knew the truth. In my case Adam knows, but that's about it. When my mother was young, she was too busy preparing

448

to be Coven leader to think about an heir. Once she became leader, she realized the Coven was faltering and decided she needed a daughter, someone she could train and prepare in her own way. So when she was fifty-two, she used magic to have a daughter. Me.'

'So that means you're . . . ?'

'The official new Coven leader.' Her lips twisted in a sardonic smile. 'It'd be funny if it wasn't so ridiculous. A twenty-two-year-old leader.' She inhaled sharply and shook her head. 'Doesn't matter. The point is that I've been trained for this. For the responsibility. I can't expect Jeremy or Kenneth or Cassandra to accept me as a fellow leader yet, but I know I can do it. Right now, though, I have to go home. There are things to be done, arrangements to be made.'

'I understand.' I leaned over her lap and lifted the notebook she'd let slip between her seat and the door. 'But if you're going home, you won't be needing this.'

She grabbed the book from me. 'Oh, actually, I do. For the Coven records.'

'You aren't going home, Paige. You're going to the compound.'

She forced a laugh. 'By myself? That'd be crazy.'

'My sentiments exactly. I understand you must want revenge for your mother, and I promise you'll get it when we go back, but there's no—'

As confusion flitted across her face, I realized revenge wasn't her motive. Then I recalled Ruth's warning, telling me not to let Paige know about Savannah or she'd insist on rescuing the girl.

'You're going after Savannah,' I said.

'I have to,' she said quietly.

'Because your Coven expects it?'

'No, because I expect it. How can I be Coven leader if I let this girl die? How could I? Live with myself? Look, I'm not stupid and I'm not suicidal. I'm not going in there, spells blazing, tearing the place apart. I couldn't do that anyway. All I want is Savannah. I'll be careful. I'll take my time, scout the place out, and find a way to get her. You guys don't need to worry about this. It's witch business. I—'

Paige's door flew open, nearly toppling her to the ground. Clay shoved his head into the car. Paige jumped and edged toward me.

'What's going on?' he asked.

'Paige wants to go after Savannah.'

'Oh, fuck!' He slammed the door and strode around to my side. 'Let me guess. She's going after the kid and she needs your help.'

'I don't—' Paige began.

'She's not asking for my help,' I said, getting out of the car. 'She wants to do it alone.'

'So she decided to tell you about it first? Call you out here, tell you what she's up to, and expect you'll let her go alone? Bullshit. She's playing on your sympathy. You'll insist on going with her and—'

'She didn't call me out,' I said. 'I followed her.'

Paige slid from the car, straightened, and met Clay's eyes. 'I'm doing this alone, Clayton. I'm not asking for or accepting any help.'

'Are you crazy?' He walked over and tried to pluck the keys

450

from her fist, but she backpedaled. He stopped and held his hand out. 'Give me those, Paige. You're not going anywhere.'

She looked from Clay to me, as if assessing her chances of escape.

'Not a prayer,' I said. 'There's two of us. We can outrun you. We can outfight you. Unless you've got a doomsday spell up your sleeve, you ain't leaving.'

She glanced over her shoulder and seemed ready to make a break for it when Jeremy stepped from the bushes behind her. She hesitated. Then her shoulders sagged and the keys slid from her hand.

'Come inside,' Jeremy said. 'We'll talk.'

'I have to get Savannah out,' Paige said as we walked into our motel room. 'You guys don't get it. I don't expect you to. Like I told Elena, it's witch business.'

'We understand that you're concerned for her,' Jeremy began.

Paige spun to face him. 'Concerned? I'm terrified for her.' She flipped through her notebook and jabbed a finger at a page. 'Look, I wrote down everything that happened that night Elena escaped. I divided the events into potential sorcerer versus telekinetic half-demon activity. There's some overlap, but between the two they cover everything. Now, what are the chances that this sorcerer and half-demon independently decided to raise hell on the same night. Sure, it's possible that one started things and the other joined in, but I doubt it. This half-demon is working with a sorcerer.'

'Okay,' I said.

Paige's gaze traveled across our faces. 'See? You *don't* get it. You can't.'

'Explain it to us,' Jeremy said.

She inhaled. 'Sorcerers hate witches. And vice versa. The biggest feud in the history of supernatural races. Our version of the Hatfields and the McCoys. Only the sorcerers do all the shooting. We're an ugly reminder—' She inhaled again. 'You guys don't need a history lesson. Just trust me on this one. If Leah is working with Katzen, and she's blaming Savannah for murder, then that's trouble. Big trouble. I can't begin to fathom their motivation, but I know Savannah is in danger. In one night, Winsloe and his cohorts have lost both their werewolves and suffered untold damage to their facility. Who will shoulder the blame for all that? The child witch. Isn't that what this Leah told you before you escaped? That Savannah did it?'

'They won't kill Savannah,' I said. 'She's too important.'

Even as I spoke the words, I heard my own doubt. With Bauer and Carmichael dead, Winsloe and Matasumi were the only principals left. Matasumi might want Savannah alive, but he was just a scientist. Winsloe had the cash, so he was in charge. I remembered the conversation I'd overheard between Matasumi and the man I assumed to be Katzen. At that time, Winsloe had already begun throwing his weight around, picking and choosing the sort of captives he wanted. Winsloe had no interest in witches. I knew that. Savannah was alone now, without even Xavier to protect her.

'This is all speculation,' Clay said.

'Which I fully admit,' Paige said. 'Which is why I'm not endangering any lives but my own.'

'You can't do that,' Jeremy said. 'If you're the new Coven leader, you have to consider the best interests of your Coven.

What happens if they lose both Ruth and her successor? You have a responsibility to stay alive, if only until you've selected and trained the next leader.'

'But—'

'Let's see what we can do,' he said. 'Give me your notes and we'll review what we have.'

RETURN

Two days later, we checked out of the motel. We were going back.

We'd spent the last two days planning. Finally Jeremy agreed that we had all the information we were likely to get and there was no sense delaying our return. Paige had chafed at the delay, but she hadn't tried to bolt, probably because either Jeremy or I had been with her nearly twenty-four hours a day, making sure she didn't. I'd even moved into her room, letting Cassandra have her own, which not only helped ensure Paige wouldn't disappear in the night but made me feel a lot better about her personal safety. As for Cassandra, well, she could look after herself.

For the trip to the compound, we split the group into two carloads, based on the two groups we'd form once we arrived. The plan was for Jeremy, Cassandra, and Kenneth to wait in the background while Clay, Adam, Paige, and I broke in and cleared all initial resistance. We'd debated which group Paige should be in. As Coven leader – and someone unaccustomed to fighting – she should have stayed back with Jeremy. However, she argued that her spells could prove invaluable in protecting the front-line group. She could unlock doors, cover us, confuse attackers, communicate with Kenneth – the list went on. Besides, she really wanted to do this, unlike Cassandra, who'd shown no interest in taking a more active role. In the end, Paige's persistence had paid off, and we'd agreed she should join my group.

I drove the second car, because Paige refused to set foot in any vehicle with Clay behind the wheel and Clay refused to take the backseat to any apprentice witch – Coven leader or not – so if we were ever going to leave the parking lot, the task of driving fell to me. Before we piled into the car, I noticed Clay shooting glances at Jeremy as he climbed into the other vehicle.

'You can go with him if you want,' I said.

'No,' Clay said. 'He's right. We need to discuss our strategies on the trip, so this makes sense. Besides, it's not like I haven't left him alone before.'

'I'm sorry.'

'About what?'

'Taking off that day. Not being careful. Getting myself kidnapped. Losing contact with you guys. Making you—'

He pressed his lips to mine, cutting me short. 'You didn't make me do anything. I chose to come after you.'

'It's just that I hate . . .' I trailed off and shrugged. 'You know, putting you in a position where . . .' I cut a look at Jeremy and exhaled. 'Making you choose.'

Clay laughed. 'Making me choose? Darling, we live with the guy. We share a house, bank accounts, even vacations. We're never alone and I've never heard you utter one word of complaint. You have *never* asked me to choose, and you have no idea how grateful I am for that, because if I ever had to pick, it would be you, no matter what that meant for the Pack.'

'I'd never do that to you.'

'Which is why I know how much you love me. Yes, I feel shitty about having abandoned Jeremy, but he understands, and I don't regret it, even if you did get yourself free without my help.' He pulled back to look at me. 'Now, are you okay with this? Going back in? 'Cause if not . . .'

'I'm fine. I want to get it over with. I want to finish this, say good-bye to all these nice people and go home, to our own home, our own beds, and be alone.'

'Reasonably alone,' Clay said with another glance toward Jeremy.

'Close enough.'

'Let's do it, then.'

When Clay and I had escaped the compound grounds, we'd used the main service road that bisected the west end of the property. Definitely not the safest route, but Clay hadn't been able to find another one. This time we were using an overgrown rutted road that dated back several property owners. Paige had discovered it by hacking into property records and old surveys. Yes, I said hacking, as in computer hacking. When she told me how she got the information, I'd asked her to repeat herself – several times. Perhaps my prejudices were showing, but when I pictured a hacker, I thought of some guy like Tyrone Winsloe, only with no money and worse hygiene. Paige quickly corrected me: She was not a hacker; she was a professional computer programmer who knew how to hack. Sounded like hairsplitting to me, but I kept my mouth shut. However she got the information, I was grateful. We all were . . . even Clay. The old surveys had shown all previous roads criss-crossing the compound property. We sampled several and chose one that fell midway between secluded and accessible. I drove a few hundred feet along it, then pulled over for our final pre-assault rendezvous with Jeremy.

Twenty minutes later, I sat on an old tree stump talking to Paige while Clay and Adam pored over the maps. Jeremy had given us our instructions and was now discussing last-minute details with Kenneth. Paige and Kenneth would act as telepathic liaisons between the two groups, allowing us to communicate without two-way radios or cell phones. Telepathic liaisons. The phrase slid so easily from my mental tongue. Scary, really. Binding spells, sorcery, astral projection, telepathy, telekinesis, teleportation – did I ever expect to hear those words outside of an *X-Files* episode? Now I was standing in a forest grove with a witch, a half-demon, a vampire, and a shaman, planning to put an end to a nefarious plot to usurp our powers and alter the path of humankind. Talk about your conspiracy theories.

After a few minutes of speaking to Kenneth, Jeremy waved Paige over. I stayed where I was.

'Does it bother you?' Cassandra asked, walking over to me. 'Being back here?'

I shrugged. We hadn't spoken much in the last few days. My choice. No matter what Cassandra may or may not have done in my absence, her abandonment of Paige at such a sensitive time was unforgivable. Despite what Clay thought of Paige, I liked her. She had spirit, wit, and a depth of altruism I truly admired. Even Clay had started cutting her some slack over the last couple of days, which only made Cassandra's callousness all the more incomprehensible. Even after I'd told Cassandra, point-blank, that I was bunking up with Paige because she was shirking her responsibilities, she hadn't shown a twinge of remorse. And I accused Clay of being self-absorbed.

'Be careful in there,' Cassandra continued. 'Remember what Jeremy said. You don't know what kind of extra security they may have taken since your escape. I meant what I said before you were taken. I'd like to get to know you better, Elena. Let's make sure we have that opportunity.' She laid her hand on my forearm and smiled, eyes sparkling with a feral gleam. 'I must admit I'm looking forward to this. Not many opportunities for mayhem in my life these days.'

Paige joined us. 'Well, Cass, if you really want some fun and excitement, you could always change your mind and join us on the front line. Oh, but that's not what you meant, right? You want controlled, risk-free mayhem.'

'My skills are better suited to the second wave of attack,' Cassandra said, smiling at Paige as if humoring a rude child.

Clay walked up. 'And I don't want anyone with us who doesn't want to be there.' He took my arm, not-so-subtly disengaging it from Cassandra's grasp. 'Jeremy has some last-minute instructions for you, darling.'

'Let me guess,' I said. 'Be careful. Don't show off. Don't take unnecessary risks.'

Clay grinned. 'Nah. Jeremy trusts you. It's more like:

"Make sure Clay's careful," "Make sure he doesn't show off," "Make sure he doesn't take unnecessary risks." Baby-sitting instructions.'

I rolled my eyes and headed for Jeremy. He was alone, leaning over a map spread on the hood of one car. As I approached, he folded the map without looking up.

'You'll be in charge out there, Elena,' he said as he turned.

'I know the routine. I look after Clay. I set the tone. I make sure he keeps it under control.'

'You call the shots. He knows that.'

'What about Adam and Paige? Do they know that?'

'It doesn't matter. Adam will follow Clay's lead. Paige will know better than to engage in leadership squabbles on the battlefield. Take control and they'll follow.'

'I'll try.'

'One more thing. Stay with Clay. If you separate, you'll be too worried about one another to concentrate on your tasks. No matter how bad things get, stick together. Don't take any chances.'

'I know.'

'I mean it.' He reached out and brushed an escaped strand of hair from my shoulder. 'I know you're sick of hearing it, but don't take any chances. Please.'

'I'll look after him.'

'That's not what I mean. You know that.'

I nodded and kissed his cheek. 'I'll be careful. For both of us.'

Step one: Inspect the grounds.

Clay, Paige, Adam, and I followed the overgrown service

road for two miles, at which point the road looped north, away from the compound, meaning we had to finish the journey with a half-mile trek through thick brush. Once we were close enough to see the compound, we stopped and circled the perimeter, staying as far in the forest as we could while still able to see the open strip of ground surrounding the building. We looked, listened, and sniffed for anyone outside the compound walls. According to Clay, from his earlier observations, people came outside for three reasons only: to smoke, to feed the dogs, and to leave the grounds. Leaving the grounds meant driving one of four SUVs stored in a nearby garage. No one left on foot and no one went for walks in the forest. Nature lovers these guys were not. Our walk around the perimeter confirmed that no one was outside.

Step two: Kill the dogs.

During Clay's earlier reconnaissance, he'd found the kennel. It was a cinder-block building tucked thirty yards into the woods, as if purposely placed away from the compound to eliminate noise. These dogs were for tracking and killing, not for guarding. As we drew near the kennel, I could tell why. Every few minutes one of the dogs would start a hellish racket, barking at something in the forest, barking at a cellmate, or just barking from sheer boredom. Although the dogs wouldn't alert anyone to our presence, we still had to get rid of them. I'd seen what they were capable of doing to me as a wolf. I didn't want to think of how much damage they could do to me when I was in human form. Once the guards realized we were in the compound, someone would get the dogs, and they'd do what they'd been trained to do, namely rip us to shreds.

We circled the kennel from the south, moving with the wind. The building was roughly twenty by ten with a fenced yard half that size. As Clay had discovered on his earlier visit, no guards were posted at the kennel. Nor were there any security measures in place to protect the animals. Only a garden-variety padlock secured the gate.

Once we were downwind of the kennel, I counted the dogs by separating their scents. Three. As Clay, Adam, and I crept forward, Paige cast a cover spell. This was the same spell Ruth had cast in the Pittsburgh alley, meaning we were invisible only if we stayed still. When we moved, our images were distorted, but visible. It worked fine with the dogs, confusing them long enough for Clay to snap the padlock and the three of us to get inside. Clay and I killed our targets easily enough. Adam fumbled the choke hold we'd shown him. Not his fault. Most people aren't neck-snapping experts. The dog managed to graze four bloody furrows in Adam's arm before Clay finished the job. Paige tried to inspect the injury, but Adam sloughed it off and helped Clay drag the dog carcasses into the kennel building.

Step three: Disable the vehicles.

This was one thing Clay and I could not do. Why? Because we were both so mechanically challenged we rarely pumped our own gas for fear we'd somehow screw up and the car would burst into flames before our eyes. Here was Adam's chance to make up for the botched chokehold. After we snapped the door locks, Adam flipped up the hoods, pulled a few wires and metal things, and declared the vehicles unusable. All Clay and I could do was watch. Worse yet, Paige advised Adam on a few ways to make the damage less detectable, so even the mechanically inclined guards couldn't quickly deduce and fix the problem. Not that I was envious. Who cared whether you could change motor oil when you could snap a rottweiler's neck in 2.8 seconds? Now there was a practical skill.

Step four: Get inside the compound.

Okay, now things got tough. In the movies, heroes always get into seemingly impenetrable buildings through a heating duct or ventilation shaft or service entrance. In real life, if someone goes through all the hassle of creating an elaborate security system, they don't have a 3' × 3' ventilation shaft secured only by a metal grate and four screws. Unless they're really, really stupid. These guys were not. Hell, they didn't even have one of those massive air vents with the slowly rotating, very sharp fan that would chew us to bits if we didn't dash through the blades at exactly the right moment. Nope. None of that fun stuff. Not even old-fashioned windows. Just one way in and out. The front door.

When Clay had scouted the compound during my captivity, he'd discovered that guards engaged in that sacred ritual of workers everywhere – the hack pack: die-hard smokers condemned to huddle together against the elements. Obviously even nefarious secret projects were smoke-free these days. Having determined there was only one way into the compound, we needed to get past the security system. That meant we needed a valid hand and retina. Since we didn't need a good pair of lungs, one of the smokers would work fine.

We positioned ourselves in the woods beside the exit door and waited. Twenty-five minutes later, two guards came out and lit up. Clay and I each targeted one and killed them. Neither guard even saw us, perhaps being too enraptured by that first flood of nicotine. They'd barely finished a quarter of their cigarette before we cured them of the habit.

We dragged the corpses a hundred feet into the woods. Then Clay dropped his and pulled a folded garbage bag from his back pocket.

'He's not going to fit in that,' Paige said.

Clay shook open the bag. 'Parts of him will.'

'You're not—' Paige paled and I could almost see flashbacks of the 'decapitated head in the bag' incident running through her mind. 'Why can't you just hold him up to the security camera?'

'Because, according to Elena, we'll need to get past more security inside, and if you'd like to drag along a two-hundred-pound corpse, be my guest.'

'I don't see why—'

Adam started to hum. As Paige turned to glare at him, I recognized the tune.

'"Little Miss Can't Be Wrong,"' I murmured . . . and tried very hard to stifle a laugh.

Adam grinned. 'Clay called her that once when you were away. If she starts getting bossy, sing it. Shuts her up every time.'

'Try singing it again and see what happens,' Paige said.

Adam's grin broadened. 'What are you going to do, turn me into a toad?'

Paige pretended not to hear him. 'Elena, did you know that one of the major accusations against witches during the Inquisition was that they caused impotence?'

'Ummm, no,' I said.

'Not just psychological impotence either,' Paige said. 'Men accused witches of literally removing their penises. They thought we collected them in little boxes where they wriggled around and ate oats and corn. There's even this story in the *Malleus Maleficarum* about a guy who went to a witch to ask for his penis back. She told him to climb a tree, where he'd find some in a bird's nest. He did and, of course, tried to take the biggest, but the witch said he couldn't have that one because it belonged to the parish priest.'

I laughed.

'Men,' Paige said. 'They'll accuse women of anything.' She paused and slanted a look at Adam. 'Of course, it's such an outlandish charge, one can't help but wonder if there isn't a grain of truth in it.'

Adam feigned a gulp. 'Personally, I'd rather be a toad.'

'Then give up the singing career or you'll be doing it as a soprano.'

I laughed and glanced at Clay. He was holding his right arm out straight and bracing it with his left hand. Sweat dappled his forehead as the muscles beneath his forearm began to pulse.

'What are you—?' Paige began.

I motioned her to silence. Now was really not a good time to pester Clay. Since we couldn't exactly lug around a box of tools, he had to improvise a way to remove the dead man's head and hand.

Adam stared at Clay's hand as it began transforming into a claw. 'That has got to be the coolest thing I've ever seen. Or the grossest.'

'Come on over here,' I said to Paige. 'This isn't something you want to see.'

We moved farther into the woods. Paige kept her gaze trained on a tree in the distance, cheek twitching, as if trying unsuccessfully not to think about what was happening behind us. There was a wet tearing sound, then a dull thud as the guard's decapitated head hit the ground.

'Nope,' Adam said. '*That* was the grossest. Hands down.'

'Heads down,' Clay deadpanned. 'The hand is next.'

Adam hurried over to Paige and me.

'You know,' Paige said, looking at Adam. 'I always thought "turning green" was only an expression. Guess not.'

'Go ahead and laugh,' Adam said. 'That's one advantage to my powers, though. Burning flesh might smell awful, but at least it's bloodless.'

'Okay,' Clay said, stepping from the woods. 'I'm ready. We're going in.'

INFILTRATION

We headed for the exit, checking first to ensure no one else had come outside for a nicotine fix. Once there, Clay removed the head and hand from the bag. I took the hand. As he lifted the head to the camera, I poised the still-warm hand beside the door handle, ready to grab it as soon as the first light turned green. Instead, the indicator stayed red and something beeped. I turned to see a numeric keypad attached to the wall. 'ID#?' flashed on the tiny screen.

'Shit!' I said. 'A key code. How did I miss that?'

'Because you were breaking out, darling, not breaking in,' Clay said. 'I didn't notice it either. Must be added security for getting inside.'

'No problem,' Paige said. 'Let's break this down logically. First, find the number of digits.' She started pressing the '9' button.

'Don't!' Adam said, snatching her hand. 'If we punch in the wrong code, we might set off an alarm.'

'I know that. All I'm doing is seeing how many digits it'll accept. Looks like five. Okay. So let's go back to this guy's body and see if we can find a five-digit number.'

'Maybe tattooed on his chest,' Adam said.

'No need for sarcasm,' she said. 'He might have a card or something with the number on it. Even if it's a secret, like a PIN number, lots of people write it down and hide it in their wallet. We just look for anything with five digits.'

'This is stupid,' Adam muttered.

'No,' I said. 'It's logical, like Paige said. I'll run back—'

'We don't have time!'

'We'll make time,' Clay said. 'You two step into the woods and stay hidden.'

Clay and I returned to the headless corpse and searched the pockets, finding neither a wallet nor anything bearing a number of any sort. When we returned, Adam was pacing just beyond the forest's edge.

'Nothing, right?' he said.

I nodded, then turned to Paige. 'Okay, so we know it's a five-digit number. Can you hack into the system? Break the code?'

'Not without a laptop and a lot of time.' She glanced at Adam, who'd strode out of earshot, then she lowered her voice. 'He's wired. I don't think he slept much last night.'

'He'll be fine,' I said. 'Let's check out that keypad again.'

We returned to the door.

'Well?' Adam said. 'Do we have a plan yet?'

'We're working on it,' I said.

'What about you two?' Paige asked. 'Can you turn into wolves and get us in?'

'How?' Clay said. 'Whine and scratch at the door until someone opens it?'

'Is that all we've got?' Adam snapped. 'What about the backup plan?'

'Cool it,' Clay said. 'We're working on one.'

'Working on one? You mean we don't have one?'

Paige laid her hand on Adam's arm. He shook it off.

'What the hell are we standing around for?' he said. His voice tightened, taking on a shrill note of panic. 'We have to hurry. Using that scanner probably set off an alarm. Even if it didn't, someone's bound to come looking for those two guards. Goddamn it!'

The whites of Adam's eyes suffused with red, as rage replaced panic. The smell of fire flared. Clay grabbed Adam by the back of the shirt just as Adam's fist connected with the door. There was a loud pop. The door shimmered. Clay hauled Adam back and threw him to the ground, then pushed Paige and me out of the way and stood over Adam.

'Control it, Adam,' Clay said. 'Concentrate.'

Adam lay face down on the ground. He balled his outstretched hands into fists, grabbing handfuls of grass and earth. The grass sizzled and smoked. When Adam started to stand, Clay put his foot on his back.

'Got it under control?' Clay asked. 'I'm not letting you up until you do.'

Adam nodded and Clay backed off, but stayed tense. Adam sat up, buried his face in his hands, and groaned like a college freshman with a killer hangover. Then he gave his head a sharp shake and looked at us.

'Sorry, guys,' he said. 'I didn't mean—' His head jerked up. 'Did I do that?'

I followed his gaze and saw that the exit door was open.

I blinked, looked again, and realized it wasn't open. It was gone. Only a pile of ash remained.

'Holy shit,' Paige whispered. 'You incinerated it.'

'I did?' Adam stood, walked to the door, and touched the edge of it, then yelped and jerked his hand away. Red welts emblazoned his fingertips. He grinned like a toddler taking his first steps. 'Look ma, no door!' He punched the air and whooped. 'Guess I'm not your average fire demon after all. See this door, Paige? Remember it next time you decide to bad-mouth me.'

'Congratulations,' Clay said. 'Now get the hell inside.'

Adam nodded and tried to plaster on a serious face, but his grin slipped through. Clay motioned for him to lead the way. As he stepped over the pile of ash, he stooped and raked his fingers through it, then turned to Paige and grinned, eyes shining. She smiled back, then proded him through the doorway. We were in.

Our next task was to disable the alarm and radio system. From my trips to and from the infirmary, I knew the communication center was located on the second floor, around the corner from the elevator. Several guards were on duty there at all times, manning the equipment. Tucker's office adjoined the guard station. With any luck, he'd be there. Killing Tucker was another high-priority job. Of all the remaining staff, Tucker was the most dangerous, not for any personal qualities – I didn't know the man well enough to assess that – but because he commanded the troops. When someone discovered that we'd infiltrated the compound, Tucker would rally them to action. Without Tucker and without the radio system, any sense of order among the guards would break down – or so we hoped. The only other person who could possibly control the men would be Winsloe. The guards might not like or respect Winsloe, but he paid their wages, which they wouldn't receive if they cut and ran at the first sign of trouble. So Winsloe would be next on our target list.

Once Winsloe and Tucker were dead, we'd be more concerned with fighting individual guards than tracking down the remaining staff members. Oh, sure, Tess might pull a nail file on us, but I could probably take her. That left Matasumi, a guy who couldn't fight his way out of a locked bathroom. Oh, right, I was forgetting someone. The sorcerer. Paige assured me she'd know Katzen if she saw him. Witches intuitively recognized sorcerers . . . or so she'd heard, though she'd never met one herself. Very comforting.

We'd planned to take our time moving from the exit to the guard station, avoiding confrontations, taking side routes if necessary. The incinerated exit door kiboshed that plan. We had to get to the guard room and disable the radios before anyone saw the damage.

Fortunately, we arrived at the communication center without incident. Our luck continued when we found only two guards manning the station. One was chomping on a granola bar. The other was doing the crossword in a week-old newspaper. We could only see slivers of their profiles, but it was enough to send a cold thrill through me. I smiled. These were two guards I recognized, two I'd never forget: Ryman and Jolliffe, the men who'd helped Winsloe hunt Lake, who'd played key roles in Armen's death, who'd taken such pride and vicious pleasure in their jobs. And now this dedicated duo was so engrossed in their work that Clay and I managed to sneak up behind them without either noticing. The temptation to shout 'Boo!' and watch them hit the rafters was almost too great. But we were in a hurry. So Clay grabbed Ryman in a headlock and I snapped Jolliffe's neck as he pondered a nine-letter synonym for stupidity. We needed to keep one guard alive and had chosen Ryman, hoping his mouth would be too full of granola for him to scream. It was. Unfortunately, it was so full that when Clay grabbed him by the throat, he almost choked to death, thereby necessitating a flurry of discussion over the proper way to perform the Heimlich maneuver. It was a sad state of affairs when you had to save someone's life before you killed him.

Ryman finally coughed up a soggy chunk of oats, then let loose a stream of vulgarity.

'Now that doesn't sound like "thank you,"' Clay said, clamping his hand over Ryman's mouth.

'There's gratitude for you,' I said. I leaned into Ryman's face. 'Remember me?'

His face went white. I grinned, baring my teeth.

'These are the two I told you about,' I said to Clay.

His eyes sparked, and he returned my grin. 'Good.'

Ryman made a noise that sounded suspiciously like a whimper. I flashed him one last smile, then stepped away, leaving him to Clay. As Adam disconnected the communication equipment, I snapped the lock on Tucker's office, leaned inside, looked, and sniffed.

'Seems our luck stops here,' I said. 'No sign of the colonel.'

'That's why we have this one.' Clay slammed Ryman's head and upper torso onto the desktop, knocking over a bottle of mineral water. 'Let's keep this brief. Where do we find Tucker?'

Blood trickled from Ryman's nose. He blinked, orienting himself, then cleared his throat and lifted his head.

'Paul Michael Ryman,' he said, voice clipped, robotic. 'Former corporal with the United States Army. Currently serving under Special Operations Colonel R. J. Tucker.'

'What the hell is that?' Clay said.

Paige muffled a laugh. 'I – uh – think it's his version of name, rank, and serial number. Sorry, Paul, but that's really not going to help us.'

Clay leaned over, stretched Ryman's hand flat against the desktop, then smashed it with his fist. There was a sickening crunch, like the snapping of bird bones. Ryman shrieked, cut off in mid-note by Clay's hand over his mouth.

'Doctors will have a hell of a time fixing that,' Clay said. 'I'd call it a write-off. That was the left hand. Next I do the right. Where is Tucker?'

'Paul Michael Ryman,' Ryman gasped when Clay uncovered his mouth. 'Former corporal with the United States Army. Currently serving under Special Operations Colonel R. J. Tucker.'

'Oh, for pity's sake,' Paige said. 'Come on, Paul. We all appreciate your loyalty, but trust me, no one else is going to give a damn. Just tell the man what he wants to know and get it over with.'

'Paul Michael Ryman. Former corporal with the United

States Army. Currently serving under Special Operations Colonel R. J. Tucker.'

'Men,' Paige muttered, shaking her head.

Clay spread Ryman's right hand on the desktop. A spurt of static from one set of speakers made me jump. Clay only glanced at Adam.

'Sorry,' Adam said. 'I'm almost done.'

He jacked down the volume on the static-spewing speaker, then bent to look at the wiring on the other one.

'Okay,' Clay said. 'One last chance. Wh—'

The still-functional speaker broke into an earsplitting whine. As Adam reached to flick it off, a voice sounded.

'Jackson to base. Base, do you read? Repeat, security has been breached. Over.'

'Hold on,' Clay whispered before Adam turned it off. He motioned for me to hold Ryman still and quiet, then snatched the mike from Adam. 'How do you work this thing?'

'Push the button to talk. Release to listen. They can't hear anything unless the button's down.'

Clay cranked up the volume on the disconnected speaker. Static filled the room. He pushed the talk button.

'Base to Jackson,' Clay said, swallowing his accent. 'Ryman here. We're having equipment problems. Repeat. Over.'

'Shit, Paul,' the voice came back. 'I can barely hear you. I said we have a breach. The fucking door's been blown off. I'm guessing explosives, but shit, you should see this. Nothing left but ash. One helluva bomb.'

'No,' Adam said, grinning. 'One helluva half-demon.'

Clay motioned him to silence, then pressed the mike button. 'Where's Tu – Colonel Tucker?'

'Last time I saw him, he was on level two, taking inventory in the gun locker. He isn't answering his radio?'

'I'll try again. Maintain your position. I'm sending backup.'

Clay handed the mike to Adam, then gestured from me to Ryman.

'You want him?' he asked.

I met Ryman's eyes with a cold stare. 'Not really. Go ahead and kill him.'

Ryman's eyes bulged. His mouth opened but before anything came out, Clay snapped his neck. Once Adam finished disconnecting the radio and security systems, we headed for the gun locker.

Now, we didn't know exactly where to find the gun locker. The guard had said level two, which narrowed it down somewhat. From my infirmary excursions, I'd learned that the second floor was laid out much like the lower level, one large block with a single corridor looping around and joining at the elevator. That made it easier. All we had to do was start at one end and check every room until we found Tucker. Getting Ryman to divulge the exact location of the gun locker would have taken too much time.

On our search, we found and killed two kitchen workers. No, they didn't threaten us. No, we didn't perceive them as a threat. The unpleasant truth was that we had to kill everyone. No matter how harmless they might seem, even the lowliest staff member possessed the most dangerous weapon of all: knowledge. They knew we existed, and for that, they couldn't be allowed to leave the compound.

While searching for Tucker, we found Matasumi in a locked room – or I should say, I smelled him through a locked door. We listened for a moment, then Paige cast a minor spell to open it. She admitted the spell worked only on simple locks, but since it was silent, we decided to try that before employing more physical techniques. It worked and we eased the door open. I peered inside and saw Matasumi seated at a computer. He was alone. I eased the door shut, bumping Paige in the chin as she craned her neck for a look inside.

'All clear,' I whispered. 'He's working at a computer. Doesn't seem to even realize there's a problem.'

'He knows,' Paige said. 'Did you see the zip disks? The knapsack? He's backing up data and clearing the hard drive before he runs.'

'And he's about to encounter a fatal error,' Adam said, grinning. 'Mind if I handle this one?'

Clay glanced at me.

'He's alone,' I said. 'There's some kind of gun on the desk. Automatic rifle, I think. Probably grabbed the biggest thing he could find. I doubt he has any idea how to use it.' I nodded to Adam. 'Sure, go ahead. We'll cover you. Just be—'

'Careful,' Adam said. 'I know.'

I eased open the door. Matasumi faced the side wall. His fingers flew across the keyboard. As Adam stepped into the room, Matasumi bent to put another disk into the drive.

He saw Adam and froze, then sneaked a glance at the gun on the corner of the desk. His hand darted out, but Adam snatched the rifle before Matasumi got close.

Adam brandished the gun and whistled. 'This is one wicked piece of firepower. You got a license for it, doc?'

Matasumi froze again, hand still outstretched.

'Didn't think so,' Adam said. 'Neither do I, so how about we get rid of this before someone gets hurt.'

Adam started to toss the gun to Clay, then thought better of it, laid it on the floor, and scooted it to us with his foot.

'Adam Vasic,' Matasumi murmured.

'You know my name? I'm flattered.'

Adam grabbed Matasumi's hand and shook it. Matasumi yelped and yanked his hand back. He stared at the bright red splotches on his palm, then gaped at Adam, as if unable to believe he'd burned him.

'Whoops,' Adam said. 'Sorry about that, doc. Haven't quite got the fiery stuff under control yet.' Adam turned to the computer. 'Whatcha working on? That's some piece of hardware. Paige, you see this? What is it? Pentium Three/Four?'

Adam bent and squinted at the tower box. He reached out and touched it. Sparks flew. Circuits popped. Matasumi jerked back.

'Damn!' Adam said. 'That looks bad. Think you can fix it, Paige?'

'Sorry, I'm not a technician.'

Adam shook his head. 'Guess we're shit outta luck, then, doc. Sorry about that. What were you doing anyway? Downloading files?' Adam popped the disk from the drive.

It sizzled, then melted like wax between his fingers. 'Oops. Hope you have backups.'

Matasumi's eyes flickered to a locked shelf overhead. Clay stepped forward and snapped it open. Adam scooped up a handful of disk cases. This time they disintegrated at his touch, leaving only charred bits of plastic and metal.

'See?' he said, showing Clay his fistful of ash. 'That's what happens when you help me strengthen my powers. Even worse than King Midas's curse. At least gold's valuable.' He turned to Matasumi and shrugged. 'Sorry, doc, but it's really for the best. We can't let that information get outside these walls, can we? Oh, wait. There's one more memory bank I need to shut down. My apologies in advance.'

Adam tore a wire from the computer and wrapped it around Matasumi's neck. For a second, Matasumi didn't seem to realize what was happening. Then his hands flew to his throat. Too late. As Adam wrenched the wire tight, it ignited, flared, then died as Matasumi slumped sideways, garroted.

'You enjoyed that far too much,' Paige said.

Adam only grinned. 'What do you expect? I'm a demon.'

'*Half*-demon.'

'And a full demon would have tortured the poor guy first. At least I was merciful.'

'Finish destroying the files and the computer,' Clay said. 'Then we move.'

'Should I contact Kenneth now?' Paige asked as we left the room.

Clay shook his head and kept walking.

'But Jeremy said to notify them once we were inside and had the systems down.'

'No, he said to notify him when Elena told you to.'

Paige glanced at me.

I shook my head. 'Not yet.'

'But we could use their help.'

'Whose help?' Clay said, stopping suddenly and wheeling on her. 'Kenneth's? He can't fight. Cassandra's? She might fight, *if* she feels like it. We'll call them in when it's clear.'

'But—'

'But nothing.' Clay glowered at Paige. 'You're asking me to put my Alpha in a potentially dangerous position where he's not only the lone fighter, but where he's responsible for two other people. I won't do that.'

'I'm sorry,' Paige murmured as Clay turned away.

Clay spun on her. 'What?'

'I said, I'm sorry.'

Clay hesitated, gave a brusque nod, then motioned us to silence and started forward again.

We found the gun locker. To my surprise, it was actually a whole room. Hey, I've never been in the military. I hear the term 'gun locker' and I picture a high-school locker stuffed with AK-47s and grenades instead of smelly socks and week-old ham sandwiches.

I sneaked up on an open doorway, peeked around the corner, and saw Tucker scribbling on a clipboard. Not only was he alone, but he had his back to us. Maybe Bauer had a point when she made that little speech about over-reliance on technology in the post-industrial age. These guys were so convinced of the impenetrability of their high-tech security system that, so long as no alarms blared, they felt safe. Tucker wasn't even armed. Really, where was the challenge?

I backed away from the door and motioned to Clay. He crept to my side, glanced around the door, and shook his head. We broke into a flurry of sign language. Then I nodded, stepped back, and waved Adam and Paige forward. Clay glided around the door, shoes silent on the linoleum. When Adam tried to follow, I put out my hands to stop him. Clay could handle this alone. Better if we stayed hidden.

I closed my eyes to sharpen my hearing and tracked the whisper of Clay's breathing, mapping it against Tucker's. The gap between them closed. Then, as I waited for the scuffle of the attack, two loud clicks shattered the silence. Guns.

I lunged into the open doorway. Paige grabbed the back of my shirt, stopping me just as two guards stepped from their hiding places, guns trained on Clay's head.

ANNIHILATION

Clay froze in mid-step. His eyes flickered from one guard to the other, but he didn't move, didn't even complete his stride. Tucker turned to face him, smiling.

'So it *is* you,' Tucker said. 'The brute that took out my men near Augusta. If we hadn't found the camera, I wouldn't have believed it. Three of my best men. Killed by one rabid dog.'

Clay said nothing. Adam, Paige, and I stood in the open doorway. Tucker ignored us.

'Not a bad idea, disabling the radios and alarms,' Tucker said. 'Not bad, but not brilliant either. You underestimated how well I've trained my men. As soon as Jackson realized we had a breach, he sent one of his team to warn me personally.'

Paige still held my arm. As Tucker spoke, she squeezed it. Thinking she was frightened, I didn't brush her off. Then she pinched me so hard I had to bite back a yelp. When I glared down at her, she nodded almost imperceptibly toward the nearer guard. I returned an equally discreet head shake. No way was I endangering Clay's life by attacking a guard.

Paige squeezed my arm harder and shot me an impatient look. I turned away.

Tucker continued, 'Yes, I know it's four to three right now. Not outstanding odds for our side, but I expect them to improve at any moment. One of my men is gathering backup as we speak.' He tilted his head. 'Do I hear foot-steps? I think I do. But you're the one with bionic hearing. Tell me, how many men are approaching? Four? Six? Ten?'

Paige murmured under her breath. It didn't sound like English . . . Shit! She was casting a spell. Before I could stop her, the guard who was farther from us tensed. He looked from side to side, only his eyes moving, slowly flooding with panic. I knew then what Paige had cast: a binding spell. Paige released her grip on my arm and I flew at the nearer guard. As I slammed into him, a shot fired at the ceiling. I wrenched the gun from his hands as we fell to the floor. The second guard was turning now, the spell broken.

Adam hurdled over me and threw the other guard into the wall. Clay grabbed Tucker by the neck. As I drove my fists into my target's gut, his knee caught me in the chest, winding me. The stink of burning flesh filled the room. The other guard screamed. At the sound, my guard hesitated just long enough for me to catch my breath. I heaved him over my head and into a set of heavy steel shelves. The back of his head slammed into the stop shelf corner. He hung there a minute, suspended in midair. His eyes blinked once, then he toppled face first to the floor, blood gushing from a crevice in the back of his skull. Clay checked the guard's pulse as I stood.

'Dead,' he said.

One glance at Tucker and the other guard told me they suffered from the same condition.

'Can you hear anyone coming, darling?' Clay asked.

'Tucker was bluffing earlier,' I said. 'But they're coming now. At least four. As many as seven. We should run.'

'Run?' Adam said. 'Their seven to our four? That's decent odds.'

'I want excellent, not decent. Seven to four almost guarantees a loss on our side. Are you volunteering for the position?'

Adam glanced at Clay.

'Elena's right,' Clay said. 'We run now and hope they split up. If they don't, we pick the battlefield. Here, we're cornered.'

We left the gun locker.

Though I could hear the guards coming, they weren't in sight yet. We made it around the corner. Then we ducked into an open doorway.

'They're at the gun locker,' I whispered as I listened. 'They're talking . . . they see Tucker. One— no, two are staying to check for vital signs. The rest are going to keep looking. They've slowed to a walk, but they're coming this way.'

'They've separated,' Clay murmured. 'But not for long.'

I turned to Paige. 'Can you cast that cover spell?'

'Sure,' she said.

'Does it work . . . reliably?'

Her face darkened. 'Of course—' She stopped herself and

nodded. 'It'll work. It's a level-three spell. I'm a level-four apprentice. Binding is fourth level, which is why it gives me some trouble.'

'Good. You three wait here in the doorway. Paige will cast her cover spell. Stay still and they won't see you. Don't cover me, Paige. I'll be the decoy and lead them past you three. Clay and Adam can attack from behind. Once the guards' attention – and their guns – are off me, I'll join the fight.'

Paige shook her head. '*I'll* be the decoy.'

'We don't have time to argue,' Clay said.

'You, Adam, and Elena are fighters. I'm not. Better to have you three attack. Besides, Elena may not look too threatening, but when these guys see me, the words "kick-ass bitch" won't even enter their minds. They won't expect a fight.'

'She's right,' Clay said.

I hesitated.

'We'll be right here,' Clay whispered to me, too low for the others to hear. 'She'll be okay.'

'Places everyone,' Paige said. 'Here they come.'

In the ensuing battle, Adam took a bullet to the shoulder. Painful, but not incapacitating. The guards died. All of them – the four who'd come around the corner, plus the two who'd stayed behind to check Tucker, plus three more who showed up before Paige finished casting a healing spell to stop Adam's bleeding. Nine guards. All dead. When it was over, Paige stood amid the dead guards, looked down at the bodies, and excused herself. She spent the next five minutes in an empty room. We didn't bother her. She wasn't the only one who'd seen enough death that day. As I thought of all the killing still to come, the guards and other staff we hadn't yet encountered, my own resolve began to falter. It was all too much. Yes, I'd killed before, but those had been mutts, stone killers themselves, and their deaths had been spaced out over all my years as a werewolf. To kill so many people in so short a time . . . I knew I'd have nightmares about this day, that I'd see their faces, wonder if they had wives, girlfriends, children. I told myself I couldn't think about that. They had to die to protect our secrets. They'd understood the danger when they signed onto this project. Knowing that didn't make it any easier. The bodies piled up, and I desperately wanted to find some way to avoid the killing. But there was no other way. Everyone had to die.

Adam, Clay, and I didn't exchange a single word while Paige was gone. When she returned, her face was pale but grim.

'Let's get this over with,' she said.

Adam blinked and looked around in confusion, like a sleepwalker waking up in the backyard. His face was as pale as Paige's. Shell shock. Clay looked from Paige to Adam to me. He rested his fingertips on my arm and half-turned from the other two, facing me.

'I'll finish,' he said. 'You guys have had enough. Show me where to look and cover my back. I'll do the rest.'

I met his eyes. He looked as tired as I felt. Not physically exhausted, but mentally wiped out. He'd had enough, too. When I touched his hand, he squeezed my fingers.

'Let's find a safe place for them,' I murmured, too low

for Paige and Adam to hear. 'Then you and I will finish.'

Clay hesitated.

'Jeremy told us to stay together,' I said. 'I'm not letting you fight alone.'

Clay searched my face, then exhaled slowly. 'Okay, darling. Let's get this over with so we can go home.'

We left Paige and Adam behind. Paige agreed without comment. Adam protested, but I took him aside and explained that we were worried about Paige and didn't dare leave her without someone to stand guard. I think Adam knew better, but after seeing a way to exit the action with his dignity intact, he accepted the change in plans and escorted Paige into an empty room.

Clay and I covered the whole second level twice. When we found no sign of Winsloe, we went upstairs, exited the compound, and checked for potential escapees. All four vehicles were still in the garage. We killed two guards frantically tinkering with a busted Bronco. Then we circled the perimeter of the compound, listening and sniffing for anyone who might have bolted into the woods. Nothing. No trace of Winsloe either.

When we returned to Paige and Adam, I asked Paige to go ahead and contact Kenneth. Time for Jeremy to join us. It would take at least thirty minutes for the three of them to get through the woods. By then, we'd be ready for their help cleaning up and destroying the evidence. First, though, we had one last task: Clear the cells.

EMANCIPATION

Paige and Adam insisted on accompanying us downstairs. By my count, most of the guards were already dead, so we let them come along. As I expected, there were only the usual two men manning the cell-block guard station. Clay and I dispatched them, then we headed into the cells. Adam's work disconnecting the system meant all the security doors were now open, so we were able to discard the bag o' body parts Clay had retrieved from outside.

Before entering the cell block, Clay and I split up. Yes, Jeremy had warned us not to, but I understood that he didn't mean we weren't to leave each other's sight at all. He trusted me to use my discretion, and that discretion said it would be better for the two of us to enter the cell block from opposite doors. We were out of contact for only a few seconds as we passed from the corridor to the cell block. Entering through separate doors meant no one could escape out the other side as we went in. An unnecessary precaution. Winsloe wasn't hiding in the cell hallway. No one was. Paige and I entered from the guard-station side, and as we walked through the door, Adam and Clay were already heading toward us from the other end.

'We should let everyone out,' I called as they approached.

Clay nodded. 'Gives us a chance to check the cells for Winsloe.'

'That's her?' Paige whispered.

I turned to see that she'd stopped at Savannah's cell. Inside, Savannah played on a Game Boy, nose scrunched in concentration.

'She's okay,' I said. 'Good.'

'Can we let her out?' Paige said, still whispering, as if Savannah could overhear us.

I shook my head. 'Let's check on Leah first. Make sure she's secured in her cell.'

Leah's cell was still next to Savannah's, and unfortunately she was also alive and well, sitting in her chair, feet propped on a table, reading *Cosmo*.

Adam peered into the cell. 'That's her? The evil Leah? Doesn't look very dangerous to me. I could take her.'

Paige rolled her eyes. 'Unbelievable. One disintegrated door and fire-boy thinks he's king of the demons.'

'Boy?' Adam sputtered. 'I'm a year older than you.'

'Move along,' Clay said. 'So long as she's secured, we'll leave her there until Jeremy decides what he wants done.'

Adam cast one last, longing glance at Leah, then turned to me. 'Now what?'

'You and Clay can check how many other cells are occupied while Paige and I talk to Savannah.'

As Clay and Adam headed down the hall, Paige and I approached Savannah's cell. Inside, she was still playing her video game. We paused outside the door.

'Did my mother tell Savannah about me?' Paige asked.

I nodded. 'She knows what to expect, that you're going to look after her. Or, that was the plan, though I suppose as long as you take her back to your Coven, that would be good enough. I doubt Ruth really expected you to adopt a twelve-year-old.'

'She did,' Paige said. 'Though I'm not sure what Savannah will think of the idea.'

'Oh, she'll be fine.' I reached for the door handle. 'Ready?'

Something akin to panic flitted across Paige's face. Then she exhaled, straightened her shirt, and ran a hand through her curls, as if prepping for a job interview.

'Okay,' she said. She stretched past me, opened the door and walked inside. 'Hello, Savannah.'

Savannah leaped up, Game Boy crashing to the floor. Her eyes flickered past Paige and saw me. Grinning, she raced over and threw her arms around me.

'I knew you'd come back,' she said.

Ouch. That hurt. Really hurt. But I had come back, hadn't I? I only wished I'd had enough faith not to abandon her in the first place.

'This is Paige Winterbourne,' I said. 'Ruth's . . .'

'Daughter,' Paige finished.

Savannah turned to Paige. They were the same height.

'This is the witch who's supposed to take me?' Savannah looked from me to Paige, then back to me. 'How old is she?'

'I'm twenty-two,' Paige said, smiling.

Savannah's eyes widened in horror. 'Twenty-two? She's barely older than me!'

'We'll discuss that later,' I said. 'Right now—'

'Who's that?' She pointed at Clay, standing in the doorway, then realized she was pointing and turned the gesture into a wave.

'Clayton,' I said. 'My—'

'Ruth told me about him. Your husband, right?'

'Uh – right.'

Savannah gave Clay the adolescent girl's version of a once-over, which didn't extend lower than his neck. She nodded approvingly, then leaned forward, nearly tripping over me.

'Who's that?'

'Adam Vasic,' Adam said stepping into the room with a mock bow.

Savannah stifled a giggle. 'Ruth mentioned you. The fire-demon. That doesn't sound *too* bad, but what can you do? Besides start fires?'

'We really should—' Paige began.

'It's Savannah Levine, right?' Adam asked.

Savannah nodded. Adam extended his hand with a flourish, paused, then put his finger to the wall. The drywall smoked. Using his finger, he scorched S. L., then drew a heart around it.

Savannah's face lit up, but she struggled to hide it under a veil of indifference. 'Not bad. But anyone can do that with a magnifying glass. Don't you have any *real* powers?'

'Later,' Clay said. 'We have two more cells to empty.'

Adam stepped aside to let Savannah pass, holding the door open for her. She pretended to ignore him, but couldn't hide a tiny smile and one last glance at his artwork on the wall. Poor Xavier. So easily ousted from Savannah's affections by a younger, more powerful half-demon. How fickle the heart of a twelve-year-old girl.

As Savannah walked past Adam, she collided with Clay blocking the exit.

'She stays here,' he said. 'Paige can look after her.'

Savannah yelped.

'We should have released her last,' Clay said. 'There could still be some guards left. I don't want her wandering about.'

'I won't wander—'

Clay cut her off with a look. They locked eyes, then Savannah dropped her gaze.

'Fine,' she said. She turned on her heel, stalked to her bed, and threw herself atop it, arms crossed, facing the wall.

'Adam, stay with them,' Clay said. 'Stand guard.'

'I don't need anyone to protect me,' Savannah said, flipping over and sitting up, pique vanishing as Adam approached. 'But you can look after *her*.' She jerked her chin toward Paige. 'She looks like she might need help.'

'This is going to be fun,' Paige murmured under her breath. 'Couldn't you have found me a sweet little eight-year-old witch?'

'It could be worse,' I said. 'She could be sixteen.'

'Someday, she will be.'

Two prisoners left. Curtis Zaid, the Vodoun priest, and a new captive in the cell across from my old one.

'What do you think he is?' I asked Clay, tilting my head to study the newcomer. 'I heard they were trying to capture a vampire, but this guy doesn't look too anemic, does he?'

That was an understatement. The man in the cell was

at least six foot three, with broad shoulders and plenty of muscles, shown off by a sleeveless sweatshirt and well-worn jeans. Definitely not anemic.

'You can stop drooling, darling,' Clay said.

I made a face at him and looked back at the stranger. 'You think he's a vampire?'

'Want me to stick my neck in and find out?'

'Maybe later. For now, I think we should leave him where he is. Just to be safe.'

We walked to Curtis Zaid's cell. I watched him through the one-way glass, trying to assess his mental stability.

'He looks okay,' I said. 'No ranting and cursing. I think the poor guy's lost it, but he isn't dangerous. He doesn't have any true power. More likely to be a nuisance than a threat.'

'Let's get him out, then,' Clay said, opening the door.

As we stepped into the cell, Zaid turned and pulled something from his head. Earphones, connected to a CD player on the table. He closed his book and laid it on top of a VCR. CDs? Books? Hell, all I ever got were old books and a television with two fuzzy stations. Maybe I should have taken up cursing.

'We're here to let you out, Curtis,' I said.

Zaid didn't appear the least bit surprised. Maybe he was too far gone. Ignoring us, he stood and headed for the door. We moved back to let him out. He stepped into the hall, stopped, and looked around, as if expecting a trap. Then he started for the exit.

'Uh, you don't want to leave just yet,' I called. 'It's a long hike to the nearest town.'

Zaid kept walking.

'Let him go,' Clay said. 'He won't get far. We'll find him before we leave.'

Savannah ran from her cell. Adam whirled from his guard-post position and tried to snatch her arm but missed.

'Are you done yet?' she called. 'Can we go now? Hey, is that Mr. Zaid?' She stopped a few feet from Zaid, stared up at him, and took a tiny step back. 'That's not a Voodoo—'

'Savannah!' Paige said, running from the cell. 'I told you to stay—'

She pulled up short. I followed her gaze to Zaid, who'd stopped and was slowly turning to face the two witches. Paige went white. Stark white. Zaid lifted his hand as if in greeting. Savannah's feet flew from under her. She sailed into the air.

'Savannah!' Paige screamed and threw herself at the girl.

Savannah's body hovered in midair for a second, then hurtled toward us like a rock from a slingshot. No, not toward *us*. Toward the wall behind us. Clay and I wheeled around, arms out to grab her. Her body struck my shoulder hard enough to slam me into the wall. Clay lunged, catching us both before we hit the floor.

I looked over Clay's shoulder and saw Paige standing five feet from Zaid. They faced one another, both silent. Zaid's lips curved in a tiny smile.

'It's been a long time since I had the pleasure of confronting a witch,' he said. 'And here I have two at once. Pity they're only apprentices. We could have had some fun.'

He fluttered one hand and Paige's knees buckled. She stumbled, but caught herself.

492

'Better an apprentice witch than a back-stabbing sorcerer,' she said.

'Katzen,' I whispered.

While I crouched on the floor holding Savannah, Adam and Clay stepped toward Katzen from opposite sides. He glanced at them and waved a circle with one hand. Clay stopped short, blinking. He reached forward. His hand seemed to hit something hard but invisible. He swung his fist, but his hand stopped in mid-swing. Katzen slanted a bored glance at us.

'Don't bother,' he said. 'This is between me and the witch. Enjoy the show, but don't make yourselves too comfortable. It won't last long.' He turned to Paige. 'I'm feeling magnanimous today, witch. Concede and I'll let you go.'

'No deal,' Paige said. 'But if you concede, I'll let *you* go.'

Katzen flipped his wrist. This time Paige mumbled a few words and stayed his hand. He flexed his fingers, easily snapping the binding spell, but when he tried the gesture again, Paige cast another spell, stopping his hand before he completed the motion.

'Good try,' he said. 'But you're wasting your time. No witch, particularly an apprentice, can hope to outfight a sorcerer. I'm sure you know your history. You witches are so *good* at remembering the past. All you have left, really. Rather sad.'

'I know my history lessons,' Paige said. 'Any true powers sorcerers have came from witches. We taught you everything, but when the Inquisition began, did you protect us? No. The moment you were targeted, you handed them our heads on a silver platter. We gave you power and you betrayed us.'

493

'Perhaps I was wrong,' Katzen said. 'History isn't all you have left. There's bitterness, too. Bitterness and envy.'

Katzen lifted both hands. Paige's lips moved, but before any spell came out, she vaulted into the air. She hit the ground rolling from the impact, then vanished. Disappeared. Katzen scanned the floor.

'A cover spell. How original.' He turned, stomped down one foot, turned again, stomped again, as if trying to squash a fleeing ant.

Katzen's barrier surrounded him and Paige, trapping Adam on the far side of the hall. Adam's eyes glowed red as he pounded at the barrier, but even his power couldn't break through it. Clay paced along our side, running his hands over the barrier, trying to find a breach. I cradled Savannah as I checked for broken bones. She seemed okay, just bruised and dazed.

Katzen continued to stomp the floor, moving a few inches with each blow. 'Tell me when I'm getting close, witch. You know I'll find you. All you have to do is move and you're caught. That's the trouble with witch spells, isn't it? You can only defend yourself. You can't fight back.'

A shape shimmered a few feet from Katzen. Paige, lips moving.

'Paige!' I shouted, warning her that she was revealing herself.

Before Katzen could turn, a fiery ball swooped from the ceiling, struck him in the chest, and exploded. He reeled back, coughing, clothing singed. He shipped his head around, searching for Paige. One of his short dreadlocks ignited and smacked his cheek, leaving a bright red patch.

He snarled and slapped the fire out, then looked around again. Paige was gone.

'Well done, witch,' he said. 'Been reading sorcerer grimoires?'

He started to say more, then stopped, turning as if something had caught his eye. His lips curved in a slow grin. I followed his gaze to Leah's cell. Katzen's grin broadened, and he flipped his hand, murmured a few words. There was a click, too soft for human ears to detect. Then Leah's door creaked open an inch. Inside, she sat up, her magazine sliding to the floor. She walked to the door, opened it, and stepped out.

DEMONSTRATION

'You're missing all the fun, my dear,' Katzen said as Leah stepped from her cell. 'Why don't you take the girl someplace safe while I deal with this one.'

Leah blinked, momentarily disoriented as she scanned the hall, gaze crossing the unfamiliar figures of Adam and Paige. I eased Savannah off my lap and stood. Leah saw the motion and turned.

'I should have guessed,' she said. 'Welcome back, Elena.'

Clay was easing toward us, trying not to attract her attention until he was close enough to lunge. On the other side of the invisible barrier, Adam paced, eyes smoldering. I sidestepped in front of Savannah.

'Don't even think about it,' I said.

'Leah?' Savannah said, still sounding dazed. She struggled to her feet behind me. 'Can – can you help us?'

Leah smiled. 'Of course I can.'

I threw myself at Leah. Something struck me in the back of the head. As I pitched forward, everything went dark. I jolted back to consciousness as I hit the cement floor. Clay's arms were around me, pulling me up.

'Savannah,' I said, clamoring to my feet.

I staggered, still woozy from the blow. The room swirled. Blood dripped hot against the back of my neck. Clay tried to steady me, but I pushed him away.

'Help Savannah,' I said.

Clay grabbed for Savannah, who now stood in front of us. But his hand didn't make contact. It stopped short as it had when he'd hit the force field around Katzen and Paige.

'No interference from you, wolf-man,' Katzen said. 'We don't need your kind or the fire-demon. Take your friend and your mate, and leave before this witch whets my appetite for a stronger challenge.'

I tottered forward and bumped into the barrier surrounding Savannah and Leah. My head still spun. When I pounded my fists against the invisible wall, the recoil from my own blows sent me stumbling back. As Clay caught me, I saw something on the floor. A book, presumably from Katzen's cell. The corner was flecked with blood. My blood. I stared at it. A book. Leah had hit me with an ordinary book, thrown hard enough to knock me out and draw blood. I looked at Savannah and fear filled me.

'Let her go,' I said. 'She's only a kid.'

Leah rolled her eyes. 'Don't go pulling that "innocent child" crap on me, Elena. Savannah is twelve years old. Hardly a little girl. And hardly innocent.' She smiled at Savannah. 'But I don't mind that. I'll look after you.'

Savannah looked from me to Leah, still confused. In that moment I realized what Leah had been up to, staging all those flying-object events and blaming Savannah. She'd tried to make herself the girl's only ally, the only one who would accept her no matter what she did. In turn, Leah had somehow allied herself with Katzen, as Paige suspected. Together they'd staged the whole horror show the night I escaped. But to what purpose? It didn't matter. Right now all that mattered was that Paige was trapped with Katzen, and Savannah was in danger of leaving with Leah. I couldn't do much about the first part, but the second . . .

'She *is* innocent,' I said. 'Innocent of everything that happened in here. Why don't you tell her who really attacked all those guards, who really killed Ruth Winterbourne. Flying objects . . . telekinetic half-demon. Hmmm, could there be a connection?'

'But—' Savannah blinking, looking from me to Leah. 'You – wouldn't do that.'

'Of course I wouldn't,' Leah said. 'I'd never hurt you, Savannah.'

'No?' I said. 'What about that flying glass? Do you think that tickled? But you weren't there, were you? You conveniently appeared after that was over.'

Savannah's gaze swiveled from Leah to me and back.

'Okay,' she said quietly. 'If you're my friend, Leah, then let them go. Tell him to let Paige go. She didn't do anything wrong. Let them go and come with us.'

'I can't do that, Savannah,' Leah said. 'They don't understand you. They'll take you away and, when things go bad, they won't understand. I'm the only one—'

'No!' Savannah shouted.

Her body jerked upright. For a moment, I thought Katzen had her again. I threw myself at the barrier, then saw the look on Savannah's face. Her eyes blazed and her features were contorted in rage. Her lips moved.

Leah reached for the girl, then froze in mid-stride. Confusion flickered in her eyes, then dawning comprehension, then the faintest stain of fear. She didn't move. Didn't even twitch a muscle. I looked at Savannah. Her eyes were fixed on Leah.

'My God,' Paige whispered. 'She's bound her.'

Katzen didn't seem to notice Paige had reappeared, breaking her cover spell. Instead he stared at Savannah, then started to laugh.

'Now there's power,' he said. He looked down at Paige sitting on the floor. '*That's* a binding spell, witch. Maybe you should have asked her for lessons before you decided to take me on. Too bad. I would have enjoyed a real workout.'

He snapped his hand and Paige sailed backward into the wall. She hit the floor rolling and vanished. Katzen renewed his stomping quest. Behind them, Savannah stood with her back to the action, binding Leah. Adam, Clay, and I watched, helpless, our attention torn between the two battles.

Paige shimmered as she cast a spell. Katzen whirled in time to see her just two feet behind him, and his foot flew out, catching her in the stomach before she finished the words. Wheezing, Paige rolled out of his way and struggled to her feet. She repeated the spell. Another fiery sphere erupted from nowhere, this one striking Katzen between the shoulder blades and knocking him to his knees. As he fell, he lifted his hands and Paige catapulted into the air, rushing at the ceiling. She said something and the sorcerer's spell broke abruptly, dropping her to the floor with a bone-jarring thud. She rolled out of his sight and disappeared behind another cover spell.

'An impressive but sadly limited repertoire,' Katzen said, getting to his feet. 'Those fire balls won't kill me, witch. You know that.'

'Oh, I know,' Paige said, appearing a dozen feet behind him.

Katzen spun to face Paige. She sat cross-legged on the floor, making no move to stand.

'But I'll bet I can kill you,' she said. 'In fact, I can do it without touching you, without even standing up.'

Katzen laughed. 'Ah, here it comes. The bluff. Do your best, witch. Then I'll do mine.'

Paige closed her eyes and said a few words. Katzen braced himself. I held my breath. But nothing happened. Katzen hesitated, then started to laugh. Paige turned her head and looked at Clay. He caught her eye and nodded, then side-stepped toward the invisible wall . . . and walked right through it. The barrier was gone. Katzen didn't notice.

'Damn,' Paige muttered. 'Can I – uh – try that again?'

Katzen roared with laughter. I sprang to my feet and leaped at him. Clay and Adam lunged at the same time, and all three of us hit Katzen together. His hands flew up to cast a spell. I snatched his wrists, clasping them so tight the bones snapped. Katzen gasped. Clay grabbed his head and twisted. The sorcerer's body convulsed, striking Adam in his wounded shoulder and knocking him backward. Then Katzen went limp. Clay checked his pulse, waited for his heart to stop, then dropped him.

'He's dead.'

The pronouncement came not from Clay, but from across the hall. From Savannah. We all turned to see her still holding Leah in the spell, her back to us. She hadn't turned. Hadn't seen the fight, unable to tear her eyes from Leah without breaking the spell.

'He's dead,' she said again, and I realized she was talking to Leah. 'It's over.'

Leah's face went white. Outrage and grief flooded her eyes. A rumbling filled the room. A loud crack. Then another. A chunk of plaster flew from the wall behind me. The lightbulbs exploded. I wheeled toward Savannah as a chair shot from Katzen's cell. It struck Savannah in the back and she crumpled. I rushed at her, but not fast enough. She toppled backward onto the floor. Paige and I grabbed her at the same time. Glass swirled around us, mingling with a whirlwind of dust from falling plaster. Clay shouted. Then Adam. Paige and I bent over Savannah, protecting her from the hailstorm of debris. Then, as suddenly as it had begun, it stopped. And Leah was gone.

Clay and I followed Leah's trail outside, but we didn't get far before a familiar voice hailed us. Jeremy stepped from the woods, Cassandra and Kenneth in tow.

'What happened?' Jeremy asked, taking in our dust-covered clothes and glass-nicked skin.

Reaching out, he wiped a dribble of blood from my cheek. I leaned against him, closing my eyes to indulge in a brief moment of peace.

'You're okay?' he murmured.

'Alive,' I said. 'Everyone is.'

I gave Jeremy a full report, concluding with Leah's escape. Although I wanted to go after her immediately, Jeremy nixed that plan. He was more concerned with stopping Tyrone Winsloe and finding any remaining staff members. If Leah was on the run, she posed no immediate danger. It was a long walk to the nearest phone. We could stop her later. Right now we needed to make sure no humans left the compound and took our secrets with them.

'Clay and I will go look for Winsloe,' I said.

'I'll come with you,' Cassandra said. 'We found only one guard, and Jeremy took care of him. Tyrone Winsloe may be my last chance for some actual combat.'

'Elena and I can handle this,' Clay said. 'If you want something to do, Cassandra, go skulk around the second floor, see if you can find any warm food.'

Cassandra only smiled. 'No, thank you, Clayton. I'll wait for Winsloe. He should be quite warm when you finish with him.'

'Oh, that reminds me,' I said. 'There's still one captive left. He might be a vampire, but we're not sure. Would you mind taking a look, Cassandra? If he is a vampire, you can tell me whether it's safe to release him. You'd know, right?'

She nodded. 'There aren't many vampires in North America. If he's one of us, I should recognize him.'

After we all returned to the cell block, I led Cassandra down the hall toward the remaining captive. As we walked, I tried to think up a way to keep Cassandra from accompanying Clay and me on our search for Winsloe. I didn't want her there. Winsloe was mine. I owed him for everything he'd done, everything he'd threatened to do. His death would be a private matter, something I would share only with Clay.

We arrived at the cell before I came up with a plan. Cassandra took one look at the man inside and blinked. Hard.

'You know him?' I asked.

She paused, seeming to debate whether to lie. 'He's a vampire.'

I interpreted that to mean she did know him. 'Is he dangerous?'

'Not really. Not very useful either. I wouldn't be in any rush to release him. He'll only get in the way. We can come back later.'

She turned to go. I grabbed her arm. Her skin was cool to the touch, like someone who'd spent the day in an air-conditioned office.

'What if something happens and we can't release him later?' I said. 'Or is that a chance you're willing to take, like when I was being held captive?'

The words were out of my mouth before I realized it. Cassandra turned and studied my face.

'So Clayton told you,' she said. 'I'd have thought he'd want to spare your feelings. It wasn't like that, Elena. You're a werewolf. A warrior. A bright, resourceful warrior. You didn't need my help to escape. There was nothing I could have done.'

'And the others? You counseled them not to help me. To let me rot here.'

Cassandra sighed. 'It wasn't like that, Elena.'

'And the thing with Clay? Making a pass at him before my side of the bed was cold?'

'I wouldn't call it a "pass." Clayton is a very intriguing man. Perhaps I was a little too intrigued, but you can hardly blame me for that. Now you're back. He's your man. I respect that. You needn't worry about me.'

I smiled, baring my teeth. 'Trust me, Cassandra, I wasn't worried.' I glanced at the man in the cell. 'But I am concerned for this poor guy. I'm letting him out.'

Cassandra blanched, then quickly recovered her composure. 'Suit yourself.'

She turned and headed down the hall, walking faster than I'd ever seen her move. Fleeing the scene? Hmmm.

I opened the cell door. The man turned and gave me a wary once-over.

'Yes?' he said, polite but cool.

'Hi, I'm Elena.' I extended my hand. 'Your rescuer for today.'

'Oh?' Still cool. Brows arching. No effort to shake my hand.

'You want out?' I asked.

He smiled, a touch of warmth defrosting the chill. 'Actually, I was getting quite comfortable here, but if you insist, I suppose I could tear myself away.'

'We have an old friend of yours with us. She's eager to see you.'

'Friend?'

'Cassandra . . . I'm not sure of the last name. Auburn hair. Green eyes. Vampire.'

'Cassandra?' His eyes narrowed. 'Where?'

'Right down that hall.'

I leaned out the door. The man brushed past me and strode into the hall.

'Cassandra!' he yelled.

Halfway down the hall, Cassandra turned. Slowly.

'Aaron!' she called. Her lips stretched in a wide smile as she headed back to us. 'My God, is that really you? How long has it been? All these years and, you know, you haven't changed a bit.'

'Very funny,' Aaron said. 'Now, Cass—'

She gathered his hands in hers and pecked his cheek. 'I can't believe this. When did I last see you? 1917, wasn't it? Philadelphia?'

'1931, Romania,' Aaron growled, disengaging himself from Cassandra's embrace. 'Fifth stop on our Grand Tour. We could have gone to Prague, Warsaw, Kiev, but no, you had to stop in some Romanian backwater so you could amuse yourself playing Dracula for the peasants. And I'm sure it would have been very amusing if *you'd* been the one locked in a church cellar for three days and almost drowned in a vat of holy water.'

'It was a mistake,' Cassandra murmured.

'Mistake? You left me there!'

'She abandoned you?' I said. 'Fancy that.'

'Oh, no,' Aaron said, glare boring through Cassandra. 'She didn't just abandon me. She *gave* me to them. Her little prank got out of hand, and when the mob came, she saved herself by handing me over.'

'It wasn't like that,' Cassandra said.

'I'm sure it wasn't,' I said. 'Well, I guess you two have a

lot of catching up to do. Go ahead, Cassandra. Clay and I can handle Winsloe on our own.'

As I walked away, Cassandra tried to follow, but Aaron grabbed her arm. They were still getting reacquainted as Clay and I left the cell block to find Winsloe.

RETALIATION

The dog was in the kennel.

We smelled Winsloe as soon as we got within twenty feet of the out building. We scouted the perimeter as I whispered my plan to Clay. Before I finished, he reached for my arm, stopping me.

'You sure about this, darling?' he asked.

'Oh, I'm sure. Aren't you?'

Clay pulled me closer and tipped my face up to his. 'I'm sure I want to do it, and I'm damned sure the bastard deserves it. It's certainly poetic justice. But is it *really* what you want?'

'It's what I want.'

'All right, then. If there's any trouble, though, I'm taking him down.'

'No, I will.'

Clay hesitated. 'Okay, darling. If we have a choice, he's yours. But I won't hold back if you're in danger.'

'Agreed.'

We headed for the kennel.

Winsloe sat in the rear of the middle dog run. His back was to the wall, knees up, pistol trained on the door. Once we'd determined his position by peering through the dusty windows, we chose a course of action. Obviously barreling through the door was out of the question. We weren't bullet-proof. Since the entrance was to Winsloe's left, I selected the window closest to his right. Clay hoisted me, and I carefully unhooked the latches, pulled the pane free, and handed it down to Clay. The opening was roughly two feet square, too small for Clay, so I had to go it alone. He boosted me higher, and I wriggled through feet first, straining to hear Winsloe below, ready to yank myself out if he so much as moved. He didn't. Once my lower torso cleared the window, I grabbed the upper sill with both hands, swung sideways, and pounced, landing on Winsloe's head and shoulders. He screamed. I grabbed his gun and flung it over the wire fence into the adjoining cage.

'Nice scream, Tyrone,' I said as I brushed straw from my jeans. 'Very macho.'

Clay strolled through the doorway. 'Sounded more like a shriek to me, darling.'

Winsloe jerked around to stare at Clay.

'Yes, that's Clayton,' I said. 'Looking pretty good for a dead guy, eh?'

As Winsloe struggled to stand, Clay strode over, grabbed him by the neck, slammed him against the wall, and patted him down.

'Unarmed,' he said, dropping Winsloe.

'What?' I said. 'No grenade? No nail gun? And you call yourself a hunter.'

'How much do you want?' Winsloe said. His voice was steady, edged more with anger than fear. 'What's a life worth these days? One million? Two?'

'Money?' I laughed. 'We don't need money, Tyrone. Jeremy has plenty and he's more than willing to share.'

'A combined net worth of maybe two million bucks?' Winsloe snorted. 'That's nothing. Here's the deal. You caught me fair and square. I'm willing to pay a forfeit. Ten million.'

Clay frowned. 'What's this? You never said nothin' about a deal, darling. You promised me a hunt.'

'I'm sorry, Ty,' I said. 'Clay's right. I promised him a hunt, and if I don't deliver, he'll sulk for days.'

'Hunt?' Trepidation flashed through Winsloe's eyes, but he quickly doused it. 'You want a hunt? Okay. That's fair. Like I said, you caught me. Here's the deal, then. Let me get my equipment and we'll have a real hunt. If I kill both of you, I win. You corner me and you'll get fifteen million.'

'The man has balls, darling,' Clay said. 'Gotta give him that.' He hauled Winsloe up by the shirtfront. 'You wanna deal? Here's the deal. We let you go. You run for your fucking life. You make it off the game field and we let you go. We catch you first, we kill you. Okay?'

'That's not fair,' Winsloe sputtered.

Clay threw back his head and laughed. 'Hear that, darling? It's not fair. Weren't those *your* rules? The rules you planned to use if you hunted Elena. She'd be released and hunted by a team of trained professionals. If she escaped the game field, she'd live. Otherwise, she'd die. Am I missing something?'

'It's not the same,' Winsloe said, glaring. 'I'm not a were-wolf. A human can't fight without weapons.'

'What about those equipment lockers you have out there?' I said.

'They're locked.'

'Fine,' I sighed. 'Let's make it "fair," then. We wouldn't want it too easy. No challenge, no fun.'

I walked into the adjoining cage and picked up the gun. Upon examining it, I figured out how to open the chamber and dumped the bullets onto the floor. Then I returned to Winsloe and handed him the empty gun.

'What the hell am I supposed to do with this?' he said.

Clay shook his head. 'I thought this guy was supposed to be bright. Let's think about this. We need to Change forms to hunt you. That means we'll be occupied for a while. We're not going to leave you with a loaded gun so you can shoot us while we're Changing.'

'You could find us and beat us over the head with the empty pistol,' I said. 'But I wouldn't recommend it. We'll take turns Changing. If you come near us, we'll kill you. While we're busy, you'll have time to do something. How much time? Well, I'm not going to tell you that. What I will tell you is that you have time to do *something*. You can run for your life. Or you can go back into the compound and find ammo for that gun. Or you can race to the nearest equipment locker and try to spring the lock. Or you can head for the garage and see if you can get one of the disabled vehicles running.'

'There,' Clay said. 'We spelled it out for you. Fair enough?'

Winsloe stood eye to eye with Clay. 'Twenty million.'

'Twenty seconds,' Clay said.

'Twenty-five mill—'

510

'Nineteen seconds.'

Winsloe set his jaw, looked from Clay to me, then stalked from the kennel.

'He's taking this remarkably well,' I said when Winsloe was gone.

'Disappointed?' Clay asked.

'I must admit, I had hoped he'd piss his pants. But this isn't so bad. At least he'll try. More challenge.'

Clay grinned. 'More fun.'

We weren't stupid enough to Change in the kennel. We went outside and found a clearing about fifty feet into the forest. Clay Changed first while I stood guard. Then we switched. When I finished, we returned to the kennel, where I picked up Winsloe's scent and followed it.

Winsloe hadn't returned to the compound. Nor had he tried the garage. He'd gone straight into the woods, either running for his life or entertaining the pitiable hope that he could jimmy the lock on an equipment shed before we caught up with him. Worse yet – at least, worse for Winsloe – he'd taken the main path. Had he cut his own trail through the undergrowth, he'd have slowed us down. On the wide path, we could run full out, side by side. Which we did. There was little need for caution. With only an empty pistol, the worst Winsloe could do was hide in the bushes and pitch it at us as we raced past. Not exactly cause for grave concern.

We passed the lookout tower. Halfway to release point two I caught a whiff of metal. My memory looped through that initial hunt with Lake and I remembered the next

511

landmark: an equipment locker. So that was Winsloe's plan? Unless he had lock picks handy, he was in for a big surprise. And we were in for a very short hunt.

I rounded the corner and saw the locker ahead. No sign of Winsloe. Had he given up and run? As I drew closer to the shed, I noticed something on the ground. Night-vision goggles. Beside them, a carton of ammunition. And binoculars. I skidded to a halt. The locker doors were open. Sunlight glinted off a metal key in the lock. Winsloe had had a key all along, or he'd known where to find one. Now he was armed with god knows what kind of artillery.

As I stared at the mess, Clay slammed against my shoulder, knocking me into the bushes. A round of gunfire shattered the silence. Clay prodded me farther into the undergrowth. When I didn't move fast enough, he bit my haunch. I scrambled into the bushes, belly scraping the ground. Clay followed. Another round of automatic gunfire showered bullets in a wide arc far above our heads. Wherever he was hiding, Winsloe couldn't see us and was aiming by sound alone. I slowed to a crawl, slinking noise-lessly through the brush. When we were out of range, I found a thicket and stopped. Clay crept in behind me. He snuffled along my flank, up to my neck, sniffing for blood. When he finished, I checked him over. We'd both escaped unscathed . . . so far. How many guns did Winsloe have now? How much ammo? Any grenades or other surprises? When I'd said I wanted a challenge, this wasn't what I'd had in mind.

We huddled in the thicket, not so much hiding as staying still and safe while we pinpointed Winsloe's location. After a few minutes, Clay nudged my shoulder and pointed his muzzle northeast. I lifted my nose, but the wind blew from the south. Clay flicked his ears. Listen, don't sniff. I closed my eyes, concentrated, and heard a faint shuffling, the sound of fabric rubbing against fabric. Winsloe was northeast, at least a hundred feet away, back by the equipment locker. Judging from the sound, he was arranging his equipment or shifting to a better vantage position, but staying close to one spot. Good. I indicated to Clay that we should split up and circle around. He snorted softly and eased from the thicket. By the time I got out, he was gone.

From Clay's scent, I could tell he'd gone left, so I went right. Giving Winsloe wide berth, I crept through the bush until I calculated I was directly north of him. Then I slowed, slunk down, and crept south. Now the wind was in my favor, blowing Winsloe's scent into my nostrils with each breath. I should have sent Clay this way. His sense of smell was poorer than mine and the wind would have helped. It didn't matter. Clay would manage fine without the extra aid. He always did.

Another twenty feet brought me close enough to see flashes of Winsloe's gray jacket as he moved. Hunkering down, I sniffed for Clay and found his scent. Honing in on it, I squinted through the trees and picked up the faint sparkle of gold fur against the drab undergrowth. Clay was closer to Winsloe than I was, so I slid forward until I'd made up the difference. Now I could poke my muzzle through the brush and see Winsloe clearly. He was crouched in a clearing, hands wrapped around a large automatic weapon, eyes darting from left to right. As I watched, he shifted position, turning south, surveying the forest, then rotating north and checking from that viewpoint, never leaving his back to any direction for long. Smart. Very smart. As he moved, I scanned his clearing for weapons but could see only the gun. I was sure he had more, likely hidden in or under his jacket.

As I watched, I heard a soft growl to my left. It was Clay, warning me he was there, rather than suddenly appearing at my side and scaring the crap out of me. As I turned, he stepped through the last stand of trees between us. This was not part of the plan. I huffed and glowered at him. He shook his head. With one look, I knew what he meant. The game was over. Winsloe was heavily armed, tipping the odds too far in his favor. Time for a quick kill. Clay made a circling motion with his muzzle, then jerked it toward Winsloe. Again, I understood. We use the usual routine, boring but reliable. Clay would circle south again. I'd scare Winsloe and drive him into Clay's waiting jaws. I exhaled a canine sigh and lay down to wait until Clay got into position. But he didn't leave. Instead he prodded me to my feet and motioned from Winsloe to me. Ah, a change in routine. Clay would roust Winsloe from the south and drive him into *my* waiting jaws. At first, I thought Clay was being considerate, granting me the kill I'd asked for. Then I realized he wanted us to switch roles because scaring Winsloe would be more dangerous than killing him. Okay, I guess he was still being considerate, not wanting me to get blown to bits or anything. I would have argued the point, but I wanted the kill too badly.

Clay disappeared into the forest. I tracked the whisper

of his footfalls. When he was partway around Winsloe's hiding place, Winsloe suddenly stood. I froze. Had he heard Clay? Tensing for the attack, I listened. All I heard were the normal chirps and rustles of the forest. Still, if Winsloe so much as pointed that gun in Clay's direction, I'd be through the bushes in a second, caution be damned. Winsloe straightened, rolled his shoulders in a stretch, then looked up into the trees, craning his neck and surveying the sky. Was Clay in position yet? If so, this would be the perfect time to attack. But I didn't smell Clay on the breeze, so he must still be working his way south. Damn! Winsloe rubbed the back of his neck, then checked his gun, gave a last look around, and stepped from the clearing, heading west.

I edged closer to the now-vacant clearing. When I reached the perimeter, I saw Clay on the southeast side, partially hidden in the bushes. Noticing me, he pulled back and vanished. Seconds later, he reappeared at my side. I looked at him. Now what? Our quarry was on the move. Scaring him and steering him in the proper direction would be ten times more difficult. An ambush would be our best bet, but that meant circling in front of Winsloe, conjecturing his path, and finding a well-hidden place to lie in wait. Difficult enough when we knew the terrain, near-suicidal when we didn't. From the look in Clay's eyes, he couldn't think up a decent plan either. Finally he snorted, brushed against me, then headed in Winsloe's direction. We'd wing it.

We emerged from the clearing into a thick stand of forest. Ahead, Winsloe's jacket bobbed among the trees. Moving carefully to avoid noisy piles of dead leaves, we crept after him. He didn't turn. He was moving fast. As we picked up speed, the forest thinned. Late-afternoon sunlight pierced the thick canopy overhead, speckling the ground with ever-widening pools of light. The forest was ending. We broke into a slow lope. Winsloe disappeared in a flood of sunlight. A clearing. A big clearing. I sniffed the air. Water. We were coming to the river. I glanced at Clay. He grunted, telling me he smelled the water and wasn't concerned. Did Winsloe think he could lose us in the river? Swim away or douse his trail? It wouldn't work. We could swim just fine, doubtless much better than Winsloe. As for losing his trail, it was true that we couldn't track him through water, but we were so close that it didn't matter. Even if we lost sight of him, I could pick up his scent in the air.

Winsloe walked to the water's edge, stopped, and wheeled fast, flourishing his gun. Seeing nothing behind him, he turned to the river, looked up and down it, then began pacing the bank. Clay snorted impatiently. So long as Winsloe was thirty feet from the forest's edge, we didn't dare move closer or he'd have time to shoot before we brought him down. If he waded in and started walking, we could move alongside him, staying in the trees until the forest weaved nearer to the riverbank, bringing us close enough to attack.

Winsloe finally stopped pacing. He stood at the foot of a huge oak, tilted his head back, and shaded his eyes to look up at it. Then he grasped the lowest branch and gave an experimental tug. As he slung the gun over his shoulder, Clay shot from the forest. Winsloe didn't notice. With his back to us, he grabbed the branch again and hauled himself up. It was then that I realized what Winsloe was doing. Climbing the tree. Okay, so I'm a bit slow on the uptake. By the time I leaped from our hiding place, Winsloe was ten feet off the ground. Still running, Clay crouched and sprang. Only then did Winsloe see him. He glanced over his shoulder a split second before Clay's teeth sunk into his knee. Winsloe howled. He kicked with his free leg, knocking Clay in the side of the skull. Clay hung on. Blood sprayed his muzzle as Winsloe flailed, shouting and fighting to keep his hold on the tree. I was still several yards away, running full out. I could see deep furrows in Winsloe's calf where Clay's teeth had ripped through his leg clear to the bone. As the flesh tore, Clay began losing his grip. He danced on his hindlegs, not daring to release Winsloe long enough to get a fresh hold. I covered the last few feet and leaped at Winsloe's free leg. He kicked at exactly the right moment, catching me in the eye. I yelped and fell back. As I got to my feet, Clay's grasp slipped to Winsloe's shoe. Before I could jump at Winsloe again, his shoe slid off and Clay tumbled backward. Winsloe swung his legs out of reach, scrambled to the next branch and grabbed his gun. We bolted. A round of gunfire rang out, but we were well clear, hidden in the forest again.

We stopped behind a thick stand of trees. Clay motioned for me to stay put, then turned and headed back for a better look at the situation. I didn't follow, not because Clay had told me not to – I'd never been good at taking orders – but because it was safer for only one of us to venture out. As much as I hated to admit it, Clay was the better stalker. If

I tried to help, I'd only triple the likelihood of making noise and getting us shot.

Winsloe climbing a tree posed a problem. A big problem. Next time, I'd be a lot more careful about asking for a challenge. I knew Winsloe was smart, but I hadn't expected him to keep so cool under pressure. Given what I'd seen of Winsloe – that cocky self-importance masking an easily bruised ego – I'd thought he'd panic when he realized his life was in danger. Maybe he didn't think it was. Maybe this was all still a game to him. Unfortunately for us, it was a game he was winning. Talk about ego-bruising. First, he'd tricked us and armed himself. Now he'd gone up a tree, the one place we couldn't follow. The tree not only provided him with safety, but it was the perfect vantage point for shooting. How could we even get close—

The forest exploded in a flurry of gunfire. I bolted from my hiding place, then stopped in mid-run. I shouldn't go out there. I was safer here. *Clay* was safer with me here. But what had happened? Was Winsloe shooting blindly? Or had he seen Clay?

Another rapid-fire round of shots. Then silence. I stood there, legs trembling as I listened. When Winsloe fired again, I nearly jumped out of my hide. That did it. I barreled down the incline toward the river clearing. More shots. I stopped on the edge of the clearing, hunkered down, and crept until I could see what was happening. Ahead was the old oak with Winsloe perched twenty feet up, squinting south, gun poised. Other than that, the clearing was empty. Empty and quiet. Suddenly a crackling of leaves broke the silence. I swung my head north. A flash of gold darted through the trees. Winsloe turned and fired, shooting at the noise. Clay was long gone. A waste of bullets. I realized that was the idea. Get Winsloe to empty his gun firing at phantasms. A good plan, and one I would have thought of . . . eventually.

I considered retreating to my hiding place, but couldn't do it. I knew it would be safer to let Clay do this alone, but I'd go crazy with worry if I couldn't see what was happening. Before long, Clay smelled me there. He came over and tried to prod me deeper into the woods, but I wouldn't budge. I laid down, put my head on my front paws, and stared into the clearing. He got the idea. I needed to watch, to be sure he was safe. He settled for a quick nuzzle, then grabbed the back of my neck in his jaws, not biting but pinning my head, telling me to stay here and stay down. I grunted my assent. He brushed his muzzle against mine, then disappeared into the forest.

Winsloe emptied his automatic quickly, going through several reloads of ammunition. Then he pulled a pistol from under his jacket. He was more careful now, less willing to waste bullets on mere noises in the woods. So Clay had to be more daring. At first, he'd only come near the edge of the clearing, allowing Winsloe to see a flash of fur. Eventually, though, even that didn't work and he had to dart into the open. By that point, my eyes were firmly closed. My heart pounded so loudly I almost expected Winsloe to hear it. Eventually, though, it was over. The last shot was fired. After several minutes, Clay slipped from the forest. He stood there, in plain view, muscles tensed, and waited. Winsloe threw the empty pistol at him and cursed. Clay walked closer, slowly, presenting the perfect target if Winsloe should have another weapon stashed under his jacket. Nothing. Winsloe was done.

Now I had a plan. Good thing, too, or my ego would have been more than just bruised. This was my hunt, and I'd done almost nothing, made no plans, taken no risks. It was my turn. While Clay ensured Winsloe was out of fire-power, I crept farther into the forest, found a likely spot, and started my Change.

Less than ten minutes later, I walked to the edge of the clearing and whistled. Winsloe's head shot up and he scanned the forest.

'Hear that?' he called to Clay. 'Someone's coming. Guess you didn't kill every guard after all.'

He leaned over the tree branch and peered down, but Clay was gone. Seconds later, Clay burst through the forest perimeter and looked up at me. His eyes flashed a question. Did I want him to Change too? I shook my head, knelt, and whispered my plan. As I talked, he moved closer, fur rubbing against my bare skin. Without thinking, I ran my fingers through his thick fur. As I finished, I realized what I was doing and stopped. My face heated. On rare occasions when the situation was reversed, and I was a wolf while Clay was human, I freaked out if he touched me. It was . . . well, it was too weird. This time, when I pulled back, Clay nudged my hand and licked between my fingers, telling me it was okay. And it was. Clay was Clay no matter what form he took. Yet another baby step toward accepting my own duality.

'Sound good?' I whispered when I'd finished outlining my plan.

He tilted his head, considering it, then snorted his agreement.

I grinned. 'Can't argue anyway, can you?'

He gave a mock growl and nipped my hand, then prodded me to my feet. I stood and we headed for the oak tree.

By the time I emerged from the forest, Winsloe had climbed partway down, staying a dozen feet from the ground, obviously thinking Clay had run away but not willing to descend completely until help arrived. When he heard me coming, he called, 'Over here!' – then saw who it was. Disappointment flitted across his face. Not fear, just disappointment. Seeing Clay at my side, he climbed to the next branch.

'How long you planning to stay up there?' I called.

'As long as it takes.' His eyes flickered over my naked body, and he managed a humorless smile. 'Hoping to entice me down?'

'If I could stomach the thought of seducing you, I'd have done it while I was trapped in that cell.'

His mouth tightened. Amazing. Even treed by two werewolves, Winsloe was more concerned about his pride than his life. I walked to the base of the tree and grabbed the bottom branch. He only watched me. It was still a game to him.

I swung onto the first branch. He climbed higher. I went to the next branch. So did he. Beneath us, Clay circled the tree. Ten more feet up and Winsloe's stockinged foot slipped. The branch he held gave way and he grabbed the tree trunk for support. After steadying himself, he squinted at the remaining branches above.

'They won't hold your weight,' I said. 'But don't take my word for it.'

He didn't. He grabbed a branch and tugged. It snapped in his hand. He hesitated, then lowered himself onto the branch under his feet until he was sitting on it. When I got close enough, he kicked at me. As if I wouldn't see that one coming. I ducked easily and seized his injured leg. He gasped and jerked back, nearly tumbling off the branch.

'You want to fight me, go ahead,' I said as I climbed onto his branch. 'But you'd better have a spare gun under that jacket if you hope to win.'

He said nothing. I teetered on the branch, getting my balance. Winsloe sat still, as if resigned to this. Then his hand shot out and smacked my ankle. I grabbed the limb overhead and steadied myself. The branch beneath us swayed.

'Don't be doing that,' I said. 'If this branch breaks, I can jump to the ground. Even if you survive the fall, you won't survive what's waiting at the bottom.'

Winsloe muttered something and made a move to settle, then slammed both hands into my calf. I grabbed his collar, hauled him to his feet, and smashed him backward into the tree trunk.

'You want to fight?' I said. 'Okay, let's fight.'

He didn't move. His gaze flicked down. I whacked his head against the tree.

'Thinking of knocking my legs out from under me? Don't bother. You do and we both fall. Now, in case you hadn't noticed, I'm not trying to kill you. In fact, I haven't laid an unprovoked hand on you, have I?'

A glimmer of cunning lit his eyes. 'You want to negotiate.'

'Maybe.'

'Fifteen million.'

'I thought we were up to twenty-five?'

'Twenty then.'

'Oh, so that's how it works? Once I show some interest, the offer goes down. A true businessman.'

His mouth tightened. 'Fine. Twenty-five.'

I pretended to consider it. 'You know, Clay was right. We don't need money. We have enough. Wanting more would be greedy.'

'Thirty million.'

I grabbed him by the shirt collar and swung him over the side. His feet scrambled for purchase, finding only air. I shifted sideways and rested my back against the tree. When he clawed at me, I thrust him out to arm's length.

'Offer me more,' I said.

His mouth tightened. I let him slip to my fingertips. He flailed, all four limbs jerking, convulsing, lashing out. I started to release my grip.

'Fifty million,' he said.

'Not enough.' I let him slip another half-inch. 'Offer me everything.'

'What?!'

I released one hand from his shirtfront.

'Okay, okay! Fine!'

I grabbed and steadied him. He gulped air, then cast a surreptitious glance at the ground and shuddered.

'Let's clarify that,' I said. 'What exactly are you offering?'

'My estate. All of it.'

'Your personal estate? Not good enough. I want your business holdings, too. Every dollar, every share, every last thing you own. Offer me that.'

'Wh— what would I live on?'

'Start over. You're a smart guy. You could make a living. At least you'll be alive. That's more than we can say for Lake and Bryce, isn't it?'

'I'll give you my holdings in everything but Promethean Fire.'

I let go. He shrieked, arms windmilling. Before he fell, I grabbed him by the shirtfront, hauled him up, and bent over him.

'Wanna try again?' I said.

His shirt tore, just an inch, but the sound ripped through the silence like a chainsaw.

'All of it,' he said. 'Goddamn you. Take it all.'

''Cause nothing's worse than dying, right? Tell me, Ty, what would you have done if Armen Haig made you the same offer? Promised you everything he had? Would you have let him live?'

Winsloe's shirt tore another inch. He stared at me, wild-eyed, lips moving soundlessly.

'Let me answer that for you, Ty. It's "no." He could have offered you millions and you still would have killed him. Why? Because his death was worth more than all the money he could give. The few seconds of amusement his death offered was worth more.'

'Please,' he said. 'Please, I'm going to—'

'Fall? Hah. Too easy. You fall. Clay rips your throat out. Game over.'

524

'It's not a fucking game!'

I cupped my hand behind my ear. 'What's that, Ty? I think I misheard you.'

'I said this isn't a fucking game. It's my life!'

'No, it's your death. Hey, there's an idea. Not a game, but a game show. *This Is Your Death*. Now, I've got to admit, I'm a bit young to have seen *This Is Your Life*. I only know the title, so I'll have to improvise. Cross it with something I do remember watching as a kid. *Let's Make a Deal*.'

I pulled him back onto the branch and held him, letting him get his balance, keeping my hands wrapped in his shirtfront.

'You – you want to negotiate.' He wiped sweat from his face and swallowed loudly. 'Okay. Good. Let's negotiate.'

'Negotiate? Hell, no. I'm making a deal regarding the *method* of your execution, Ty. You're going to die. That's a given. The only question is *how?*'

'N— no. No. Wait. Let's talk—'

'About what? You've already offered me everything you own. You have nothing else to offer, do you?'

He stared, mouth working soundlessly.

'You've offered everything. I rejected that offer. So you're going to die. Why? Because I finally see your point of view. You've convinced me. Watching someone die can be worth more than all the money in the world.'

His face drained of blood, mouth opening and closing like a fish on land.

'Behind door number one we have the most obvious choice. You fall from this tree. Only I'll make sure Clay doesn't kill you. And I won't drop you, I'll throw you. Hard enough to break every limb, but not hard enough to kill you. Then we'll gag you and leave you to die, slowly and painfully.

'Behind door number two—'

'No,' he said, his voice nearly inaudible. 'No. Don't—'

'Hey, I'm just getting warmed up. You know what I admire most about you, Ty. Your creativity. Your ingenuity. Like giving me the choice between killing Armen or being gang-raped. You've inspired me to new heights of creativity, so shut up and listen.

'Option two. Remember that video you saw of me fighting Lake? The one where I change my hand into a claw? Cool trick, huh? Well, here's my idea. I change my hand and slice open your guts. Not a lot, maybe pull out a bit of intestine, start a steady blood drip. You know what they say about gunshot wounds? That gut shot is the absolute worst. Takes forever to die and hurts like the fires of Hell. Which, if you ask me, would be a good precursor to what you can expect from your eternity. I kind of like that one. Very appropriate. To hell with the game, I'm going for this one.'

I pressed my hand against his stomach. He convulsed and a strong, acrid scent wafted up. I looked down to see a wet stain spreading down his pant leg.

'Shit. Ty. I was only kidding.' I waved my hand in front of him.

'Stop it,' he whispered. 'Just stop—'

'Can't. You remember *Let's Make a Deal*, don't you? You're about my age, so you must have seen it as a kid. There's a door number three left. And behind this one we have . . . hmmm.' I looked around, then caught a glimpse of something overhead. 'There. See that bird flying to the east? Know what that is? A turkey vulture. Also known as a buzzard. A scavenger. That will be the last choice. Death by scavenger. I take you down from this tree and stake you out on the ground. Then I slice you up. Lots of little, nonlethal slices, just enough to draw blood. Before long, you'll get a firsthand view of every scavenger in these woods. Oh, and I'll need to cut out your tongue so you can't scream. A definite sadistic improvement over gagging, don't you think? You should be proud of me, Ty. I'm your star pupil. Oh, speaking of pupils, I won't blindfold you. That way you can see the vultures and stray dogs as they feed on you. Well, until the vultures take your eyes at least—'

'Stop!' His voice rose, nearly shrill. 'I know what you're doing. You want me to beg for my life. To offer you more.'

'What more? You've offered everything, Ty. And I said no.'

His eyes rolled, rabid with fear and denial. 'No. You won't kill me. I'm worth too much.'

'You're worth nothing. Only your death is worth something to me.'

'No! You won't do it, Elena. I know you won't. You want to scare me, but you'd never—'

'Never?'

'You don't have it in you.'

'Option one, two, or three. Pick now.'

'You're torturing me. That's all. You only want to see me squirm. You don't have it—'

I grabbed him by the throat and hauled him off his feet. Then I pressed my face against his.

'Don't tell me what I don't have in me.'

I growled. Saw the terror in his eyes and drank it in. Then I let him go. Clay ripped out his throat before his body hit the ground.

CLEANUP

After killing Winsloe, Clay Changed, and we returned to our clothing. No time for lingering. There was still work to be done at the compound. Every bit of evidence had to be found and destroyed. Then we had to remove all traces of our presence. Eventually someone would find the compound and the bodies within. To decrease the likelihood of a large-scale police investigation, Paige had hacked into the computer system early this morning and transferred the property deed to a Colombian drug cartel. Don't ask me how she even knew the name of a South American dope lord. Some questions are better left unanswered. As for Winsloe, we'd disposed of his body in a way that ensured he'd never be found. How? Well, that's another one of those questions. The point was that no one would ever find Winsloe or link him to the compound, which would avoid the media blitz that would surround his death.

'Did Savannah look okay to you?' I asked as we finished dressing. 'She hit that wall pretty hard.'

'She seemed fine. Jeremy will look after her.'

'Do you think Paige will be able to handle her?'

'If Paige could handle that sorcerer, she can handle a twelve-year-old kid. She'll be fine, darling. They both will.'

'I hope so.'

Clay pushed aside a branch for me. 'Watching you with Savannah, I was thinking—'

'Don't.'

'I didn't say anything.'

'Good. Don't.'

'I was just thinking—'

'No kids.'

He laughed and put his arm around me. 'That sounds definite.'

'It is. Me as a mother?' I shuddered. 'I can only imagine one thing worse. You as a father.'

'Thanks a hell of a lot. I'd make a . . . fairly good father. And if not, there's Jeremy. He's a great parent. He'd compensate for my shortcomings.'

'Great idea. We have the kids and dump the responsibility on him. He'd love that.'

'He wouldn't mind.'

I groaned. 'No kids.'

Clay walked a few more feet, then grinned. 'Hey, you know what else? If we had children, you couldn't leave. You'd be stuck with me. Now there's a thought.'

'You – that's – oh!'

I threw up my hands and stomped off. Clay's laugh echoed through the forest. He jogged up, swung me off the ground, and tickled me.

'I'm hiding my birth control pills,' I said, gasping for breath.

'We'll discuss it later.'

'Nev—'

He cut me off with a kiss. A few minutes later, there came a rustling in the bushes.

'They're kissing.' A young voice. Savannah.

I twisted to see Jeremy yank Savannah back. Then he peered through the bushes.

'Oh, you're dressed,' he said, and released Savannah.

I wriggled out of Clay's grasp. 'Of course we're dressed. Since when have we ever stopped in the middle of a dangerous situation to have' – I glanced at Savannah '— a rest.'

Jeremy rolled his eyes.

'Did you kill Winsloe?' Savannah asked.

'Kill—' I choked. 'Um, no, we – uh—'

'He's been taken care of,' Jeremy said. 'Now I think we should get you back to Paige before—'

'There you are!' Paige said, bursting through the bushes, face glistening with sweat. 'I told you to stay close.'

'I did stay close,' Savannah said. 'You didn't say who I had to stay close to.'

'I was out here trying to pick up Leah's trail,' Jeremy explained to us. 'There's no trace of her. Perhaps you two can do a better job.'

'I'll go with Elena,' Savannah said. 'If we find Leah, I can use my binding spell again.'

Paige and I both opened our mouths to protest, but Jeremy beat us to it.

'Why don't we go find Adam?' he said. 'Perhaps we can help him.'

Savannah's eyes sparked at the mention of Adam, but she only shrugged and allowed that she *supposed* that would be an acceptable alternative. When Jeremy headed toward the compound, Savannah trailed behind him.

Paige sighed. 'I may have finally met a challenge I'm not ready for. Thank God I have my Coven sisters. They'll probably die of shock when I actually admit I need help.'

'Do you want to come with us and look for Leah?' I asked. 'Take a break?'

'No, you two go on. Be careful.'

I grinned. 'Now what would be the fun in that?'

Paige laughed and jogged after Jeremy and Savannah.

When we left the compound at dawn there was no evidence to suggest anything out of the ordinary had happened there. Okay, a building filled with dead bodies isn't exactly commonplace, but there was no evidence of anything supernatural. Before leaving, Adam started a series of small fires, not enough to be seen by passing planes, but enough to fill the building with thick smoke, further damaging anything that remained.

Oh, and Leah? We never did find her. I spent two hours scouring the grounds outside the compound. If she'd left, I should have found a trail. Since I didn't, we had to assume she'd holed up somewhere in the compound, where she would have eventually been overcome by smoke. And if she did manage to escape? Well, let's just say none of us planned to visit her home state of Wisconsin anytime soon.

Dime Store Magic
Kelley Armstrong

Did you know you could have a real witch living
right next door to you, and never even guess?

Take Paige, for instance. Just an ordinary young woman,
runs her own website design company, worries about her
weight, wonders if she'll ever find a boyfriend. Okay, so
she has an adopted daughter, Savannah, who wants to
raise her mother from the dead. And who would rather
be living with a certain female werewolf called Elena.
And who is being stalked by a telekinetic demon and a
renegade sorcerer. But other than that – really ordinary
(you might even say boring) life. That is, until the
neighbours find out who Paige Winterbourne really is,
and all hell breaks loose. Literally . . .

Dime Store Magic, Kelley Armstrong's third novel, is as
thrilling, hip and funny as its predecessors, *Bitten* and
Stolen. Prepare to be enchanted . . .

Orbit
1 84149 323 6